TO J

Eleanore Gray

GOLDIE M. LUCAS

with
James N. Lucas and Sarah M. Anderson

ISBN-13:9781463523206

Eleanore Gray

This is a work of fiction. Names, characters, places, and incidents are either the product of the author's imagination or are used fictitiously, and any resemblance to actual persons, living or dead, business establishments, events, or locales is entirely coincidental.

Printed in the U.S.A.

To Goldie and Walter
And all who came after them

Acknowledgements

The following people contributed to saving and preserving this novel: James N. Lucas; John and Carolyn Lucas; Faith and James H. Lucas; Cindy Lucas; and Sarah M. Anderson. Additional thanks go to Mary Dieterich and Leah Hanlin.

Preface

HILL COUNTRY

There lies a dragon in my valley.
Its tentacles stretch from the old town of Linn Creek to Gravois Mills
to the sleepy village of Warsaw on the banks of the Osage River.
The foaming head is near the logging depot at Bagnell, Missouri.
The dragon arrived ten years ago amid a flurry of protests and fighting.
The dragon rules still.

TODAY, THERE ARE RIBBONS of concrete running through the Missouri hills which are crisscrossed by lesser ribbons of smoothed gravel and slate-colored macadam. Sleek Packard, Studebaker, and Cadillac motor cars speed along these roads like glimmering multi-colored beetles propelled by foothill winds. Tourists come every day to Hill Country by driving just a few miles southwest of Jefferson City. They come and they go. Color brochures lure them to the Ozarks to fish, hunt, camp, and explore the tourist sites. Flies, heat, and the business affairs of home send them off again with their Kodaks, bass-catching equipment, and a superficial vision of Hill Country.

Tourists have been known to glance through the windows of their vehicles to take note of the passing landscape. Women have probably murmured, "Isn't it just lovely across those hills?" while masculine companions, thrilled by the sight of rabbit and squirrel rushing for thicket cover, have surely responded, "Ought to be good hunting, but those rocks look difficult. A person would really earn his game trying."

Sometimes, the cars come to complete stops. The passengers get out to stretch their legs and take in the breathtaking views of the huge lakes that have formed by water backing up from the manmade dams. The lake is deep and pure blue-green, surrounded by forest, divided by public access areas, cluttered with summer homes of tourists and retired city men. The water is seldom disturbed except by the motorboats, which cut white foam paths through the mirror-like surface of the water. Some might say, "We should come here next summer with the kids to ski and fish."

Nasal-twanged proprietors of lodgings, waitresses, and gas station attendants have been known to be the suppliers of local history and color for many a tourist. More than once, they've offered a slow and deliberate cataloging of regional offerings that has amused many a city visitor.

"Did you folks come fer? Chicago! You don't say! A fellow stopped here 'while back truckin' hogs up thar. Yeah, we git people from all o'er the country, pert near. Huntin', ye know, is good 'round here. Met a feller from St. Louis killed fifty-four squirrel up the Glaze a piece. Ought to be a law agin' it though if ye don't need the meat, I always say. Fishin's real good, too. Plenty of bass you city folk like. Us hillbillies don't mind suckers and hog mollies, ha, ha! Best country in the world 'round here, but then I ain't been no place else! Ye gotta be goin' already? Welp, t'was nice meetin' ye. Ye come back.'"

Such speech has caused city folk to twitter, to suspect the intelligence of the speaker, and to set the dialogue to memory to be repeated at a cocktail party in Chicago.

Little do those visitors know that local dialects vary, and carry with them Anglo-Saxon roots that are as deep and as pure as those of many in old time New England. Likewise, they do not realize that the true Hill people have uncanny intelligence and honor that has been cultivated and preserved through generations of isolation. Few tourists realize that the joke has been at their expense. Many a vendor and café charge "furriners" higher prices for goods and services than they do their own folk. Most likely, in fact, Hill people have taken joy in the double standard of pricing as they've watched the visitors depart with sugar-cured hams, sorghum, woven rag rugs, and simple cedar wood carvings.

Hill Country is a part of the Ozarks, which spreads across the southern part of Missouri and extends into Oklahoma and Arkansas. There are 60,000 square miles of green hills, rugged hollows, caverns, springs, and creeks, as well as oak, maple, and cedar timbers. A half century before the Civil War, people came to settle in this region from the Appalachians. Their ancestry was purely Anglo-Saxon. They had originally come from England, Wales, Cornwall, and Scotland. Some later moved on when the lure of gold in California beckoned, but a great many remained contently in isolation for generations. The farming was not the best in the country, but the people managed. They married within the region. They sometimes married cousins; first, last, and those in between. Unlike most of the nation, it was no "melting pot." Despite the age of industrialization, they clung to farming methods that had served them well for generations. And, despite the invasion by social workers during the

1930s, they maintained the standard and style of living taught by ancestors.

The region is rich with a heritage that is seldom appreciated by the visitors who seek lake recreation. Many, in fact, are appalled by what seems to be unruly poverty and ignorance. It's not at all the truth. The past has been carefully preserved here. The modern eye misses it.

Only with determination and a good deal of shin-barking has anyone seen the heartbreaking loveliness of cedar-topped bluffs and the pure blue green of the swift, unfettered Osage River. Unseen are the rutted old wagon roads that twist and turn around rocky hills, and through the valleys of wild grass. Fence rails and log cabins so narrow that the forest branches have entwined a shelter above them stay hidden from ordinary sight.

In 1902, however, all of these sights were revealed to the eyes of a pioneer woman who, with three children and a wagon of household goods, traveled the road to a new home in Dean's Creek, Missouri. Her name was Eleanore Gray.

Chapter I

CEDARVILLE, 1902

DOCTOR BOB GRAY DID not come home one night. He had been called up across the river to attend to a pneumonia case. Instead of traveling by the long bridge road, he rowed himself across a river swollen with spring rains to see his patient. On his return, a large piece of driftwood struck his frail craft, sinking it and plunging him into the tow of a sucking current. He came up once, called out, and then was hauled under again. He was found the next morning when, quite ironically, his body was caught by a piece of driftwood and flung up onto shore.

Eleanore Gray stayed up all night awaiting her husband's return. Well after midnight, she sat by a window with a glowing lamp, scanning the streets of Cedarville for the figure of a man. She never slept. Shortly after sunrise, a cluster of men arrived on her doorstep to confirm her dread. Breaking the news to such a frail-looking and gentle woman was a fearful undertaking.

Eleanore stood still and stiff as a man explained that a body had been found on the river bank. She vaguely heard him say the name of the fisherman who found it. Her muscles and senses were frozen. All she said was, "Where is he? May I go to him?"

"Ye'd best not for a spell, Ellie. He's at my place," said Cousin Jim. "You stay here with the youngsters for a bit and I'll send my wife down. Your sister-in-law is on her way." Cousin Jim issued his gentle orders, and then gave an uneasy look to the men with him who stood, looking down at their shoes with their hats in their hands. "We'd best be going now, Ellie," he announced. Jim and the men, with muttered expressions of sympathy, then filed away.

A moment later, Emmy Gray entered the cottage. No words were necessary between the two women. Emmy hugged Eleanore to her ample bosom and they silently rocked in a shared pain.

Although Emmy had come to help Eleanore, it was oddly Eleanore herself who set about tackling chores and coping with the three children. With her own hands, she started a morning fire, found clothing for her children, roused them, dressed them, and fed them. The responsibility of telling Nancy and Paul, aged ten and eight, and a two year-old Janey that their Daddy had gone to Heaven was solely her own.

Her home became the terrible house of mourning. The blinds were drawn, and black linsey-woolsey dresses were unpacked from cedar chests. Nancy and Paul vowed to "take care of Mama," while weeping cousins in black alpaca and crews of aunts cooked meals in the tiny kitchen and consumed large portions of food in the dining room. Eleanore refused to eat. It sickened her. The grim silence in the house of mourning seemed, at times, only broken by washed-out utterances of sympathy and incessant chewing that filled the dining area.

A coffin was built, and Bob's body was placed in it. It was moved into Eleanore's parlor. She stood at the head of it, clutching Janey against her heart for strength, as she gazed at the still face of her beloved. She allowed no well-meaning relative to coax her away, to take the baby from her arms, or even to cease her vigil to "take some food for strength" because, as she repeatedly explained, "I have such a little while to be with him that I cannot spare a minute of it."

The women shook their heads and whispered behind the closed kitchen door. "Mark my words, she'll break when they bury him," Cousin Sarah announced. Another declared, "She's going to be sick and maybe die because this is hurting her worse than she knows. Anybody can see she's not strong enough to hold up." Cousin Carrie then whispered to Emmy Gray, "Cousin Ellie ain't like me when Dave died. He was so sick for so long that the end weren't no surprise. I don't think Ellie realizes everything yet. I pity her when she does." In a less solemn tone she concluded with, "Let's open that jar of pickle peaches to go with the cake Sarah brought. Look at that ham! I do declare, it's done and ready for the table. Sure wish we could get Ellie to eat something."

While the women whispered predictions in the kitchen, men congregated in the yard to share their own observations. Someone remarked that it seemed a pity that Dr. Bob had spent his savings on starting up his practice in Cedarville. "I wonder," asked a practical cousin, Fred, "if he didn't have a little set aside to fall back on."

"Well," said Eben Strange, president of the small local bank, "she'll have just enough to bury him and that's all, as far as I know. People around here are pretty healthy, farm folks were always too poor to pay him, and the people out in the hills seldom called him out because they still persist in treating their own ailments with weeds and roots. It amazed me that he managed as well as he did when ye consider that a parcel of wheat or corn sufficed as payment for his aid more often than not. 'Course, I warned him to get a side business, but he wasn't one for taking advice. This house here is already mortgaged for all it is worth. I doubt Mrs. Gray will ever be able to pay it off, but I don't aim to be hard on her. If she were stronger, I suppose she could get a job doing laundry or cleaning, but I doubt she weighs even a hundred pounds. Emmy will probably take her into the millinery shop with her though, and that seems more fittin' work for her sort."

As Eben Strange concluded his appraisal of Eleanore's financial situation, a clatter of fast horse hooves sounded on the hard-packed road leading to the yard where the men were congregated. The rider was recognized on sight, and loudly identified as Will Gray, Dr. Bob's brother from Dean's Creek. As Will Gray dismounted, hands went out to greet him. Will had once been a familiar member of the Cedarville community before he had given up his job as vice-president of the bank. When his wife, Jessica, died in childbirth, Will left the town to farm in Dean's Creek. That was twelve years ago. Now he was thirty-five, tall, clean-shaven, and well established as a successful farmer. This return to Cedarville was painful. Will's face, drawn with fatigue and grief, revealed just how badly his brother's death had affected him.

"I just heard this morning about Bob and came as fast as I could. They haven't buried him yet, have they?" asked Will.

"No," replied Jim. "The funeral is set for tomorrow, Will."

For a brief moment, Will allowed his eyes to meet Jim's in an exchange of sympathy and understanding. "I can hardly believe this, you know," said Will as he dropped his head and fought back the tears.

"Eleanore's as well as can be expected, Will," mumbled Jim, "but they can't get her to eat anything or rest at all. I'm afraid she won't hold up well at all."

Will nodded acknowledgement, then left the gentlemen in the yard. He opened the cottage door and walked into the parlor. The room, though occupied by mourners, was so still that breathing seemed to pour loudly and distinctly from each black-clad body present. Aunt Martha, Clara Strange, and Cousin Sarah were on the sofa. Will, with hat in hand, nodded his head toward the women and turned his attention to the woman standing at the head of the coffin. Eleanore still stood, looking at Bob Gray. Her eyes had never moved from the sight before her. Will's entrance and presence registered no response.

Will watched her for a long time before he finally crossed the room. Eleanore's face, he thought, seemed as white as the lilies resting on the foot of the black-stained pine coffin. Her dark eyes were clear and vacant. She seemed smaller and far more frail than he recalled her being. He hoped this was only an illusion created by the folds of black wool that draped her. Her hands were tightly clasped before her, and she seemed to scarcely breathe at all.

Will crossed the floor to Eleanore's side and took her hands in his. She looked up, met his eyes, and finally gave a soft cry of recognition, "Oh, Will, I am so glad you came!" For a moment she allowed her head to rest against his shoulder.

"Eleanore, I came as quickly as I could. I cannot believe our Bob is gone," whispered Will.

"He's not gone at all, Will. I believe that he is here now in this room with us. I have to believe that."

"I understand, Eleanore," said Will as his own heart drifted back to recall the death of Jessica and his child. "Please go rest for awhile now. They say you haven't rested at all."

"Yes, I think I can rest now that you are here," answered Eleanore. Cousin Sarah rose from the couch and guided Eleanore like a weary child up to her room.

Chapter II
THE FUNERAL

ELEANORE DID NOT BREAK down at the church during the minister's lengthy praising of the deceased and comforting of the bereaved. Nor did she break down at the Hill Cemetery when the body of her husband was at last lowered with harness straps into the cold March ground. While aunts and cousins moaned and sobbed, in fact, Eleanore stood silent and tearless. She managed to defy predictions.

Through it all, Eleanore stroked Nancy's head and clasped Paul's hand. After the casket had been lowered and the men prepared to spade it over, however, Eleanore refused the arms and assistance of friends and relatives who wished to guide her to a carriage. "No," she responded over and over, "I thank you, but the children and I will walk home." And finally, with Paul and Nancy, Eleanore left the crowd.

They watched her walk. With an uplifted face and erect posture, she led her family through the gravestones toward the road. They saw her remove the mourning veil that Emmy had so carefully draped over her plain black hat, fold it, and place it in her coat pocket. It was an unexpected gesture; one not in keeping with customs of the time and produced a wave of shock and surprise that made heads shake and whispering well up. It was not at all what the women in the kitchen or the men on the front lawn had expected from Eleanore Gray.

"Just ain't natural for her not to take on any more than this. Why, I don't believe that woman's shed a single tear for her husband," commented the red-eyed and snuffling Martha.

And Cousin Ida added in an amazed tone, "You don't suppose that she's glad he's gone, do ye?"

Only Eleanore's sister-in-law, Emmy Gray, offered a kinder interpretation. "Ridiculous, Ida! It's just that she doesn't realize her loss yet. She acts like she's dreaming."

Though well meant, the observation was not an accurate one. Eleanore did indeed realize her loss, and more. She knew that self pity could be fatal. For days, she had felt like a child lost in the depths of a timber. There had been no light or exit. Now, above all, she knew the two children by her side and little Janey could not be abandoned to a wife's grief.

As if to confirm her thoughts, her young son said, "Mama, I'm glad you came away from all those people hollering and crying, because if Daddy's in Heaven, they shouldn't be acting like that." And Paul, adding proof to his philosophy, abruptly wiped the last traces of tears from his eyes.

"You are right, Paul, and I am so very fortunate to have such brave and wise children," said Eleanore. "Let's walk down this path a ways to see if any cowslips or violets are out yet. It's nearly April, you know. See! There are violets! They're up by that rock. Aren't they just lovely? Tomorrow, if you like, we'll bring a trowel up and dig some to plant on your Daddy's grave."

"Please, let's," said Nancy in a controlled voice. "He'd like that so. Maybe we could find some fern to put with them."

"You're right, Nancy. It doesn't seem that the winter snow has touched the fern at all. There are already buds on the oak trees. They're starting to swell and they're always the last to get leaves."

"We should take some violets to Granny Duncan," added Paul.

Eleanore watched her children pull up clumps of violets and fern fronds along the path home to Granny Duncan's where baby Janey awaited them. She felt a new calm spread over her as she watched them trudge ahead over the moss rocks that lined the lane. She watched their sturdy backs, Paul's square-toed shoes kicking up sodden leaves, Nancy's braids wagging within the bounds of black satin ribbons, and their small fists clutching clumps of early spring promises. They filled her with tenderness. She felt the mourning veil in her pocket, and it seemed like a silken lump of remembrance. It was time for her to place her yearning for the presence of Bob Gray deep inside her. "Dear God," she thought, "I thank you for my children. Please help me. Please guide me."

Chapter III

PICKING UP THE PIECES

THREE WEEKS AFTER THE funeral, Eleanore and Emmy again sat on the sofa in the front parlor. The place where Bob Gray's coffin had been, though now arranged with a small fern stand and a side chair, still loomed conspicuously before Eleanore's eyes. She kept her vision framed on the white lace curtains, Emmy, an ecru doily, and anything else on the far side of the room away from the fern stand. Emmy, acutely aware of the deliberate course of Eleanore's eyes, pretended to take no notice. She kept talking. Once again, she asked Eleanore to join her at the millinery shop.

"Emmy," sighed Eleanore with as much firmness as she could muster, "I thank you kindly for your offer, but there are other considerations. I've given the matter much thought, and I must decline your help. In the first place, you barely make enough to support yourself in that shop. I have three children to feed and provide for. A shop that barely supports one could hardly be expected to support five. In addition, my home is mortgaged and the interest is due. I know what you're thinking, Emmy, but even Eben Strange's generosity will end. I cannot see any point in prolonging a painful event if there is no hope of preventing it. I've returned much of Bob's medicines to the drug company in St. Louis. I expect to get fifty dollars or so from it. If need be, I can also sell the horses and the calf to get me started."

"Started?" asked Emmy most quizzically. "Are you suggesting that you've found a solution? You are a sly one, you are!"

"I'm going to farm, Emmy," announced Eleanore.

Emmy's mouth gaped open. "Have you taken leave of your wits? You are barely strong enough to beat a rug! And how, by the way, does one get a farm for fifty dollars?"

"Hush a minute so I can explain," replied Eleanore to Emmy's outburst. "My husband took care of a family called Chaney down by Dean's Creek near Will's place. He doctored that family through three childbirths, a siege of measles, and a bad case of pneumonia. And, as usual, he never got a dime for all his care and travel. Last spring, however, the family moved back to Texas. They needed travel money so they tried to strike a bargain with Bob. If he would mark their bill paid and give them fifty dollars in cash, they would sign the farm over to us. Bob hoped that we would someday retire there. I've never seen it myself, but he always talked about how pretty it was. I suppose the fact that Will lived there tended to make it even more attractive to him."

Emmy, a practical woman who had a deep love for Eleanore, was startled by the whole idea. "Excuse me, Ellie; I'll be back in a moment. I need to get us some tea," she said as she rose from the sofa.

Eleanore continued to stare at the curtains as they swayed to and fro with the spring breeze that aired the parlor. She fell into a daze, thinking not of the curtains, but of her past. She remembered watching Bob and Will as young men skating on the river during their years at the Academy on the hill. They had been her admirers and rivals for her attentions. When Bob returned from medical school in St. Louis, she consented to marry him. Will had been terribly hurt when the announcement was made. Eleanore unconsciously twisted the thin gold band on her finger. It had belonged to Bob's grandmother.

Emmy brought Eleanore out of her reverie when she carried in a tray with tea. "Dear, I just can't see how you could possibly manage a farm by yourself. That place is probably as poor as Job's turkey and the house is probably little more than a pig sty. You seem too delicate to earn your living on a rocky farm out in the brush. If I were you, I would sell that place and put the money down on this house."

"Yes," interpreted Eleanore with impatience, "the solution would be to spend life as yet another Cedarville widow. There are enough of them now. Forgive me, Emmy, but just look at yourself! Tom's been dead nine years and you still wear black and tire yourself out making pretty hats for other people to wear. You'd never think of wearing one yourself. You are thirty-five and may as well be ninety! On the other hand, there's Melinda Smitty. That fine widow crimps her hair, giggles too much, and makes sheep's eyes at any man that passes by. The other variety is Kate Duncan; six children and a tumble-down shack. She takes in washing and works herself to the bone. Her children still go hungry and dress in rags. No, Emmy, I can't do it! I won't become another Cedarville widow!"

"Oh, Ellie, I didn't intend to get you so wrought up!" cried Emmy. "I know you wouldn't say such unkind things about me and the others if you weren't half sick with grief. It can be forgiven, but taking those three children out to live in those hills may not be. Please be practical. There are no doctors, no shops, and no stores; no anything out there! They have a church of sorts, but those Hill people haven't taken much note of it. If there is a school at all, it certainly isn't as fine a school as we have here. Moving there is moving backwards."

Eleanore's eyes narrowed. "My children will not starve or freeze. They will not become heathens, and they most certainly will not become illiterate. I had enough strength to bring them into this world, and I have even more to see that they are taken care of. I'm small, but I'm not nearly as frail as everyone thinks. I may not be able to make a decent living out there, but I know I can't do it here. I grant you that it will be different and that there will be inconveniences, but I assure you they will be small when weighed against widowhood in the booming town of Cedarville! As a matter of fact, it will be nice to live somewhere where I don't have to wear black and contend with people like Ida and Florence and Eben Strange. They can whisper about me all they want once I'm gone, and it won't bother me a bit. In fact, it might keep 'em busy."

"You tempt me, Ellie," said Emmy as she reached out to squeeze Eleanore's arm. "I think, however, that I'll stay put and make hats like a sensible widow. And, by the way, I have so tried on a hat or two. I've grown partial to one with a cluster of grapes on it!" she added with a conspirator's giggle.

Chapter IV

PACKING UP

IT WAS HARD TO tear up the house, hard to watch the years be sold and traded for what everyone thought was a foolhardy dream. The sofa, organ, and oak dining table set sold to a neighbor. The kitchen cupboard, parlor stove, and Brussels rugs were used to buy a large springwagon. Eleanore sold the buggy to the minister to buy supplies. She sold the calf to a farmer whose cow had lost her calf. Eleanore hoped that, with regular milking, her cow Jersey would continue to give milk for several months yet.

She stood in the empty parlor, twisting the gold band on her finger as she called off the inventory for Nancy to check off the list. "Sugar, flour, cornmeal, a stand of lard, salt, pepper, cinnamon, nutmeg, soda powder, pickling spices, cloves, dry sage, bacon sides, smoked hams, dried beans, molasses, ginger, and dried apples. That should start out the larder. You have them all checked off, Nancy?"

"Yes, Mama," replied Nancy, as she and Paul started putting the smaller packages into a crate. "The garden seeds are packed, too."

As Eleanore helped the children with a sack of seed corn, she made a mental inventory of tools they would need to get. "And," she thought, "I better see about soap, medicine, and clothes."

She had already written to Will Gray. He answered at once to tell her that he would put the house in order and have the garden broke. He also gave her a list of things to bring. The final paragraphs read:

> You won't need all your furniture, Eleanore. Sell it for what you can get until crops come in. I've made plans for someone to break ground for a dollar a day. You needn't bring a stove. There is a big fireplace and an old cook stove. It's rusty, but I'll clean it and put up a new pipe. There are only two rooms, but the house is log and fairly tight. I'll do some patching on the roof.
>
> I want you to know, Ellie, that I am glad you are coming. I hope and pray you will find peace here as I have.
>
> Will Gray

Will's note comforted her nearly as much as Dr. Gray's study disconcerted her. The bare shelves and uncurtained windows made a lump rise in her throat. "He's really gone," thought Eleanore. "I wish I could recall what I told the children yesterday. My words seemed to heal wounds in them that I'll never be able to heal in myself."

She had gone with the children to her husband's grave to plant flowers. She had uprooted a favorite rose bush from the yard and transplanted it on the plot. Beneath the small bush, the children had planted their clumps of wild violets and fern. Before they left she had whispered, "I won't say goodbye, Beloved, because I know that you will be with me always. I love you so dearly." To the children who were by then wrestling back tears, she had comforted, "Come and be brave now. Your Daddy wants us to be happy. Look up to the sky and think of how fine it would be to walk with the Lord. Let's all stop crying now."

Nancy had looked skyward. Then, in a choked little voice, she said, "Oh, Mama, I hate to leave him here. I'm so afraid he will miss us!"

Eleanore had replied, "Dear, Daddy is a spirit now. His body can no longer hold him beneath this stone or to any place he doesn't want to be. Although you cannot see him, he is with us wherever we go. Remember that."

Eleanore forced herself to turn and leave the study. It was like leaving Bob Gray's grave yesterday. "Nothing is like it was," she thought. "After tomorrow, I will never have to be reminded of that." However, as she entered the parlor, she corrected herself with, "Liar!" She knew that walking away from death was not equivalent to forgetting death.

The wagon was loaded the next morning. Her big bed and the two little iron beds were on board. They also took the baby's cradle, the wash tubs carefully packed with her best dishes in linen, and a walnut dresser full of clothing. The doctor's books and some medical supplies were in a small trunk. The feather beds and pattern quilts were tied with ropes to the top of the wagon. A favorite rocking chair and a coop of Plymouth Rock hens were precariously fastened to the back of the wagon. The cow, Jersey, was expected to walk, tethered behind the wagon. She was still bawling and fretful, since her calf had been taken away. Toby, the children's black and white shepherd, would follow the caravan to nip at the cow's heels when she lagged.

Jim and Maud, the gentle team of many years, were finally hitched to the wagon. They laid back their ears and tucked their tails in when they realized the weight of the load. But Eleanore soothed the horses with gentle murmurs. After buttoning their coats and pulling their caps over their ears, Nancy and Paul climbed into a nest of hay in the wagon, which would protect them from the April chill. A sleepy little Janey was nestled between them, oblivious to the excitement around her.

Eleanore was dressed in a long plaid coat with a gray mull scarf tied around her curly brown hair. She climbed up without assistance and took the reins in her small hands. She knew that the friends and relatives who had gathered in the dawn to see them off thought her foolish. She didn't care any longer. She thanked them and said her goodbyes brusquely and without sentimentality. She drove the team on toward the new swinging bridge. Cousin Tom and Toby walked behind. The little caravan rumbled and creaked down the bottom road through the early dawn. The dog barked some, and the children shouted a great deal. Tom left them just before they reached the bridge. They were on their way. The journey into Hill Country had at last begun.

The town people silently watched the departure until the Gray family was no longer visible. The watchers were unusually quiet for a long spell. They were awed. They had seen something remarkable occur, something almost sacred. As soon as the wagon was out of sight, however, they began to buzz and swarm like bees over a honey pot. Some commended Eleanore for her courage. Others persisted in calling it all sheer foolishness. Both camps had to agree, however, that they had all been mistaken in thinking that the Gray woman was weak.

Chapter V

THE JOURNEY

IT DID NOT SEEM possible that the spindly and treacherous-looking affair that swayed before Eleanore was really a wire bridge that could support a wagon loaded with house and family. She knew the knot of terror taking hold of her was irrational. Bob had told her that the steel wires of cables could support tons. It certainly didn't look capable. The horses, of course, seemed to sense Eleanore's fear. Instead of moving with her fear, however, they stepped bravely forward onto the planks just as they had done many a time with Dr. Gray.

The cow had other notions. She had never crossed before, and made it plain that a first crossing was not at the top of her list of pleasant pastimes. No matter how hard Maud and Jim pulled, Jersey remained steadfast. She rolled her eyes and counter-pulled. The caravan was at an obvious impasse, and Eleanore was grateful that the troupe that saw them off was no longer in viewing distance. Eleanore considered her alternatives. She could untie Jersey and try to lead her over after the wagon crossed, or she could have Paul run back to town to get help. Pride prevented the latter, and physics prevented the former. A woman who weighed a bit less than a hundred pounds could hardly be expected, even with the aid of a barking dog and three shouting children, to lead a terrified cow over a bridge it refused to cross. The pull of the horses, however, might offer her an advantage.

Eleanore's hands shook as she handed Nancy the reins. She then dismounted, went to the cow, got a firm grasp on the ropes holding it, and issued instructions to her children. "Okay, children, listen carefully. When I tell you to, start the team across. Do not let them stop, and do not frighten them," she said.

"But Mama, we're really high up and there's lots of water down there. What if the horses run into the rail and smash us up?" asked Paul. He managed to sound brave.

"Trust the horses. They've done this before and they know what they are doing. I promise they'll walk straight and keep on the tracks," replied Eleanore with false confidence.

Eleanore spent some time soothing Jersey into calmness. When Eleanore gave the word, the team started out. Maud and Jim never faltered in their struggle with the wagon and the cow. Jersey fought and lashed against Eleanore's fierce jerks and Toby's false ferociousness. The cow crossed the bridge. Everyone, including the cow, heaved with relief when they were on land again. Eleanore, still trembling from fear and exertion, climbed up and resumed the thirty-mile journey to Dean's Creek.

The road ahead of them turned at the hill's top to reveal a view of all Cedarville nestled at its foot. The green dome of the native stone courthouse glistened and sparkled in the morning sun. Everything was uniquely still and bright. Even the markers in the cemetery were distinct. Smoke from breakfast fires twisted and wound up from houses into the light green of new trees and the deep green of the magnificent cedars. They saw their own home sitting empty and smokeless. The children stood up, waved, and shouted, "Goodbye, goodbye!" The wagon wheels turned on, and Cedarville soon vanished as the caravan followed the route to the hills.

Baby Janey, warm and comfortable, had laid her fat cheek against her big sister and fallen placidly asleep. Nancy and Paul turned their attentions to the birds that called and fluttered past them. "Oh, Mama!" cried Nancy. "See a red bird fly to the right, see your true love before tonight!" Nancy and Paul named birds, imitated their calls, and giggled at the silly rhymes they knew about different birds. The sun rose higher in the sky. The horses swished their tails in a rhythmic fashion to ward off flies as they continued to pull the loaded wagon on.

Jersey had discovered the hay that was stuffed between the furniture in the wagon and was keeping as close as possible to pull out wisps with her long tongue. Toby, deciding the cow was no longer worthy of his attentions, trotted on ahead, waving his tail like a banner. Though he paused every so often to bark at a rabbit or to chase a squirrel, he always returned to lead the family on. More than once, the errant escort would suddenly emerge from the thickets and charge at the wagon with enthusiastic speed. His mouth would hang open wide as if he were laughing at a very fine joke of his own.

Sometimes, they could spy farmhouses at the base of a hill. Some were clean and prosperous with fat livestock and tidy barn lofts. If there were children, their chubby faces would press against the window glass in attempts to see the passing wagon. Other times, however, the houses looked like mere shacks. Pillows, stained and yellowed, were stuffed into broken glass panes to keep the cold out. Bony horses stood with hanging heads and matted tails, scarcely able to stand in the filthy barnyards. Half-dressed children and countless lean hounds cavorted in littered yards. There was a meanness to poverty that turned even dogs into fierce creatures. Sometimes the dogs would snarl and growl at the wagon.

Once, Nancy and Paul cried with fright as a pack of hounds raced for the wagon. Toby, a veteran fighter, was undaunted by the onslaught of a few bony hounds. He knew where to bite. His thick hair protected him, and he emerged victorious from a bloody scuffle. The conquered foes, whining with pain and humiliation, returned to their shack where their master, a huge bearded creature with red eyes, directed his wrath toward the wagon. He slowly turned and sulked into the shack, however, when Toby bared his fangs and bristled up. Eleanore hurried the horses on as fast as she could. From then on, it became policy to pass such dwellings with haste.

By noon, they had covered the first ten miles of their journey. The horses could not be pushed harder because the road was deeply rutted. The steep hills made the load nearly unbearable. Eleanore always felt a surge of terror rise when they had to go down the other side of a huge hill. She was barely strong enough to hold the brake in place and feared they would tumble into a ravine. The strength and intelligence of Maud and Jim, however, always prevented the caravan from becoming a pile of wreckage. At noon, they stopped in a beautiful little clearing where a creek wound between grassy banks. The horses and cow were allowed to drink their fill, and a bag of oats was opened. The chickens received a pan of the cool water and some feed.

Eleanore brought the big picnic basket down from the seat. The supreme moment had come and the children squealed with delight when their mother uncovered the goodies Aunt Emmy had packed the day before. The basket held chicken, beet pickles, and a large loaf of soft bread that the children smeared with plum jelly. The real treasure, though, was a brown paper sack of raisin-dotted cookies from Aunt Emmy's pantry. They felt capable of devouring all of the basket's contents in one sitting, but they soon found themselves full, and enough food remained for a second meal.

"It's a good thing there is extra food. We'll have it for supper. We have a long way to travel yet, so I don't think we'll have a house to sleep in tonight," said Eleanore to the children.

"Oh, Mama!" yelped Nancy with obvious glee. "Do you mean we'll sleep outside in a place like this? My, won't that be fun!"

"Yeah," answered Paul in his most grown-up voice. "I'm almost a man, so I'll see to it that nothing bothers you women."

Nancy snorted at Paul's overtones to adulthood, but Eleanore only smiled and turned her head toward Toby, who was finishing out the meal's scraps. That beast, she thought, was her real protector.

The journey was resumed and the family rode through a long and sunny afternoon. The cow tired, and Toby felt obligated to bark at her heels to maintain progress. Sometimes Jersey let a foot fly wildly at the dog, but he always managed to dodge. The kicks were a professional challenge, and they seemed to elevate the dog's enthusiasm for herding.

Chapter VI

THE LAST TOWN

IT WAS NEARLY FIVE o'clock when they reached the first and only town between Cedarville and Dean's Creek. It was called Big Town. The naming of the town proved to be an act of jest or generosity, for the town itself consisted only of a rocky street lined with a general store, post office, blacksmith shop, a church in need of paint, and half a dozen dwellings. At the foot of the hill, beside a swiftly flowing creek, was a mill for grinding corn and wheat.

The porch of Harper's General Store was thickly littered with men and boys. Some sat on a well-worn bench, while others seemed to support the porch posts. Still others rested full length on the plank flooring. Many had straw hats tilted over their heads to either protect them from the sun, or to camouflage catnapping eyes. There were farmers with long moustaches who were neatly dressed in clean overalls and handmade checked shirts. There were also a few drummers in derby hats. They smoked cigars and wore store clothes. Some of the boys were pretending to be asleep, but everyone knew they were keenly tuned to every oath and tale of the elders. There were also other sorts on the porch. They sported stained whiskers, ragged clothes, and eyes like those of hungry dogs. Nearly everyone used a sawdust box for spitting out tobacco juice; accuracy was not mandatory. Bored horses stood patiently tied to posts, waiting for their masters to rise and go home. Eleanore imagined that any number of wives pretended to believe that their husbands had come into town to take care of business affairs. They surely knew they had come into town to hold court on the front porch of the store.

Eleanore hated to walk through them, but she had to go into the store to get directions. The road now broke off in three directions, and she had no idea which turn led to Dean's Creek. When she climbed down from the wagon, she knew she had an audience. The onlookers nudged each other at the sight of her white embroidered petticoat and trim ankles.

One of the farmers whispered, "That must be Doc Gray's wife from Cedarville." His announcement quieted the men. They had all known the doctor. The men stood politely aside to allow Eleanore to pass through the door.

Stepping inside was like entering a blackened room. When her eyes adjusted to the dimness, she surveyed the room. All of the walls were lined with shelves of dry goods and foods. There were barrels of this and that cluttering the floor. At the far end, she spotted the proprietor busily measuring off yellow calico for a squat woman in a plaid dress. When the owner finally spied Eleanore, he yelled, "Hey, Nell, there's somebody in the store!"

"All right, Pa, coming," came a voice from a doorway that evidently led to living quarters. From it emerged a tall, raw-boned young woman with a booming voice. "Something fer ye, ma'am?" she asked as sweetly as her unfortunate voice would allow.

"Yes," replied Eleanore with hesitation. "I wonder if you could tell me which road goes to Dean's Creek."

"Sure. Ye jes' goes straight 'til ye cross the creek and then ye turns left. I think it's the left. Ain't it, Pa?" When Pa yelled back the confirmation, the woman asked, "What are ye goin' up thar fer?"

"I'm moving there."

"Well, for pity sake, why?" she asked incredulously.

"I have a farm there," replied Eleanore as politely as possible.

"Land's sakes alive!" bellowed the hearty Nell. "I can't see why a body would want to go there after that drought we had las' year. I'll take town living myself!"

Eleanore suppressed a wry smile that might have implied impertinence. Instead she said softly, "Well, to each his own."

"Don't ye wanna buy nothing?" asked Nell in disappointment.

"Come to think of it, there are three children in my wagon who may just appreciate a dime's worth of peppermint candy," said Eleanore as she pointed to a glass jar on the far end of the counter.

Nell's curiosity seemed to grow as she counted out the sticks. "What's yer name, if you don't mind me being so bold?"

"Eleanore Gray."

"Oh!" exclaimed a flustered Nell. "I'll be! Well, thank ye. Anything else ye be wantin'?"

Nell's sudden change of manner let Eleanore know that her husband had clearly impressed people here. Undoubtedly, news of his death had traveled fast. As Eleanore turned to leave, Nell hollered out, "I wish ye luck, ma'am. I guess a farm ain't bad for them that likes it."

The men on the porch hushed as Eleanore swept through them to the wagon. She tossed the bag to Nancy who immediately squealed and divided up the sticks of candy. When Eleanore was in her seat again leading the team down the hill, Nancy handed her the bag. "And, Mama, there are four sticks left for you." As Eleanore took a bite of the red sweet, she chuckled aloud over Nell Harper and Big Town. The children suddenly looked up at their mother. It was the first time they had heard real laughter from her in many weeks.

The day's light was not going to last forever. The sun was already hanging low in the western sky. Layers of mauve, lavender, and coral clouds moved eastward. Maud and Jim were tired. Each turn of the wheel strained them. The roads were rougher and less traveled now. Sometimes the trees grew so close that the hubs would scrape the trunks as they passed through. Even Toby's spirits suffered. His usual energetic trot was reduced to a slow and deliberate walk. Eleanore was exhausted and her arms, unaccustomed to driving a team, felt lead heavy. They had traveled twenty-two miles since sunrise, and a camp had to be found before sunset.

A small creek ran over a rocky bed in the tiny clearing they chose for the night. The animals were allowed to graze and drink their fill. The children stretched their cramped legs, and little Janey whimpered at the sight of the shadowed valley of dark trees. Although the cow held out, Eleanore managed to get milk to comfort the baby and feed the older children. Without fanfare, the lunch basket was opened and its contents were consumed in silence.

Eleanore spread a pallet for the children in the wagon below the seat. The down pillows and feather tick were as comfortable as their little iron beds from home had been. As she covered them with quilts, Nancy asked, "Where are you going to sleep, Mama?"

"Don't you worry. I'm going to be down here near you on the grass. I've got a pillow and plenty of blankets. I'll be just fine."

"I'm scared for you, Mama," said Paul, who remembered his promise of protection. "What if a wildcat or snake comes up to get you?" Paul's fear was evident in his voice and little Janey picked it up and howled with renewed terror.

"Oh, Paul! Now see what you've done, you bad boy!" scolded Nancy. "Mama, can't you crowd in with us? We can make room."

"No, dear. We all need real rest, and we won't get it if we're all bunched up. You don't need to fret. Toby will stay with me. See, Maud and Jim and Jersey aren't frightened. Now, now, Janey! Lay your wee tiny head down on the pillow and go to sleepy town. Mama will sing you a song."

Eleanore, despite weariness, sang "Jesus, Lover of My Soul" until the baby's clenched fists unwound and rested partially open. Her children had fallen asleep before the second verse was complete.

Eleanore found her own sleep more elusive. The ground was hard, and small sticks and stones poked through the bottom quilt. She tossed and turned on the hard damp ground until she finally laid flat on her back to watch the sky. Stars filled it and she traced their patterns. She ached.

She thought of the loafers on the porch in Big Town. It frightened her. She heard a screech owl, and Toby left her to investigate. She thought she would never sleep. The dew chilled her and she went to the wagon for another blanket.

She recovered the sleepy youngsters and returned with an extra quilt to her bed on the ground. What was it, she thought, that she had sung to the children? She sang "Jesus, Lover of My Soul" to herself. Toby returned from his prowl and thumped down beside her. He thrust his cold but reassuring nose into her palm.

Eleanore slept.

Chapter VII
DEAN'S CREEK

THE SUN PEEPING OVER the ridge woke Eleanore. She felt rested despite the hardness of her bed and the dampness of the dew. Toby was up and prowling. The children had covered their faces with a blanket and continued to sleep. She left them to feed the team and chickens and to milk the cow. She had always found these early morning chores pleasant. When she finished, she went to the creek to wash herself.

The cold spring water stung her hands and face, but it made them glow with a rosiness that betrayed her weariness. She undid her hair to comb the tangles out. Grass and burrs were matted in. When she finally replaced the mass of curls high on her head, she thought she looked like a lady in a fashion magazine. "Really, Mrs. Gray!" she mimicked aloud. "That's a brazen notion for a would-be Cedarville widow!"

Her sleepy-eyed children tumbled and squealed down toward the creek to join her. Toby also returned from the thicket. He splashed through the water and shook furiously. He rolled in the grass and growled with happiness while Nancy and Paul washed in the cold water. Janey protested, but even she was scrubbed until she squeaked. When they were all freshly dressed, Eleanore gathered them for a breakfast of bread with plum jelly and fresh milk. Restored by sleep and invigorated by the creek bath, they chattered with animation and cheer. Their fears of the previous night were forgotten.

"Mama, can I have more jelly bread?" asked Paul. "See those trees blooming on the hill? I think they're redbud trees. Ain't they pretty, Nancy?"

"Yes, it's so pretty here I wish we could stay forever. Why couldn't we? We could make a house with brush under the trees like they do for brush arbor meetings! Couldn't we, Mama?" Nancy liked the idea.

"I suppose we could, but it would get cold in winter," replied Eleanore.

"Oh," said Nancy, "I forgot about that, and the rain, too. Looks like we'll have to keep going. I'll pack the basket, Mama. Get down, Toby! You've had your share."

This day's journey was more promising. There were, after all, only eight miles left to Dean's Creek, and the horses and passengers were anxious to start out. They passed through meadows lined by forests, and the songs of jays, cardinals, robins and small yellow and black birds filled the air. The children joined the birds in song. Nancy, with her high, clear voice, and Paul, with his childish treble, sang "Dear Nellie Gray," "The Little Rosewood Casket," and "Sweet Evelina" with joyful relish. The miles passed.

By ten o'clock, they passed a long, rocky bald with bluffs of honeycomb rock and scrub trees. The road crept higher and higher until it finally revealed a view that left even Eleanore breathless. It was magnificent. Dean's Creek, shining in the morning sun, ran through its bed like a silver serpent. Large, whitened sycamores extended their branches to the sky. Pale green willows dipped their fringes into the sparkling water. On both sides of the creek, set like an exotic quilt pattern, were fields. Some were dark brown with freshly turned soil, while others were green with clover and wheat. Placid cattle grazed in pastures, and homes could be spotted at half-mile intervals up the valley. Blue gray wood smoke curled up from chimneys. Orchards burst with bloom. Clustered around homes were the rosy mists of peach blossoms, white clouds of plum blossoms, and the pale green auras of budding apple trees. On both sides of the valley rose rounded hills, which were covered with the rich, green denseness of leaf and bloom.

As Eleanore drove on, however, the vision of prosperity diminished. The first dwelling she approached was set back from the road in a little draw. The log structure looked more like a corn crib than a true house. A small baby was stationed in a dry-good box that served as an improvised crib. On the front steps was one of the most vicious-looking men Eleanore had ever seen. He wore a stubby beard that seemed to serve no purpose but to collect the foul tobacco juice that drooled from the corners of his thick, coarse lips. His clothes appeared to be a cut above the thin rags worn by his wife. He even had boots on; the wife, despite the chill, was barefoot.

Eleanore felt a deep pity for the woman. She nodded and spoke, "Good morning," but the woman only nodded very slightly and returned to her digging as if her life depended on it. The man, however, leered and raised a huge, hairy arm in seeming friendliness.

When they were out of earshot, Nancy whispered, "Wasn't that an awful man!" Paul consented, "Gosh, he scared me terrible. Did you see how dirty his face was?" Eleanore, in an effort to preserve optimism, said, "Yes, dears, and we can hope he's not our nearest neighbor."

This was the case, though, and they realized it as soon as they recrossed the creek and turned up the hill to their own cabin. The hill rising up to their new home was steep, rocky, and unused. Will Gray stood at the gate to welcome them. He hurried forth with outstretched arms and helped them all down from the wagon. As he undid the team and cow, he said, "I was getting worried about you. You've no idea what a relief it is to see you safe and sound. I kept thinking I should have gone to Cedarville to fetch you myself, but it's a bad season for taking time out. Are you all feeling okay? Was the trip much for you? The kids look fine. Here, let's go in and take a look around!"

Eleanore smiled at his enthusiasm. They entered the open gate and, after they passed through, she noticed that Will made a deliberate gesture to keep it ajar. He knew Eleanore had spotted him, and he sheepishly explained that local superstition prohibited closing an open gate. "It's foolishness, I know, but it's not my gate to close!"

The log house was low and weathered to a silvery gray color. Well-worn steps led them through a vine-shaded doorway. Honeysuckle, perhaps planted by some young bride's hands, ran riot over the doorway to mingle with a lush Virginia creeper from the other side. On each side of the path were gooseberry bushes as round and perfect as city manicured shrubbery. Bees hummed as they worked away on yellow blossoms. Rose bushes grew in a corner of the yard. Although they had not been cared for, the new green stems gave promise, and Eleanore hoped they would bloom. Lilacs, with huge lavender clumps hanging thick and sweet between heart-shaped leaves, held posts of honor against the front corners of the house. "Please, Will," said Eleanore as Will reached to turn the door latch, "Let's look around out here before we go in."

The backyard was shaded by gnarled orchard trees. Apple, peach, and plum trees mingled limb and blossom above, and the ground below was covered with emerald green grass that had been delicately littered with fallen blossoms. Nancy and Paul ran about, peeping between bushes, into the well house, and inside the log stable. Fresh hay scented the stable with a crisp and pungent aroma. The freed Plymouth hens ran about on their stiff legs, eating grass and gravel with comic fury.

With Janey in her arms, Eleanore was hesitant to leave the beauty of the yard for the interior of the dark doorway. "It's so beautiful! I never dreamed it would be as fine as this. Just look at the view and that creek!"

"It's pretty, Eleanore, but don't be misled," said Will. "The land itself is poor; it's been corned to death. The people wouldn't raise anything but corn year after year, and now the fields are washed away. See those ditches?"

The bare fields stretching to the west were marred by red clay ditches. "I admit it doesn't look fertile now, but I can't believe that a place so beautiful has to stay poor. Everything is going to be just fine. The children already love it. Just look at them! They're as busy as the chickens. Even Janey seems mesmerized." She sighed, eyeing those ditches. "I hope I've done right to bring them here."

"Well, there are plenty of youngsters here about for them to play with. Some of them are mighty nice and come from good families. I want all of you to find happiness here, Ellie, but you need to know just what you're getting into," said Will.

"Bob would want us to be happy. I feel near to him here, closer than I felt to him in Cedarville. This was his special place. Do you think perhaps that the spirits of loved ones guide us to happiness?"

"I don't know about that, Ellie, but it is a nice way of looking at things. I'll warn you though, and don't take it lightly, that you'd best not speak of spirits and such to folks around here. It's surprising, but most people around here carry superstitious notions. They take talk about spirits seriously. They still think uneasy spirits haunt people!"

"What are 'haunts'?" cried Paul.

"Nothing you need to know about," answered Eleanore.

"What's a 'haunt'? I want to see a haunt!" yelled Paul as he danced up and down between the two adults.

"You wouldn't want to see one if it came up behind you and yelled 'BOO!'" taunted the wise Nancy. The children then ran off behind the house, laughing and shouting, "Boo...Boo...Boo!!!"

Will and Eleanore finally crossed the threshold and entered the cabin itself. The wide-planked oak floor had been scrubbed until it looked new. The walls, though rough, had been white-washed, and they made a lovely contrast against the log beams that ran over the ceiling. Tiny windows, set high up, glimmered. On the far end of the room was a large fireplace of native stone. Logs were already laid on the andirons. A mottled yellow spatterware bowl filled with sprays of dogwood and crabapple had been placed on the carved walnut mantle. Eleanore rushed to them and buried her face in the heady fragrance.

The reserve and control that had prohibited tears for weeks suddenly failed her. Torrents of tears and sobs shook her apart. With almost womanly tenderness, Will stepped forward to take the baby from her arms. He held Janey and placed a heavy hand on Eleanore's shoulder and gently said, "I'll take them away, Ellie. I didn't mean to make you feel badly."

"It's not the flowers, Will," she managed to gasp out between sobs. "I'm being selfish to do this in front of you. I can't seem to help it. You've done so much for us."

When she had regained composure, Will left to find the children and begin unloading the wagon. He returned with the box of pantry supplies and scuffled through the packages until he found the salt and pepper. He held them up and grinned. "These are the first articles any self-respecting Hill person unpacks. Rumor has it that it will bring you good luck if you place these on the shelves before you move in!"

He single-handedly managed the large four poster bed and set it up under one of the high windows. The dresser and pine table were placed near it, and the hobnailed lamp was placed on the table. The lean-to kitchen shelves were slowly loaded with provisions. Eleanore made a fire on the cook stove and put a kettle of water on to boil. While Will and Paul put up an extra shelf for her best dishes, Eleanore covered the table with blue check homespun. Nancy moved the rocker near the fire, and made up her mother's bed with a gay wedding ring quilt as a spread.

"Really, I think I like this way of living! There's something about the fireplace that will make this room look grand no matter how it's furnished. That portrait of your and Bob's mother looks just right over the mantle. Her curls and clothes seem almost fashionable again. What do you think, Nancy? Do you want your pictures put up now? Over the bed or above the dresser?"

"Both! Let's put the 'Guardian Angel' over the bed and 'Rock of Ages' with the baby Jesus above the dresser." Nancy helped to hang and straighten them, and then she jumped down from the chair and picked up a picture of her father. "Let's put this one next to the bed on the little table. That way, we can look at him if we wake up at night." She reverently polished the frame and arranged the picture on the table.

"Mama, I'm hungry!" announced Paul from the kitchen end of the cabin.

They all laughed at this as Eleanore replied, "Your appetite is on schedule. It's past lunchtime. The water's boiling and I'll have something ready shortly. One of you needs to keep an eye on Janey for me so I can work." They soon sat down to biscuits with jelly, bacon, and coffee.

Will, as he was about to bite into his fourth biscuit, teased, "I see my little playmate has grown up to be a real cook!"

Eleanore flushed, and Paul piped up, "Why does he call you his 'little playmate'?"

Will spared Eleanore by answering for her. "Well, when she was about your size, we used to have grand times playing house, riding horse sticks, and even climbing trees."

Eleanore interjected, "And fighting, too, if I remember correctly. My head still aches when I remember how hard my braids were tugged!"

Will, not to be undone, added, "The time you blackened my eye caused my mother to call you a 'terrible tomboy'!"

The children laughed loudly. They could hardly picture their mother being involved in such antics. Uncle Will and Mama smiled, too. Biscuits and jelly and laughter filled their mouths, and life seemed strangely safe.

"By the way, Will, we seem to have some rather unpleasant-looking neighbors," said Eleanore with renewed seriousness.

"Say no more, Ellie. You must have met Hank Leffert. Yep, he's a true brute and a mean drunk. His wife was a nice woman 'til she married him. I wouldn't dwell on them if I were you, though. There are far nicer people here about. The Adamses, the Smalls, and the Petersons live in the bottom, and they're all more respectable than the likes of Hank Leffert. The women, as a matter of fact, are to be expected any time now!"

Will brushed a lock of hair off his forehead, paused, and then continued his conversation. "These hills are not like Cedarville, Ellie. Cedarville is something of a town that has kept pace with progress in a commercial and social sense. Many of the people here have never been out of here, never had exposure to ideas we've had. Most of the people are pleasantly refreshing and un-touched by the sort of corruptions seen in modern towns. There are bad sorts, though. There are moonshiners and troublemak-

ers, and folk so ignorant that their survival seems a mercy. Some
of us have tried to help. We built a church, you know. It's on the
hill above my place. It's just a Christian church in general. We
rotate preachers of different faiths. The Hill women have started to come, and they seem anxious to learn. Some have even
started going to school. It's not uncommon to see a woman
twenty years-old at a desk behind a seven year-old child. Mrs.
Wetherby is a wonderful teacher. The men and boys, however,
are a different lot. Stubborn, ignorant, and sometimes plainly
mean, they are. I must warn you to keep your doors locked at
night. You need a loaded pistol, too. A beautiful woman without
a husband may seem like easy prey to some."

"How you flatter me, Will! I'm sure I can take care of myself. Should I ever need you, I'll fire a gun three times. I'm sure
you'd be at my doorstep in a moment," laughed Eleanore. She
never dreamed this would ever be necessary.

Chapter VIII

PLANTING

ELEANORE ROSE AT DAYBREAK. Her rest, though broken twice during the night, was thorough. Once, only hours after she had gone to bed, she had sat bolt upright and panicked. The new room disoriented her momentarily. She actually rose and climbed the narrow stairs to the attic loft where Will had set up the iron beds for the children. Nancy and Paul had apparently suffered no trouble and slept soundly. Janey provided a second interruption to her already broken rest by crying out loudly an hour later. Eleanore had again left her bed to give the child water and comfort her to sleep. Her first resolution for the morning was to move the children down to sleep near her. Her second was to survey her property alone before the children awoke.

Eleanore dressed silently and quickly, lifted the oak door latch, and stepped into the April dawn. Streaks of orange and orchid already touched the eastern sky. Birds shattered an otherwise silent world with a variety of melodies that made the low cackling of her hens mere trumpery by comparison. She investigated the henhouse first, made mental resolve to improve it as soon as possible, and moved on to the barn. It had been cleaned out by Will, but more work remained for her. A huge pile of rotting manure lay only a few feet from the entrance. "I must get busy," she said to herself. The manure, she thought, might be suitable for gardening. Cracks in the stable wall would have to be repaired before winter, and the adjoining lot would require fence mending before she could raise pigs.

The fields in back of the house caused her to frown. Barren except for a profusion of weeds, the fields clearly appeared to be as unfertile and unpromising as Will's warning had indicated. She would have to learn if there were ways to recover fertility, ways to stop the washing off. She turned her back and gazed out over the more pleasing prospect of the valley. Will had plowed a ten acre stretch along the road near the creek. It belonged to her. He had told them that the stretch would raise their "bread and beans" during the next year. Eleanore smiled at the phrase yesterday. Today, it was a dismal notion. Ten acres of rich land, and huge stretches of eroded land; ten acres would not make much of a farm. "If I don't learn more, it will be bread and beans for the rest of our lives," she said aloud. She'd plant corn, a cash crop, on those precious ten acres.

She fetched the pail from the house and returned to look for the cow. Jersey was placidly nibbling away on the new grass on the hill above the barn. When Eleanore called to her, she barely raised her head and returned to her eating. Eleanore called Toby away from the rat hole he was investigating. He knew her wishes instantly, and tore up the hill to chase the cow home. Jersey, however, recalled the grudge that had developed between them during the journey to Dean's Creek and decided to take action against the hairy little beast. She lowered her head, raised her tail over her back, and, with an angry snort, lunged for him. The dog apparently thought discretion was the better part of valor.

He tucked his tail between his legs and ran for protection behind a paling face. The cow gave chase and stood glaring down at him from the other side of the fence.

The encounter amused and half alarmed Eleanore. She laughed aloud when Toby, the brave and fearless, barked furiously at the plainly unpardoning cow. He continued to glance at Eleanore every so often during the harangue as if to say, "I got her here, so now you better do something!" Eleanore obliged by taking Jersey into the stable to be milked. The woman climbed into the loft and tossed a forkful of hay down to the cow to abate her temper. Jersey quickly changed from an untamed beast into a gentle, middle-aged cow. She allowed her mistress an abundance of milk.

The children, roused by the racket in the yard, stood in the doorway, rubbing sleep from their eyes and shivering from the chill of the morning air. When she saw them, Eleanore called, "Get into your clothes! Nancy, you dress the baby. We have lots to do today. I'll fix breakfast." The children were obedient and instantly retreated to fulfill the commands. Eleanore finished milking and went inside to prepare hot mush.

Nancy, Paul, and Janey were unusually gay over breakfast, so much so that their mother had to stamp her feet and scold them over the excessive chatter and play at the table. Janey gurgled and gabbed in her baby voice and spilled so much on her bib that her mother finally took the spoon from her and fed her herself. Paul spilled milk across the tablecloth and Nancy nearly choked on her food from laughter. Although Eleanore was usually calm and fairly permissive about the behavior of her children, she felt they had to be pulled into her work.

"Children, I know you are excited about being here, but I need your help and cooperation as I've never needed it before. Your father took a great responsibility upon himself to provide for us. Now we must band together and assume that job ourselves. Do you understand?"

"This farm needs more work than we have imagined, and we cannot ever again postpone work when it needs to be done. This is an important time of the year for a farm family. Our gardens must be put in now. I need you to work with me. I want Nancy to bring out a bucket of fresh water to wash the dishes while I tidy the other rooms. Paul, you must feed Toby and the chickens."

The children caught the spirit at once. While Janey played, Nancy and her mother washed the bowls and put them away, swept the floors and turned back the bedcovers for airing. Paul, in addition to his chores, emptied the dirty water and wrung out the rags and spread them over the gooseberry bushes to dry. Eleanore opened a big trunk and found a practical split bonnet for herself and smaller bonnets for Janey and Nancy. She pinned a large denim apron around her waist and appraised everyone's work with a businesslike air. With her children at her heels, the family went out to the newly-plowed garden patch.

Will Gray had plowed and harrowed already, so the worst part was done. Eleanore shook her head at the rather thin clay loam that lay exposed. She picked up a handful and let it run through her fist. Paul imitated her motion and then looked up at her for further instruction. "Well, I think the first thing we must do is move that pile of old manure from the barn to the garden. This soil is too poor as it is for vegetables. The problem is how to move it. We don't have a cart or wheelbarrow."

Paul looked helplessly around. "Mama, see that old tub over in that junk? Could we use that?" Nancy instantly ran over and hauled a battered old tub out from a pile of abandoned odds and ends. "It's alright except for a few holes in the bottom," she announced. "Mama, maybe you and I together could carry it."

"What can I do?" cried Paul.

"You stay here under the tree and play with Janey, son. That would be a big help, and you're really too small to lift this tub when it's loaded."

"Naw, I don't want to stay here. Toby can watch Janey, and I could help you. I'm strong, Mama. I thought I could take this old bucket and carry it full," he said as he ran off with the bucket to get the first load of manure. Toby, as always, seemed to understand their conversation. He trotted over and sank down, panting next to the baby girl under the tree.

At first the work went quickly. Children can do a lot of work if they choose to, and both Paul and Nancy were willing, but as the sun rose higher, little arms began to ache and little legs lagged. By noon, the pile had been only half moved. "I'm tired," sighed Nancy as she sank down on the soft turf by her sister. Paul dropped his bucket with a bang and flopped down by her side. "I'm hungry, Mama. Aren't we gonna have something to eat?"

"Pretty soon, dear. You and Nancy sit there and rest awhile and I'll spread this out and work it into the soil. This afternoon we'll plant some seeds."

After dinner, Janey was put to bed for a nap, and Nancy and Eleanore went back to gardening. After much raking and breaking, the clods were spread and rows were scored for planting. They planted lettuce, beets, radishes and peas. The tiny seeds were planted and spaced by Paul's small grimy hands. They all went to work on hands and knees, inserting onion sets. When they were done, they stood back and admired the result of their labors. A weary woman with two weary children stood arms akimbo with perspiration, dirt, and manure clinging to them. They all grinned with satisfaction. "How long before they are big enough to eat?" asked Paul with a child's impatience.

"Not long for some, Paul. Tomorrow we'll plant potatoes and start getting ready to tackle the corn. There'll always be weeding and hoeing to do, too."

"Doesn't sound like much fun to me," grumbled a tired child.

"Well, as the Indians used to say, no work 'um, no eat 'um!" laughed a teasing Eleanore as she headed for the house to rouse the sleeping Janey.

When the sun set, a dampish breeze sprung up and carried a chill up from the creek. Frogs began their evening serenade in the lowlands. The chickens went to roost, and Jersey was at the gate chewing her cud, waiting to be milked. Eleanore hurried the three children into the house with her, set a fire to ward off the chill, and brought out a tub of water and soap. She put it near the fire, washed her hands, and told the children to scrub themselves up while she tended to the cow. When she returned with a foaming pail, she found the children scrubbed and sitting in the rocker, singing in their soft, sweet voices.

They were unaware of her quiet entrance. She paused on the threshold to look at the scene before her in motherly appreciation. The firelight caught in the blonde curls of Paul's head made him appear as if he were wearing a halo of spun gold. Nancy's young face was filled with a Madonna-like glow of love and innocence as she cuddled little Janey and Paul. Eleanore felt her throat tighten with a possessive love for her daughter and the two little ones. The children suddenly looked up at her with smiling faces. She gently placed the pail on the floor and ran to them, gathered them in her arms, and covered faces and hands with playful kisses. The baby squealed with pleasure while Paul and Nancy returned her kisses, kiss for kiss. Paul, always the boy, finally ended the playful attack by saying, "Ain't we gonna' eat?" They all laughed and their mother rose and headed for the kitchen.

"We're having dinner in the parlor tonight, my loves, so remain seated until the cook brings it in!" she called. They all laughed at this, and while Eleanore prepared the meal, the little ones play-acted a formal dinner scene. Their mother returned with great squares of cornbread left from lunch and thick slices of home-cured ham to be toasted over the fire. As a special treat, a jar of canned peaches was opened and served with thick yellow cream in Eleanore's nicest hand-painted dessert dishes.

They were full and satisfied. Nancy said, "Isn't this just like a party, Mama?" Paul echoed, "Just like a party."

Janey was tucked into her cradle. True to her resolve, Eleanore covered Nancy and Paul in her own bed. She felt a sudden let-down. She was almost too tired herself to face the dishes and washing up, but she knew not to postpone chores. It was slow going for a weary woman to wash dishes, scrub, and sweep, but she managed. She finally bolted the doors, combed out her hair, and replaced her soiled dress with a clean, light wrapper. She sat down before the dying embers. "Oh, help me, kind Heavenly Father, make me brave and strong for my children's sake," she prayed. "Keep me from making too many mistakes and keep us well and happy. I ask this in Jesus' name. Amen." Scalding tears poured down her cheeks as she thought of the husband she missed so dearly. "I don't know how we'll do without you. I love you, Bob Gray." The tears relieved her aching heart, and when she finally snuggled down next to her sleeping children, slumber fell upon her.

Chapter IX

NANCY

THE DAYS FLEW BY. Eleanore and the children rose early each morning, hurried through breakfast and domestic chores, and headed for the fields. Janey was placed in the shade to play under the supervision of the big black and white dog. The bottom field was planted in corn. Vic Small, an awkward half-grown boy, harrowed the roughly plowed ground and laid off check rows for two dollars a day. Nancy and Paul followed him and dropped the white grains into the furrows, two seeds in each cross. Eleanore followed with a hoe to cover each check with pulverized soil, and to press it firmly in place with a pat of the hoe. Following the family came the birds, friendly black birds with purplish feathers that glistened in the sun, rusty-breasted robins and homely, little sparrows. Each bird desired either a tasty worm from the turned up soil, or an occasional grain of corn left uncovered or spilled. Sometimes a hoarse crow would fly down, gather up the coveted grain, and then swerve off for a tree to call out his claim. The birds afforded the hard-working children a little amusement, and they often left an intentional stray grain for the birds to swoop upon.

Life had become work, work, and more work. Eleanore's hands, always a great source of pride to her and of envy to her friends, changed from their soft whiteness to a firmly calloused brown. Freckles appeared on her nose. Her soft, dark curls became rebellious under the gingham bonnet and escaped to blow and batter around her face in the winds. Damp, tight rings of hair covered her sweaty forehead. The children were equally freckled and grubby from the week of outdoor labor. Nancy could do almost as much work as her mother. Paul, in boyish enthusiasm, often did more harm than good. He frequently dropped the wrong number of grains, spilled more in an effort to retrieve the first error, and usually ended up falling in the cloddy soil in frustration. Each mistake was forgiven, though, and work well done was rewarded by his mother's accolades of praise. That seemed to be the secret of her success with the children. Even little Janey received her share of praise. No one neglected to notice that she behaved like a lamb as she patiently and quietly occupied herself playing with rocks, rag dolls, insects, and leaves during the long days of planting.

Will Gray dropped by on Friday. He saw the progress the family had made and smiled widely. "Have you had any visitors yet, Ellie?"

"None but you. I kept expecting a flock any minute from the way you talked the other day, but I'm starting to think we're the only ones out here!"

"They'll be by. I suggested they hold off a spell so you could get settled in. Besides, everybody around here looks as dirty as you do right now, it being plantin' time and all. The women wouldn't want you seeing them looking like that any more than you'd want company seeing you right now. Just look at that apron! You're a sight!"

"Very funny, Mr. Gray. I don't suppose there's a way to do this and still look presentable? If there is, you best let me in on it."

"No secret there, Eleanore. When you work for a living, you get damn dirty and so tired you think you won't survive the season. I must admit, you've done a sight more than expected and looks like you've done it well. I have to get back to my own work, but I wanted to stop and see if you needed anything."

Eleanore felt her cheeks warm at Will's language. "Nothing that a tub of hot water won't fix. Thanks for coming, though."

The days had been filled with work. Evenings were loaded with scrubbing, chores, getting supper, and crawling into bed, bone weary and grateful for a place to drop. Sleep came instantly to all of them. By Saturday afternoon, in addition to the vegetable plot, the bottom field had been planted all in corn, except for a half acre set with seed potatoes. Eleanore and the children stood on a knoll looking down on their achievement. Eleanore remembered her small garden back in Cedarville. It seemed so tiny compared to this.

"We're done, children. Tomorrow is Sunday, and were going to spend it resting and playing," she announced with satisfaction.

"Aren't we gonna go to church like at home?" asked Paul.

"Maybe next Sunday. You've worked so hard and deserve a chance to act like youngsters for a change instead of a team of horses! Besides, I need a chance to collect my thoughts without worrying about meeting new people looking like this," she said as she held out her hands to examine her blistered palms.

"I know what we'll do!" cried Nancy. She grabbed Janey's pudgy little hand and trotted the wobbling baby up the hill leading to the house. "We'll make a playhouse under that black hawthorn tree up here. See how it spreads out like a roof and the grass is like a carpet!" she called. As they were admiring

Nancy's plan, Nancy suddenly let out a shrill scream and came running back, pulling the baby so forcefully that they stumbled and fell in a heap. Her face was pasty white. Her eyes stared in terror at a large copperhead only a few feet away. It writhed and twisted and raised its head to strike. Eleanore was stricken with horror. She reached for Nancy to pull her back, but paused when the snake jutted out.

Suddenly, a black and white streak flashed past her. Toby had seen the danger and, with lightning speed, he had jumped over Nancy, sank his teeth into the snake's middle, and shook it violently. When he threw it some six feet away, it was clearly dead. Toby wasn't satisfied. He again seized it and shook it with intensity until he was certain he had done his duty well. He sniffed it, pawed it, and then turned to Eleanore with much wagging and grinning. Eleanore helped the girls to their feet and held them to her. Tears of terror and relief streamed down their cheeks. Paul jumped up and down with excitement. "Good boy, Toby! You fixed him good, didn't you, boy? You ain't afraid of snakes, are you, feller?"

"Oh, Toby, I could kiss you," said Eleanore, and she and Nancy fell to their knees and hugged the dog tightly. They hurried away from the scene as quickly as their trembling legs would permit. It was a wise maneuver, as it was mating season and the dead snake's companion was probably nearby.

The house seemed like a haven after the harrowing experience. The hens were cackling and strutting in the yard, and bees hovered in the afternoon sun over the honeysuckle blooms. It was good to be home, good to have the hardest jobs done. The wide poster bed, smooth and clean with sheets and coverlet, seemed inviting. The water from the well tasted better than ever when Eleanore drew up a fresh bucketful. They sat in the kitchen with bread and milk after the hard day. Eleanore washed her face and hands, then fetched the box containing her husband's medical supplies. She cleaned her blisters and spread them with salve, then wound them with strips of clean white cloth. She was glad her children had been spared hoeing.

After lunch, they scrubbed themselves. Although the sun was still high in the sky, the children were grateful to be put to bed. Eleanore turned down the covers, settled the tired children, and stretched out beside them. Every muscle ached, and a weariness that comes from hard labor swept over them. How good it felt to be resting in a bed after bending and stooping for six days!

Janey and Paul fell asleep instantly, but sleep eluded Nancy, who kept her eyes closed as her mind turned. She felt her mother's body relax and listened to her breathing. Mother was asleep. Nancy opened her eyes. She watched her mother intently. Her mother's face looked white against her dark lashes and dark hair. Her hair spread over the pillowslip like a crown of feathers. How young she looked, mused Nancy. She looked like a young girl. The sleeping woman's hands, pitifully battered and bandaged, stung the little girl's heart. Her pearly nails were cracked and scarred with traces of dirt that would not wash out. "They are not much bigger than mine," thought the girl. "Oh, why can't I do something to help her? If I were bigger, I could do the cooking and she wouldn't have to do that, at least after working out there all day." Nancy suddenly got an idea. "I know! I'll milk old Jersey for her tonight and feed the chickens. She'll like that."

Nancy stayed awake, making plans. "I won't go to sleep. I'll get up and have it all done before she gets up." It wasn't hard to stay awake. Every time she closed her eyes, a vision of the plaid-backed snake with his threatening tongue loomed before her. The terror of not being able to get away filled her. Her mother had tried to pull her away. "Dear, dear Mama," she repeated to herself. "Oh, Dear God, why did you take Daddy away from us and leave us alone like this? We need him," she thought as hot tears scored her soft cheeks.

Nancy softly crept from the bed, picked up her shoes, and tip-toed into the kitchen. She got the milk pail and let herself out the door to put her shoes on. Everything seemed still with the other children asleep. She went into the dim interior of the corn crib and filled her apron with feed for the chickens. The corn, like the hay in the stable, had come from Will Gray. She thought about her uncle. "How good he is to us!" she thought as she sat at the door shelling corn. "He's sort of like Daddy, but I think Daddy was smarter because he was a doctor." She had always been proud of her father's profession. When people came to the door to ask for him, it filled her with a sense of importance. Daddy had called her his little nurse. He even let her hold the instrument tray and fetch supplies. "Well, at least I know one thing is for certain. When I grow up, I'm going to be a nurse," she told herself with childlike assurance.

She finished shelling the corn, scattered it to the hungry chickens, and shook the cobs and chaff from her apron. The cow had come over the hill from the back pasture. She came of her own accord for an evening forkful of hay and a few ears of allowed corn. It was great inducement and saved them from having to chase her about at milking time. Nancy climbed up into the stable loft and threw down the hay. "Gosh, it's dark up here. What if there are snakes?"

She peered anxiously into corners. To her surprise there appeared, in a neat little hollow, something distinctly white and unfamiliar. It startled her at first, but curiosity prompted investigation. She giggled at herself, "What a scaredy-cat I am!" It was not a white pile of snakes. It was a nest of chicken eggs. "Small wonder Mama couldn't find any in the henhouse. The chickens have been hiding out here. There are fifteen eggs up here!"

She carefully lifted the eggs and placed all but one in her apron. She knew one must be left for a nest egg. With great care, she climbed down the ladder and carried her precious burden into the house. Everything inside was still quiet and the family slept. It was only with great difficulty that she restrained herself from waking her mother to announce the news. She placed the eggs in a pan and set it on the table before she hurried back out to milk the cow.

Jersey was busy devouring hay, and Nancy bravely approached her with pail in hand. Jersey turned, sniffed at her, and backed off a few feet. "Now, Jersey, don't be mean," pleaded the little girl. "Back your leg up now." The girl stroked the cow's neck until the cow returned to her chewing. Nancy then started to milk her. "How big your hooves look from down here!" thought the child. It was hard to squeeze the milk out. "I'm not gonna sit on a stool and use both hands like Mama because I want to be able to run if I have to!" She experimented until she felt comfortable milking the placid beast. Her fingers cramped, but she finally saw the bucket filling.

Eleanore opened her eyes. It was almost dark. The bed was so nice. She dreaded having to stir to begin choring, but duty always motivated her. She had dreamt about Nancy and the snake. She reached out to touch Nancy for reassurance, but found the child gone. Alarm spread through her and she sat up. Paul was sleeping. His face was flushed and his hair was damp. Janey was visible in her crib. Nancy was gone! Eleanore ran barefoot over the rough plank flooring, glanced into the empty kitchen, then hurried out, calling, "Nancy! Nancy!" in a frightened voice. She suddenly spotted her daughter crossing the yard. Her hair was tousled, a braid had come loose, and hay clung to her gingham dress. Her mouth was spread wide in a grin. A big pail of foaming milk, almost too much for the little girl to manage, gently beat against her bare legs. Her daughter had never looked so dear.

"Oh, sweetheart, what have you been doing?"

"I milked the cow," said Nancy proudly. "I fed the chickens for you, and I liked doing it, and I'm always going to do it all the time now."

"Honey, it's too hard for you!" protested Eleanore.

"No, it isn't. Did you see the surprise on the table?"

Nancy grabbed her mother's hand, put down the bucket, and led her mother into the house. She ran to the table and held up the pan of eggs. Eleanore beamed and held her tightly. "I have the best little daughter in the world!"

Chapter X
VISITORS

POETS HAVE DESCRIBED, ACCLAIMED, categorized, and reveled in the delights of May, but mere mortals, with a multitude of fancy words, could never do justice to a May morning in the Ozark Mountains. The first faint lights in the eastern sky make night stars pale, as if a thin gray gauze veil were being slowly drawn across them. The curtains of true color are then flung wide; mauve, orchid, pale pink, and fiery red, all growing in intensity to herald a new day. The stage is set for a mountain's waking. The songs of a thousand trilling birds hum and vibrate through the hills in symphony. The trees, dignified in every shade of green, bow and wave their leafy hands in conductor's ecstasy. The sun, a golden ball over the rocky summit, grows larger and larger until its life-nurturing beams have enclosed the entire panorama. New hope is given to the disheartened. New strength is administered to the weary.

Habit is a perfected alarm clock. Eleanore Gray woke early. The knowledge that she had no grueling labor to perform did not permit late waking. She finished the outdoor chores as quickly as possible, fixed the most lavish breakfast a meager larder could provide, and called her children. Laughing and eager to begin the holiday, they rumbled out of bed and came into the savory scented kitchen. They seated themselves at the attractively arranged table and instantly fell upon the meal before them. Lean bacon and perfectly fried eggs were heaped on a large, indigo-bordered platter. Canned applesauce, liberally sprinkled with cinnamon and nutmeg, made miniature mountains in individual amber glass dishes. A silver tray held luscious, flaky brown biscuits. The meal was accompanied by a pitcher of fresh yellow cream and a pat of smooth butter. They ate with keen appetites and a sense of frivolity and freedom.

Eleanore sent the children out to play in the orchard. While Janey tumbled and squealed over the large shepherd, Paul and Nancy, like conspiring architects, used a stick to draw out plans for a playhouse in the soil. The junk pile rendered ample materials for construction. They rummaged through the debris until suitable treasures were accumulated. Imagination transformed bits of broken china and a lidless rusty tea kettle into bowls, platters, plates, and a cook stove. Nancy became the "mother," Paul the "father," and little Janey became the "eldest daughter." Nancy's Raggedy Ann, who had indeed grown raggedy through years of loving abuse, became an errant and frivolous daughter. A chipped, grinning clown toy was appointed to be the prodigal son. The three Gray children spent hours acting out domestic scenes with grand-scale gaiety.

When the dishes were washed, the floors scrubbed, and the entire cabin was finally dustless, Eleanore opened a large trunk and began some rummaging of her own that required both imagination and skill. She pulled out a light lawn dress that she had worn the summer before. Its white background was peppered with gay sprigs of pink and lavender flowers and tiny green leaves. There were yards and yards of fabric in the full skirt and double picot bottom ruffles. This would make lovely curtains with ruffles for edging and tie-backs. With needles, thread, thimble, and scissors, she concocted beautiful curtains for the bare cabin windows. A crocheted doily from the trunk was removed and placed under the lamp on the pine table, and a large floral cushion was found for the rocker. She removed the withered blossoms from the spatterware bowl on the mantle and replaced them with newly opened honeysuckle, stolen from the bees. She finally stood back to admire her skills as an interior decorator, and was not at all displeased with the results. Just as she turned to call the children to see the transformation, the front door opened and Nancy stood there crying out, "Mother! Mother! We're going to have company!"

Eleanore instantly ran to the mirror, tucked her curls into place, removed her stained apron and shoved it in a bureau drawer, and issued orders to Nancy to get the younger children cleaned up. "Take them around back and wash their faces and tell them to be really good and I'll…well, I'll make them cookies tonight." As Nancy flew in haste, her mother hurried out to welcome the guests.

Three women were walking up the grassy lane to the cabin. They walked with the lazy, strolling gait typical of mountain women. Their appearances, however, seemed incongruous to the hills. A middle-aged woman, short with snapping black eyes wedged between a mound of gray hair and a rotund little body swayed along with a cluster of bright red cherries dangling over the brim of a modest black hat. She was dressed and corseted all in black taffeta, though the dress was obviously worn to a shiny blue-black. She held her skirts back with a dainty pinched thumb and forefinger to reveal high-laced black kid shoes. A tiny gold watch on a grosgrain ribbon ornamented her full bosom. Though of similar age, a second woman, dressed in severe black, was tall and thin and void of decoration. The third woman was another sight entirely. This woman was young and unusually beautiful, with big brown eyes, a pink and white complexion, and a large-brimmed picture hat. Soft, long, blonde curls clung to her shoulders. A long, printed mull dress gathered at her slim waist. The full sleeves drew in at the elbow and finished out with row on row of creamy lace. She carried a parasol in one hand, a beaded bag in the other, and a clump of violets was pinned at her throat.

Eleanore studied them. They looked peculiar against the tall trees and broken-down fence rail. When they finally neared the house, Eleanore hurried down to the gate to greet them. The plump lady spoke first. "How do you do, Mrs. Gray? I am Mrs. Adams, and this is my sister Miss Britton," she said, indicating the tall woman. "And this is my daughter, Nelle. We knew your husband and surely sympathize with you. They say the good die young, and your husband, I'm sure, will rest in peace. We missed you at church this morning, and wished to come by to welcome you to Dean's Creek." The formality of her diction did not hide a friendliness and warmth. Mrs. Adams grabbed Eleanore's hands and patted them. As Eleanore shook hands with the other two women, tears welled in her eyes and she was filled with the pleasure of establishing new friendships. No matter how contented she may have been with the exclusive companionship of her children, adult company was a blessing.

"This touches me deeply," said Eleanore to the three women. "It makes me feel as if this will be a real home to us. Please come into the house." As she led them over the threshold, she wrung her calloused hands and wondered if her handshake had revealed her week's labor in the fields.

The light muslin curtains and special touches drew exclamations of delight from the guests. "My, my!" said Mrs. Adams. "You have really done your house up pretty. I can't say when I've seen a nicer living room. Sure looks a sight different than it did when those awful Brunes lived here. Poor white trash, you know. Long time ago. Even Sophie Dean's parlor don't look any prettier, in spite of her Brussels rug and piano." Mrs. Adams sat down in the rocker and fanned herself with her lace handkerchief.

"Should I know her?" asked Eleanore, as she carried in the tall-back chairs from the kitchen for Miss Britton and Miss Adams.

"My goodness, yes! Or at least, you will if you don't!" laughed the amiable Mrs. Adams. "Sophie plays the organ in church and is really quite cultured. In fact, I guess we were all quite crude 'til she took us in hand!"

Nelle laughed merrily at this, and even the dour Miss Britton permitted herself a smile. Nelle explained, "It's for Sophie's benefit that Mother wears that watch. Only between us, though, it won't run at all!" Nelle laughed louder and Mrs. Adams flushed.

"How about you?" retorted her mother without dignity. "Just because Sophie has a pink parasol from St. Louis, you had to get that silly thing there! Don't even think it would hold up against a few rain drops." They all laughed some more until Miss Britton cleared her throat and made a grave observation.

"I dare say we all needed a touch of Sophie's culture. I'm quite sure she wouldn't laugh so loudly about it, either. Imagine what we'd look like to Mrs. Gray if it hadn't been for Sophie. We'd come here barefoot and speaking some foreign English like we used to. At least now we're presentable and not so bad as some Hill folk."

It occurred to Eleanore then that the clothing and demeanor of her guests was the work of an outsider, someone who had lived beyond the hills. She wondered how extensive this Mrs. Dean's cultural missionary work really was. Perhaps these three women, dressed like Cinderella's sisters, were even a bit embarrassed by pretenses and what they had been. "I think your parasol is lovely, Miss Adams, and your mother's watch is actually quite charming!"

The children entered the cabin with solemn timidity. Their faces were washed, and Eleanore was pleased to see that they looked presentable. They were introduced formally, complimented accordingly, and, much to their relief, dismissed to return to their play. They stole glances over their shoulders as they exited, were clearly amazed by the costumes of the three country ladies and even giggled some as they closed the door.

When they were gone, Mrs. Adams spoke. "If you'll excuse me for asking, what church do you belong to? We are Baptists ourselves." Eleanore replied that she was Methodist. Mrs. Adams quickly added, "Of course, I always think that denomination isn't as important as how you act. That's why we have a church union. As there are not yet enough goers to make any one congregation, we sort of combine them all. Now, the Petersons are awful strong Methodists, too."

"Yes," said Miss Britton. "Sometimes I feel like taking Joe Peterson and wringing his neck for it. He's the most stubborn man alive."

"You see," interrupted Nelle, "Aunt Melinda used to go with Joe Peterson. He wouldn't marry her though, because she was Baptist. He married another gal instead." Nelle laughed at her aunt's embarrassment.

"I'm sure there are better fish in the sea," retorted the aunt. "As I've told you before, Nelle Adams, I didn't marry that man because I didn't want to. He was too stubborn for me to put up with." Melinda Britton lifted up her pointy chin in a last attempt at preserving dignity before a stranger. It quenched Nelle's fire and she pursed her lips and folded her hands primly in her lap.

Eleanore interrupted the unaffordable silence by saying, "I'm sorry I wasn't in church this morning. We seldom ever missed a service at home, but the children and I worked quite hard this week getting settled in, and we really needed a day to recuperate."

Mrs. Adams quickly consoled Eleanore. "Don't worry, dear, we quite understand. Your absence is to be forgiven. A great many didn't make it. Some were still planting. Some farmers plant at special times, and May Day is one of them. Lots of others weren't there because they still hold to heathenish ways."

"Yes, I understand from Will Gray that there's been some trouble getting people to accept the church," replied Eleanore with sympathy.

"That's not at all what she's talking about," cut in Miss Britton with stiffness. "They come some, but whenever there's some reason to drop the Lord's way, they run for it. See, May Day is important around here for more than planting reasons. Why, they still hold with dumb suppers and egg hunting and all sorts of foolishness. Not a one is willing to let God take care of courtship!"

"Now, Melinda," said Mrs. Adams. "We used to do the same things when we were young. No real harm to it."

"Not unless Mrs. Dean catches wind of it," snorted Nelle.

"I'm not sure what you're talking about," said Eleanore who had never heard of dumb supper.

"I forgot that you're not from around here. Well, Hill people believe in some ideas and notions that are odd to educated folk. Young girls around here are anxious to catch husbands, and they resort to old ways to predict their futures. When I was a girl, we used to wet a white handkerchief on the last night in April and hang it outside to dry. In the morning we would examine the wrinkles and see if they made the initials of a man or boy we knew. That would be a way of predicting our lover. Sometimes, we would spend all of May Day hunting out bird nests. If we found one with eggs in it, it meant we'd marry and have a family. If it was empty, we'd end up as an old maid!" explained Mrs. Adams with a tender smile.

"Did it work, Mama?" teased Nelle. Mrs. Adams blushed and grinned, but never answered.

"A dumb supper is even more foolishness. Girls all missed church this morning to get ready for it. I did it myself as a girl, and it sure didn't get me much!" said Miss Britton with vehemence. "Bunch of us went to one girl's house and prepared a fake supper. We had to work in silence. Weren't even allowed a giggle or a whisper or it would break the spell and we'd have to wait a whole year before we could do it again. We had to walk backwards and do everything backwards looking over our left shoulders. We'd set places at the table and everything. After we pulled the chairs to the table, we'd stand behind our chairs with our heads bowed. If a wraith or spirit showed itself to us, it would be our lover. If nobody showed, well, you guess what that means. I never saw a thing, and I'm growing into an old maid. If you saw a black figure, it meant you'd die before the next dumb supper. Maybe we done it wrong. Some people said to look into the plate to see a reflection of the spirit. I don't know about any of it. It's certainly not Christian."

"And you, Mrs. Gray, are lucky you don't hold with those ways," said Nelle with playfulness. "They make widows hang horseshoes out over their front doors on May Day. First creature to come through under it supposedly will have the same coloring as your next husband. Lordy! Since Ma came through first, you'd end up married to an old feller with white hair and pink skin! Might even have cherries hanging off his head!" All three of the women roared with laughter and Eleanore grinned widely.

"Maybe Mrs. Gray will think we're all crazy if we gone on so," said Miss Britton. "Not everybody around here acts so silly. You've got some good people for neighbors."

"Please tell me about them. I'm very interested," declared Eleanore.

"Well," replied Mrs. Adams. "There are the Smalls. They're good people; Methodists, too. Heard their boy did some work for you. They're a hard-working lot. Then there's the Sloans. There's seven of 'em. Mrs. Sloan's a good woman, but superstitious. They live in that old house up the creek. I'm telling you, the stories she tells about that place makes yer hair stand on end. They all think that house is haunted. To look at it, I wouldn't be surprised if it were. All surrounded by locust trees and a dug well, and the whole place is full of closets; gives me the creeps."

"Why do they live there if they're so scared?" asked Eleanore.

"Well, it's really the finest house in these parts, and it's been in their family for years. Mr. Sloan's grandfather homesteaded that place. He came from England. Our land belonged to them, too. My Frank bought it from them and built our house. Ours is that frame house you can see from the bottom field. I'm sure glad we moved into a new house. I'd sure hate to be Mary Sloan. The stories she tells about her place gives me goose bumps!"

"Well, I think it's nothing but imagination," said Miss Britton hotly. "And, really Becky, I don't think you need to scare Mrs. Gray."

"I'm not scared at all, actually. I rather think these stories are fascinating!" said Eleanore to her guests. It provided the three women with motivation to continue filling Eleanore's ears with more stories, gossip, and scandal.

One ghost story in particular interested Eleanore. During the Civil War, the Sloan house was apparently occupied by Confederates. They had a spy in the Union army posted to warn them of approaching Union soldiers. If they approached, he was supposed to ride up on a black horse, knock on the door, and then quickly ride away again. When the night came that Union soldiers neared the house, the Confederate family knew something strange was going on. They waited for their son, the Union spy, to bring them news. They were finally aroused at night by a rapping on the door. They saw their son ride off on a black horse, and they took refuge in caves along the creek. They later learned that their son had been caught and killed on his way to warn them! They decided then that it was his ghost that had warned them. The Sloans still heard horses galloping up. They still heard rapping on the door, but they never saw the rider. The story had been told so convincingly for so long, that more than half the people in Dean's Creek believed in it.

Mrs. Adams also told the tale of Julie Holler, a wide valley of some fifteen hundred or so acres about four miles off in the hills. A neighbor woman had lost her cows out there. She wandered the Holler for seven days looking for them. When they finally found the woman, she was a raving maniac. People still believed they could hear a woman screaming in the Holler when they rode along the ridge above the hollow. Some said the sound echoed and reechoed from bluff to bluff. Others said it was only the noise of a panther or wolf.

"But," added Miss Britton, "I'd far rather run into poor old Julie than a panther or wolf!"

Eleanore enjoyed the visit greatly. The warm Mrs. Adams, her taciturn sister, and the gay Nelle had succeeded in breaking the monotony of her life. She walked them to the gate and expressed her pleasure clearly. "You must come see us now. Come spend a day! We'd love to have you," invited Mrs. Adams.

"And do come to church next Sunday. It's Methodist next week, but we'll be there, too. We're broad-minded," said Miss Britton with an air of congeniality.

"I will! I think you're doing wonderful work to bring people together for worship. I'm sure you're doing a lot of good."

Nelle Adams laughed. "I'm afraid they don't all come to worship. Some come for entertainment! There will be as many drunks as sober people present. It's the only regular social event around here! The funniest thing you'll see is a line of boys waiting at the door to escort the girls home. Some of the boys ask five or six girls in a row and get sacked every time!"

"I notice you do your share of the sacking, Nelle," laughed her mother.

"Well, when I marry, it won't be to some hillbilly from these parts," declared Nelle with her chin up.

"You best take what you can get, girl," admonished her maiden aunt gravely. "Time may come when you'll wish you had!"

The women shook hands again, said goodbyes, and the visitors departed with their skirts held high. The lively Nelle strolled along, clipping the leaves of trees with the spike of her parasol as if she were beheading the offensive male population of the hills.

When Eleanore returned to the house, she found her tired and hungry children rummaging through the kitchen in search of supper. True to her promise, she made them huge sugar cookies. After they had been fed, the chores completed, and bathing finished, she tucked them into bed. She knew well that a stolen cookie or two was stashed beneath the pillows, but she pretended ignorance and allowed one night's indulgence. She went outside and sat on the front step and watched the moon rise. The night was pleasantly warm. Frogs were holding a loud court session in the moonlit creek bottom. A whippoorwill called to its mate. "Horseshoes, indeed!" she said aloud as she looked up at the barren door above her head.

Crickets and katydids chattered away furiously. She could hear the horses snorting with pleasure as they crunched away at the hay in the stable. Toby came down and sat by her feet. It was peaceful there, safe and sane. She drowsed and recalled the day with contentment. All at once, however, Toby pricked up his ears. Horse hooves could be heard galloping down the bottom road. They grew louder and louder. Drunken voices could be heard singing a wildly obscene refrain to some tavern-quality ditty. They grew louder and louder until they finally passed.

Eleanore gave a sigh of relief. She sat still, listening to the noise fade into the night. Peace was broken for her. She rose and went into the house. Fear prompted her to bar the door with care. The wooden bar banged loudly down with her severe thrust. She paused to see if it woke the children. They slept on. She lit the lamp and went to the big trunk. Down at the bottom rested Bob Gray's revolver. She loaded the gun as her husband had taught her, and hung it on a nail over the bed. She raised a window to let in the spring breeze, and lay down with her children. Sleep came easily. Outside, the big dog paced recklessly to and fro, perking his ears up at the slightest sound. He was a noble beast who kept guard while his charges slept.

Chapter XI

THE DEAN'S CREEK CHURCH

ALTHOUGH HER PLANTING WAS completed, Eleanore found
the next week no less demanding. One task crowded another.
The family cleared brush, mended and patched the barn and
gaps in fences, weeded flower beds, burnt off debris and brush,
split wood from Will's pile, and cut a path down to the creek.
Eleanore single-handedly washed, dried, and pressed smooth a
mountain of laundry, mended torn overalls and calico dresses,
cooked, scrubbed, and cared for her children. She worked until
her senses were drugged.

On Saturday morning, however, she woke to the hard pat-
ter of rain on the window panes. It would cease the plans for
another day's work outdoors, and it would be a boon to the
newly planted garden and field, but it was a gloomy prospect for
Eleanore to wake to. She looked out to see the trees furiously
swaying and the livestock huddled by the barn. The pink petals
of the climbing rose were covered with dripping mud. The sky
was overcast with low clouds, white and swift, crouched below

an ominous, deep gray ceiling. Puddles had formed everywhere. Tiny rivers of dirty water ran down the paths with a swooshing sound. Everything seemed to drain to the creek, which foamed and gurgled with wash off and bits of trees. In her mind's eye, she saw the angry river that had carried her husband to a brutal death. She turned with a shudder. The dreadful ache of loss, despite the preoccupation afforded by hard toil, had not yet dissipated. Every day, some sight or some word would make her husband's dead white face rise before her.

The children woke in good spirits and demanded feeding, their mother's smile, and rainy day play. A fire was lit to send the chill out of the cabin, and the three Gray children spent the morning playing games, singing, and telling tales in the fire's glow. Eleanore made gingerbread and was pestered into sitting down with the children after lunch to tell them a story. She told Paul's favorite about an Indian and Nancy's favorite about a crippled little girl. She had always made the stories up as she went along, so they often varied. This time, she concluded by having the Indian steal the crippled girl off to live in the forest. The children clamored for more, but Eleanore distracted them into another game. She simply wasn't up to the energies of her brood. As she stood up to return to work in the kitchen, a loud knock was heard at the door. It frightened her, and she stood shock still for a moment before she answered it. There stood Will Gray in dripping clothes, hat in hand, hair plastered down and beaming through a face covered with beads of water.

"Well, aren't you going to invite me in?" he laughed.

"Of course! Of course! You took me a bit by surprise. What ever is the idea of stomping through this downpour? Why on earth is your hat off?" she scolded.

"I always remove my hat before royalty," Will stated with a bow as he created a puddle on the floor. "And you are Queen of the mountain!"

"You might at least spare me blushing in front of the children," she said as she recovered from her confusion, and led the wet man to a rocker.

"Far be it from me to steal the most comfortable chair in the house from a lady," he declared as he sat down on the floor and stretched his wet feet toward the fire. The children crowded close to him as he began rummaging through his pockets. "You know, I thought I had something for you kids, but I reckon I must of lost it on my way here." He laughed at the downcast expressions the announcement produced on the children's faces, and produced a damp paper sack. He handed it ceremoniously to Nancy. There were shouts of joy.

"Oh, Mama, it's candy!" said Paul before he joined Nancy in thanking the donor. There was candy indeed. The sack contained chocolate drops, coconut squares, peppermint and lemon sticks, and a great slab of peanut brittle.

"You're spoiling them terribly, Will Gray," said Eleanore with a smile. She and Will joined the children in eating some of the sweets.

"Can't a crabby old bachelor have any fun?" retorted Will. He took another bite of the peanut brittle and between sticky chews explained, "I was over to Big Town yesterday to get supplies and market my eggs. I stopped at the Adamses on the way over and heard favorable reports about you, Mrs. Gray. Miss Britton said you were a very sensible young woman. Coming from her, that's praise of the highest order."

"I only hope I could be of some help here," explained Eleanore with a pretense of modesty.

"You may begin on Sunday. I'll be by for you to take you to church myself. It's high time you and your children met the rest of Dean's Creek."

Eleanore felt the blush returning to her cheeks. "Will, don't you think it would be more seemly if the children and I went alone?"

"Old Miss Prudence herself!" sighed Will in mock frustration. "If you must, then I'll give you directions. Go past my place until you come to a fork. Turn left there and go about a half mile up in the woods. The church will be there. It's built of logs, but it's bigger than most of the cabins. Start out about ten o'clock. Methodist this week, preacher's from Big Town. He's not much of a preacher, but he can sing like a canary, so the turnout will be good."

Will was exceptionally jovial and talkative. He delivered a lengthy and colorful inventory of the neighbors. The Smalls had many children; the Deans had none. The Carsons, Davises, and Brimmers each had three sets of children, and they were locally identified as "his," "hers," and "theirs." The Mattersons had intermarried so much and so closely that the clan was marked by a dozen or so who were either blind, deformed, or "touched in the head." He also spoke of the Lefferts. The wife, Sadie, had been a Matterson. She left home to marry Hank to escape her father's beatings. It was a case, Will said, of "out of the frying pan and into the fire" because Hank was noted for a violent temper and Sadie certainly received the brunt of it.

Eleanore walked Will to the gate after several hours of talking. The rain had stopped, the sun was slowly lowering, and the sky was a clouded mass. A perfect double rainbow, "fairy boys," had formed. Eleanore caught her breath at the mystic loveliness of it. Will called the children out and they watched until the bright colors began to fade. They had all seen rainbows before, but this one was notable for an awesome brilliance of hue. It seemed to Eleanore that a heavenly message of hope and promise was being radiated.

Sunday morning dawned clear and bright. The scent of rain lingered. The grass and flowers seemed more luxuriant from the storm. The gloom of Saturday had vanished, washed itself clean. There was a great deal of bustling and hurrying going on in the Gray cabin that morning. Eleanore managed to get chores done, tidy the house, and dress her three children in Sunday best in record time. While the three children sat primly on chairs, Eleanore made a last attempt to look less like a weary farmer and more like a young mother. She was already tired from the frantic pace of the morning, but a brisk bath and fresh clothes helped restore her. She stood before the mirror to come to terms with her hair. It was an unruly mess that seemed bent on flying every which way like a little girl's. She pinned the curls up as tightly as she could, and added two side combs set with brilliants for security. Would they disapprove of her for not wearing a widow's black dress? Her husband hated black. The dress she wore now had been one of his favorites. It was a soft, half-silk, beige gown that gathered tightly to her waist and fell in soft pleats to the floor. Bands of the same fabric were sewn around the entire bottom skirting like ribbons. The three-quarter length sleeves in a leg o'mutton style became her. They made her seem less thin, more graceful. The high collar was certainly appropriate for church. She pulled on a pair of white gloves and arranged her hat over the pinned curls. The hat had been made by Emmy Gray. It was magnificent, with beige silk banding and a multitude of pastel, satin roses. The children applauded her finery. It was more pleasing than the drab and faded calicos she had been wearing. Had they forgotten, she wondered, that she was capable of beauty?

Since they had no proper carriage, the family walked to church. They walked very slowly over the grassy paths to accommodate Janey's tiny, unsteady legs. Honeycomb limestone rock and mammoth, mossy slabs bordered the path. A small, cold spring bubbled below an ancient elm tree and raced down the hillside in miniature waterfalls. The water had washed the limestone white and clean. Spice wood, hawthorn, redbuds, and hazelnut trees abounded. The unexpected beauty of it all tempted the children. Eleanore repeatedly hurried them back to the main track in an effort to restrain them from muddying themselves in the water. She finally resorted to a mother's bribery and announced that they could play here in the afternoon.

On top of a high hill that overlooked this magnificent glen, Will Gray had built his home. The house, low and roomy, was painted white. It was surrounded by fruit trees and grape arbors. Blooming bridal wreath and roses clustered around the doorway and front of the house. There was a surprising neatness about this bachelor's house, as if a woman's hand had touched it. Hens with downy chicks in tow strutted about the yard, and cows chewed and swayed beneath a big hickory tree. It seemed as if the owner was gone already, but Will suddenly appeared at the side of the house. He strolled toward the family, grinning widely at Eleanore's amazement.

"Howdy, folks!" he said cordially. "Going my way?"

Eleanore laughed and scolded, "I thought you'd be gone already, Will Gray. Whatever will people think?"

A bit of mischief twinkled in his eyes. "Whatever they please, I imagine. Fact is, little Janey there needs a horse, or she'll get so tired from the walk that she'll miss out on that Methodist's singing!" He bent down and scooped the starched, beribboned little girl up on his shoulders, where she cooed and giggled all the way across the meadows and through the woods to the church.

A crowd had already gathered in front of the log building, and more people continued to arrive for quite some time. Some came in wagons loaded down with scruffy bands of children. Others came in shiny new buggies with red tassels and polished buckles. The handsome horses with arched necks passed their leaner neighbors with haughtiness. Horses were tied everywhere; under trees and on posts. Some sported richly ornamented saddles, and others had no more than torn blankets wrapped around their bellies as saddles.

The people who gathered in the churchyard were not unlike their horses in contrast. Men in fancy dress mingled with those in soiled overalls. Some had an air of polished dignity, others looked awkward and dumb. Some seemed upright and educated, others seemed mean, with ratty faces and bloodshot eyes that came from whiskey. As Eleanore approached the door to the church, she noticed one particularly vile creature crouched behind a skinny horse. He was furtively gulping whiskey from a brown quart bottle.

She grabbed the hands of her youngest children and followed Will into the meeting house. The rough plank benches were partially full, and every head turned as the newcomers entered. There was much whispering and even some girlish giggling at the sight of big Will Gray, the most elusive bachelor in the hills, escorting a dimpled baby girl down the center aisle. Eleanore at first wondered why Will led them through the crowd to the front of the church, but she understood when the crowd of rowdy boys and men eventually entered and positioned themselves on all the back benches. They whispered and joked in rough tones, so boldly and loudly that she was grateful to be removed from their company.

The song leader stood and signaled the beginning of the service. A tall, thin woman stood gracefully then seated herself at the organ. She pumped the ancient instrument with her feet and fingered the yellowed keys until she managed to squeeze out the opening bars of the first hymn. The song leader threw his arms wide in a birdlike gesture and the entire congregation broke into song.

Despite the squeaking organ and the ill-organized efforts of the song leader, the off-key singers produced a strange, wild harmony that moved Eleanore's heart. As they sang, Eleanore studied the parishioners. She identified the woman at the organ as Sophie Dean. The woman wore a rich, deep blue taffeta dress with a white collar of crocheted grape clusters. A highly ornamental gold watch was fastened to her bosom on a filigree chain. A pink parasol rested against the bench beside her. Eleanore secretly longed to see the pretty thing opened over the large blue feathered hat that angled over the woman's head. The thin, anemic-looking song leader, she gathered, must be Mr. Dean. The mighty voice that issued from his frail body was a wonder to her.

The Adamses sat before Eleanore, and the family on the next bench consisted of two parents and a great many children. They surely, she thought, must be the Smalls. They all looked harassed. Even the tiniest baby sported a wrinkled, pink scowl. The other people in front of her were obviously backwoods people. One of the girls appeared to be about fourteen or fifteen years old. She wore a plaid cotton dress that had seen far too many scrubbings with strong lye soap. Her thick, brown hair was parted and neatly braided into two very long braids, but as Eleanore studied the child, she nearly admitted an audible gasp of astonishment. The girl's hair was literally working with lice. Eleanore shuddered and looked away. She found it difficult to concentrate on the sermon delivered by the stately, mustached preacher. She had seen poverty before, and she had seen illness and dirt before, but never had she encountered such an abundance of vermin; never, at least, in the House of God. It amazed her that nicely dressed men and women could sit smugly and piously within a few feet of a bench loaded so with the earmarks of poverty.

The unfortunate family in front sat quietly, absorbing every word of the sermon. The grandmother was perhaps only the mother, aged by the hardness of life. It was impossible for Eleanore to put their ages and relations into perspective. The woman sat beside the lice-ridden girl. She was wrinkled and beat. A faded calico bonnet sat askew over limp gray hair. There was an unmistakable aroma of tobacco around her. When they rose to sing, a pouch and pipe were clearly visible in the gaping pocket of her apron.

The sermon was long and loud. Each phase of it was chorused by determined "amens" and "hallelujahs" from the benches. More than once, some inspired soul rose and dramatically bellowed, "Praise the Lord!" The sincere declarations were frequently mimicked and guffawed by the drunken lips in the rear benches of the church. It amazed Eleanore that the minister did not break concentration and composure during the rough outbursts.

Suddenly, in mid-sentence, the clergyman broke into song to explain a point. It drowned the other noises and rendered the back rows silent. She remembered what Will had said about the man's voice. The crowd listened intently to "The Dear Old Sweet Hour of Prayer" which was sung in a rich baritone. Eleanore scarcely breathed during the hymn and its beauty caused her to study the singer intently. She wondered what he was like behind the moustache and wooly sideburns. His teeth were strong and white. He wore a stiff celluloid collar with a carefully tied bowtie. His clothes were shabby, but clean and well pressed. She turned to survey the congregation, and her eyes rested on Nelle Adams. Clearly written on the girl's face were the signs of adoration and worship, not spiritual but worldly. Evidently, the tall, middle-aged preacher had captured the girl. "Dear, dear," Eleanore thought to herself. "I wonder…"

The service concluded, and joiners were called forth to accept Jesus Christ as their Savior. Everyone prayed for penitence after that. Formalities were finalized, and the service turned into a singing session. One hymn after another was sung with power and zeal. The back bench antics increased conspicuously during the final hymns, but the congregation was undaunted. After the final amen, the crowd rose and broke into talk. As people shook hands, they exchanged gossip, local news, appraisals of the services, and plans for Sunday afternoon.

Eleanore smiled with amusement as she watched the lads line up for the honor of walking their maids home for a hearty Sunday meal. Mrs. Adams took Eleanore in hand and introduced her to the higher-ups. She was introduced to the stylish Sophie, the flock of Smalls, the sickly Mrs. Peterson and her delicate daughter Flora. Mrs. Sloan, the woman with the haunted house, turned out to be a likeable soul with an outrageous laugh. Eleanore felt that she had been introduced to more people than she would ever remember, but was secretly relieved that she had been spared an encounter with the shabby tribe that had been seated before her during the service. Relief turned into pity, though, when she noticed the Hill girl still sitting on the edge of the bench watching her. Her eyes revealed the bitterness of having been deliberately ignored during introductions. Everything existed in those eyes—the mirrors of poverty, humiliation, and hurt. Eleanore suddenly turned to Will Gray and asked loudly, "And who is this young lady, Will?"

"Why, this is Rachel Matterson, Ellie," he said with barely concealed surprise. "Rachel, this is Mrs. Gray."

A sudden joy leaped into the girl's hurt, gray eyes. There was pride. With a swift curtsy, the girl acknowledged the introduction and then was prompted by her guardian to leave. Eleanore watched the faded plaid dress slip into the crowd and exit.

As they once again walked down the wood's road, Will, after a long silence, remarked, "You shook hands with the Matterson girl. I think I should warn you that they are a lousy bunch, and they've been known to have the itch. It was an admirable gesture, Ellie, but it might be regrettable."

"I couldn't help it. Did you see the look in her eyes? It cut me to the quick. Will, I want to help those people."

"They won't let you. Don't you realize that they are that way by choice?"

"I don't care. I'll help them in spite of them!" She realized too late that she had snapped at him.

He looked at her with great tenderness. "My dear, you don't understand these people. They won't let you interfere. They have their own ways, and they don't like any others."

"I am going to help them. And you are going to help me," announced Eleanore. She pursed her lips in resolve.

After a moment, Will laughed loudly. "Alright, where do we begin, Hill angel?"

"I don't know. The opportunity will rise, though, and we will take advantage of it then. Now, will you come home with us for a decent meal?"

"On the contrary, Mrs. Gray, you are expected for dinner at my house."

They eventually reached the gate to Will's house. He opened it and admitted the small family. The children scrambled about trying to capture the downy little chicks. Their mother left them to their play as she entered the house with Will. The living room was roomy. Bookshelves lined the walls on both sides of the fireplace. The highly varnished floors and woodwork were real walnut. Will caught the small woman's admiration, and he eagerly explained that he had sacrificed a few of the walnut trees on his property to do this room. There was a soft leather couch in one corner and a mahogany piano in the opposite corner. On top of the piano was a violin. Over the mantle hung a shotgun and a rifle. There were comfortable chairs and a highly carved table. It was obviously a man's room, but any woman would have found it attractive.

"What do you think, Ellie?" asked Will.

Eleanore turned to again survey the room. She was struck by its richness, by its unexpected beauty. "I think I'm ashamed of myself! I had somehow pictured your house as a rustic shack full of dogs and junk! Forgive me, but this place is magnificent!"

Will Gray beamed as he escorted her through the rest of the house. The kitchen was spotless and cheery. The floor was scrubbed to a clean white, shining pots and pans hung along the walls, and his mother's dishes were carefully arranged on the shelves. A handmade table covered with red oilcloth was set with covered dishes. She carefully lifted the edge of a muslin cloth to see the contents of a crock. It contained baked beans. Other dishes were filled with boiled potatoes, boiled eggs, spiced pickles, and a huge hunk of ham. Will began making a fire in the stove. "Now, Mrs. Gray, if you'll be so kind as to produce some of your delectable biscuits while I make potato salad, we can soon sit down to a feast."

He put the beans into the oven to warm, produced a huge denim apron for "Milady's dress," and set out the ingredients for biscuits. Eleanore worked quickly and quietly. Will went out to fetch cottage cheese and cooled butter. When the biscuits were safely in the oven, she walked over to the small glass window to search for her children. They were not visible. She turned and walked to a doorway and peered out. The children were absorbed by a flock of wobbling ducklings gathered by a small pond.

Nancy happily looked up at her mother's call, but the cheer dissolved visibly as the young girl studied her mother. She saw her silhouetted against the door frame, beaming through a mask of smeared flour. Her mother looked radiant, almost too happy and too at home. "Mama and Uncle Will..." she said half aloud. "No one can take Daddy's place, not ever." The little girl became gripped by a sort of fear that made her solemn through the entire meal.

Chapter XII

FLORA

THE DAYS GREW HOTTER, the nights stifling. The Grays found little relief by sleeping on the floor before the open door on late June nights, but some relief was better than none at all. Eleanore often found sleep impossible. Her skin itched with sweat, and the heat made her head swirl and ache. Little Janey's brow was always damp now, and her small curls had transformed into tight coils. Eleanore often rose in the middle of the night and paced the yard with Toby. They had not had rain for many weeks. Even in the moonlight, it was evident that the corn in the bottom field, the corn that had cost her family great toil, was beginning to burn up in the hot winds. She was always filled with a panic, a fear that the drought of the previous year would be repeated.

Every day she and the children hauled buckets of water up from the creek to drench the vegetable patch. They kept the soil pulverized and they pulled the healthy flock of water-sucking weeds out, but she even feared for her small garden. The creek provided the Grays with escapes from their labors. It was spring fed and always cool for wading and splashing. They often saw snakes now but had grown accustomed to their disconcerting presence. All four of them had shed long sleeves and sunbonnets. Her children went barefoot, bare-armed, and bare-headed. They were all too hot and too weary to pay attention to such proprieties.

Nancy, however, sometimes thought enviously about the pink and white prettiness of Flora Peterson. In a vain effort to remove the brown and freckles from her arms and face, she would scrub her skin raw with cucumbers, vinegar, and sour cream. It never worked. She even cut up a pair of leggings to cover her arms when she worked in the garden with her mother, but even they failed. The girl eventually grew disgusted with the poor results of her beauty efforts. She threw the leggings into the junk heap by the barn, ran free down the rocky slope to the creek path, crossed a burning sand bar, and leaped into the welcome coolness of the creek. One of her greatest joys was to stand on a grassy knoll below the house and sing at the top of her lungs. She only hoped that Flora Peterson down the valley could hear her. Nancy had a fine, high voice that carried well. It was the one treasure that gave her hope of outdoing Flora.

One afternoon, Flora Peterson came to the Gray house. It was a first visit, the first opportunity Nancy had had to see the girl outside of church. Nancy saw her coming up the hill and ran down to greet her. She extended her hand shyly to the frail girl and gave a welcoming hello. Flora offered her hand with grown-up politeness. "How do you do, Miss Nancy? My mother suggested I should pay you a visit. She said you were unlike the other rural children. You see, she does not allow me to play with just anyone."

Nancy was greatly flattered by the compliment, but looked dubiously at the dainty finery of her guest. "You have a very pretty dress on, Flora, but I'm afraid if we play much that it will get dirty."

Flora glanced down at her china silk frock as if she hated the thing. "No, I must absolutely not get my dress soiled. If I did, Mother would think we had been playing roughly and she'd never again allow me to come here."

Nancy sighed sympathetically. "Yes, that would be terrible. Perhaps we could find something to do that wouldn't get you dirty. What do you like?"

"Well, Mother lets me play tic-tac-toe and guessing games and drop the handkerchief."

"Oh, dear! I'm afraid that I'm not much good at those, and it's much too hot to play drop the handkerchief."

As the two girls talked, they had climbed the hill to the yard. They rested in the shade of a big maple tree. Both children were drenched with sweat, but Flora, with her large hat, silk dress and white stockings, looked nearly ill from the heat. Nancy regarded her costume with pity. "Flora, don't you go barefoot, even at home?"

"No, it's absolutely forbidden. Mother says it isn't ladylike."

"But you aren't a lady yet! You're not even as old as I am, are you?"

"Mother said you are eleven. I'm past eleven, though I don't look very strong or big. Mother said it's a blessing not to be overgrown."

Nancy doubted the validity of such sentiments. She looked down at her own sturdy brown legs. Both children were silent and uncomfortable for a few minutes. It was Flora who broke the impasse by volunteering information. "If Father could sell the farm, we would move to Kansas City. I have two aunts who live there, and Mother says we shall never be satisfied until we move there, too."

An unflattering portrait of Flora's mother was forming in Nancy's mind. "I kind of like it here, Flora," she announced apologetically. "Paul and I have a dandy place to play down by the spring. There's a clay bank there and we make the keenest bowls and pots. Would you like to see them?"

Flora clapped her hands enthusiastically. "Oh, yes, please!"

"Wait until I tell Mama you are here." Nancy left Flora, ran up the path to the house, and peeped in. Janey was curled asleep on the bed. Nancy tiptoed into the kitchen and found her mother stirring berry jam. Paul was scraping remains from a pot that had already been emptied into small square jars. The heat in the kitchen was unbearable. Her mother's face was beet red, her head and dress soaked with sweat. "Oh, Mama," cried Nancy, "Flora Peterson is here to visit me and we're going down by the spring to see the clay pots that Paul and I have made. Paul can come if he wants to." Nancy and Paul immediately started for the door.

"Children," called their mother after them, "when you get back, please bring Flora in to see me." The children agreed.

"Flora, this is my brother, Paul," said Nancy with politeness.

"Must he come, too?" asked Flora with pettiness.

"Oh, Paul's not like most boys," Nancy asserted. "Tell you what; let's race down the hill to the spring. One…two…three… go!" Paul and Nancy instantly ran down the grassy slope with great speed, leaping rocks and jumping ditches with the agility of goats. They raced to the top of the next bank before they skidded to a stop. They looked back to see Flora sedately walking down the slope. It was obvious that child's play had been forfeited to preserve patent leather shoes. "What a sissy!" exclaimed Paul to Nancy.

"Shush! She might hear you," cautioned Nancy. "Flora, do be careful! I'm sorry we ran off so quickly. I forgot about your clothes. Be careful coming up this bank. It's dreadfully slippery."

Nancy issued her apologies and warnings from the crest of the bank. She pitied the frilly girl's efforts to climb it, and finally came part way down and extended a hand to Flora. "Here, I'll help you. Easy now. Oh! Oh! Ohhh!" The last issued cry was directed at Flora's feet, which, even with Nancy's helping hand, flew from under the girl and sent her sliding and tumbling down the bank. Flora landed prone on her stomach. Paul roared with laughter. Flora started to cry.

"Oh, Flora, are you hurt?" asked Nancy as she scrambled down to aid the girl. "I'm so very sorry. It's all my fault," she declared with false politeness.

"I'm not hurt, but my dress is all dirty and Mother will whip me!" sobbed the little girl. Her pink silks were covered with mud and grass.

"Never mind, Flora. My Mama will fix that. You're dirty anyway, so we might as well have some fun. Take those shoes off and let's wade in the spring!"

"I guess I might as well," sighed the conceding Flora, whose strength had given way to temptation. She sat down, removed her shoes and stockings, folded them neatly, and placed them on a convenient flat rock before she skipped off to join the others. She was delighted by the place; by the miniature waterfalls, the cool clear water, the pine woods and the dense shade. "It's too wonderful! I've never played in a place like this before."

She and Nancy splashed across the brook. Flora paid no heed to the water-splashed pink dress. She screamed with a pleasure she had never known before. The afternoon was spent molding clay dishes, wading and splashing, nibbling at spice wood and peppermint, creating dams and bridges, and decorating a rock garden with moss and ferns. While the two girls scrambled off to gather bright columbine and May apple umbrellas, Paul disappeared and returned to the house to raid the vegetable garden.

Paul returned with pockets stuffed with tomatoes, cucumbers, and salt. The children feasted on these in the shade of a huge tree. Paul used his toad sticker to peel the cucumbers for the girls. They ate with relish, with the delight of unfettered freedom.

For the first time in her life, Flora walked barefoot through mud. It squashed and curled up between her toes. She squealed with ecstasy. Equally surprising was the joy she found in watching Paul's antics and amusements. No matter how often the boy fell, he rose beaming and ready to perform another feat for her amusement. His energy seemed to be unquenchable. Flora was actually learning to play and laugh without fear of her mother.

They found a perfect, tiny Indian dart sticking out from the moss on the hill. Nancy presented it to Flora as a gift, a token to cement their new friendship. Flora accepted it gravely and with sentiment. She swore she would keep it always to remember Nancy by. A large gray lizard streaked by to interrupt her ceremonious declaration. It horrified Flora as much as it delighted Paul. Suddenly, Flora looked up from where the lizard had emerged to see the sun sinking low in the valley. The valley was shadowed, but on the opposite hill over moss-covered Indian graves, there was a brilliant golden cast. It made the burial grounds glimmer as if they were covered by the coveted gold that so many a person had longed to discover.

"Oh, Nancy, I must go home. Mother said I was to be home before sunset at the very latest. Look at my dress! What shall I do?" moaned Flora in despair.

"Don't worry so, Flora. Mama will fix you up. Let's hurry, though." The children helped Flora gather up her belongings, and they ran to the house as quickly as their legs would carry them. Dirty and wet, they flew into the kitchen, where Eleanore was washing the pans and bowls from the berry jam. She turned and opened her eyes in horror at the sight of Flora's dress, but refrained from scolding when she recognized the tears in the little girl's large blue eyes.

"Mama," began Nancy in explanation, "she fell down and got ever so dirty, but she had great fun. She has to go home now, but she's afraid her mother will whip her and never let her come again because she got so dirty. Can't you help her?"

Eleanore looked at the muddy dress. Although she was painfully tired and hot from her day's efforts, she could not resist her daughter's pleas or the tear-filled eyes of a terrified child.

"Run to the well and draw a bucket of water, Nancy. Flora, please take off your dress and slip. Paul, take Janey out for a walk or something." Eleanore poured the girl a big basin of water and commanded her to scrub herself with soap. Eleanore put the flat irons on the hot part of the stove, fresh wood into the firebox, and the girl's clothing into a steaming bucket of soapy water. With swift hands, she washed the clothes, wrung them out in a big bath towel, and ironed them dry. She brushed the girl's hair, ironed and retied the ribbons, and scrubbed the clay from her fingernails. Miraculously, the girl was transformed. She stood neat and freshly scrubbed.

Flora stood and gazed into Mrs. Gray's face for some time, and then she did something she had never done before. She impulsively threw her arms around the woman's neck and kissed her. "Oh, thank you, Mrs. Gray. I just love you." Eleanore gave a kind and reassuring pat to the girl's back and kissed her clean cheek. "I have to go now, Mrs. Gray. Will you let me come back?"

"Of course! You must come and play with Nancy often."

Nancy walked hand in hand with Flora down the rocky hill road. They parted with reluctance, promising again and again to meet soon. They waved to each other three or four times as Flora continued on alone. Although they did not know it, a friendship had been initiated that would endure for many years.

Nancy Gray continued her trips to the knoll to sing nearly every day. She no longer sang loudly to preen, to voice a sort of superiority that would echo down to the Peterson home; she now sang in hopes that her strong voice would extend to the pale little Flora, to the frail creature with golden curls and smart frocks who was forbidden childish pleasures.

They were permitted by Flora's mother to play again often, but the girls preferred Flora's visits to the Gray home to the sedate and dull afternoons on the Peterson's porch. When they played at the Peterson's, their activities were restricted to sitting on the porch, looking through family albums that contained pictures of the supposedly wealthy Kansas City branch of Peterson relatives. Every activity, gesture, and conversation was impeded by the cold, supercilious direction of Mrs. Peterson. At Nancy's home, however, the children were permitted the luxury of relatively free play. Eleanore always had Flora remove her finery, don an old and faded dress of Nancy's, and play with the liberty of bare feet. Flora would transform from a stiff, small adult into a happy child. Her mother did not know a thing about it. The girl always returned home in clean clothes, and she never failed to resume the airs of propriety demanded by her mother.

The drought that threatened finally broke in torrents of rain. It was a much prayed-for event that was met with equaled prayers of thanks in the Gray household. Some Hill people, however, attributed the longed-for rain to special spells and incantations. When Will explained local efforts to bring on the rain, Eleanore reacted with amusement and horror. Men had plowed dusty fields and hung dead snakes on their fences to bring it on. Boys had stabbed frogs and toads and spread them on the dry road. A woman had suspended and submerged a cat in sulfur water to beckon the aid of nature. While Will and her children laughed uproariously over these efforts to bring on rain, Eleanore became almost grim. It was to her a sign that superstition held priority over religious faith. She was slowly becoming aware that Hill people were not only stubborn and misguided, but blatantly straying from the teachings of the Dean's Creek Church.

Two days after the rains had ceased, Eleanore mounted old Jim to ride to the country store and post office. It was a three mile journey. She dreaded leaving her children alone, but travel alone would be more efficient. She had saved up several dozen eggs for market and she hoped to buy some material to make Nancy a few new school dresses. She cautioned the older children to watch young Janey carefully, and to run into the house if a strange man came near. She left them standing in the doorway as she rode slowly off.

The little crossroad store was a busy place on the bank of the swift and narrow Glaize River. A dam had been constructed there to power a mill that ground corn, wheat, and feed for several small Hill communities. There were numerous horses tied to hitching rails, and seven farm wagons piled high with sacks of wheat from recently threshed fields. As Eleanore approached the store and dismounted, an unusually rotund bald-headed storekeeper hurried out to relieve her of the egg basket. She followed the little man in, and was approached by a motherly little woman, the obvious mate of the storekeeper, who offered to assist her.

The woman was eager to chat. She and Eleanore talked of dress goods, latest styles, gardening, poultry, and the incredible turn of the weather. Although the store had only a limited selection of ginghams and prints, they were all of fine quality and coloring. She purchased a deep blue plaid for Nancy's dress and light percale shirting for Paul. She weakened over a pink print with a gay floral pattern and purchased enough to make dresses for both her daughters. To these yards she added a bulk of white muslin, threads, rick-rack, and embroidery floss for trims. Several neighbors from church recognized Eleanore and chatted with her amiably. Time was slipping away, but Eleanore welcomed the pleasant diversion. The cluster of chattering people broke, however, when a burly farmer strode in and boomed out, "Looks like we might be gonna get more rain, big cloud coming up in the west!"

Eleanore and others ran to the windows. A stiff breeze was riling the trees and a big black bank of clouds loomed. She thought instantly of her children, of how frightened they might be of a booming storm. She hastily gathered up her parcels, added a sack of candy, packed her goods in the egg basket, and mounted Jim for the trip home. The clouds were coming quickly, the sky was darkening, and the low roll of thunder chased them on. Old Jim sensed the storm and broke into a run that Eleanore appreciated. Before they had covered a mile, the sunlight was blotted out and the wind had grown to a roar that bent trees and greenery to the ground. When they turned the corner, Jim skidded to a stop. Sprawling prone in the road was a man. Eleanore rode closer and recognized Hank Leffert. She hardly knew what to do, but she finally dismounted and bent low over the body. A bottle was clasped tightly in his hand. He opened his red-rimmed eyes and delivered a drunken grin.

"Thass alright, lady... I'm okay. Don't you worry 'bout me." Then, in a cocky, loud voice, he said, "Would ye care come and lay down by me?"

Eleanore drew back in alarm as the man made an aimless grab for her ankle. She sprang to her saddle and rode away as quickly as Jim could, leaving the body of Hank Leffert still laughing in the road.

Huge, scattered drops of rain fell as if they were being flung from Heaven. The sky turned a sickly green that forewarned Eleanore of hail. She leaned over the basket in an attempt to shield it from rain. She neared her home with relief. She approached Hank Leffert's shack and peered at it with disgust and contempt. She wondered if his wife was in there, if the woman knew where her husband was. All at once, above the noise of wind and rain, she heard the agonized wail of a woman. In the crooked doorway of the shack stood Sadie Leffert, baby in her arms, pleading for Eleanore to stop. Eleanore rode up, sprang down from Jim, and rushed to the woman.

"Oh, Missus, my baby is dying!" Sadie screamed with terror. Eleanore looked at the child. He was nearly black, his eyes were rolled into his head, and his limbs were stiff.

"Have you any hot water, Mrs. Leffert? The pan on that stove would be adequate," she said, indicating through the open doorway a steaming pan that was visible on an old stove. With lightning fingers, Eleanore unclothed the child and gently lowered it into the pan of hot water.

"What are you doing?" screamed the frantic mother. "You'll burn him up!"

"No," explained Eleanore. "It's not that hot. He's having a spasm and this will help. What in Heaven's name has he been into?"

"Hank came home at noon," explained Sadie. "He'd been drinking. The baby reached for those plums in that pan." Sadie pointed to a pan of damaged plums on the rickety table by the stove. "I didn't want him to have them. They weren't right, and I was gonna go through them to see if I'd missed any good parts, but Hank hit me and took the baby away from me and fed him all he would eat. Oh, Missus Gray, is it gonna kill my baby?"

"I doubt it. See, he's getting his color back." The baby then issued a strangled cry and Eleanore lifted him from the pan, scrubbed him briskly with a piece of coarse cloth, and placed him in her lap. She held him between her knees and shoved her finger down his throat. The child squirmed, convulsed, and began retching up soured milk and unchewed bits of plums.

He vomited considerably. He obviously consumed enough of the fruit to make an adult ill. "There now," soothed Eleanore as she cradled the vomit-covered infant against her. The baby rested, weak and spent, with regular breathing against the woman's breast. "He'll be fine, Mrs. Leffert. Give me his clothes and we'll get him cleaned up and dressed. He's all tired out and will be sleepy. Don't feed him much for a few days, and make his milk part water. I saw your husband as I came home from the store. He was quite drunk. I thought you'd be worried."

"Worried!" said the young mother with a bitter laugh. "I wish that dirty dog was dead. I wish he'd go off and never come back. If you hadn't stopped, my baby would have died and he'd have been the murderer." The broken little child-mother slumped on the side of the bed next to her baby, buried her face in her hands and sobbed.

Eleanore did not know how to comfort her. The storm was growing worse and her own children needed her. She rose to go, but returned to the cabin with her bundle of muslin. She tore off a length of the snowy fabric and handed it, with a small wad of blue floss, to the Leffert woman. "Here, my dear, make your baby a new dress with this. I wish I could help you more." Sadie Leffert beamed up at Eleanore. Her tear-stained face seemed almost happy.

"Missus Gray, you saved my baby. I couldn't ask another human being to do more for me. I thank you, too, for this material. You're an angel, aren't you?"

Eleanore left. She called out, "Any time you need me, you come." She got aboard the wet saddle and broke Jim into a run. As they hurried to their home, Eleanore wondered if Sadie Leffert literally meant that she was an angel. The girl didn't say it as if it were a simple expression of speech. She smiled with tenderness and pity. When she entered her home, she was shocked to find it empty. The terror was momentary, however, because she realized that the quilt on the bed covered three small bodies. They had not heard her entrance above the noise of the storm. When she walked over to the bed and lifted back the quilt, six very round, frightened eyes peered up at her. Suddenly, all three of her children embraced her with arms and legs and wet kisses.

"Whatever are you all doing in bed?" asked Eleanore.

"Well, I heard that lightning won't strike feathers. Everybody was scared of it, so we got in bed," replied Nancy.

"I wasn't scared for myself," declared Paul as he hugged his mother tightly, "But I was worried for you out there!"

"You are all good children and I love you very much!" said their mother with a smile. "Our crops are saved, you know, and everything is perfect. Let's open up these packages!"

Chapter XIII

THE ADAMSES

THE RAINS HAD LEFT their marks on the Dean's Creek valley. The storms had cooled the air, turned the browning stalks of corn green again, and renewed the fading grass to a lustrous blue hue. People went about their daily affairs with vigor, with songs over household tasks and a lightness of heart over field work. The rains also turned the creek into a foaming torrent of mud, but the foot logs had been spared.

While Eleanore set about morning chores, her children played down by their spring. Even the small spring had turned muddy from wash off. When Nancy attempted to wade across, she discovered the water had risen well above her knees. To their dismay, the children found their clay dishes in ruins, their dams and bridges fallen, and their rock gardens battered by the increased flow of the bubbling little waterfalls. They invented a new pleasure in throwing sticks and rocks into the rapid falls, which would madly toss and whirl the fragments about, submerge them, and turn them out again at the foot of the falls. It was slim compensation for the collapse of their artistic endeavors, but it satisfied them for several hours.

When they finally heard their mother's fourth call, they scrambled up the muddy banks for home. Nancy and Paul each took one of Janey's pudgy hands and pulled and carried the little mite along at a reckless pace. Their mother was leaning in the doorway, framed between blooming honeysuckle and Virginia creeper. She was dressed in a fresh blue print dress. A jaunty blue bow was nestled in her dark curls. She was laughing at the wet and muddy youngsters as they struggled with the baby girl. She hurried the three into the house where a hot bath awaited them. "Hurry, Nancy, wash Janey so I can dress her while you and Paul clean up. Today, we are going visiting!"

The sick Leffert baby had left its impression on Eleanore's mind. She had prayed and contemplated over the infant for two days. Still, the image of the tormented infant and its horrified mother pressed her heart like a bruise. She had finally decided to visit Sadie Leffert again. She planned to take the children along, but only so far as the Adamses house, where she hoped she would be able to leave them for the afternoon. She also hoped she could persuade Nelle to accompany her to the Leffert cabin. She disliked the notion of venturing alone; she feared that the loutish Hank might be home. She had taken some medicines from her husband's supply box. Eleanore was familiar with their uses and hoped to minister to the baby. He was obviously undernourished and probably suffering from diarrhea as a result of the plum episode. The possibility of dehydration existed. "I'll treat the symptoms, but I don't know how to deal with the source. No medicine on earth can rid that child of Hank Leffert," she thought.

After the children had scrubbed and pulled on starched, second-best clothes, the family leisurely strolled down the road to the creek. Toby trotted along with them, sniffing and snorting. The novelty of visiting seemed contagious. The creek had indeed risen, so much so that the foot logs were barely above the muddy flow. The foot log at this pass point was actually a large old sycamore that was chained on each end to the opposite banks. Sometimes, big rains washed it free of a bank and farmers would come to restore the convenient "bridge" over the creek. Janey was afraid to walk across it and Eleanore was not strong enough or steady enough to carry her over. They stood debating for a spell before it was decided that Nancy, who was active and agile as a cat, should attempt to bring the little one across. As she carried Janey over, she nearly ran with swift ease. Eleanore was amazed. For the first time, she had to acknowledge that her first born was nearly as tall as she and decidedly stronger. Nancy was well built and beautifully proportioned. The girl could have won a prize for health. There was something of Dr. Bob Gray in her erect carriage, the proud angle of her head, and in her fearlessness. Nancy carried Janey, a squirming mass of starched skirts and chubbiness, further on over a gravel bar and up a weedy path. All mothers watched their girl children suddenly spring from babies into young women. The recognition is often colored by mingled feelings of pride and loss. Eleanore surely felt both.

Mrs. Adams was out in the garden picking beans. Miss Britton was sitting on the front porch, crocheting a rag rug. Nelle Adams was inside singing at the top of her lungs as she dusted the front parlor. All three women nearly ran to greet Eleanore and her children. Their house was a large, two-story weatherboard affair that was ornately trimmed with carved posts, spindle rails, and gingerbread eaves. It was so white that the green trim and shutters nearly jumped out against their background. The yard, unlike most farm yards, was formally arranged with maples, cedars and shrubbery contained within an ornate wire fence with a decorative iron gate.

They ushered the visitors into the parlor, a large room papered in green and tan stripes. A large, green plush sofa was
heaped with embroidered cushions that sported mottos. "Home
Sweet Home" and "Sweet Bunch o' Daisies" were done in a huge
satin stitch that made it plain that the Adams women were adept with the needle. There was an organ with a crimson plush
stool, an oak center table draped with a fascinating crocheted
scarf, and strategically-arranged, burgundy photo albums and
leather-bound Bibles. A large, green wool rug with enormous
pink and tan roses at its center covered much of the wooden
floor. The remaining polished wood was littered with smaller
rugs, some with sleeping dog decorations, others with cat family
portraits and beauty's heads. It was a charming room, a reflection of all that was considered to be in good taste during the pe-
riod. Such parlors, though now faded and worn, still sport this
splendor in the hills today. Although immobility does not come
easily to a two year-old child, little Janey held her mother's hand
and stood as if paralyzed as she surveyed the Nottingham lace
curtains, the oval glass portrait frames and the dark center table.
"Purty, Mama!" she finally announced.

After complimenting Mrs. Adams on her home, Eleanore
hastened to explain the purpose of her visit. She concluded
with, "The baby was so sick and I think I should call on them
to give it some medicines that my husband used in such cases.
I am, however, a bit put off about dealing with Hank Leffert.
I was wondering if you might watch the children here for me,
and if one of you would go with me."

"Certainly, dear!" Mrs. Adams beamed. "We'd be just tickled
to death to have them here. Nelle, you go change your apron and
go along with Mrs. Gray. I'll finish up the housework. Melinda,
would you take the little folks out to see the goslings?"

Melinda's faded cheeks turned pink with happiness. She
took obvious pleasure in being entrusted with the children's en-

tertainment. She beamed as she took Janey's hand and led the children through the door.

Nelle soon came down the stairs with a starched bonnet on her pretty hair, and she and Eleanore hurried out. Nelle was talkative, and prattled as they walked down the road. "Really, I do feel sorry for Sadie Leffert, but there's really not much to be done. Hank Leffert is the meanest man I know. I've heard he doesn't even let her eat until he's had his fill! No wonder that woman is a bag of bones!"

"I don't doubt that you're right, Nelle. It seems unbelievable that anyone would treat a woman and a child as he does. The whole situation is cruel. The baby is a sweet little thing, but far too thin."

Nelle ceased her long striding and suddenly turned to Eleanore with both hands placed on her hips. "I know what I'd do if he were my man! I'd slip a spider in his biscuits!" Both women laughed merrily and resumed their course. As they walked, Eleanore listened to Nelle.

She learned the girl was only twenty and just crazy about the preacher, Brother Davis. "But he's so pious, Mrs. Gray, that he can't see a woman!"

Eleanore smiled. "Isn't he rather old for you?"

"Only thirty-eight, and his voice…oh, it just thrills me through and through. I don't even give a hoot if it is a Methodist voice. Don't you think he has a grand voice?"

"Yes, of course. Please, Nelle, could you possibly start calling me Eleanore?" Eleanore took over the conversation and told Nelle all about her own life, of her husband's education in St. Louis, his practice in Cedarville, of her own teaching certificate, and of the antics of her children. The two women soon felt they had been acquainted for years, and the trip to the Leffert cabin passed quickly and pleasantly.

The mile to the Leffert house was over. They were pleased to see the young woman hoeing in the garden, the baby nearby, and the dreaded husband nowhere in sight. As the visitors approached, Sadie put her fingers to her mouth to silence them. She scooped up her son and motioned them to follow her. They silently walked around the bend in the road, out of sight of the cabin, and up to a mossy bank. They sat down.

Sadie said, "He's drunk a lyin' on the bed. I slept in the loft last night. Pulled the ladder up after me, I did. I'm purty safe up there unless he takes a notion to burn the house down." She laughed bitterly. "I made a little dress for the baby from the goods you give me, Missus Gray. I hid it so he wouldn't find it. He hates for me or the baby to have anything purty." Nelle and Eleanore both uttered sympathetic words and offered the small woman their help, but Sadie was a realist. "If I knowed what to do, I'd leave him, but there's no place for me to go. My folks won't have me. Granny'd help me if she could, but Pa won't let her. Said I made my own bed and I best sleep in it. I'd go off to a city if I could find some work and someone to care for the baby, but there ain't no place like that for the likes of me. Guess we'll just go on 'til he kills one of us."

Eleanore cried out in horror, "But surely he wouldn't do a thing like that!"

Sadie sighed and rolled up her sleeves. "Oh, he wouldn't, eh? Just look at my arms. I've got even more bruises on my back and maybe I'm just lucky to be alive right now."

"Can't the sheriff arrest him for that?" asked the appalled Nelle.

"Ha! Not when Hank sells the best moonshine in the county and gives it free to the sheriff to leave him be."

"Well, here's some medicine for the baby's stomach. I wish I could do more."

"Ain't nothing anybody can do, Missus Gray. The medicine is help enough. I'll just hide it here under this stump and bring the child up for it when Hank ain't around. He'd probably pour it out if he knew about it. That man ain't got no mercy."

"We should probably go now, Mrs. Leffert. We wouldn't want to cause any more trouble for you should your husband wake up," announced Nelle. Nelle was obviously as distressed over the Lefferts as Eleanore was. Huge tears welled up in her eyes. The women rose to take their leave, and Sadie stood up with her child to say goodbye.

"I want you to know that I appreciate your thinking of me. Things ain't easy and I think some folks just soon forget all this. I don't think that you should fret so. Many a woman's had a bad man and many a woman's stuck it out. Thank you for all your kindness, both of you." Sadie looked down to her bare feet for a moment.

Nelle made yet another effort to help the woman. "If you need some butter or milk, Mrs. Leffert, Mother will let you have it for the asking. We have plenty, and it sometimes gets wasted."

"I thank you. I wouldn't care for myself, but my baby gets hungry. I want to tell you something I've been ashamed of. I've been milking a quart jar from your old brindle cow for a spell now. She grazes along the lower field, you know. I wouldn't have done it, but I worry so over the baby. You make me more ashamed now by telling me I don't have to steal." Sadie made her confession without ever once raising her eyes from the ground. The baby whimpered in her arms and tears spilled down the front of Sadie's dress.

Nelle and Eleanore looked at each other. Nelle could not speak, and felt a small shame in having motivated Sadie Leffert to reveal her crime. It was no wrong act to steal for a child, thought Eleanore. She reached over and gently lifted Sadie's wet chin up, looked into her eyes, and said, "Any fine mother would have done the same if her baby was hungry."

Nelle found her tongue. "Any time you need milk, you are to take it from Brindle. She's my cow anyway. We have extra vegetables and eggs as well. I want you to come by regularly to fetch them when your husband is gone. You are not to feel ashamed. Your husband is to blame!"

"How can I ever thank you or repay you?" the woman cried.

Nelle and Eleanore hurried away. They walked well beyond the Leffert cabin before they spoke a word.

"That poor thing! That poor thing!" uttered Nelle.

"Isn't there anything to be done? I feel as if we've not helped at all. We can feed them and doctor them into health so Hank Leffert can drain them!" said Eleanore with contempt.

"We'd be more charitable if we would take Hank Leffert out and hang him!" was Nelle's vehement response.

The visit to the Leffert cabin had darkened the day for both women. They walked in near silence all the way back to the Adams home. They saw the children gathered about the porch. Melinda Britton was patiently attempting to teach Nancy to crochet and the other children were fascinated by the lesson. Janey was undoing a huge ball of yarn and stringing it over the porch railings. Paul, who had been peering through a stereoscope, had put the instrument aside to snort at Nancy's endeavors. Melinda Britton was in her glory. Her eyes were bright and her face reflected a motherly joy. As they approached the porch, Nelle whispered, "Melinda is a born mother!" Eleanore nodded her head in silent agreement.

Mrs. Adams was in the kitchen putting the finishing touches to the Saturday dinner. Eleanore went in to thank her for her help and to bid her goodbye. Mrs. Adams protested. "Now, you simply cannot leave right now at dinnertime! I already have your places set at the table, and I baked a cherry cobbler just for the children."

"Yes, you simply must stay," announced Nelle, as she dried her hands on a white muslin towel. "Pa's coming up from the field now. He's expecting company for dinner and will be a sorry soul if he's disappointed!"

It was an enjoyable meal. Bowls of fresh green beans, slaw, mashed potatoes, and cream gravy were heaped upon the table to accompany fried chicken and the cobbler. Everyone chattered wildly between mouthfuls. Mr. Adams, a quiet man, chuckled to himself and added small comments to every discourse. Eleanore was secretly glad that her children remembered the many lessons on manners that she had drilled into them. Melinda Adams insisted on waiting on the children. Not a drop was spilled, and the children used 'thank yous' liberally. Janey even refrained from attacking her food with creative flourishes and flings.

After the meal, Mr. Adams took the children outside to play on the porch. Eleanore joined the women in the kitchen. As they washed the dishes, they discussed the visit to the Leffert cabin. Each woman vowed to make a special effort to assist the little mother down the valley.

Mr. Adams herded the children into the parlor to join the ladies after the dishes were arranged again, cleaned and dried and in the shelves. While Miss Britton explained the pictures in the photograph album to the children, Nelle convinced Eleanore to play the organ for them. Everyone gradually rose and clustered about the organ to sing favorite hymns and old-time songs. Their voices blended well. When the sun began to fall, Eleanore rose to go. Nelle walked the Grays to the creek and they parted reluctantly, promising to again visit.

Eleanore finished her chores that evening and sat down in her doorway to rest and consider the day's events. Melinda Britton, she thought, was bound to an old maid's life. She

seemed to be fine motherhood material, and her natural incli-
nations were destined to be wasted because Mr. Peterson had
married a shrew. "Such a pity," sighed Eleanore. Sadie Leffert
still bothered Eleanore. The woman was reduced to tolerating
her husband's brutality, stealing food for her children, and living
in constant fear because her husband produced a fine enough
moonshine to ward off the interference of the law. It seemed
odd to Eleanore that a man like Hank Leffert was left free to
roam the earth when a good man like her own Bob, a man who
had dedicated his short life to helping mankind, had met an
early death. "But who am I to question the ways of the Lord?
Lord, indeed! Hank Leffert is Satan himself!" she thought.
Bitterness crept into Eleanore's heart. "I'm going to Granny
Matterson. She is Sadie's surviving grandmother. There ought
to be something she can do."

Chapter XIV

THE SILVER CREEK SCHOOL

Nancy and Paul started school in August. School started early in the hills, and attendance was at best scattered, depending upon finances and the demands of farming. It cost forty dollars a month to pay Mrs. Wetherby to teach for six months. Families donated to the salary as they were able, and frequently supplemented it with gifts of food or goods when cash was scarce. The teacher's job was a difficult one. Fifty-five pupils were enrolled in the Silver Creek School that served the Dean's Creek valley. One teacher was responsible for all of the instruction, and students varied in age from five years to twenty. Skills varied even more widely. The alphabet was often taught to tiny children and fully grown adults alike. Discipline was a skill that a Hill teacher had to acquire rapidly.

The Gray children were eager to begin school, and the first morning of lessons caused great commotion in the household. Paul required a fresh haircut, an extra rough scrubbing, new blue overalls, and the newly sewn percale shirt. Nancy wore her pink dress with a full gathered skirt and huge bow. Her hair was dampened and braided tightly the night before and it was unwound and combed into shimmering waves that ran to her waist. Each child was given a new denim book satchel, new readers, new arithmetics, spelling books, thick writing tablets, and sharpened pencils. Nancy also carried a new geography book filled with maps of exciting places and pictures of people in native costumes. Their shiny tin lunch pails were loaded with homemade bread and butter sandwiches, hard-boiled eggs, ripe tomatoes with little packets of salt in paper and four big cookies apiece.

Eleanore accompanied the children to school this first day to inspect the school and see that her children were properly enrolled. The road to the school was sided by bushes and fields glittered with dew. Goldenrod and black-eyed Susans trimmed the meadows with color. Small clumps of wild blue asters seldom escaped a child's picking. The fields were nearly white with daisies. When they reached the point where they were to cut through the fields to a footpath, a covey of quail burst into flight.

The Silver Creek School was a new structure composed of cement, creek gravel, and sand. It sported big windows and a well-tailored roof, the essentials of a modern country school. The teacher's buggy was behind the building, her horse tethered under a tree nearby. The yard was full of children. Some were cleaned and combed, others were shaggy and barefoot. They all mingled in schoolyard games with great enthusiasm.

Eleanore ushered the children into the schoolhouse. Mrs. Wetherby was seated at her desk with a large ledger open before her. She was tall and sparse, weathered and graying. Her stern exterior was, however, betrayed by a set of kindly eyes that twinkled in the sober face. Her graying hair was swept into a moderate pompadour which was efficiently secured with a multitude of studded celluloid combs. She wore a dark serge skirt and a striped blouse. Around her neck was a tight velvet choker. Long jet earrings hung from her ears. She wore a thick gold wedding band on one finger, and a thinner ring set with seed pearls and emeralds on another finger. Nancy could barely take her eyes off the pearl and emerald ring. Paul, however, was fascinated by an ornate gold watch that hung from a chain on her bosom.

Mrs. Wetherby was efficient and businesslike. She looked up, requested the children's names and ages, and entered them in the ledger. She scrutinized Nancy. "Are you quite certain that you can make the sixth grade this year, young lady? You look a bit young." Nancy brought out her Cedarville report card and handed it to her new teacher. Mrs. Wetherby regarded it carefully and finally returned it to Nancy with a smile. "I knew your father when he was a boy. I think you may take after him. If that be the case, sixth grade should be managed easily."

The instructor rose and ushered the children to their seats. Nancy was alarmed to discover that a Matterson girl was assigned to sit directly behind her. Eleanore crooked a finger at Nancy to beckon her over to a corner where she was issuing final instructions to Paul. "Nancy," she whispered, "do be careful. For pity's sake, don't let other children handle your books, and try to keep a distance from the Matterson children. I think you know why. Watch out for Paul, and be a good girl."

Eleanore took Janey's hand and left. Outside, she spotted Rachel Matterson with two small brothers and a tiny sister leaning against the side of the building. It was evident that other mothers had cautioned their children not to play with the Mattersons. They were the only children excluded from the games. Their clothes were horribly shabby. The boys wore pants so covered by patches that the original fabric could only be guessed at. The girls wore faded calico dresses that were wrinkled. They were barefoot. As Eleanore studied the children, she noticed a large boil on the little girl's leg. It was red-rimmed and obviously infected. Someone had tied a rancid piece of salt pork against it with a dingy rag that had slipped down. Eleanore knew the child had to be in pain. She walked over and said, "How do you do, Rachel?" The girl responded with a bashful grunt. The little ones just stared. "Listen, Rachel, your mother ought to attend to that boil on your sister's leg."

"Ma's dead," stated the girl in a trembling voice. "They ain't nobody but Granny and Pa. Granny made a fat meat poultice to draw the pizen out, but it won't stay put."

"My husband was a doctor," said Eleanore. "I have some wonderful medicine for boils. If you would bring her by after school, I'd be glad to attend to it."

"You would?" asked Rachel doubtfully. "It hurts Peggy something fierce. Nobody has anything to do with us, Missus Gray, 'cause we're poor trash. I just thought I'd tell ye."

"Never mind that. You come to my house just the same."

The teacher suddenly appeared in the doorway and rang a little bell in her hand furiously. The children instantly rushed to form a line. The children consisted of tots, small girls and boys, half grown girls and boys, adolescents, and young women. "Mrs. Wetherby must be a magician to manage a bunch like this!" mused Eleanore as she and Janey went down the steep hill. The sun had burnt off the dew by now. Save for a breeze that fanned their faces, the day promised heat.

Eleanore suddenly felt unbearably lonely. Nancy and Paul, though young, had been excellent companions to their mother. Now she was alone with a tiny girl who had a limited vocabulary, a brief attention span, and a need for constant entertainment. Eleanore and her youngest sat on a log by the creek to rest. Janey pointed to the water. "Purty, Mama!" then Janey turned to a rock. "Purty, Mama!" She continued to point at a sumac bush and every bit of vegetation nearby and declared them, "Purty, Mama!" However, her observations failed to break through Eleanore's thoughts.

Eleanore reflected on the changes in her life. When the children were in school in Cedarville, Eleanore was never alone. Bob was usually home, the office was full of patients or friends, and cousins were forever stopping by for tea or gossip. She sometimes snuck away to go to Emmy's to admire the hats in creation. The children always came home at noon, hungry as wolves. The days never seemed long enough. In Dean's Creek, though, life was stilled. She dreaded going home to the cabin, to the silence of chipped whitewash and bare floors. She had been too occupied with canning and the children during the summer to take notice of her house, but memory of the Adams home made her wistful now. The wallpaper, the rugs, the carved woodwork had been so pleasing. She wondered if surroundings affected one's morale.

Daydreams had a way of turning into plans with Eleanore. Even as she and Janey sat looking at the "purty" things by the stream, a plot was hatching in Eleanore's mind. She had forty dollars reserved in cash. The corn crop was going to be a success. Will had dropped by on Sunday and told her that it should have a very high yield to the bushel per acre. He estimated that the Grays would have about 450 bushels for market. Eleanore had plenty of canned fruit. There were already canned and pre-served blackberries, gooseberries, plums, cherries, tomatoes, pickles, green beans, and sweet corn lined in row after row on the wide shelves under the stair to the loft. Peaches and apples would be added to the stock later. The potatoes, though planted late, promised good yield as well. Cabbage and turnips would be buried for winter eating. Eleanore now had over one hundred chickens. Except for the hired plowing help, Eleanore and her family had provided for themselves for the coming winter and spring. They had done well. The only expenses that she could foresee would be to get new shoes and some heavy garments for the winter. It did not seem unreasonable to splurge to make the cabin more like a proper home.

Will had told her that Mr. Dean was the community carpenter. Eleanore decided to visit Mr. Dean that instant before returning home. Her mind brimmed with excitement. As she and Janey walked down the creek bottom to the wagon road that led to the Dean home, she prattled to Janey about her plans. "We'll have the kitchen and big room plastered first, then you and I will put up pretty blue and white garland paper. We'll get a rug, a soft brown one with blue flowers and a border. Won't that be pretty? Then we'll make a side room just for you and Paul and Nancy. We'll do it in rose and green. We could paint your beds white again and make wild rose quilts for them! Best of all, Janey, we'll have a little porch built so we can sit outside in the evenings."

The Dean home sat on a little knoll. The house was not large, but the compact neatness revealed the skill of its carpenter. Small gables and a bay window graced the building. A large poplar tree, not a native of the hills, had been brought in. It towered beside the home, its soft leaves quivering in the sultry breeze. The home was still, void of rowdy children and barking dogs. Even the buff-colored hens carried on their efficient business in near silence. Mr. Dean could be seen in the open barn repairing a bit of harness. When Eleanore knocked on the front door, it was almost immediately opened by Sophie Dean.

Sophie, with graceful dramatic flourishes, beckoned Eleanore to enter. She seated the mother and child in a big velvet arm chair. The house did not contain gaudy rugs and the usually ever-present Mission oak furniture that Eleanore was prepared to face. There was instead a deep piled mulberry-colored rug, spindly Windsor chairs, a golden brown plush sofa, and wine damask draperies that were edged with gold threading and tassels. A polished grand piano occupied an entire corner. Colored glass and pottery vases sat atop the marble tables. An oil lamp, decorated with an abundance of polished glass prisms, was suspended from the ceiling. It was a charming room; a room with a sense of art to it. It told of its mistress' cultured background.

Sophie Dean, however, was not as stylish and poised as she usually was at church. She wore a faded wrapper and her hair was done up on kid curlers. She looked every bit of her forty years. Her face, devoid of powder, was pale and delicately lined. Sophie begged Eleanore to forgive her appearance, the effect created by a dreadful headache that had plagued the woman for two days. Eleanore complimented her on her house and, not wanting to distress the woman who obviously was not up to having callers, rapidly explained the nature of her visit. Mrs. Dean hurried out to fetch her husband.

While the women waited for Mr. Dean, they chatted amiably. Sophie seemed to welcome the opportunity to explain her history to Eleanore. "I suppose you find this house a bit different from most farmhouses, Mrs. Gray. My husband and I come from St. Louis, where he was engaged as a master cabinetmaker. Mr. Dean is not a strong man, though, so when an opportunity presented itself to lead a quieter life, we moved here. His uncle, a bachelor of distant relationship to the other Deans in these parts, promised us this farm if we would care for the gentleman in his old age. Most regrettably, the man died during the first year we lived here and the farm then became our own.

"Living here has been very good for us, though I do confess the adjustment was at first difficult. Once I became involved with the community, however, I felt as if I had a valuable contribution to give to the Hill people. I have organized a Sunday school for the young people and have offered free music lessons. I had been a music teacher as a girl. Unfortunately, it is seldom that I find any natural talent here. My husband and I always longed for children of our own, but we were never blessed in that way. The chance to involve myself with children has had to suffice." Eleanore was not put off by Sophie's pretentiousness. It occurred to her that the stilted speech and stiff mannerisms were merely an effort to retain the background that seemed so precious to her. There was a sincere gentleness, an earnestness to the woman's endeavors to improve the valley. "I would so enjoy to hear you play, Mrs. Dean," announced Eleanore. Sophie assured her that she would relish the chance and then inquired if Eleanore played. Eleanore modestly responded, "Mostly plain songs and a few waltzes, nothing very difficult. With the children and all, I simply have had no time to practice. Before we moved here, I had to sell my organ."

Tom Dean came in, and the building project was discussed. Sophie was thrilled by Eleanore's descriptions. Tom agreed to do the work. He also agreed to accept some corn as partial payment. "Mrs. Gray, I believe I can have it all done before winter," he said as negotiations concluded.

"I like to see people improve their surroundings. In fact, I think it is an important part of raising a family. Having a nice home is encouraging to a youngster. That is part of the trouble, I believe, with these mountain people. They live in dark and dingy huts. Women get tired of scrubbing. When it fails to improve things, they eventually give up and reside in filth and dirt. It drags them down, it weighs on their spirits and ambitions," commented Mrs. Dean with taunt assuredness.

Eleanore was inclined to agree with Sophie Dean. She told her about the Matterson children, about her plans to attend to them that evening. With graphic detail, she described the boil in the child's leg. "And," she went on, "I intend to put some medicine on their itch and hair to get rid of the lice. My children must associate with them in school and church, and they can hardly do so if the lice forbid any friendships."

Sophie, though obviously disgusted by the lice topic, praised Eleanore. "It shames me to think that those of us who have lived here for so long with an awareness of the problem have not done a thing to make amends. We've pitied the Mattersons and shunned them, but then you, a total stranger, come in and actually try to do something. I think, Mrs. Gray, that you will be a blessing to this valley."

Eleanore changed the topic by asking Mrs. Dean to play the piano. Little Janey had long ago fallen asleep in her mother's lap. Tom Dean, with a pipe to his mouth, had settled back in a leather chair to watch his wife's nimble fingers chase over the keyboard. She played piece after piece; Chopin, Beethoven, Bach. Eleanore sometimes glanced at Tom Dean. He was very much in love with his wife. Adoration was evident in his gentle scrutiny of the woman's face. They listened for nearly an hour before Sophie tired. She finished the last composition and turned to Eleanore. "It is so seldom that I play for anyone who really appreciates fine music. Usually the people here want to hear a jig or some chords and they sit talking the entire time. It irritates me terribly, but you are the perfect audience!"

"It was just wonderful, Mrs. Dean," murmured Eleanore. "I must really excuse myself now. There is work waiting for me at home. I first dreaded going home to an empty house this morning, but I think now it may be lovely to have the children off to school. You've improved my spirits considerably."

Sophie strolled with Eleanore and a sleepy Janey out to the gate. Mrs. Dean watched the baby girl with tenderness. "You know, it hardly seems worthwhile to cook a decent meal for just Tom and myself. He has poor digestion and cannot eat well. You, on the other hand, have your lovely children to care for. The little ones are probably hungry when they come home. And full of news about their first day at school, I imagine. Family life with its little quarrels, songs, and stories is something I'll always envy you for. I've pictured tucking a child into bed many a time in my imagination. I've always longed so for a daughter. You may think it silly, but I have daydreamed of brushing her long brown hair, of teaching her to play the piano, of teaching her to sing. I've cried at night for the sound of a child's song. Whenever I've gone shopping, I've looked at yard goods and toys and even penny candy with a dream child in mind. You must think me a little mad, I suppose."

Eleanore bravely grasped Sophie Dean's hands. "I think I understand very well, Mrs. Dean. When your husband comes up to work on the house, please come along and spend time with us. I'm sure we have much in common."

The afternoon passed quickly at the Gray cabin. Eleanore baked cookies, churned butter, and made yeast dough for bread. All afternoon, she went over her plans to redo the home. She gave Janey a bath in the tub. Eleanore and her baby were playing in the grass under the trees in the backyard when she spied her other children walking up from the fields after school. The Matterson children tailed them at a safe distance. Peggy was limping badly. Rachel and the other children looked sheepish as they came along, perhaps fearing harsh words instead of kindness. Eleanore was prepared for these uncomely guests. She hurried them into the kitchen. A large kettle of water was already steaming on the stove and work began instantly. While her own Nancy and Paul excitedly described the events of the day, Eleanore tackled the silent Mattersons. They looked like sheep being led to slaughter, and Eleanore knew no way to ease their fears. A mixture of coal oil, Vaseline, and carbolic acid was rubbed into each tousled and crawling head. Each louse twisted in death under her merciless attack. She left the mixture to stand on each head and bade them to hold out their itchy hands.

She covered the red skin with ammonia and then rubbing alcohol. Each child winced, a few cried, and they all came to accept the treatment as the only way to play with the other children at school. Finally, Eleanore spread the hands with a soothing salve.

It was time to investigate Peggy's leg. Eleanore opened the wound and twisted out the hard center, bathed the injury in hot water and soap, and coated it with an antiseptic salve and a bandage. Peggy gave a teary sigh as Eleanore rose from her ministering. The Mattersons allowed her to fiercely scrub their heads with a coarse brush, steaming water, and laundry soap. When each of them had been dried and combed, the woman was astonished to note the alterations in their appearances. They had nice features, especially Rachel Matterson. A clear complexion had risen from the layers of filmy dirt.

As a reward for their trials, and as encouragement, Eleanore seated the Mattersons with her own family around the table, and all of the children shyly shared cookies and milk. She made up a parcel of cookies for the children to carry home with them. She eventually saw them off with final instructions. "Keep your pillows clean. Here are some clean combs. Keep them clean and use them frequently. Rachel, you see to it that all of you wash your heads regularly. If you don't, you'll have lice again. Stop in tomorrow evening so I can change Peggy's bandage. Now run along home. I hope I haven't gotten you in any trouble and that you won't be scolded for being late."

"Pa won't be home anyway, and Granny won't care. She'll be glad!" The Mattersons delivered this as a sort of thank you and scurried up the hill into the growing twilight. When they were gone, Nancy turned to her mother and said, "Mama, I'm glad you did that for them. I kind of like Rachel. You should hear her sing! It's better than me!"

"Mama," added Paul, "you should hear Peter Matterson cuss!"

"Listen up, Paul Gray!" said Eleanore with sternness. "Don't ever let me hear you repeating any of those words." Paul looked alarmed as he replied, "Yes, Mama."

Nancy, in a small effort to save Paul declared, "Rachel slapped Peter for saying those words."

Eleanore returned to her work. She wondered if she had done right in taking the Matterson children into her care. She remembered the biblical instruction, "Take care not to cast your pearls amongst the swine, lest they turn again and rend you." She comforted herself by repeating, "If you have done it unto the least of these, my children, then you have done it unto Me."

Chapter XV

THE BLUE RUG

AUTUMN WAS GLORIOUS. A slight frost came early to the valley. It left light coloring to the leaves and transformed into a lazy Indian summer. The peaches were canned. Soft rosy clings were made into a spicy pickle, and the large free stones were cut and left to dry on the kitchen roof. The apples, mealy Ben Davises and tangy Winesaps, were picked and dried or made into apple-sauce for canning. Though the orchard was in need of care and its produce was imperfect, it yielded enough fruit to serve the family through the winter and spring. With the help of a neighbor boy, the corn was harvested.

The months of work in Dean's Creek wrought a change in Eleanore. She was thinner than ever. Working outdoors had peppered her face with freckles. Her hands were no longer white and delicate, but tanned, reddened, rough, and strong. She could easily wield a corn knife and drive a team. She could chop a load of wood in record time, and shell corn with the ease that usually only comes with years of practice. Will Gray visited frequently, and he could not help but feel that the woman no longer needed his aid as she had in the beginning.

Once the crops were in, Tom Dean started work on the Gray home. Will Gray donated some oak siding left from his own construction. It was enough for an extra room. Tom Dean worked faithfully and without complaint. He seemed happiest when wood was under his hands.

One Saturday while the remodeling was still in progress, Will Gray took his wagon and team to the Gray house. He loaded Eleanore and her brood of excited children and they set off for Benchfield, a town to the east, for lime, wallpaper, paint, and the new rug Eleanore had longed for.

The journey was thrilling for the children, for they saw their first train. Puffing and belching out black smoke, the locomotive raced through the town. The engineer pulled the whistle three mighty blasts and waved cheerfully to his audience. It frightened Janey. Will hoisted her up on his shoulders so that she could see the source of the dreaded noise, but this only increased her terror and the little girl buried her face in his hair.

They ate dinner in a little café. They gobbled down hot soup, roast beef, fried potatoes, and a sample of desserts. Paul chose a lemon pie with a mountain of meringue. Nancy selected a jelly roll slice. She and Janey both studied the swirl of yellow cake and red apple jelly before she ever lifted a fork to her mouth. They later went to a furniture store to look at rugs and wallpaper. Nancy and Paul were intrigued by the variety; they explored and admired every object carefully. A new kitchen range, black and highly polished, particularly caught Paul's eye. He ran his hands over the nickel-plated towel bars and scrutinized the large hot water reservoir. "Nancy," he whispered solemnly, "I'm gonna buy one of those for Mama when I get big."

Nancy was awed by the large dressers with giant plate glass mirrors, and she actually exclaimed aloud in rapture over a leather folding davenette seat. Her mother called to them to join her in selecting wallpaper. They felt quite grown up and important as they argued the merits of each paper before the patiently-waiting, dapper clerk in a salt and pepper suit. Nancy favored a print paper with Japanese ladies in pink and blue kimonos with delicate parasols traipsing over silver bridges. Her desires waned, however, when Eleanore whispered that the dear ladies cost fifty cents a roll. Nancy then turned her attention to a roll that consisted of silver stripes and tiny pink roses. Her heart was set on it. Paul liked it and it only cost fifteen cents a roll. They bought it. The all-important matter of selecting a rug now took preeminence.

"It must be blue," stated Eleanore.

"The blue rugs run about fifty dollars, ma'am," stated the clerk as politely as he could. "Many other colors run somewhat less, however."

Eleanore was crestfallen, and her feelings were plainly visible to both the clerk and her family. Without enthusiasm, they selected a gray rug with unnatural blue and green roses in the corners for twenty-five dollars. As soon as the selection was finalized and the merchandise paid for, Eleanore and the children left the store. She was embarrassed by her disappointment, by her desire to pout like a willful child that did not get its prize, and she longed to be away from the eyes of the clerk, who obviously pitied her and her inadequate pocketbook. Will, much to her relief, stayed behind to have the rug wrapped and loaded.

She and the children stood outside the store. Paul nudged his mother and whispered, "This is just like a big city, ain't it Mama?"

Eleanore smiled. She was still brooding over the rug, and could not even manage to bother to correct Paul's grammar. The "ain'ts" were obviously a sign that he had adopted Hill speech. Nancy persisted in drawing Eleanore out by pointing to the gay

Saturday town crowd. Buggies, wagons, buckboards, and surreys were hitched to every immovable object in sight. Farmers, town people, drummers, and loafers crowded the streets. Women passed in long trailing skirts and hoop skirts and the latest hobble skirts. Enormous hats drifted past with bird wings, fruit, and velvet flowers as ornamentation. The finer women sported patent leather, high-heeled pumps, and fancy topped kid shoes with intricate stitching. Farm women shuffled along in heavy brogans and calico dresses, with plain bonnets or scarves tied over their heads. Their faces, brown and weathered, seemed worried by the unfamiliar noise and urgency of the visit. Their sometimes frightened children clung to them.

Eleanore hurried her family into a general store to buy new overshoes and stockings. It took every bit of her chicken money to outfit the youngsters. "We had better go home now, children. We've spent all of the money and if we stay any longer we'll have to apply for a loan from the bank!" Her spirits had improved considerably, although she still longed for the blue rug of her dreams. She loathed the longing and eventually dismissed it as foolishness unbecoming to a grown woman.

No one really wanted to leave, but it was time. The rug, the rolls of wallpaper, lime, paint, and nails were loaded. Will Gray was leaning against the wagon talking to another man. As Eleanore and her flock approached with stockings and shoes in parcels tucked under their arms, the man tilted his straw hat at Eleanore and bid Will goodbye. The children climbed aboard and leaned against a mound of straw that was to buffer their treasured purchases against the jostle and jolt of the ride home. From behind his back, Will brought forth a mysterious paper bag and held it high for all to see. It was too large for a candy bag. It smelled enticing, but wholly unfamiliar. He finally tossed it up to Nancy. "My treat, but wait a bit before you eat it."

Nancy and Paul peeked inside the bag. It was filled with a huge, spicy, garlic bologna, a sausage, crackers, and a wonderful big hank of bananas. Just as they cried out with delight and thanks, the wagon lurched and began the rough roll down the rutted wagon road for Dean's Creek. As they traveled homeward, Eleanore realized how grand the day had really been, how much fun it had afforded her children, and how generous Will Gray was with her family. Eleanor sighed aloud, and Will turned to her with a puzzled expression. "Oh, Will it's really been a fine day. The only thing is, I still can't get that fifty-dollar blue rug out of my mind!"

Will Gray laughed. "Now isn't that just like a woman?"

It was nearly dark when they came up the hill to their house. Although the children were weary, all three helped to unload the treasures. Nancy and Paul ran back and forth like relay runners, carrying in the lighter parcels, while little Janey proudly struggled with a parcel of stockings. Eleanore and Will grappled with the awkward rug and finally emptied the wagon completely. Since a neighbor had done the chores for both Will and Eleanore, there was no urgency to set about farm work. Eleanore proposed that Will should stay for supper. He kindly agreed and kindled a great fire in the hearth. The children, thoroughly chilled from the journey home, huddled near the blaze, soaking up the warmth while their mother prepared a meal.

After supper, they sat before the fire admiring the mountain of parcels. Even the nails and the lime were treasures to be appreciated. The children undid their shoes and tried them on again. Eleanore finally decided to unwrap the rug. "Now that I have this thing at home, I want to see if it will fit in. It really isn't a bad rug at all." As she lifted one corner, she let out a cry of surprise. "It's my blue rug!" Clearly amazed, she looked to Will Gray's grinning face for explanation. "You did this, didn't you?" she accused with mock fierceness.

"What's the matter, Ellie? Don't you like it?" laughed Will.

"Like it? Oh, but it's wonderful! You shouldn't have done that, though. I simply cannot accept so much from you."

"Forget that. It's a loan. When your children grow up, they can pay me back."

"We will, too!" cried out Paul. Both of the older children were clapping and dancing about in glee in their new shoes. Janey foraged through the wrappings and laid her cheek against the blue softness of the coveted rug.

"Please keep it, Mama," begged Nancy. After much coaxing, Eleanore agreed. The blue rug was forever to be referred to as "Will Gray's rug."

Chapter XVI

CHRISTMAS

EVERY DAY, PAUL AND Nancy walked down the path through the fading weeds, the long strip of bare woods, the thick layer of fallen leaves, and up the hill to the school. More often than not, they spied pheasants and quail now, and usually, they paused to watch the frightened flight of whirring wings. Squirrel abounded now. They would race up the tall bare trees to perch, chatter, and scold the children who stood below. A timid bunny would hop away from them into the tall brush, leaving only his snowball tail visible like a signal of light. After the early frost, persimmons, black haws, and tangy purple grapes ripened. The children usually ate their fill on the way to school and on the way home. Their mother worried over their apparent loss of appetites, until the children volunteered an explanation. After that, she, too, went along the path with Janey and a basket to gather the fruits from the rotting rail fences and small trees. Grapes were converted into jellies and canned juice.

When nuts began falling from the trees, the family collected them. With large sacks and baskets in hand, they gathered walnuts, butternuts, hard-shelled hickory nuts, and precious hazelnuts. Every Saturday morning, they worked at prying the nut meats from their protective shells. As they worked, cold winds blew down from the north, browning leaves and whispering a cold song of death to every bush and vine in the valley. The goldenrod and late asters were affected, and they turned an ugly black. Only the cedars withstood the blast and wail of the winds. Persimmons shriveled and dried in the cold, but the children discovered that they still retained a sugary sweetness that was more delicious than ever before.

Eleanore brought out coats and caps for the children, and knitted mittens to protect their reddened hands. When ice formed pools along the creek edges, out came new overshoes and extra scarves to tie around their necks. The Matterson children, like their half-kin Davis brothers and sisters and the Carson children, however, went barefoot to the Silver Creek School long after frost. Their skin was mottled red and purple by the time they arrived. They would cluster around the schoolhouse fire, shivering in their thinly patched clothes until classes began. Eventually the cold became too much for them to bear, and they ceased to come. Rachel was the only one of the clan to persist. Every day, she came over the hill with bare feet, hair whipped wild from the winds, and eyes bleared from the cold. The girl even braved storms to walk the three miles to school. Her craving for knowledge was unquenchable. Eleanore learned of Rachel's determination through Nancy. Eleanore's funds were low from work on the house, but she turned to her friends the Adamses to obtain shoes for the girl. Eleanore gave Rachel a pair of her own warm stockings and Sophie Dean provided the child with a coat cut down from one of her own. Miss Britton crocheted a lavender scarf to cover the girl's head and shoulders.

Rachel sometimes stopped by the Gray cabin with Nancy on her way home. Once, as the Hill girl stood before the fire warming herself for the rest of her long walk home, Eleanore asked her to sing. She at first hesitated, but finally agreed when pushed by Eleanore. Both Eleanore and Nancy held their breath in astonishment as Rachel, in an untrained but unusually fine voice, shyly sang a wild mountain ballad with strong, high notes. She held some of the high notes for a minute without the strain normal to a young voice. Eleanore hugged her tightly when the song was over. "Child, child!" she cried. "You have a wonderful voice. You have a gift that must be given a chance!" The Hill girl, abashed but pleased, wondered what the generous woman meant.

The house, under the hands of Mr. Dean and Eleanore, was completed by Thanksgiving. Everyone marveled at the change. The children continued to enter each room with pride for weeks on end. "Mama, our house is the nicest in the county!" they would exclaim. Little Janey, equally pleased by the remodeling but still limited by her vocabulary, would sum it all up by yelling, "Purty!" as she rubbed her palms over the striped wallpaper.

Eleanore's friendships with the Deans and the Adamses flourished with each meeting. Thanksgiving was celebrated at the Adams farm. Will Gray and the Deans joined the festivities. Eleanore could not, however, achieve such intimacy with Mrs. Peterson, a fussy woman who was far too stiff and formal for country life. Flora Peterson, on the other hand, eagerly dropped her mother's pretensions and became an "adopted" member of the Gray family through her friendship with Nancy. Through Flora it was learned that the Smalls, a prolific family of simple, hard-working Hill people, were related to the Petersons. Mrs. Small was Mr. Peterson's sister. The city-bred Mrs. Peterson forbade Flora to associate with her own Small cousins because they were "beneath her," and thus unsuitable. Eleanore found

Mrs. Peterson's dictates hard to swallow. She, for one, had been impressed by the Smalls. The family had ten children, ranging from age eighteen to eighteen months. The eldest son, always eager to earn a dollar, had helped Eleanore with her farm. He tackled even the most unpleasant chores with great energy and no inclination to complain.

When he was not hired out for work, even this young man attended school. In the winter months he joined the school children. Nancy explained that Mrs. Wetherby permitted older children to attend school in the winter even two or three years after they had completed their eighth grade studies. In the absence of any regular janitor, they were helpful. The big boys cut wood and tended the fire; the big girls tidied the schoolroom and assisted in dressing and undressing the little ones. Older children often heard lessons and corrected the younger pupils while Mrs. Wetherby graded essays and fractions. She encouraged these nearly grown children to set examples for the younger ones. They were a special resource to her, particularly when preparing one of the three major school-year festivities.

Every year, money had to be raised to purchase school supplies. A new globe, more chalk, books, maps, or spellers might be needed. The solution was a traditional "pie supper," which consisted of a lengthy program of student recitations and songs followed by an auctioning off of pies made by the girls. The boys bid for favorite pies or, more likely, for the pie made by a favored sweetheart. Once a pie was sold, the fellow was permitted to eat it with the baker. It thrilled the girls to watch their lad bid up to two dollars for the privilege of sharing a pie. The honor was sometimes undone when an unfortunate lad selected a poor baker whose pie lacked enough sugar to sweeten the gooseberries. Similar festivities were held in the spring to honor the graduates, but the very highlight of the year fell at Christmastime.

In early December, Nancy and Paul came home nearly bursting with excitement over the planned Christmas program. There was to be a big tree, a real Santa Claus, a program of verse, songs, and skits, and presents for everyone. Eleanore's children stayed up late every night memorizing their parts of the program. Eleanore listened to Paul repeat his one line, "The boy stood on the burning dock," so frequently that she nearly screamed in protest. Nancy had three parts to prepare. First, she and Rachel Matterson were to sing a duet. Listening to those rehearsals was a joy. Nancy was also to play an old maid school marm in a comic skit. Most importantly, though, she would recite, "Curfew Shall Not Ring Tonight." Day after day, the child would repeat the many verses over and over until they were firm in her memory. Each stanza ended with the title refrain. Eventually, even little Janey learned to repeat the refrain in her garbled speech.

At last the great day arrived. There had been some snow, but it melted into just a few scattered patches. The weather was mild, the sun shone, and the mud was knee deep. Will Gray arrived early by buggy to collect the Grays. Bundled in warm coats and lap robes, Nancy burned with an excitement that was nearly smothering. The schoolhouse eventually came into view. The yard was full of vehicles. Buggies, surreys, hacks, and wagons, as well as an odd assortment of horses and mules had piled into the yard. Groups of people stood around the door, beside their vehicles and near-bare trees. There were the inevitable roughnecks sharing moonshine. One had already imbibed too heartily and his vexing yell of drunken obscenities afforded his seedy companions with an opportunity to echo in staggering hilarity the phrases that had already turned more than one sober head. Eleanore pointed Hank Leffert out to Will. Leffert was red-eyed and snarling with his pack of drunken curs.

Will said, "I only hope he drinks himself unconscious before the program starts." He then took Eleanore's arm and guided her into the building. It was packed. Every seat, save but a very few, was occupied. Even the planks that had been put up in the back were crowded. Nancy and Paul hurried off behind a muslin curtain. Mr. Adams gave up his seat to Eleanore and Janey, and he stood next to Will in the aisle by her side. Nearly every family in the valley was present. Sadie Leffert had even managed to come. Sadie, in a threadbare coat and broken shoes, clutched her tiny son against her. The infant was wearing the muslin and embroidery Eleanore had provided. His bare feet were wrapped in a worn woolen shawl. He looked healthier and he had certainly grown since the plum accident. As Eleanore turned away from her study of Sadie, she glanced up to see Sophie Dean smiling at her. Mrs. Dean was elegantly bedecked in a black silk dress, a velvet hat and a gray fur scarf and muff. Eleanore nodded her head to Sophie and looked around the audience. The severe Mrs. Peterson, dressed also in silks and velvet, was keeping a protective watch over Flora. Flora looked like a miniature sophisticate, with curled blonde hair, a blue silk dress, and new patent leather shoes. Eleanore smiled as she thought of Flora running barefoot through her own yard. The shabby Davises and Carsons were present. It was hard to believe that some of them were cousins and half-kin to the lovely Rachel. The Smalls, the Sloans, and the Adamses were a part of the audience as well.

Mrs. Wetherby eventually came forth and made a little speech to introduce the program. As the program began, Eleanore was drawn to look at Mrs. Small's face. The mother of ten performers looked anxious and proud as little Danny Small came out to make a welcome speech in his five year-old lisp. When he exited with a stiff little bow, everyone applauded and his mother gave a heavy sigh of relief that was barely covered by the clapping of hands. Danny's speech was followed by school

songs, more speeches, and at last Paul's recitation. Paul's stage
fright caused him to botch his verses. He spoke as quickly as
he could. There was a whisper of sympathetic laughter from the
crowd, but applause was given liberally. Nancy, unlike her shy
brother, was at ease on the platform. She handled herself admi-
rably, and her mother blushed with pleasure at the whispered
wave of praise that ran through the audience.

Eleanore's high point, however, came when Nancy and
Rachel, angels clad in muslin, sang "Away in a Manger." For
once, the crowd, even rowdier than the elements, was silent and
breathless. Every note was full and tender. Their voices blended
in perfect harmony. As the last note faded off, the crowd remained immobile and silent for a moment, and then abruptly
burst into deafening applause. Eleanore's eyes were wet with
tears, and Sophie Dean dipped and dabbed a lacy swatch of
handkerchief at her own brimming eyes. Perhaps for a moment,
unknown to all but Mr. Dean and Eleanore, Sophie Dean had
imagined the girl standing next to Nancy as her own longed-
for daughter. Eleanore cast a glance at Sadie Leffert, wondering
how the misused woman responded to the singing of her half-
sister, Rachel. Sadie's face was buried in her son's tiny shoulder
and her back was shaking with sobs. She suddenly turned her
face at Eleanore and beamed through the tears.

The moving performance of the two singers was followed
by a comic skit that allowed the audience to recover its composure. Santa Claus appeared, strangely enough looking a bit
like Mr. Adams, and distributed presents from beneath a dazzling cedar tree that was coated with the decorations of children. The crowd was gay, and when the teacher commanded
two big girls to pass out assorted candy sticks to the crowd, the
laughter and cheer reached thundering heights. Over the chatter and whooping, there suddenly rose a hoarse scream that was
followed by drunken shouting. It was as if a mighty hand struck

down the merriment. Every voice was suddenly stilled and every
ear tuned in to the unpleasant racket. The men nearest the door
rushed out. Some women swept out after them. Will looked at
Eleanore's now-white face. "Don't look so horrified, Ellie," he
whispered. "It's probably some drunken fight that won't amount
to much."

Eleanore, like the others remaining in the schoolhouse,
twisted her head around to wait for an all's well sign from the
doorway. None came, but the sound of a pistol shot drove her to
her feet. The bullet missed its mark, chipped off some concrete
from the school's exterior, and prompted a wealth of screams.
Nancy and Paul, hand in hand, pulled through the crowd for
sanctuary at their mother's side. She pulled them closely to her.
A second shot rang out that jarred them all. Will, who had been
holding Janey, turned her over to her mother and headed for
the door. The shot initiated more screaming. Over the din, a
woman's scream from outside pierced the schoolroom. Sophie
Dean shouted, "That's Stella Carson. It must be her menfolk in
trouble!" Mr. Adams, half in his Santa garb, ran in the door and
announced, "Don't get alarmed. The fight is over."

He strode toward Will and whispered, "We want to use your
buggy. You've got the fastest team and young Ned Carson is
pretty badly hurt—real cut up. He and Leffert, Buck Matterson,
and Slim Davis were a-fighting with knives. We'll have to hurry if we expect to save that boy." Eleanore overheard the announcement. She turned her children over to Mrs. Adams and
followed the two men out.

Ned Carson, covered with blood and looking very near
death, was lying in his mother's blood-covered arms. Strong
hands were holding Leffert and the Matterson boy at bay. Young
Slim Davis held out a severely cut wrist. Blood poured from the
wound. "I was helping Ned," he explained. "Them damned dogs
jumped onto him, but there weren't much I could do. They had

knives." Heads turned toward Leffert and Matterson. The offenders sported no mean wounds. They leered with a sort of
sick triumph that earned them the crowd's malice. As someone tended Slim's wounds, Will prepared the team to take Ned
Carson to a doctor.

"Just a minute!" Eleanore cried. "If you're going to take that
boy to Benchfield for the doctor bleeding like he is, your journey will be for nothing. He'll be dead long before you get there.
Has anyone any rags or bandages?" Mrs. Wetherby nodded
vigorously and retreated into the school. She returned with a
showy petticoat and, as she ran back to Eleanore with an ath-
lete's skill, she tore the garment into strips. The men cut back
Ned's clothing to expose his wounds. There was a deep gash in
his chest that probably touched his lung. A long cut on his face
had covered his features with a red mask, and a severed vein
in his wrist pumped out spurts of blood. While Eleanore set
to work, the mob backed off. She had seen her husband take
care of such cases before, and she prayed for a touch of his skill.
She packed fresh snow against the chest wound and bade Stella
Carson to apply pressure to the wrist wound. The wrist was
the worst. With Will's help, while a tourniquet was applied to
his arm with precision, Eleanore delicately probed for the cut
vein. By the light of a kerosene lantern, she worked at the wrist
until she managed to tie off the vein. The watching crowd was
amazed. It was tightly bandaged to stop the bleeding. "This will
have to be stitched," she instructed.

Ned Carson remained unconscious and barely breathing through the entire repair. They packed more snow against
his wounds, wrapped him in a borrowed overcoat, and tenderly lifted him into the buggy. He lay like a corpse. Will got up
to drive, and Mr. Adams climbed in to tend to Ned. The team
broke into a run with one crack of the whip. The buggy swayed
and lurched off down the uneven road. Stella Dean, still cry-

ing, looked gratefully at Eleanore. Eleanore put her arms over the woman's shoulders and walked her to the school door. Two women met her. As they attempted to guide her into the building, Stella turned fiercely and stared with burning hatred at the two men who had attacked Ned. She turned her heels and proudly marched into the safety of the schoolhouse.

Eleanore went over to bandage Slim's wrist. Mrs. Wetherby, with all the courage and sensibility of a wartime nurse, had already cared for his wound. Nancy appeared in the doorway. Seeing her mother's hands and dress covered with blood, she screamed and fell into the arms of a nearby bystander. The child had fainted. The day that had been so longed for had ended in utter tragedy. When Eleanore's tasks were finally done, Tom Dean took her and the children home in his buggy. Nancy remained silent, weak and pale. She leaned against her mother's breast.

Sophie Dean cradled Janey in her arms. Paul, wide-eyed and shocked, sat beside Mr. Dean like a brave little man. Home had never looked so good to Eleanore. She sunk into the rocker. Tom Dean silently made a fire and lit the lantern. Sophie hurried the youngsters into the kitchen to make tea. They drank tea in silence before Sophie put the children to bed. Eleanore was thankful for their kindness.

Eleanore and the Deans sat silently before the fire. Eleanore prayed to herself not only for Ned's recovery, but also for justice. Sophie Dean, the friend that Eleanore was so grateful to, finally broke the silence. "It's a pity that this happened to spoil the Christmas program for the children. Four houses have been made miserable by that fool Hank Leffert."

"He was the one who started it. I imagine he was the one who cut up Ned like that. No one else would have the stomach for it," added Mr. Dean dryly.

"I mustn't let it spoil my Christmas for the children," declared Eleanore with characteristic determination. She stood up and walked over to the cedar tree that Will had cut for them. It was set in a kraut crock of water, weighted and supported by rocks. The Christmas tree was bare of ornaments. Eleanore wheeled around, arms on hips, and said, "Mr. and Mrs. Dean, would you do us the honor of trimming this tree?"

With Sophie's help, Eleanore hauled a wicker basket of handmade ornaments out from under the bed. Out came cookie and tin ornaments, paper chains, and acorns painted with white, gold and silver paint. The adults knew that the children had gone to bed believing that Santa would come despite Leffert's folly. They could not be disappointed. They toiled for hours until the tree at last stood in glory. Hidden gifts were pulled out and arranged beneath the tree. There was a book for Nancy called <u>Heidi</u>, a rag doll for Janey, and a homemade sled for Paul that Will had secreted away in the barn some days earlier. There were new red mittens and handkerchiefs for each child and the inevitable box of stick and peanut candy. In bright green paper was a store-bought set of dominoes. By eleven o'clock, the tree was completed, and Eleanore and the Deans had settled back before the fire with hot tea. Mr. Dean dozed while Sophie and Eleanore exchanged tales of their own childhood Christmases. Sophie didn't really want to go home yet. They talked on and on, secretly hoping that word of Ned Carson would come before long. It did. Old Toby bristled at the sound of jingling harnesses, rattling wheels, and the pounding of horse hooves.

A soft knock came on the door. "It's me—Will. May I come in?" Eleanore unbolted the door. Sophie roused her husband. "I'm glad you've got company, Eleanore. I hurried back, thinking you might be alone. Not a very good way to spend Christmas Eve."

"How is Ned?" they all asked at once.

"He'll be fine," replied Will with a pleasant smile. "If it hadn't been for Eleanore, though, Hank Leffert would have to swing for murder." Will turned and went outside again to return with a mysterious bundle. "Santa Claus in person!" he announced as he undid the bundle and produced two dolls with fine china heads and real hair, a jack-in-the-box, and a big bag of fruit and firecrackers. "I got the storekeeper in Benchfield out of bed to serve these up!"

They sat before the fire for nearly an hour after Will's arrival. Eleanore wondered if the bells were doing the sacred midnight chimes in Cedarville. She wondered, too, if Bob Gray knew how peaceful and happy she felt this night in the company of good friends. She imagined that Tom and Sophie Dean were tasting their first Christmas since childhood. She urged them to spend the night, to take her big bed and allow her to creep in beside Nancy. They were delighted. Neither the prospect of the journey home, nor the thought of their own cheerless hearth appealed to them.

Will Gray studied Eleanore. As the woman stared into the flames, he knew that at last she was beginning to forget her grief. It was a time he had hungered for. "I have to go now, folks, but you can count on me first thing in the morning. By the way, Ellie, did you know that Hill folk believe that the beasts are blessed with the power of speech at midnight on Christmas Eve?"

"I suppose you've heard them, Will Gray," laughed Eleanore.

"No. The spell breaks if they're overheard! Besides, they still think real Christmas happens on January sixth according to some ancient calendar!" he replied as he closed the door.

Chapter XVII

GRANNY MATTERSON

SCHOOL CLOSED DURING THE month of February. Attendance was so hampered by the cold and the snow that a recess was deemed practical. While the long dark days of February were perhaps dismal for grown-ups, the month spelled romance and recreation for the children. Outside tasks were few then, and a great deal of time was spent indoors. Eleanore no longer milked Jersey. The cow was, as she politely explained to the children, "expecting the stork." Everyday, Eleanore walked up the hill to Will's to get a bucket of milk from one of his cows. Although the walk was cold and occasional snows made it a cumbersome journey, the walk gave Eleanore a rest from her children and restored her dampened winter spirits.

The children spent many hours cozily seated before a roaring hearth or beside the cook stove, diving into the world of storybooks. Outside, the cold north winds shrieked and moaned through the bare maples as they piled drifts of snow against the fence rows. Sometimes they brought gusts of stinging sleet that would batter against the glass windows like gunfire, or a steady, drizzling rain that would freeze as it fell over each branch, bush, or broken weed. On many a morning, Eleanore would travel up the hill to Will's through a landscape of icy sparkles and gleams that resembled an illustration from a child's book.

Paul read <u>King Arthur</u> for days on end. He would stretch out the length of the blue rug, cushion his head, and pour over each page with carefulness. Nancy had borrowed an armful of books from Mrs. Dean, mostly novels and romances. The girl floated through romance after romance. <u>Joshural</u> and <u>Self Raised</u> became her favorites, and she cried so much over the sorrows of poor Joshural that her mother threatened to take the novel away. Eventually, Eleanore read a chapter or two for herself, found her own eyes full of tears, and was forced to return the book to her daughter, saying, "I suppose a good cry does no harm every now and then." Janey was less easily occupied by reading, but she enjoyed studying the illustrations and drawing pictures of her own.

When they wearied of reading, the children turned to Eleanore for entertainment. She often popped big pans of corn or made a bit of molasses candy. The children returned to earth long enough to help make the treats and devour them, and then they usually returned to a bookish world of make-believe. Nancy, unlike the others, found it hard to break away from her books. She read everything, laughing loudly over the yellow volumes of <u>Peck's Bad Boy</u> and shuddering over a big picture book about the Johnstown flood.

Eleanore spent the long days piecing quilts or braiding a rug to protect her cherished blue rug from the wet and mud that came through the front door. After a snowstorm, she would grease the sled runners with lard and permit the youngsters to frolic in the snow. She noticed, too, that heavy eating and indoor confinement had fattened them all up. A sluggish tiredness grew over them as the months of winter wore on. When spring signaled, she went out with a hoe and basket to dig sassafras roots. She washed and boiled them, made a tangy red tea, and sweetened it ever-so-lightly. As her children consumed the brew, she was relieved to acknowledge that they were at last receiving long-belated vitamins. Some time before the garden vegetables came in, greens matured. Down by the brooks and along the fence rows, at the first true moment of spring, they picked square weed, lamb's quarters, and dock. Eleanore stewed them with seasoning and served them with vinegar. It took only a bit of coaxing to get the little ones to eat these.

One mild day in early spring, a Saturday long after the children had resumed school, Eleanore was surprised by the arrival of unexpected visitors. Granny Matterson, Rachel, little Peggy, and the boys stoically trooped toward the house. Nancy and Eleanore hurried out to greet them. Granny was a wrinkled and weathered old bird, certainly past age seventy, who had mothered the brood since her daughter's death. Without a word, Granny led her unruly pack into the cabin, took a look about, turned on her heels, and squawked out, "Rachel and Peter and you all, git yer tails back out to the porch. Ye gotta wipe yer feets." For a split second, Eleanore thought the woman was canceling the visit altogether. She was relieved to learn they were only being commanded to clean off their shoes. With comic earnestness, the horde of untidy people began scraping off huge globs of mud onto the porch front and rails. Granny personally inspected her troops before she permitted passage through, but her eyesight wasn't nearly as sharp as her tongue, so a good many brown smears and streaks were nonetheless left on the blue rug.

"My, my, you sure did fix this here place up purty. Law sakes, I usta come here purt' often when Sal Brown lived here. Tweren't any better than the rest of poor folk cabins then. That's what

comes of book learnin', I says. That's reason why I'm so fixed on
Rachel and the others going to school. You know, Rachel's been
a hovering o'er me all winter to come and pay ye a call. Thinks
the sun rises and sets on ye, she does. T'was such a purty day, I
figured it to be the day to visit." The toothless woman grinned.
Her face was consumed by wrinkles and mouth, twisted into
distortion.

"I'm glad to hear that. I'm most honored to have you, Mrs.
Matterson," replied Eleanore.

"You call me Granny." The old woman seated herself in the
rocker, dismissed the children with a wave of her hand to go
off and play, and brought out a pipe from the depths of some
invisible pocket in her baggy clothing. She lit the thing with
a fire coal, inhaled deeply, and continued her speech. "I don't
want Rachel to be like the rest of the tribe. Look at Sadie. She
was a good enough girl, but her pa, one of my daughter's husbands, was a might hard on her and she run off an' married that
Leffert, who's a no-good devil. Out of the fryin' pan and into
the fire. Seems the women folk in my family ain't never had no
luck or sense when it comes to men. Take my datter which married up to Rachel's pa. Couldn't have done worse blindfolded.
All that family is so low down nobody else would have 'em, so
they marries their kin. My datter's funeral was one I never shed
a tear at. I couldn't help thinking as I saw my baby girl a laying there in the pine box, 'Yer better off, gal. No more being
knocked around an' cussed at anymo'." The old lady wiped a tear
off her leathery cheek.

Eleanore was not sure what to say, so she tried to change
the subject. "Your grandchild, Rachel, has a wonderful voice for
singing. Sophie Dean and I predict a great future for her if she
has a chance to study."

"Sophie Dean, ugh! City folks and their crazy notions. Guess singing in church is good enough for Rachel." The old lady was stern. She looked like an Indian at war.

"But, Granny," pleaded Eleanore, "don't you see that when God gives a person such a gift, it's sinful to throw it away? It should be used to inspire others."

"My ambition fer Rachel is to marry a good man," the woman replied with finality. "We're put here to wed and make children, not to act like wild canaries. I want her to have a good man who will make a living and treat her decent and take care of her brothers and Peg. Then I kin lay these ol' bones down and die in peace, the first peace I'll ever know. The girl's thirteen now and I've done tol' her to start a lookin'. Said she favors Slim Davis. Seems like his gittin' cut up at Christmas got her stuck on him. Davises don't have no money, but they's good to their women and provide enough to eat. Not like Rachel's pa. He wouldn't put up with me fer a second if he could help hisself. He thinks twice about cussin' me 'cause he knows I'm more apt than not to land him o'er the head with a stove stick. He knows he'd never git anybody else to come in and do fer him and his youngsters for free like I does."

Eleanore was horrified. She wondered what would become of the girl with such a dismal background. "But why," she asked, "do you want her to live like a hillbilly if you think book learning is so important?"

"If she has book learnin' she'll be able to fix a house up like this one!" The old woman was firm. "So's she'll be able to bake a purty cake like some ladies bring to basket dinners, and so she'll be able to make a dress as fine as the one you got on," she pronounced as she pointed to Eleanore's worn blue print.

Eleanore, though still unsettled by the woman's plans for Rachel, suppressed a smile. Evidently, the Granny didn't know what Mrs. Wetherby actually taught at the Silver Creek School.

It might have been funny had it not been so pitiful. After a bit, Eleanore excused herself and retreated into the kitchen to bring out fresh coffee and a cake she had made the day before. Hungry from the long walk and unused to sweets, Granny enjoyed the honor immensely. She maintained a running conversation as she mauled the cake with toothless gums and sipped the steaming black brew from her saucer.

Eleanore brought the children away from their game of tag in the yard. Nancy and Rachel, faces aglow from exertion, ran through the door. They outran the boys. Eleanore watched her daughter break off her slice of cake and eat it in small pieces with the delicacy of a cat. Rachel studied Nancy's attack of the sweet and imitated her every movement. The boys, however, bolted theirs and showed no inclination for manners. As she watched the children, she became secretly determined that the talented older girl should have a chance at a better life, at least in so much as she could promote it.

Chapter XVIII

WILL GRAY

KENNETH SMALL CAME TO help with the heavy work in the spring. Eleanore launched her attack on the barren fields to the west in hopes of revitalizing fertility. She talked to farmers, she borrowed agricultural journals from Will Gray, and she formed a plan of great labor that was permeated with hope. From sunup to sundown, they cut brush and hauled rock to fill the deepest ditches that had been created by years of erosion. She loaded and hauled wagonloads of manure from neighboring farms. Not realizing that the manure was gold to the woman, farmers were pleased to have their barn lots cleared. In the fall, after the barren land was prodded and enriched, she would sow it and plant wheat as a cover crop for rich red clover. Her hands became distorted by blisters, calluses, and stains.

One evening, after a hard day's work and after the children had been fed and bedded down, she sat on the porch in the twilight to rest. She was worn out, but not willing to end her day without the well-earned moment or two of absolute rest. The air was perfumed with the scent of orchard blooms, and the frogs chirped gleefully after the long freeze of winter. The indomitable courage of nature awed her. Tiny fireflies flickered about. It was a still night, but to Eleanore's ears there was a symphony of katydid, whippoorwill, and catbird calls that meshed in harmony with the low mooing of the cow and the stomping of horse hooves in the barn lot. It was the music of the night.

Will Gray came out of the gathering shadows. Eleanore was startled by the unexpected figure and gave a little cry of surprise that ceased when recognition came. She welcomed him gladly. He sat down beside her. "I was thinking of you, Will."

"Granny Matterson would tell you that it's an omen of good fortune to think of someone who suddenly appears, or maybe she'd say you had conjuring powers!" replied Will good naturedly. "Pleasant thoughts, I hope."

"Who would have imagined," she mused, "years ago, when you and Bob and I were growing up, that we'd be sitting out on a porch in the middle of nowhere alone and lonely. Bit maudlin for a spring night, don't you think?"

"Eleanore, my dear, dear woman!" Will cried out. "How often in this past year I have wanted to speak to you of this, but have been unable or unwilling. You have no idea how it wounds me to watch you slave away, bearing tasks unfit for any man, let alone a woman like yourself. Your hands have performed hard labor for a year now. I've wondered not so much about your hands, but about your heart. You've used your hands and your back to escape your heart, to defy loss and loneliness, haven't you, Ellie?"

When she couldn't meet his gaze, Will continued, "More than anything else on this earth, I want you. I want to take care of you. I know no one can take Bob's place, but I wish you would let me in. I've loved you always. I love you more than ever now," he declared. He took her in his arms. For a moment she rested passively against his chest, feeling his heart pound, smelling the sweet and pungent aroma of tobacco and shaving soap. His arms were powerful and gentle.

Then she gently pushed herself away. "No, Will. No one will have me. I love you. You know that. I've always loved you. I have loved you as my childhood playmate, as Bob's brother, and even as the brother I never had, but I cannot love you or anyone else as my husband. My husband is dead and too much of me died with him. I am making another sort of life for myself now and there is no room in it, no room at all, for more love or for more hurt." It did not escape Eleanore that these words did, in fact, bring a small pain to her heart.

"Think of your children, Ellie," Will begged. His voice had grown husky with emotion. "I can do so much for them and love them as my own. You do not know how many nights I've been sleepless with worry over you, with a longing for you. I thought at first I should give you time to get on your feet, to have a try at this life, but I've secretly hoped that it would drive you to me."

She felt a flash of anger at this hoped-for failure. "My life is full, Will. My children need me—all of me. While they love you as an uncle, they could never call you father. Janey might, perhaps, but Nancy and Paul would consider it a betrayal of Bob. I've watched them, overheard them. They fear that I might love you. If I were to marry you, they would think me a quitter. It would also fire up Ida and the others who already have been quick and loud to declare that I've had ulterior motives for moving here."

The two adults sat silently, side by side in suffering. Eleanore knew she had hurt Will. Will knew he had pushed Eleanore and lost her. The moon, the lilacs, the splash of water of the creek rocks, and the scent of a man created a spell that was hard for Eleanore to resist. It seemed as if all nature contrived to drive her into Will's arms and she felt powerless to resist. However, the spell was quickly broken when Janey cried out, "Mama, want a drink!"

Eleanore turned to Will and, with a sorry laugh, said, "See? This is my job. Please, dear, try to understand that I have to see my way through."

He raised her bowed head and kissed her on the cheek. "You are a brave woman, Ellie. I think I do understand." He bid goodnight in a broken voice that ended in a heavy sigh, put his hat on, and hurried down the path into the shadows. Eleanore watched him leave, grateful that he didn't suspect how near she had been to surrender.

Eleanore attended to Janey. She gave the child a drink, crushed her to her breast, and covered her tiny warm face with kisses before tucking her in again. As she tiptoed away to her own bed, she whispered, "Damn him!"

Sleep did not come. Her head swam with words and remembrances. For over a year she had lived without an inner life. Her movements and thoughts were channeled into mechanical activities. Her love for Bob Gray had gone through phases normal to grief, but now she was forced to acknowledge that loss had grown bitter. His death had caused not only the loneliness that pervaded her life, but the inclination to remain alone—which deprived her of Will Gray. Paths were no longer clear. Men, one dead and one alive, had clouded her directions. She resolved to think only of her children and the barren fields.

While spring proved to be an uncomfortable time for their mother, it was a joyful time for the children. Eleanore relieved her own children of much of the drudgery by hiring two large neighbor boys to work for fifty cents a day. Nancy, Paul, and the toddling Janey were free to roam with the Small children and Flora Peterson. The children often went out to pick wildflowers and even attempted to uproot and transplant their finds in the yard. Under rotting trees they collected mushrooms. They went down to the creek frequently with limber poles to fish. They would return proudly bearing a string of perch or bass for their lunch.

Eleanore retained a fear of water long after her husband's drowning. She knew it was not justified, but it existed all the same. She fought off inner misgivings when she knew her children had been fishing or wading in deep holes. One evening, they returned home dripping, carrying bundles of wet and muddied clothes. Eleanore actually cried out in alarm. They told her they had learned to swim under the guidance of a neighbor child. Nancy confessed they had tried to learn on their own all summer, but that the secret seemed to be to tackle the deeper holes instead of the small stream. Nancy exclaimed excitedly, "I tried it first. I went out to the water up to my shoulders, held my breath like they told me to, and just kicked off! It was the easiest thing in the world! I never had such fun before. Paul wasn't scared after I tried, and he can swim ten feet now without stopping!"

Eleanore shuddered as Paul beamed broadly. She imagined them drowning, leaving her as their father had. Nancy saw the fear and quickly reassured her by saying, "Why, Mama, there must have been fifteen of us down there and all of us can swim like crazy now! Kenneth Small is a terrific diver. He said he could pull any one of us out if we needed help. Nothing can happen."

Paul was quick to add, "Why, even Flora Peterson can swim. She's not such a 'fraidy cat anymore, but I don't think her Mama knows!"

Eleanore gave her children a warm smile. "I'm sorry you have a 'fraidy cat for a mother! I'll try to be brave for you from now on." This was all she needed to say to drive her children to the stream day after day during the hot months.

Chapter XIX

THE HAUNTED HOUSE

ON A SUNNY AFTERNOON in early summer, Eleanore and her children, dressed in their Sunday best, made their way up the ancient weed-covered wagon trail that climbed to the Sloan house. The roly-poly, black-eyed mistress of the decaying manor had repeatedly invited the Grays to visit after Sunday services. The children persistently badgered their mother for a glimpse of the reputedly haunted house, and she finally gave in. It was a hot trek, a battle against gnats and flies that sought refuge in the shady lane. They circled and buzzed around the heads of the Grays, and Toby, the constant companion of the family, nipped and snorted at the insects with savage fury. Under their feet lay a dense carpet of rotting leaves and molding undercover. Thick brush, hawthorn, post oak, and hazel bush grew so closely on both sides of the path that visibility was hampered. Eleanore drew her breath in alarm as a long black snake slithered across the path before them, rustling dry leaves. Toby gave chase with a wagging tail. Peering anxiously through the brush, Paul whispered in a low voice, "Mama, do you reckon there's any wild animals like panthers around here?"

"Of course not, child!" declared Eleanore with a reassuring laugh that failed to be convincing. Suddenly, Nancy screamed in shocked terror as a huge black shape pushed its way through the bushes. Hysteria turned to mirth, however, when they realized the villainous creature was only a black steer that had thrust its head through the brush. The animal took one terrified look at the strangers and the barking dog before it quickly bounded away through the bushes.

They soon arrived at a clearing that revealed a house standing off about another half mile that was bordered by wide, fertile fields and a willow-lined creek bed. The house was large and square, graying white and shadowed by gnarled locust thorn trees. It was built in a day of limited architectural knowledge, a day when the multiplicity of rooms was more important that actual structure or design. A great many rooms had then meant a great deal of wealth. It was one of many poorly constructed frame monsters that still linger in the hills today. They were once more plentiful, but old chimneys caused the burning of many. The Sloan house was unique for its highly carved porch, tall narrow windows, and impractically high ceilings. Behind the building stood the tumbled down remains of slave quarters that spoke of richer and more powerful days. Long vacant, they stood with rotted roofs and caved-in walls. Some were still in use as corn cribs, but those that were too far gone were permitted the mercies of nature. The dwellers, at least a good many of them, moldered in an overgrown cemetery below the house.

The Grays crossed a gravel-bottom gulch that was bordered by green scum pools. During heavy rains, the gulch turned into a raging stream. Nearby was a stone-walled well with a rope-tied tin bucket hanging beside it. Stella Sloan had already spotted her visitors as soon as they entered the clearing. She hurried out and stood under one of the formidably ugly locust trees to wait out their climb up to the house. Chickens, ducks, turkeys, and guineas ran free and wild everywhere. Gooseberry bushes and purple Washington bower vine tangled around the porch. A few brave hollyhocks displayed their color near the vegetable garden where rows of lush cabbages, beans, and potatoes attested to the skills of their mistress. Mary Sloan gladly welcomed the weary walkers, picked Janey up in her arms, and showed the family into the big parlor where her husband's feeble-minded sister, Sarah, sat pasting pictures in a scrapbook. She glanced up when they entered. Her eyes were bright for a second, but returned to their vacant stare quite quickly, much as if a cloud had passed before them.

The parlor was a strange mixture of old and new. A faded, grainy carpet warped its way over the floor, long muslin curtains drooped at the high windows, and an old spinning wheel in need of repair stood beside a new oak Climax sewing machine. A what-not shelf of red cherry wood held an odd assortment of miniatures, a small vase of dried cock's comb, several dishes of vintage value, a paper fan, and a box of protruding postcards most likely saved for Sarah's amusement. Over a mammoth stone fireplace mantel hung a battered musket with powder horn, a revolver, and a brace of ivory-handled pistols. Comfortable wood rockers, complete with ruffled cushions and dainty crocheted backs, were scattered throughout the room. Jaded prints, a charcoal portrait, and embroidered samplers hung on the papered walls. A long hall ran the length of the house, a curving stairway led to the second story.

After they were seated, the Gray children looked about with sharp interest. It was not, after all, too difficult to imagine ghostly horse hooves and strange goings-on in such a place. Eleanore inquired after the Sloan children. "Oh, my dear, most all of 'em have up and married or gone off to school now. We had our family long ago, you see. Two of the boys still stay here, but they hire out for work when they aren't in our fields," giggled Mary.

Nancy, with polite curiosity, studied Sarah, the poor creature in the rocker, and shuddered. With precise movements, the tormented woman was busily pasting headless hoop-skirted women, legless men with derby hats, and pieces of children into her book. Nancy wondered how her mother and Mrs. Sloan could so easily sit and discuss weather and gardens and chickens and church in the presence of this disconcerting, feeble-minded woman. A shadow moved across the carpet before Nancy's very eyes, darting and twisting with unfamiliar movements. Her eyes were riveted on the shadow and she followed it to its source. It was relieving to discover that its creator was only a sprig of purple blossom, swaying in the breeze.

With a slightly audible sigh, she glanced over at Paul, who was also fascinated by the bewitching shadow. He wore an expression of helpless terror. Perhaps he thought a ghost was about to seize him and fly him off. Nancy could contain herself no longer. She suddenly broke into the adult conversation and asked, "Did you ever see the ghost, Mrs. Sloan?"

Mrs. Sloan smiled. "No, child. I never have seen it, but I've heard it several times." Despite the polite smile, her eyes glowed with solemn blackness.

"How thrilling! Do tell us about it, please!" pleaded Nancy. Although Eleanore was secretly longing for the tale herself, she glowered at Nancy's impudence.

Mrs. Sloan did not need more encouragement. She eagerly dove into the tale. It was not often that she had newcomers to give a first recitation to. "Well, let's see. The last night the ghost came was the night my husband's mother died. My, but it was a wild night, too! The old lady was in bed in that room across the hall, all hunched up and skinny, waiting for the death rattle. The locust trees were nearly bent double from the rain that was a pourin'. All at once, the storm seemed to let up and turn silent, quick as a flash. And during that lull, we heard the feet of horses coming up, splash through the gulch, and stop dead flat in front of the house. Three times we heard the rapping on the door that night. Me and my husband and his brother, Ben, all three ran to the door and opened it. Not a thing was there, just more rain and black clouds. When we came back inside, the lamps had somehow blown out. When we got the place lit up again and checked on Mother Sloan, she was as dead as could be, her eyes wide open as if she'd seen something terrible."

The Grays gasped with astonishment. Sarah Stevens, however, showed no emotion. She sat staring out the window with blank eyes, her paste brush poised and dripping. "Was that the only time you heard it?" asked Nancy, who was eager for yet another gruesome story. She wanted to probe the horror to its depth.

"No," continued Mrs. Sloan. "I had heard it before, and the old woman had, too. When Mother Sloan was first married and came here to live with her husband's folks, she learned of it firsthand when tragedy happened. 'Twas her new brother-in-law that got killed during the war. She was here then. It was before Sarah was born. The ghost rapped, and she fell in a faint. Heard it again when she was carryin' Sarah, too. Everybody always says that's what turned Sarah queer."

Eleanore wanted to change the subject. She remarked upon the comfortable atmosphere created by the largeness of the rooms. It was a weak diversion, but it worked. Their hostess eagerly offered them a tour. Each room, however, was described in full with ghoulish associations and remembrances that only helped to illuminate the atmosphere of haunting. Paul, still timid master of misgivings and fears, openly displayed his terror. He jumped once when a white curtain brushed against him in the breeze. He skirted each of the huge mahogany wardrobes in the bedrooms as if he feared some weird specter hidden inside. Eleanore herself wondered how anyone who put faith in the peculiar tales could possibly endure life in the house. Only Nancy seemed bold and curious enough to ask direct questions. Mrs. Sloan was not unaware of the discomforted guests. She stopped at the top of the landing, turned to the Grays, and gently explained that the ghost came only to warn the family of dangers and misfortunes, never to do an injustice to them. Paul looked instantly relieved to learn this; Nancy saw it as greater embellishment of her romantic notions.

The kitchen of the house proved to be its very heart. It contained both a huge smoke-blackened fireplace, a cast iron stove of immense proportions, a large handmade oaken table that had been made by a Civil-War-era grandfather, and an off assortment of ladder-back chairs. It was obvious that the home once served a great family with many servants and members. The delight of the children grew when Mary Sloan opened a stone cookie jar and brought forth a handful of ginger cakes. The guests sat at the long table, enjoying the refreshments. Sarah joined them. She seemed somewhat more animated and alert in the room. She told them once that a band of fearsome Indians had sat at the very same table while old Granny Sloan cooked mush and beans for them over the fireplace. As soon as she finished her slurred tale, she resumed her half-asleep state and silently stared out the window.

Eleanore could not help but fall under the spell of the old room. She gazed thoughtfully at the charcoaled beams overhead and wondered what scenes they had been witness to through the years. She imagined they must have been hewn and put in place by the gentleman from England, Charles Sloan, who sired the future of the family. Perhaps he had lived to see wedding feasts prepared in this very room. Perhaps he had watched gen-

erations of Sloan offspring line up along the rough pine bench
on one side of the oak table for special allotments of cookies and
milk. She was certain that the room had, like her own kitchen
in Cedarville, been the center of mumbled gossip and proph-
ecy during many a morning. She glanced out Sarah's window
toward the mossy brown stones that marked the cemetery and
knew that the house had withstood many a death. Her imaginings were finally interrupted when Sarah stood up and mumbled a few unintelligible words to her sister-in-law. Mary smiled
and interpreted, "She wants to show the children her kittens."
The children shyly rose and followed the sleepwalker through
the kitchen door and down a cobbled path to a log outbuilding.
Mary beckoned Eleanore to follow.

In the cool shady interior, nestled in a mound of sweet
straw, was a tabby with a litter of tiny varicolored kittens. Nancy
scolded Toby, who nosed through the cluster of children to bark
at the defensive mother cat. Dismayed, the dog trotted off with
hung head to await his flock under a locust tree. The children
gleefully chattered at the kittens and laughed at their antics.
Janey, at that age when a child sees with its hands, lovingly fon-
dled a small mass of yellow fluff. As she watched the toddler
play with the kitten, a ray of light suddenly passed over Sarah
Sloan's eyes. She haltingly spoke. "Baby…have…kitty."

Mary smiled. "Sarah wants Janey to have that kitten."

Eleanore was at a loss, but she felt it would be a kindness to
Sarah Sloan to accept her gift. "Yes, children, you may have it."
The children beamed and devoted full attention to the newly
awarded pet. Nancy, remembering her manners, thanked Sarah,
who was once again in a dream state and unable to acknowledge the polite expression. Sarah had sat down in the door sill.
Her gray apron was brimming with kittens, the mother cat was
wrapped around her shoulders, and little Janey was playing with
her prize at the feet of the woman. Eleanore studied the wom-

an's face. It bore the smile of a sleeping infant. The activities of
the material world escaped Sarah. It was as if she existed in a
world of spirits beyond, a world invisible to most. Mary turned
to Eleanore. "Mrs. Gray, I can't say I've ever seen her take such
a liking to anyone before. She's always seemed to like children,
but she's never offered a kitten to one before. She loves her
cats so. It's kind of aggravating sometimes to have thirty of the
things rambling around underfoot, but we never dared to get
rid of one because she's so particular to 'em. Just look at her! I
haven't seen her so happy for a long spell!"

The Grays, moved by the fading sun and new evening wind,
had to depart. They waved goodbyes to the two women, one fat
and jolly, and the other like a frail flower hovering in the neth-
erworld, both bonded by love.

The walk back out from the Sloan house was equally as terrifying as the walk in, perhaps more so because the sun had sunk
low and the trees swished and swayed with the wind. Eleanore
was secretly fearful that the weird stories had only added to the
anxiety obvious on her children's faces. The kitten, uncomfortable in the flour sack that had been provided for the trek home,
squirmed and mewed against Eleanore's chest. Toby sometimes
abandoned his lead ahead to take a sniff at the cloth parcel. A
bat darted across the path in front of their faces and the children screamed in terror. They shrank even closer to their mother. Farther down the darkening valley, a screech owl tormented
them with eerie cries. Their mother hoped her forced expression
of calm would be of comfort. Paul held onto her skirt for dear
life. When home appeared, the children scattered and ran up
the lane.

Gloom was broken by the three cozy rooms, the lighting of
the lamps and the presence of the familiar. Eleanore went out to
tend to Jersey and her offspring. When she returned, she made a
fire in the cook stove and prepared a simple evening meal. Janey

and her kitten played in the kitchen. Paul went out to draw water and get wood chips for the next morning, and Nancy helped her mother by setting the table. Eleanore had seldom asked her children to perform such chores. She was grateful and pleased that they considered helping a privilege, an expression of appreciation for all she did alone.

They ate bacon, mashed potatoes, and wilted lettuce. The children looked as if the eventful day left no mark. Eleanore asked, "Do you feel better now that we're home? Safer?" The children laughed at their own terrors. Bed came soon after dinner. The children were washed and tucked between freshly aired white sheets. Eleanore opened the windows wide to admit the gentle night breeze.

Once Janey was sleeping soundly, she went into Paul and Nancy's room to blow out the reading light and bid them goodnight. Nancy sat up and said, "Mama, Rachel Matterson says if you sleep with the windows open that you'll get sick. Is that true?"

Eleanore frowned. "Now, Nancy, you know that's not so. It's just Hill superstition. You don't think I'd open the windows if I thought it would hurt you? Now, settle down and quit fretting."

Paul, who always dreaded the dark, still had more questions before he would allow Eleanore to blow out the light. His were more serious. "Mama?"

"Yes, son?" replied Eleanore with some impatience.

"Ah..." he faltered. "Do you think Daddy might haunt us?"

Eleanore sat down on the bed beside him and felt his forehead. "Let me ask you a question for once, Paul. Did Daddy ever scare us when he was with us—I mean really scare us?"

"No, not really. Only when we played, I guess," he replied doubtfully.

"Then I'm sure he wouldn't do it now. In fact, I'm sure he'd be very angry if anybody ever scared you. Ghosts are only for those who believe in them. To someone who believes in ghosts, every door creaking and every shutter blowing closed in the wind is the work of evil spirits. You and I know that strange noises are only the works of wind and mice and birds and such. Our Daddy is safe and happy in Heaven. He watches over us, but he doesn't haunt us."

"That's good," murmured the little boy sleepily.

Chapter XX

BENCHFIELD CELEBRATION

DURING THE SUMMER, THE sun beat down with relentless force and hot winds, once again scorching the entire valley and threatening drought. A few thunderstorms and swift showers, however, saved crops and spirits alike. On the fourth of July, the annual Civil War encampment was held at Benchfield. The gathering not only honored those who lost their lives in the terrible war, but afforded the Hill people with opportunity for celebration and entertainment. This particular year, because crops promised great yield and the weather relieved the farming community of the burden of coping with drought, brought more people to the annual celebration than ever before.

People traveled to Benchfield from miles around in wagons, surreys, buggies, as well as on horseback for four days of frivolities and camping. Like flies drawn to an open dish of honey, hundreds of pleasure-starved mountaineers and farmers hurried

to the "big doings." Baskets and washtubs were brought loaded
with sumptuous edibles prepared by the women folk. The best
of everything had been saved aside and tenderly prepared for
the feasting celebration. The fattest hens were dressed, the prize
hams were boiled with cider and honey, and the choicest pickles
and preserves were brought out with due honor. For days on
end, the women and girls had spent hot days in the kitchens
and outbuildings baking cakes, great loaves of fine bread, cookies, and the tempting fruit pies that were eaten with relish.

There had been much sewing and washing and pressing going on in many a cabin as well. Up in the hills, new calico dresses were sewn by hand, sunbonnets were washed, starched and
pressed while wet to render them stiff and shiny as celluloid,
overalls were mended, and seldom-used shoes and boots were
polished with blacking. In better homes, long lengths of taffeta,
lawn lace, and fine printed muslin were cut and sewn with care
into fashionable dresses duplicated from magazine and cata-
logue illustrations. Hair was curled, ribbons were pressed, and
pocket money was horded away for the special days. Children
went about in a daze of excitement, the threat of not getting
to go hanging like a swift and terrifying sword over their heads
should they make a crooked move. Grandmothers and old aunts,
those who had lost husbands, brothers, sons, and sweethearts to
the Civil War, moved with sad ceremony as they brought out
their black widow's weeds for the occasion.

To young ladies who were eager to catch husbands, the gathering supplied ample opportunity to survey the Hill's offerings
and engage in a bit of sparking. Because store-bought cosmetics
were yet unfamiliar in many Hill cabins, the girls spent weeks
trying out homemade magic to improve their looks. This had to
be experimented with on the sly, away from the disapproving
eyes of the older women who eschewed "face whitening" and
rouges as artificial beauty befitting only the vain and promis-

cuous. Flour and corn starch disappeared from the larders to cover the freckled and tanned faces of Hill beauties. Some girls gathered a weed known as cow slobber to redden their cheeks; various mixtures of buttermilk and wild honey were covertly applied to many a face to lessen the effects of the elements. Some even went so far as to swallow raw chicken hearts in the belief that they could produce both beauty and sexual charm. Hair was wound tightly in rags, washed in springs, and fretted over. Spells and love charms were explored with enthusiasm, and more than one girl certainly traveled to Benchfield with bits of wasp nests, the beard of a wild turkey, or a carved peach stone tucked secretly into her clothing for luck in love.

Though the Hill people usually hoped for rain during the summer, they were pleased when the day of the encampment dawned bright and clear. In the Gray home, excitement reigned supreme. Will Gray had promised to escort the family to the first day of the encampment. Preparations were a matter of bustling, hustling, running back, and forth, tying and retying hair bows, polishing shoes, trying on finery, and taking countless peeks into the luncheon hamper. Fresh water and extra feed were put out for the poultry. Janey begged to bring her kitten, but was coerced with tearfulness to leave the tiny "Bur" behind. Her face had to be scrubbed once again to remove the marks of tears before Will's arrival. Toby was much put out to be left behind with only a ham bone and pan of water to console him under the plum tree that Nancy had tied him to.

At last, Will's wagon wheels rattled up the road. Eleanore was filled with as much anticipation as her children, who sat squirming and fidgeting with impatience. Her anticipation was compounded, though, by some uneasiness; she had not been alone with Will Gray since the spring night that had caused them both great sorrow. During the few meetings at church he had spoken to her as usual, but not without a glimmer of hurt in his gray eyes—an expression that did not escape her notice but served instead to make her feel uncomfortable about her rejection of the generous man. To some extent, she dreaded the journey to Benchfield. In spite of the presence of the children, she feared there might be some personal conversation, some words with double meanings that would extend his heart out to her. As Will herded the children out to the wagon, she glanced at her face in the mirror by the door. "Cowardly soul you have, Mrs. Gray. Heart of steel," she whispered to her reflection. She adjusted her bonnet and closed the door.

The long journey was not sober, but filled with gay good humor and bantering. Paul was permitted to sit between Will's knees to have a go at the reins, and Nancy was invited, with a great show of gallantry, to take the place of honor next to Uncle Will. Will had grunted with pretended fatigue as he hoisted the lunch hamper into the back of the wagon. He had peeked beneath the covering, smacked his lips in exaggerated pleasure over the fried chicken, and asked the children what they planned to eat since he was sure he could devour the quantity alone. He handed Janey to her mother with a flourish, cautioning her not to crush her mother's pretty dress and not, "for pity's sake," to step on her corns. So it was in the midst of laughter that he touched the whip to his team and sent them all rumbling down the road in a cloud of dust.

They roared down the weedy bottom, past the Sloan house where they frightened the chickens into squawking hysteria, and splashed across the creek. They flew along at high speed. The wagon swayed and wobbled precariously. Eleanore's heart was in her throat, but she stoically remained silent. When they reached the main road, they encountered other hurrying vehicles. Will's sleek horses, well-bred and spared from hard labor, easily outstripped the plodding work horses that carried other families. The children cried with glee each time they passed another traveler, and Paul said proudly, "You've got the best team in the country, ain't cha, Uncle Will! Look at them eating our dust!" Will responded by speeding up more. Eleanore finally scolded, tried to keep her grip on Janey, who was bouncing wildly, and somehow managed to keep her broad-brimmed straw hat secured.

The long road cut like a wound through the wide patchwork fields. They sped past wild roses, pink and opened, that clung to fence rows. They soared through groves of heavy timber, black oaks, white oaks, and walnuts that grew menacingly close to the actual road. The branches, entwined with vine, frequently meshed overhead to form an arbor tunnel. Tendrils and delicate leaves brushed their heads as they ripped through. Far to their left, blurred by the blue summer haze, rose the high crest of Julie's Mountain.

Scrawny pine and post covered Julie's Mountain like an ill-kempt beard—a beard matched with a majestic face that proudly scanned the valley below. The valley spread through wooded miles of mankindless realms where bird and squirrel squired and lorded over free-range cows or goats that had run off. Julie's Mountain dawns were never silent, save a second or two between the exuberant calls of saucy crows, the rattle of squirrels coursing the trees, and the perpetual jabber of song from every small bird that soared through. A buzzard patrolled overhead, lazily hunting for carrion. It was no longer difficult for Eleanore to believe the story she had been told about the woman who had become lost and demented in this shadowed valley. To a first-time explorer on foot, each tree in awful sameness would confuse the sharpest to distraction.

Soon they encountered the Adamses. The family, dressed in all their finery, looked quite distinguished traveling along in their hack. The older ladies struggled with huge black parasols and beribboned bonnets that threatened to become entangled in the wind. Mr. Adams, hunched and hot at the reins, tipped his derby at Eleanore and winked at her children. He looked uncomfortable in a stiff celluloid collar and shiny serge suit. His moustache drooped despite a generous application of wax. His demeanor seemed to imply, "I'll be stylish for the ladies if it kills me."

Nelle Adams sat on her hard seat with the grace and dignity of a queen on a throne. She was surrounded by the lengths of her blue taffeta dress. The bodice fit snugly around her tightly laced waist, and a large berth of cream-colored lace spilled over her shoulders. Her hair was piled up under a magnificent blue lace hat. The seriousness of her gray eyes had almost completely given way to coquettishness. As they passed the Adamses, Will feigned a lusty sigh and pronounced, "Many a noble swain's heart shall be landed this day, I'll warrant!"

"Never mind," defended Eleanore. "Nelle Adams is a very beautiful girl, but all the flattery in the world won't turn the intelligence of her mind. I like her very much."

"So do I!" cried Nancy and Paul in unison.

"And so do I!" laughed the unquenchable Will with a roar.

"You might do worse," declared Eleanore with meaning.

"Woman, have you no shame?" scolded Will. Flush had crept up his face and, feeling her own embarrassment, Eleanore hastened to alter the subject.

A few miles before Benchfield, the Gray wagon overtook a rickety farm wagon drawn by two mangy mules. On the dangerously sloping seat, Granny Matterson perched. She sported a dark calico bonnet that almost looked clean. Her son-in-law, huge and bewhiskered, sat by her side at the reins.

The Matterson children were heaped in the back on a quilt that covered a mound of not-too-clean straw. They grinned openly at the Grays. In their midst was Sadie Leffert, who was trying to shade her son's fair face from the sun. She wore an expression of happiness that Eleanore had never imagined possible for her. Eleanore secretly wondered what pressure Granny had applied upon her son-in-law to persuade him to take the family on this outing. The old lady's face was clearly triumphant. She wrinkled her face and waved her cheap poplin handbag at them as they passed. Will and Eleanore returned her greeting with dignified bows of respect. Rachel's face, noted Eleanore, bore a strange expression, one that was indecipherable.

"Granny Matterson is a wonder," said Will in admiration. "She's obviously proud as a peacock to be taking the youngsters to this outing."

"She must have taken a wood stick to that surly man's head to get him to take them!" said Eleanore.

"I dunno. Buck is an odd man. He's hard as nails, tough and mean, likes his liquor, and only works just enough to keep his kids from starving. On the other hand, he's got a soft spot for those kids somewhere under that hard hide. You won't believe it, but he's just crazy about Sadie's baby. Last time I went to the mill, he was standing around bragging about his grandson to one and all, and seemed tickled to death that the little fellow called him 'Granpaw'!"

"You'd think he'd take Hank Leffert to task if he cared so much," argued Eleanore. "I'm still confused about the whole thing. If he isn't a Matterson, why are his children called Mattersons? What happened to his first wife, and who was she?"

"It's a mess, but it's not too hard to figure out. He's kin to Mattersons. His first wife was, too. She had Sadie. Got childbed fever and died. Granny took him and the baby in, and he ended up marrying Granny's daughter. Had a bunch of kids, then she died, too. He's considered, as are his children, to be of the Matterson clan."

"A great many Hill people operate as family clans up here," Will went on. "Technically, they are related by both marriage and blood, and the clan often chooses to ignore any outside intermarriage as just being a bit of straying from home, so to speak. I think he doesn't interfere with Sadie's marriage because he believes she did wrong to marry outside. He thinks such hardness is a parental privilege. Perhaps he thinks Hank's hardness is a husband's right."

By now, the main gravel road approaching Benchfield Post was crowded with vehicles. The sidewalks were alive with figures. Townspeople hustled along with ease in their store-bought clothes. They made little effort to hide their distaste for the Country Jakes who skirted between them in homemade clothes. Will drove the buggy into an alley behind a feed store, unhitched the team, and tied the horses near the back of the wagon where they could stuff themselves on hay. He helped the children down. Wrinkles were smoothed out, curls were recaptured, bows were perked up, and smudges of dirt were wiped off Janey's face. Will watched the primping with pretended intolerance. He finally surveyed the results with critical amusement. "Missus Gray," he said solemnly, "I firmly believe your hat is crooked."

Eleanore gave the hat a tug. She looked at Will for an appraisal.

"No! No!" he protested. "Let me fix it." Eleanore wondered if it was her imagination or if the man's hands actually trembled as they lingered on her hair as the hat was set aright. Will laughed, Eleanore gave his bowtie an appreciative pat, and they jointly grasped Janey's hands and headed for the street.

The campground was far down at the end of a grassy meadow near the railroad. A band played at the center. Streamers of bunting fluttered from posts, and a large flag waved ceremoniously from a pole in the center of the campsite. Rows of flimsy fabric draped from refreshment booths. Other booths were marked by gaudy signs that identified them as sites for games of chance and luck. Numerous tents were already set up as temporary homes for those who had come a great distance. One could spy children playing on hard dirt floors or sleeping peacefully on makeshift pallets inside the hastily erected shelters.

At midmorning came the signal for the grand march, a procession of flag-carrying and music-making. First, came a staff bearer with a crisply waving flag. He was followed by a loud, if not harmonious, brass band. There followed, four abreast, slowly plodding and rather grizzled veterans of the War Between the States. Their weathered faces were proud and happy. Though freshly brushed and pressed, their threadbare and faded old uniforms reeked of cedar and moth repellents. Shout after shout rose from the crowd as they marched past. Many eyes were blurred by pride. Behind them came the dozen or so nattily dressed Spanish-American War veterans who were trying in vain to equal the pompous dignity of their elders. The crowd closed in behind the procession and followed them toward the bandstand. "The Star-Spangled Banner" was played with fervor. Several dignitaries were then to take the stand to speak. A state representative was present. An elderly Civil War captain was on the agenda and a veteran clergyman was to follow him.

The children, eager to explore the promises of booths and mischief, found it nearly impossible to sit through the long-winded speeches of these gentlemen. Many begged permission to escape the rough plank seats to watch the man play the calliope on the far side of the campground. Patient mothers gave them coins and instructions and watched them excitedly disappear into the crowd. More than once, an old man's faltering speech was covered by the fascinating reedy sound of the steam calliope. More than one respectful parent wished to join the children.

"Must be great to be young and think that a merry-go-round ride is the loftiest of pastimes!" sighed Will to Eleanore, who had packed off Paul and Nancy.

"Though I'm certainly not young anymore, I confess that the notion of riding one does seem a bit alluring," replied Eleanore with a twinkle in her eyes.

"Come on then, you shameless tomboy!" cried Will. He instantly hoisted Janey onto his shoulders and pulled Eleanore from her seat. They laughingly followed the children, who had fled the dullness of speech-making. Many a head swiveled around to watch the undignified departure.

As it so happened, Sophie Dean strolled down from the stand at the conclusion of the speeches and was amazed to discover her neighbor, the proper Mrs. Gray, whirling past on a painted red pig on the children's merry-go-round! Her skirts flew everywhere, and her hat seemed to fall lower and lower over her face as the creature swept around. Mrs. Dean's astonishment nearly turned to pure horror, however, when she spied the school director, Mrs. Wetherby, in an equally compromising situation. Mrs. Wetherby, with the joyfully screaming Janey in her arms, rocked past on a polka-dotted steed. Sophie Dean's gloved hand actually went to her mouth for a second, but she regained composure, and with liberal blessing, turned to her husband and said, "It's great to be young. I nearly wish I wasn't too nice for a merry-go-round ride myself!"

Everyone seemed determined to obtain the very last morsel of day, which rivaled even Christmas. It would be difficult to decide just how much each pink lemonade and ginger beer contributed. Band music, sticky popcorn, chance meetings with old friends, penny prizes, and bouts of sentimental storytelling created a most intense pleasure for the young and old alike. The children, when they had grown up and had children of their own, would tell their youngsters of a year when the Annual

Encampment at Benchfield was so grand and so crowded they thought they had spent a day in Heaven. It would be likewise told that this particular encampment was most special because the school marm, Mrs. Wetherby, had actually purchased ice cream cones for them all.

Eleanore spent a part of that memorable day talking to Granny Matterson. She found the old woman sitting on a bench, hunched over her clay pipe, observing all of humanity with a decided flash of animation to her watch. Sadie, who sat nearby swaying her child in her tired arms, patiently allowed her son to reach out to Eleanore with his sticky fat hands. Eleanore studied Sadie as she pretended to play with the little one's fingers. She wondered how they had managed to escape from Hank's malicious grip for this special day. It was Granny who read her thoughts. "Hank came into the picnic this morning. He didn't know Sadie was figuring on coming. He came early, got good and drunk, and now the constable has him locked up in the jig. He's there sleeping it off and Sadie got herself a rest! Heh, heh!" laughed the wizened old lady. Her pipe rattled dangerously. Sadie, with equally childish pleasure, added, "I figured he'd do just what he did. Me and the baby are going to have some fun for ourselves for once!"

There were moments when Eleanore was as repelled by these Mattersons as she was attracted to them. She gave pennies and nickels to the Matterson children for candy sticks, games, and merry-go-round rides. They beamed at her. They were greedy, happy children, lice and all, who had cornered her heart. Rachel still shone in Eleanore's eyes as a creature far above the others. Eleanore watched her by the bandstand. The girl had her hand wrapped about the width of her throat as she stood listening to a medley of Stephen Foster songs. If she removed her hand, Eleanore was certain that jewels would burst from her mouth, diamond high notes and ruby lows. Mrs. Dean, who happened to be standing near Eleanore, also studied the girl and she whispered, "That girl will be the center of attraction some day."

Eleanore was, at first, inclined to agree, but doubt crept in when she caught a glimpse of Rachel later standing on the far edge of the grounds, half-hidden behind a buggy, talking earnestly to Slim Davis. When Rachel caught sight of Eleanore's watch, she backed further out of sight with the flush of shame spreading over her young face. Eleanore did not miss the telltale red blush, the implication that the girl's secrecy was somehow shameful to her. Eleanore had to face facts. The girl was a Matterson, a child of the hills who was ultimately victim to Hill culture and thinking. She could very easily forfeit the promise of her voice to the lure of Slim Davis. For a brief second, Eleanore actually regretted having mended the young man's severed arm.

By mid afternoon, lunch baskets had been emptied and recovered, and most of the celebrants were resting off heavy meals in the shade of trees and beneath the tent shelters. Important news spread around the camp, news that an automobile was going to come. It had been rumored for some time that Dr. Lackland planned to buy a gasoline buggy to enable him to travel more quickly through the counties on medical calls. The contraption had arrived the day before the encampment on the afternoon freight and stored at the blacksmith's shop. It would first be brought out for the encampment. Only a few cattlemen and merchants had ever seen such a vehicle during excursions to St. Louis or Kansas City. Although some folks had seen pictures of the invention, there was nothing as thrilling as a firsthand encounter. Word spread across the camp like a brush fire.

"You reckon the Doc knows how to drive the thing?" asked one doubting farmer.

"Heard a feller in St. Louie showed him how when he was there to pick it out," replied another.

"Will it really run up a hill by itself?" wondered many.

The mysterious nature of the invention was intensified by a quick spreading announcement that gasoline was as powerful an explosive as dynamite. "Awful goldarned dangerous, if you ask me, with all them spark plugs flying 'round!" remarked a stout man who seemed quite unwilling to see any good at all in new-fangled ways of travel.

Information, rumors, and conjectures whirled through the crowd, and the children, who were most impressed by words of danger, became terrified of the prospect of having a real gasoline buggy in their midst. They imagined it might look like two bicycles bound together with a lot of fire surrounding it, or something perhaps like a locomotive on land. In either case, it was certainly a machine that seemed menacing.

At last, someone mounted the bandstand and bawled out through the megaphone that the long awaited look at the rumored-about gasoline vehicle was at hand. "Ladies and gentlemen! We now have a surprise for you. The good Doctor Lackland, who has strived to make our community the most progressive and modern town in the Ozarks, has brought to us an automobile. He will drive it from one end of the park to the other three times so that every one of you may have an opportunity to study the amazing machine up close. As you well know, the machine is as easy to drive as a team of horses, but even a team of horses is liable to get frolicsome in a crowd. Because of this, we ask that you stand back and give the doctor plenty of room. Clear the road! Here she comes!" The band struck up some brassy hoopla to introduce the gasoline buggy with befitting ceremony.

There was a mad scramble to clear the road. Above the racket of the crowd came the thundering phut-phut of the gasoline buggy. Children hid their faces in their mother's skirts. Those who had wandered from their parents took refuge behind trees and buggies. They peeped out, frightened but equally curious.

The buggy roared over the rough road, leaving a cloud of acrid smoke in its wake. The doctor, seated high on the leather seat, wrestled with the high wheel as nonchalantly as great exertion would permit. He looked daring and triumphant. He wore a gay checkered suit, a scarlet tie that matched the paint of the automobile, and a derby hat. A long black cigar was clenched between his teeth. All in all, he was the very picture of a blood-and-adventurous traveler.

The driver had a few rough attempts at turns, but his performance was otherwise a grand success. When he finally exited, children released the comforts of skirts and opened up eyes that had been squeezed tightly shut against the vision of the monster. Older children marveled at what they had peeked at. The better-off menfolk resolved to purchase such machines as soon as possible. Some women smirked and remarked that their husbands were like boys with toys. Some farmers of the old school vehemently shook their heads and swore it was all foolishness, some trend that wouldn't last long against a good team of horses. "You try that thing out over the flint rocks and up in the hills, and I bet you'd wish you had a mule instead!" one barked before he spit out chew in contempt.

Will looked down at Eleanore's excited face and asked, "Would you like a chariot ride in that, Mrs. Gray?"

"I'm not sure that I'd mind the bumpiness, Will, but the stench is a bit fierce!"

The excitement for the first day concluded. In late afternoon, many families prepared to travel home. Children were reluctant to leave the gaudy stands and remainders of festivity, but they knew that the mountain trails were too treacherous at dark for them to linger any longer. Only the townspeople and the campers from afar were content to settle in with the knowledge that they had yet another two days of merriment due them. Will and Eleanore decided to leave a bit early to avoid crowds on the road. Nancy and Paul were almost tearful in their protests. Janey seemed indifferent. Eleanore knew how hard it was for her older children to surrender this rare day of perfect pleasures.

After the fury of the day's excitement, the journey home seemed exceptionally peaceful and restoring. A fresh, sweet breeze had sprung up, gently sweeping across the woodlands and perfuming the traveler's faces with longed-for coolness. Placid cows grazed and gathered at ponds, awaiting the return of their keepers. Bands of sheep, gray and white blobs on the hillsides, looked up and bleated inquiringly at the wagon as it passed. They neared Julie's Mountain at dusk. It loomed older and wilder in the growing shadows. Only the croak of frogs, the rampant sound of cicadas, and the tumble of the wagon wheels could be heard now. Janey, wearied by a day of strangeness, fell asleep in her mother's arms. Paul's head nodded.

The team was stopped in the middle of a creek to have a cool drink. Will stepped out to let out their check so that they could drink their fill. The water splashed over the rocky bed in constant tempo. Eleanore watched and listened to the hypnotic rhythm. It was like her life was being transcribed. Turbulence and disorder was momentary, always restored to a normalness that paid little heed to interruptions.

Will entertained his own thoughts. Eleanore had seemed unusually happy during the day. The merry-go-round ride was like an antic from their carefree youth. Perhaps, he thought, she was actually getting over that dour, impenetrable distance that she had maintained since Bob's death. Maybe she was starting to leave the past. If not, he feared. Bob would always be like the Sloan ghost, a dim silhouette against a distant hill that haunted year after year with imaginary rappings. Eleanore must have sensed his very thoughts, for she suddenly spoke softly.

"I've been very happy today, Will."

"I'm glad, Ellie. This trip wasn't meant just for the children, you know."

"I had thought I would never be happy, not for a second, since Bob's death. Maybe the old saying that time heals all wounds has some truth to it."

Will patted Eleanore's hand. His touch was hot, sincere with love for her. She was grateful. She smiled at Will and at herself. Nancy, who had been laying silently in the back of the wagon with Paul, suddenly sat up and whispered, "Mama, you know I never knew what that saying meant before."

Chapter XXI

BATHING DRESSES

ONE AFTERNOON IN LATE July, when the children had wandered down to the creek to splash and play with the Smalls, Eleanore took a basket of mending outside and arranged herself and the sleeping Janey under the shade of a maple to tackle the most unpleasant domestic chore. It was unbearably hot. It was difficult to finish the irksome task of darning and patching when one's hands were slick with perspiration. Rivulets of sweat crept like annoying insects down Eleanore's back, her hair clung in damp rings, and her high collar seemed to stifle her. The air was dense and difficult to breathe in. "Our clothes aren't going to go to ruin just because I'm uncomfortable," said Eleanore with resolve as she threaded her needle and set to work. She twisted the needle in and out of a torn seam in Nancy's dress. The torturous process was broken, however, by the shout of a gay "hello" in the lane. With welcome relief, Eleanore craned her head and caught sight of Nelle Adams hurrying up the lane. Nelle's sunbonnet was pushed back, her high collar was unfastened, and much to Eleanore's surprise, two narrow bare ankles shown under the hem of the woman's uplifted skirt. Even in disarray, Nelle Adams was regal and fetching.

"Sit still!" she called. "Don't make a single unnecessary move in this heat, Ellie!" She finally reached Eleanore's perch, refused Eleanore's offer of a proper chair, and plopped down on the lawn beside the sewing basket. She untied her bonnet and sent it spinning.

"Eleanore, why on earth were we born women?" Eleanore smiled in reply, attempted to search her mind for some reasonable answer, and shrugged. Nelle continued, "Look at our dresses! Tight collars, tight waists, enough petticoats for a brigade, and a corset that promises nothing more than pure torture! Look at the men. You wouldn't catch them dressing like this. They seem to have more sense, less inclination to kill themselves off. Church martyrs didn't even have to endure this. The fellow who invented the corset should have been hanged! And I'm sure it was a fellow!"

"At least you've shed your shoes, Nelle," said Eleanore with approval.

"Yes, and if this heat keeps on, I'll most likely shed everything else. Mother and Aunt Melinda were near death at the sight of my bare feet. They cried out that I was shameless to go traipsing off to visit in this state. To add insult to injury, I had to pass a flock of children at the creek. They were nice and cool, having the time of their lives I think, and I had to roast along. Mother thinks bare feet are for children only, that modesty is the supreme concern for young ladies. Modesty be damned, I say!"

"I quite agree. We'll have to do something about this," said Eleanore with a conspirator's enthusiasm. Nelle obviously had a secret method of her own in mind. With an air of furtive secrecy, she extracted a scrap of folded paper from her bosom and handed it to Eleanore. The paper proved to be an ink drawing from a mail order catalog. It featured an assortment of women in bathing dresses. For only seven dollars and ninety-five cents, read the advertisement, one could be the owner of this modern attire. Eleanore studied the long belted smock, the sateen bloomers, the saucy bow-trimmed caps, and high-laced canvas shoes that comprised the costume.

Nelle waited patiently as Eleanore inventoried the page. Finally she asked, "Does this put any notions into your head?"

"We could make them much more cheaply, I believe," was Eleanore's reply.

"Yes, and I hardly think we'd need the shoes if our feet were covered by water," Nelle added excitedly.

Eleanore ran her hand over her forehead and frowned. "Nelle, it would mean an awful scandal if anyone ever saw us at all, you know."

"Of course, but I'd certainly prefer scandal to being boiled in oil every summer for the rest of my life. I came close to feeling murderous when I passed those kids at the creek. If New York and Chicago women can wear these costumes in front of men, I certainly can't see the harm in us wearing them out in the brush!"

Eleanore was clearly enthusiastic, despite her weak attempts to remember proprieties. Nelle Adams spoke what Eleanore had frequently only thought. It relieved her to recognize that she was not the only woman in the county who felt hindered and trapped by social law. She felt compelled to reinforce Nelle's speech. "We are, after all, grown, God-fearing women living in a supposedly enlightened age. It's time a speck of emancipation hit these dusty hills, Nelle. I suggest you cart yourself home this afternoon and look up the price of that sateen fabric. Order as much as you think we'd need. I'll buy my share of it. I'd like enough for the girls, too."

Nelle giggled. She grabbed Eleanore's hand and shook on the proposal. It was a gentlewoman's agreement, a pact between the two of them. Nelle declared, "Oh, but I can just feel the cool waters swirling over me. I'm going to learn to execute a dive from the sycamore!"

"I'm afraid the only water you are going to feel pouring over you for the next few weeks at least shall be the sweat flowing from your own tortured body!"

Nelle laughed. "Just you wait, Ellie!"

Nelle did indeed return home to pour over the gaudily decorated mail-order book. In absolute secrecy, she sent off for the yard goods and daily waited for the parcel to come. In due time, a mysterious parcel arrived. Every day for nearly a week after that, Nelle Adams trudged through August heat down to Eleanore's house. The two women measured, cut, pinned, and sewed with great energy. The products of their labors only vaguely resembled the catalog drawing, but they both agreed that the results were satisfactory.

When the new suits were tried on by Nancy and Janey, there was much proud prancing and preening. Janey hopped around the cabin like a red bunny with sturdy brown legs. Nancy ran her hands over and over the softness of the fabric in rapturous admiration. "Oh," said Janey, "very purty, Mama!" It was with some trepidation, however, that Eleanore and Nelle emerged from the recesses of the bedroom in their own costumes. To actually venture into the glittering sunlight of the warm afternoon required a further collection of courage. The children were eager to share their delights at the creek. They anxiously led the two shy women down the bank.

"It is silly for us to feel so nervous, Eleanore. Chances are that no one will see us at all," said Nelle with a giggle.

It was almost cool under the burr oaks and sycamores by the creek. The shallows were dotted with flecks of sunlight that danced like yellow sapphires on the water's surface. Tiny minnows darted playfully up and down over the shoals where they were safe from the hungry mouths of older fish. Fat, lazy crawdads scooted out of clouds of sand dust and slid across the bottom. Frogs suddenly appeared and dove in fright with the coming tramp of the trespasser's feet. They emerged at different points to stare with bulging eyes at the red-covered, two-legged intruders.

Nelle and Eleanore nimbly leaped across the rock shelves and painfully minced their way along over creek gravel. Janey screamed with delight as she imitated her brother and dove into a sand bank. She emerged flushed and laughing, her curls and suit glistening with sand and water. With some alarm, she tried to get the grit out of her eyes. Nancy scooped her up and dipped her in a clear pool. Eleanore and Nelle faced each other with shock when Nancy rose up to her feet. Her bathing dress dripped not only sand and water, but rich, red blood! For a moment, Eleanore was horrified.

"They fade!" declared Eleanore and Nelle in unison when the source of the "blood" became evident.

Nelle gazed ruefully down at her own smock. "After all that work!"

"Oh, gosh!" sighed Nancy. "What difference does it make? Let's go swimming! Last one in is a baby!" Nancy herself earned the title by pausing in a sprint to tuck Janey under her arm. Other neighbor children joined them, and there rose shouts and screams for a good length down the creek as children ducked and splashed with glee. There were diving exhibitions, races, and shouts of "Who can float the longest?" and "Who can swim the farthest?" and "Who can do this?" Both Eleanore and Nelle were repeatedly asked to watch various feats and maneuvers, each more daring than the last. The Smalls, right down to the youngest towhead, scrambled and mixed with the pack. The air rang with joyfulness. Dainty Flora Peterson, on a pretend visit to the Grays, joined in the afternoon fun. She wore a faded old brown dress donated by Nancy. It was her bathing costume. She looked like a woodland creature when she dove from the limb of a sycamore. Boys and girls alike, in a hodgepodge of costumes and bare knees, shared the banks of Dean's Creek with little regard to modesty.

Eleanore was content to paddle along with Janey in the shallow water. She delighted in the coolness of the clear water, which caressed her slim figure. Nelle, however, was no shallow water paddler. She had learned to swim, like many a Dean's Creek child, during a time not long past. The tricks and skills of her childhood were not forgotten. She captured an admiring audience. Nancy and Paul attempted to dunk the able swimmer's head in a secret attack, but they found themselves instead coming up for quick gasps of air amid the squeals and shouts of their friends.

When the children felt chilled by the cooling waters, they sprawled on the sandbars to soak up sun through their much-exposed hides. The shadows began to lengthen, and everyone knew that it would soon be time to walk homeward for an evening meal. Eleanore gathered her brood.

Nelle walked with them back to the cabin to change her clothes. Cool and tired, yet strangely calm and exhilarated, they trudged up the road. Flora and Nancy sauntered along arm in arm. Paul, who brought up the rear with Toby, spent most of the walk terrorizing the two girls with a katydid that he threatened to put down their backs. The troupe had nearly reached the rocky trail to the Gray house when they heard voices coming from the main road. A high-pitched soprano voice was discussing some topic with fervent indignation, while two more subdued contraltos chimed in soothingly. Eleanore's flock paused. Flora Peterson turned a sickly green. "It's my mother!" she announced in terror. She held onto Nancy's arm with all her strength.

Nelle Adams flushed deeply. "Flora, you are not alone in this. If I'm not mistaken, my mother and my aunt are about to discover my most unladylike antic to date as soon as they turn at the fork!"

Paul grinned. "Maybe we ought to duck in the bushes!" His notion was kind, but not nearly quick enough. Already, Mrs. Peterson's words penetrated throughout the brush with remarkable clarity. "I'm telling you, ladies, it is a shame the way Mrs. Small raises her children! She permits them to carry on disgracefully. Why, I'm actually ashamed to acknowledge that she is my husband's sister. It's a burden to be kin to them. The woman actually told me that it was none of my affair when I warned her against allowing Amanda and Ida to go to the creek with those boys. Amanda will soon be twelve, and Ida, I dare say, knows more about certain things than I do!"

"Well, I dare say Mrs. Small meant no harm," wheedled Mrs. Adams in a comforting tone. Aunt Melinda broke in, "Well, her young ones are healthy and sturdy, even if their manners are a bit crude."

"Crude? Ha!" scorned Mrs. Peterson with a hoot through her well-bred nose. "Savages...well...I...I...," sputtered the woman with a gasp of air as she rounded the turn, which exposed a huddle of dripping swimmers. Her steely eyes scanned their wet clothing—what there was of it.

"The old battle axe is actually speechless," muttered Nelle under her breath. She pulled together a smile and approached the three harpies. "Why, hello, Mother! Aunt Melinda. Where are you off to?"

Mrs. Adams turned brick red as she surveyed the wet red satin that clung immodestly to her daughter's shapely, uncorseted figure. She quite suddenly spied Flora hiding behind Nancy.

It gave her some comfort, enough in fact to make an uncontrolled smile form on her face. For once, Mrs. Peterson's spiritless little girl was causing shock.

Eleanore kept her balance. "Good afternoon, ladies," she said with a nod of her dripping head. It seemed wisest to take the bull by the horns. "You should have joined us down at the creek. We had a perfectly heavenly afternoon."

"So, I see!" said Mrs. Peterson as she advanced menacingly toward the cowering Flora. Mrs. Peterson's skinny hands were extended like talons to tear her apart.

Eleanore consciously stepped in front of the child and continued with her explanations. "Nelle and I thought it wisest, you see, to chaperone and supervise down at the creek."

Mrs. Peterson was temporarily confused by the noble sentiments attached to the most disgraceful of scenes. Aunt Melinda, who was obviously much sharper than her companion, asked, "And where did you get those creations you're wearing?"

Nelle struck a hands-on-hip model's pose for the benefit of her aunt. "We made these stunning bathing dresses with our own fair hands. We copied them from your mail order catalog, Aunt Melinda!"

While not a natural liar, Eleanore could not resist the opportunity to get the better of the haughty Mrs. Peterson. She decided the story needed more embellishment. "Yes," she cut in. "My cousin in Chicago, Mrs. Warthington-Howard, wrote to tell me that all the finer ladies in Chicago are wearing suits like these and bathing in Lake Michigan. She says it has caught on rather well. I really do think it pays for us country women to be modern. Even if we are in the backwoods of this nation, we should make an effort to keep up with the times. Don't you think so, Mrs. Peterson?"

At the mention of the hastily invented but distinguished cousin's name, Mrs. Peterson's ears pricked up. She could not bear to think that she had missed out on anything pertaining to city existence. She drew a deep breath and replied, "Oh, yes indeed! My sister in Kansas City neglected to mention anything about swimming styles in her letters or I would have sent for a proper suit for Flora long ago. My sister probably thought we knew all about such things. It is so hard for city people to know how isolated we are out here. I sometimes just think I will suffocate out here for lack of city ways. I intend to get my husband to take us soon." Mrs. Peterson concluded with an affected laugh.

Eleanore was quite pleased with the success of her fictitious cousin. Much to Nancy's astonishment, she continued to chatter on about the Mrs. Warthington-Howard who had saved the day. Mrs. Peterson hung on her every word. Mrs. Adams and Miss Britton smothered potential laughter that welled in them. Mrs. Peterson had been tamed. After Flora had gone with the other children to the house to change, Mrs. Peterson treated her with a new respect, a respect that came with a vague affiliation to the Chicago woman. Although she was in better humor when her daughter reappeared in clothes and ribbons, she could not resist a parting shot at Nelle Adams. "I do think, Nelle, that with a figure like yours, you really should wear a corset. Wet satin clings so."

Nelle was content to be let off so easily. "Thank you, Mrs. Peterson. I do think I shall consider your advice."

The day ended as merrily as it began. Eleanore's quick thinking and her ability to weave a tale from thin air spared Flora a beating. Swimming became fashionable in Dean's Creek. The final weeks of summer passed at a snail's pace. The children spent every last hot afternoon dear to them by the banks of Dean's Creek. It afforded them an escape from the grueling heat that would last an entire afternoon. More than once, the children were surprised to see the tormenting sun turn a hot red as it fell behind the blue haze of ridges and valleys. It was a signal that another day of summer had passed, that it was time to wander home.

Although Eleanore sometimes joined the antics by the creek, she often put aside her red satin dress and remained at home to preserve and store the produce and fruit that would be so precious during the winter to come. The children, wet and dripping from a day's swimming, would run into the kitchen to test the remains of a batch of jam, or to simply sit and watch their mother's efficient skills with peaches and apples. It became fairly traditional that summer to have Flora Peterson join them on Friday afternoons for hot baked cobbler before she headed for home. Flora Peterson had a store-bought royal blue bathing dress before the summer was out.

Chapter XXII

HARVEST TIME

WHILE FARMERS UP AND down the creek harvested abundant corn crops and planned for winter wheat, their wives, when not helping in the fields or feeding those who came to help with the harvest, spent many hot hours putting up jams, jellies, catsup sauce, chow-chow, kraut, and pickles. Children, when not choring or lending a hand to their parents, spent the few idle hours they had pouring over the new mail order catalogs that had arrived. In the kitchens, perched between baskets of apples and jars of preserves, they fantasized about which plumed bonnets or ankle-length skirts or guns or boots they would choose if they were rich. More than one child certainly was swatted on the top of his tousled head for such idle daydreaming in the peak of a work season. Mothers wondered if the scent of cooking apples made the children so dizzy and dreamy.

Farther up the ridge, deep into the hills, cellars lacked and pantries wanted even at harvest time. Many a Cooney Ridge household relied on raids on the valley stone houses for their stores for winter. Pilfering was common and often necessary to make up for the laziness of a backwoodsman. Many a father did not worry over winter meat. Squirrels and rabbits tided them over. There were persimmons to put up for the picking if a wife or daughter would do so. While the men in the hills were proud of their positions as family heads, they felt no compunction to assume duties and responsibilities usually associated with the honor.

It would be erroneous, however, to assume that all their waking hours were spent in mindless idleness. Just because they had given up notions of attempting to grow crops on the boulder-strewn hills, did not mean that they forfeited income altogether. Moonshining was a booming business. Many small stills produced a wealth of sorts in rocky ravines. Further enrichment could be gained if one were also adept at poker. Winnings were sometimes only pocket knives or coon skins, but they served as a sort of legal tender. Still earnings, poker winnings, and wild game were the chief contributions of menfolk up on the Cooney Ridge.

Ridge women were industrious enough to produce, in addition to numerous offspring, scanty crops of tobacco, sorghum, bleached beans, corn, and potatoes. Their skin turned leathery and wrinkled from working long hours in rather hopeless garden patches. They invariably looked older and worse for the wear than their husbands.

Children hired out to help the valley farmers sometimes. Otherwise, they were expected to work with their mothers in the gardens or act as principal gatherers of wild gooseberries, plums, and herbs. Day after day, they were fed on the inevitable diet of cornbread made with water, fried potatoes, and cabbage or pinto beans boiled with rinds or meat ends when they were available. When fishing or hunting was good, they had meat, but seldom very much of it. The children grew up skinny and hungry. A woman who could prevail upon her man to get a cow or some hens would offer heartier fare, but only one family in four might know such luxury. At an early age, children acquired a hankering for sweets and the ability to chew on a wad of tobacco to get them by.

Life up in the hills was not without some pleasure. School doings, pie suppers, church revivals, and the Civil War Encampment provided an opportunity for them to mingle with their betters. Unfortunately, they also provided opportunity for disturbing the peace and creating mischief that did little to improve their already tarnished reputations. Those who could not take joy in the valley doings were able to enjoy entertainment that was strictly reserved for the hills. They had hoedowns and dances, weddings, spoonings and sparkings, and the excitement of birthings. These events, when combined with liquor, satisfied many an unhappy soul.

The fear of hunger was second only to the fear of sickness on Cooney Ridge. If herb tea, horehound, or a mustard plaster couldn't cure the ailing, they died and were put to rest as soon as possible. If Granny Matterson or Granny Davis couldn't handle a birthing, mothers and infants perished in many an instance. After a decent interval of a couple weeks, the bereaved father usually wed some sturdier girl and picked up where he left off. Although many a man was no prize, it was not hard to find another woman to risk her life to his care and keeping.

In general, Hill women were expected to bear their husband's burdens. A smart wife could, with just a cow and a couple of apple trees, overcome the sore life produced by a husband's laziness. When laziness was tainted with meanness, however, her life was certain to be a hell. Industriousness did little to combat cruelty. Many a woman's body was seldom free of bruises. First her father beat her, and then her husband beat her. When a rawboned, bearded giant came for her, she endured. Children were frequently protected from the onslaught by clever mothers who would hurriedly send them up to the attic when a drunken husband came home. They would lie frightened and stiff while their mother fought it out with the old man below. The men did not always win these battles, though. More than one drunken tyrant had his head soundly cracked by a stick of stove wood. He would awake the next day with a sour tongue, an aching head, and some newly produced respect for the woman who downed him.

By Hill standards, Matterson himself was not an especially mean man. Although he was lazy and ignorant, he was regarded as the pick of the clan. He boasted that his Rachel went to school and made friends of the rich valley families. He also boasted about his cabin. It had two downstairs rooms and one large room above with a real stairway. Families larger than his frequently lived in only one room. When he came home drunk, he would pass out without disturbing everyone.

Again to his credit, Matterson played the fiddle. Hill folks swore no one could match his sawing off of "Green Corn" or "Drunkard's Dream" at a Hill gathering. He was proud, too, when Rachel accompanied his fiddling with song. She could sing every mountain ballad that had been passed on through generations. The popular "Kitty Wells" and "Butcher Boy" brought tears to the eyes of listeners. Unlike the rest of the hillbillies, she sang through her throat instead of her nose. She was regarded as a human songbird.

Matterson had had two wives; both died. After that, Granny took over the rearing of his offspring. Folks wondered why he didn't take another wife, but a hellcat like Granny Matterson would probably put off the most ardent of the prospective. She reigned supreme. What she may have lacked in housewifery skills, she made up for by idolizing her charges. Although Matterson prohibited her caring for Sadie anymore, she turned full attention to Rachel, the two boys, and young Peggy. They were the center of the old woman's universe. Ever since Rachel earned the respect and interest of the well-to-do valley people, it was Granny Matterson who made her charges endure a Saturday night bathing ritual that was practically unheard of in the hills.

On a particularly fine autumn evening that blended the color of October with the warmth of an Indian summer, Rachel bent over a tub of warm water, scrubbing the few articles of clothing that sufficed as wardrobe for the family. She scrubbed with a yellow cake of hard soap. She scrubbed as if she were trying to remove every trace of poverty from their lives. Her back heaved and bowed, her hair slid forward over her face, and her arms pumped so furiously that muscles bulged. She washed the boys' overalls and hickory-striped shirts, Peggy's blue gingham dress and flour sack drawers, an apron for Granny, a big lumpy garment that was meant to be her Pa's shirt, and two calico dresses for herself. A heap of gray rags that were used as dish towels awaited her abuse.

While their only outfits were being scrubbed, the two boys spent wash time in bed, covered up with a suspicious looking patchwork quilt. They had a fine time playing with a big button and length of string that made a kind of perpetual motion machine. Granny sat in a rocking chair by the cook stove. She alternately supervised over Rachel's chore and the kettle of cabbage that had already been stewing for two hours. It wouldn't be done for another hour, when the sodden vegetable would finally turn a rusty brown color that rendered it fit for consumption. Peggy, nearly naked, sat on the porch making mud pies. Granny didn't mind her mess. The child was obviously as dirty as she could get, and a dab more dirt couldn't hurt.

When Rachel had rinsed the clothes and strewn them over the bushes to dry, Granny commanded the children to prepare for a bath. It produced howls, screams, threats, and a chase, but Granny had a vicious gleam in her eye that meant serious business. Each youngster was scrubbed until its skin shown red. The naked little ones were then sent to bed until their clothes dried. Rachel, with Granny's help, poured the tub of soapy water on the cabin floor. She scrubbed it into the wood with a buck brush broom, and then swept the mucky remnants out the door. The rinse water from a second tub was then poured over the planks and splashed around until the wood was left fairly clean. She rinsed out the tubs and hung them on nails by the door, and then she flopped down in a chair near Granny to rest. Granny grinned at the wet and tired girl. She looked around the room with great satisfaction. "You know, Rachel honey, things look a heap nicer when they're clean! Ain't a nicer cabin on Cooney Ridge. Ever since you whitewashed the walls, it seems like light poured in here. I never dreamed anything could make such a difference."

Rachel was a dreamy-eyed, fourteen year-old. She regarded the transformation of the cabin as if she had turned it into a palace. "Granny, don't those curtains make a heap o' difference? It was sure swell of Mrs. Gray to give them to us, don't you think?"

"Yep, and that plant Mrs. Dean give ye is doing itself proud," said Granny as she pointed a gnarled finger at a Wandering Jew that piled out of a battered granite pan hung in the front window between the appliquéd muslin curtains.

"I'm gonna have lots of flowers here next year. Mrs. Dean is saving out some zinnia seeds for me."

"Well, honey, fixin' up never hurt nobody. While we're waitin' fer them clothes to dry, do ye think ye could fix up one of those 'lasses cakes like Mrs. Gray makes? There's a half sack of flour and grease. Them cakes are the best thing I ever ate!"

Rachel rose to check on the children. Peggy and the boys, with faces hot and red from recent scrubbing, were sprawled sound asleep. She then tiptoed down and got out the ingredients for the cake. Granny studied her as she began beating up the batter. "Ye know, honey," said Granny between draws on her clay pipe, "That feller 'at gets ye fer a wife is gonna get a prize. Still got yer eye on Slim Davis?"

Rachel blushed and beat harder. "I don't know, Granny. If I marry now, I'll be just like the other ridge women, jes having babies and washing and scrubbing all the time. Maybe if I go on and study hard and get more schoolin', I might amount to something like Mrs. Dean says."

"Fiddlesticks! Stuff and nonsense! Ye best take yer chances on Slim, girl, while he's of the notion. He'll do ye fine. A Davis is a good stock. Marry that feller and ye'll be the envy of every woman around here. Handsome, too. Ye love him now, don't ye?"

"Don't know. When he hugs me, I get all hot and shaky inside like I'm gonna fall sick. I like him in the moonlight alright, but I don't know if that's love or not," replied Rachel as she closed the oven door.

The old woman nodded her head knowingly. Her answer came from the depths of her seventy years. "Rachel, ye can stake yer life on it that it's love. Nothing else makes ye feel so bad and good at the same time. Felt the same way o'er my man that's been dead and gone these twenty-five years. Felt the same way fer each of my children that was borned and buried. I'll never forget how yer Ma was o'er yer Pa. When she was jes' about yer age, she tole me she been meeting him on the sly down in the holler. Scared I was gonna put a stop to it, but I knew how she felt, so I tole her to go and marry him. Good thing, too, 'cause she was a carryin' you!" The old dame chuckled with fond remembrance.

Rachel turned pale, and the expression of a cornered puppy spread across her face. With a rough little hand, she pushed her hair back off her face. She wondered if her own body was carrying a secret, hidden even from herself. She tried to remember what Slim had said to her the last time they were together. She'd have to ask him when they met at night down by the big black oak tree.

The little ones were stirring. The cake was cooling. She gathered the stiff dry clothes and brought them in to press. While she and Granny set up supper, the children were sent out in their fresh clothes to run about. They leaped over stumps and fired rocks at birds and yelled with joy. They acted like wet hounds shaking off a creek soaking.

After the supper dishes were cleared, Rachel put on a fresh dress and her one pair of beat-up shoes. She left the cabin to meet Slim in the moonlight. Her thoughts were not light. She wondered at the meaning of her life. She wondered if it just meant the feeling she had with Slim, and the drudgery that would follow if she married him. Her own mother was only thirty when she died of it. She could not decide if Sophie Dean's picture of silks and velvets and high-stepping horses had any substance to it. The lure of shiny automobiles, roses in winter, and handsome admirers in fancy clothes appealed to her. Maybe such would offer more than Slim, who always seemed to be demanding something. Instead of a wilted bunch of wild weeds, she'd get diamonds and pearls and bonbons just for the privilege of kissing her hands. Her hands! They'd be lily white, untouched by the curse of lye soap and cold hill winds. To live by singing would be the easiest thing in the world. Sophie told her that her high notes were approached with an ease most singers envied. As she strolled toward the big black oak, she practiced warbling the high notes of the "Jewel" song Sophie had played for her.

Slim Davis, who stood waiting for her, heard the notes waiver through the stillness; he shivered.

Slim Davis was tall and handsome in a blonde, boyish way. He loved Rachel Matterson with all the impetuous passion mustered in his eighteen year-old heart. As soon as she got over that nonsense about singing, he aimed to take her over to Benchfield to get married by Parson Ford. Slim was willing and, unlike other Hill boys, he didn't think it right to lead her on deceptively. Nelle Adams wasn't as pretty in his eyes as Rachel was. He knew she was brighter than any girl on the ridge or in the valley. He watched her with longing as she made her way down the path, her face and figure clearly outlined in the brilliant moonlight. The last notes of her song hung on her lips. Her eyes were mysterious pools. She seemed to Slim like an enchantress from another land.

"Rachel, my honey!" he whispered as she slipped into his arms. Eagerly, their lips joined and for one long moment the two figures made a single shadow. When Slim tried to draw her down in the grassy softness under the oak, she shuddered and pushed away. The boy was hurt. "Rachel, ain't you gonna love me tonight? What's the matter?"

"Oh, Slim, I'm all mixed up! I reckon I love you right enough, but my mind's been turning on other things. Granny said something tonight that scared me. She said my Ma was carrying me before she married and it was dumb luck that she got married in time. She didn't even know she was with child. I've heard about wood's colts all my life, but I'm scared something like that could happen to us."

"Maybe we should jes git married and quit all this worrying," said Slim with a sense of down-to-earth rationality. Something suddenly flashed in his mind and he quickly asked, "Rachel, you ain't been feeling poorly or sick, have you?"

"That's just it, Slim. I've been weak at the stomach every morning lately and I can't owe it to anything I've been eating."

"Oh, Rachel," Slim's voice quavered as recognition struck. Rachel broke into tears. He tried to take her in his arms to soothe her. "Don't you cry now, honey. I'm sorry. I never aimed to hurt you. I'll make it right with you. We'll get married and everything will be fine."

The frightened girl pushed the earnest youth angrily aside. "Slim, I hate you! You hear me? You done this on purpose so's I'd have no choice but to marry you!" Her eyes blazed as she continued to blast Slim Davis with the wealth of anger and resentment that had filled her soul. "You knew I wanted to go away and be a singer. You swore a little loving never did no harm. Now I'm lost, destroyed! Everything is ruined!" Her slim shoulders shook with sobs. The bewildered boy tried again to comfort her in his arms, but she only sprang away and put more distance between them. "I'm not going to marry you, Slim, and I'm not going to have a baby for you, either! I'm not going to be tricked. Since yer so smart and know all about this, you best jes tell me how to keep from having it!"

"Lordy, Rachel, I dunno. Ma jumped off a cliff to rid one and Bertha Simmons took some pills, but most folks jes git hurt. I don't know what to tell you if you mean this. It wouldn't be so bad being married, Rachel!"

"I'd sooner die than have a wood's colt for you or any other dirty man. Don't you come around me anymore, Slim Davis, or I'll tell my Pa to shoot you for vermin!" The girl whirled around and ran up the path.

Slim followed a spell. She wouldn't answer his calls. He retraced his steps back to the oak tree. He buried his face in his arms and sobbed against the roughness of the tree. His young heart, the heart filled with love and remorse, broke and the night echoed with his question, "Why, Lord? Why?" Slim Davis never went home until daybreak. He spent the night shivering and staring at the heavens.

Chapter XXIII

REVEREND LITTLEFIELD

WITH THE COMPLETION OF harvest came Camp Meeting, a sort of church revival that served a multitude of purposes. To some, it represented an opportunity to cleanse the soul of besetting sin through confession and baptism; to others it was an opportunity to open the heart and pour forth a song of praise and thanksgiving for the bountiful harvest that had softened their lives. Camp Meeting was also a family reunion on a grand scale. Between the morning church meeting and the evening church meeting, friends and relatives from all corners of the valley met to sample suppers and seep in the exchange of a whole year's gossip. Like all Hill gatherings of importance, Camp Meeting gave shy lasses opportunity to blush and parade past longing young men. Long buggy rides and walks, standard transports for courting, moved many a young heart. It was an unsuccessful meeting that didn't boast at least half a dozen weddings to its credit.

To the budding roughnecks from Cooney Ridge and wilder parts of the realm, Camp Meeting was the pass to devilry. They consumed liberal quantities of corn liquor and raced their horses madly, frightening timid children out of their wits. They seldom went inside the church unless they spotted some particularly dainty miss they might embarrass. She would nearly fall into a faint when one of the ill-mannered creatures crouched beside her to leer. When such victims were unavailable, they would peep in windows and bounce pebbles off the clapboard roof. During particularly fervent sermons, they would, much to the disgust of the pious inside, hide in the bushes near the church and shout out insincere "Glory Be's" and misplaced "Amens." When their antics became too obstreperous, a deputy who served as deacon would corner the culprit and directly escort him to a make-do jail for the duration of the meeting.

Although the children frequently found the sermonizing hard to bear, they still regarded Camp Meeting as an exciting break in the year. They managed to escape the routine of school on the pretext that religion held priority over book learning. It was fun to dress up and go somewhere twice a day. Parental authority relaxed during these days when higher matters were given full attention. Every day of Camp Meeting was highlighted, at least in younger minds, by the consumption of platters of fried chicken, cakes of every description, crocks full of potato salads, and mounds of yeasty breads. A child could manage at least a dozen bits of cake before he became noticed. No one objected when a growing boy devoured enough food to feed a family. Children were allowed to sleep in so they wouldn't doze during services. The piety of a parent, after all, was usually reflected in the wakefulness of a child during a tedious scripture lesson.

Several conditions indicated that this was to be a fruitful year for Camp Meeting. A good farm season nurtured the desire to be thankful. A number of farmers who weren't usually inclined toward churchgoing felt that Camp Meeting should be attended just to insure further "good luck." As far as the deacons could predict, the weather would encourage even the crustiest of sinners to come down from a Hill perch to socialize. It was an Indian summer that no one could resist. The woods were showing their earliest colors, little bits of scarlet and gold peppered through the green. Goldenrod and blue asters swayed in the warm breeze that rustled their roadside posts. The roads were neither dusty nor muddy. The evenings were cool and crisp. The moon was full enough to guide gatherers home.

The deacons also congratulated themselves on their selection of missionary preachers. Two of Springfield's finest had been delivered for Dean's Creek duty. One was Brother Holderness. He had a strong jaw, a resonant voice, and the ability to mingle perfectly quoted scripture with threatening utterances that made the sinner in every soul cower in fear of Hell's fires. Holderness hit the hardest of hearts with accuracy.

The second missionary was the Brother Harvey Littlefield. He was a quiet man, and a handsome one. His young, lean face was chiefly remarkable for a set of large brown eyes that moved and twinkled with intelligence. His dark auburn hair was brushed back in smooth waves from a high, pale forehead. His voice was always, both in church and out, soothing and persuasive. Holderness and Littlefield, though they certainly contrasted, created a perfect team. After Holderness had used his booming voice to work the audience to a fanatical pitch, Littlefield would take quiet command. As Holderness sat down to swab his brow and recover from the near-prostration produced by his own vehemence, Brother Littlefield changed terror to tears with a few well-chosen passages. "Let not your hearts be troubled, neither let it be afraid. In my Father's house are many mansions and if it were not so I would have told you. Lo, I go to prepare a place for you, and if I go I shall come again." The congregation of straying lambs could not help but be moved back into the comfort of the fold.

The old timers spent much time speculating on the merits of the two. Some favored Littlefield so much that they claimed he had the ability to save more souls in five minutes than Holderness could in an hour. Others, however, argued that it took Brother Holderness to put the fear of God into the core of a sinner. He made them ripe for picking. All Brother Littlefield had to do was shake the tree.

During Camp Meeting, the missionaries stayed at the Adams home. They spent some of their days visiting parishioners. They frequently ate a large noon meal at the home of a churchgoer who was moved to the point of gratitude by a service. It was whispered that they made friends with those who cooked the best, in hopes of another well-laid table. After all, even missionaries had stomachs. Most everyone felt flattered to have their visitors in the valley. The Adamses were secretly envied for their proximity to the two men. Envy bred gossip as well. It was rumored that Melinda Britton had complained of the ability of the houseguests to consume great quantities of linens. Somebody said that somebody said that Miss Britton had said, "It takes a mess o' sheets to keep up with the preachers. They sleep between them and want fresh ones every night. I'm quite worn out with washing and ironing and will be glad when this is over." As the rumored conversation whirled through the hills, several matrons sneered and were quick to explain that a crabby old maid who has never had to care for a man simply couldn't appreciate the honor she had in thus serving the Lord.

The Camp Meeting had not progressed but a few days before it became apparent to the more observing that Nelle Adams was struck in the heart by the handsome Brother Littlefield. Of course, some just laughed at the infatuation; it was remembered that the young lady had a crush on every revival minister since she was twelve years old. The year of the first crush produced her baptism by a Brother Stevens, a handlebar mustached man who had a wife and eleven children. It seemed that Nelle placed a halo over the head of every visiting clergyman and nothing could be done to tarnish it or lessen its impact. Nelle, however, was certain that this year's crush was no laughing matter, no simple turn of a schoolgirl's heart.

She first made the gentleman's acquaintance after he had traveled by train from Springfield to Benchfield. Her father fetched him in the surrey and took him over the rough roads to the Adams home. Hot and dusty, a bit worse for the wear, the young minister finally stepped down from the surrey to shake hands with the host family. After depositing niceties upon Mrs. Adams and Miss Britton, he finally extended a graceful hand to Nelle. Her charm and grace did not escape his notice. The moment he pressed her hand, Nelle became moonstruck. His every gesture, his every word, and his flashing smile sent a thrill through her that spread from the blush on her cheek to the tip of her toes.

Brother Littlefield was not entirely unmindful of Nelle's regard. Experience, however brief, had taught him that an unmarried minister held an interesting attraction in the mind of any rural deacon's daughter. Though he usually regarded such an attraction as an occupational hazard of great annoyance, he felt a responding emotion in his own manly breast with the meeting of Nelle Adams. He tried to put it from him. He feared it was only a passing fancy, and the temptation of a pretty face. Marriage, he felt, should not be entertained as a state of personal gratification. Should he marry, it would have to be for the betterment of the kingdom. Nelle Adams was certainly far from his vague picture of a preacher's wife. The many he had met were usually scrawny, homely, self-effacing creatures that lacked all outward signs of physical allurement. They had made notable contributions to the calling of their husbands. Harvey Littlefield had difficulty, though, paying attention to higher matters. In spite of any grand resolves, he found himself gazing covetingly at Nelle. He wondered how any creature could be so lovely. He watched the pulse in her throat quiver above the cream lace collar. When he came upon her as she worked in the house, he noticed that she blushed softly and stared at him with eyes that glittered with a fever. He imagined finding a way to contrive meeting her alone, but his imagination was inexperienced in this matter, and Brother Holderness hindered any hopes. Holderness, the eagle-eyed elder, stuck to Littlefield like glue, and went out of his way to involve the younger Brother in tedious theological discussions. Even if Holderness had not intercepted, the continual company of the family and neighbors certainly made a private meeting all the more unobtainable.

The only dignified way to gain proximity to the girl was during hymn practice in the afternoons. Littlefield managed to make himself available to stand beside her as she practiced on the organ in the parlor. He turned the pages for her. They always had an audience for practice sessions, but Littlefield could still brush against her shoulder as he flipped the pages of the songbook. Every time he was that close to her body, a wave of talcum and soapy sweetness filled his head like burning opium. Once, his chin grazed her crown of unruly hair. His chest constricted around his heart and he thought he was near collapse. Indeed, he became so distracted at times that he quite forgot to turn the pages at all. Nelle would stop playing, he would come to his senses with a start, and mumble an apology before they resumed again.

Aunt Melinda noticed the symptoms. She remembered them well. She finally met her sister in the kitchen to discuss the situation. "I tell you, Rebecca, there's trouble brewing with

Nelle. I believe she's got it bad this time. It's a shame he's a preacher when you consider how handsome he is."

Mrs. Adams ceased cutting out biscuits long enough to face her sister and corrected her, "Melinda, you'd think from the way you talk that it is a disgrace to be a minister. You have a peculiar way of expressing yourself."

"I don't mean that it's a disgraceful vocation, but I cannot imagine Nelle as a preacher's wife. She's scatter-brained and silly. Do you think she could pull off being prim and prissy in the amen corner?"

"Well now, I don't know, Melinda." The mother was obviously fond of her only child and refused to acknowledge any shortcomings. "It seems to me that Nelle would make a fine wife for any man. I know she's always been a little crazy for preachers. I don't know, but a preacher man might be just right for her. Pa inquired of Holderness about the Littlefield family. They are fine people. His father was preacher in the biggest church in Springfield. Since his father's death, Littlefield has taken care of the family alone. They have some money and he's well-educated and all. Nelle is getting to the age when she's either going to have to marry or turn old-maidish."

Melinda rolled her eyes. "Really, sister, there are far worse fates. As a matter of fact, I'd think some married women would have fared better had they not married at all." Melinda tossed her head emphatically.

"Oh, I wasn't meaning anything personal, Melinda. Don't get your fur ruffled. We all know how disappointed in love you were. I'm sure Joe Peterson rues the day he said he'd quit ye for that snappy shrew of his. But, getting back to Nelle, you know I always favored Will Gray for her. He's handsome, well-to-do, and kind as could be. That house of his is a palace. He'd be the finest son-in-law a woman could hanker after. Why, just look at how he is so kind to Mrs. Gray and the children. He watches over them like a father." Mrs. Adams sighed appreciatively as she closed the oven door on the biscuits.

"Father? Fiddlesticks, Becky Adams!" cried Melinda as she poked a slab of sizzling ham side on the stove. "You must be plain blind. Will Gray is just crazy over Eleanore. Unless I miss my guess, I'd say he's been that way for years. I suspect that's the reason why he's never noticed Nelle all this time. The way he looks at Eleanore sends chills up my spine. Disappointment in love is not reserved for just us old maids."

"Oh, pooh! Your brain's growing soft. I still say Nelle could have Will if she'd put her mind off preachers long enough," announced Rebecca. She dried her hands on a roller towel, tucked a stray lock behind her ear, and waddled towards the parlor door to announce that supper was ready.

Melinda tore off her apron with an impatient jerk, flung it over a chair, and smoothed her dress front. "Brains going soft, indeed!" she muttered.

With typical confusion, the family and its guests were seated at the table. Holderness delivered a lengthy and fervent prayer that allowed the steaming bowls and platters to cool completely. The meal was then attacked with enthusiasm and parlor discussion resumed. Table talk, as all things, was overshadowed by Holderness.

"Yes, indeed, Brother Peterson, it would be best if we could unite this here community under Baptist leadership and have one creed, one denomination for all. What a wonderful thing it would be! It is most difficult indeed to continually sheer away doctrine to appease the various groups and spare feelings. More ham, please, Sister Adams. Ah, thank you. Delicious. As I was saying, unification as Baptists would spare the finger-counting of converts and set these hills straight. Situation here is depressing and I view it with apprehension. Too much division and competition between faiths."

Mr. Adams at last felt moved to interrupt the Brother's usually endless discussion of the problem. "It ain't the people that worry me, Brother Holderness. We live together, side by side in peace, with only an occasional argument to break the peace in the church. It's been working fine. If we restricted any more than we do, I fear we'd lose a great many. These people around here value their differences and won't cotton to doctrinal restriction."

Before Holderness could clear his mouth and begin again, Mr. Adams surprised family and guests alike with an observation. "We have some trouble waiting to burst out during this Camp Meeting, Brothers, and I think we need to discuss it. It's an unpleasant matter that causes the valley to shake its head in shame and fear. There are bad elements in these hills. They've come down to do mischief. I saw Hank Leffert last night talking to a pack of no-goods from Cooney Ridge. Mark my words, they are up to trouble. Hank Leffert isn't good for anything but trouble. It's been nearly a year now since he went on a spree and cut up the Carson boy. He's due to pull something again."

"Why, surely Papa, even Hank Leffert wouldn't do anything to break up Revival?" asked Nelle with horror. She looked at Brother Littlefield who sat opposite her.

"Nelle, don't get worried, but be warned. You can't tell about Hank. We have to keep our eyes on him. I've noticed his wife in church every night. Should Sadie decide to join, I fear Hank will use the opportunity to make us all regret that we ever encouraged her so," replied Mr. Adams.

Brother Holderness, who was clearly unfamiliar with Hank Leffert's potential, regarded Mr. Adams' worries lightly and reached for a slab of apple pie. He cleared his throat and said, "Preposterous! The law can step in and take care of troublemakers. A woman can surely join the church if she so wishes!"

Melinda Britton took Mr. Adams' defense. "If the sheriff here held every ruffian and drunken bum in custody, we'd go broke feeding them. You are in the hills now, Brother Holderness. Hank Leffert is not your garden-variety criminal." Melinda bit her tongue to hold back explaining that the sheriff himself allowed such antics in exchange for corn liquor. She had no stomach for hanging out the community's dirty laundry before guests.

Brother Littlefield was as naïve as Holderness. His suggestion was so dreamy that even Nelle was inclined to giggle. "The answer, of course, is to convert the man, drive the sin from him, and solve the whole matter in one mighty sweep."

Melinda sniffed. "The only cure for Hank Leffert will be six feet of earth over his stinking body!"

"Now, Melinda!" reproved Mrs. Adams, who was more concerned with her duties as hostess than she was with the problem of Hank Leffert. Her reproval ended the meal and everyone set about preparing for evening service.

The evening was clear and nippy. Nelle liked the luxury of a shawl over her shoulders. As everyone piled into the surrey for the trip to church, Nelle announced that she was going to walk up with Eleanore Gray and her children. If facts be known, she simply could no longer stomach another of the observations offered by Holderness. To be confined in a surrey with the man would ruin a beautiful evening.

Much to everyone's surprise, Brother Littlefield said, "If you do not mind, Miss Adams, I shall walk with you. This air would do me good. It's a fine evening." Nelle, of course, did not decline the company. Her delight was visible to all but Brother Holderness, who had started on yet another theological discourse.

The sun had just gone down, and traces of gold and mauve lingered along the horizon. Here and there a bold star made an early appearance. The man and woman made their way silently toward the creek, side by side in the twilight. The footbridge appeared quite precarious to the visiting clergyman. He politely offered Nelle his arm. She politely accepted his help. Her inward trembling made it almost necessary. When she attempted to withdraw her arm after they had made their way across, Brother Littlefield held it firmly in place and it remained so as they walked up the rocky road. They walked in silence. Although both had longed for an opportunity to be alone, neither was at ease. Nelle thought, "He can speak now if he pleases. I wonder why he's so quiet." Brother Littlefield thought, "Life would be like Heaven with this girl by my side, yet I dare not say a word for fear of breaking this spell or offending her." Nelle toyed with the notion of pretending to stumble on the rocks so that she might fall into his arms, but she did not do so for fear he would see through the ruse.

As they neared Eleanore's house, Nelle silently prayed that the Grays would already be gone. Surely, she thought, with a little more time alone he might be encouraged to speak. The Gray cabin, however, was well lit and a chorus of barking dog and shouting children greeted them. "Mama, Mama! It's Nelle and the preacher!" announced the children.

Eleanore met them at the door and ushered them in. Eleanore read too well the look of shy embarrassment on the young Nelle's face. She approached her guests with graceful tact. "Hello, you two! I was hoping someone would come by to see us up to the meeting. It's such a fine night for a walk; very thoughtful of you both to remember us!" She motioned for her guests to take seats while she finished buttoning up Janey and oversaw the wrapping up of her two older children.

It was a merry group that climbed the well-worn mountain trail. The children bounded ahead, chattering like monkeys. Nelle and the young minister found their tongues strangely

loosened in the company of Eleanore. When they came to Will
Gray's place, they found the man waiting at the gate. He at
once realized that the two young adults probably wished to be
alone, so he offered his arm to Eleanore and paced themselves
far enough behind Nelle and her gentleman to grant them pri-
vacy. He whispered to Eleanore, "I see the ice has finally been
broken, eh, Mrs. Gray?" Eleanore smiled warmly in reply. When
the others were out of earshot, he said, "I almost wish you hadn't
come tonight, Ellie. I've got a feeling there's going to be some
trouble one of these nights. I'd rather you and the children were
safely home in bed, should push come to shove. If the rowdies
should start up, promise me that you will find the children and
keep them away from the windows."

"Worry wart! What could possibly happen? It's been a good
meeting so far. Successful, too. Sadie Leffert told me she's going
to join tonight! I'm so glad for her. To have faith will be a great
comfort to her in her troubles."

"My dear little idealist, that may well be the light to the fuse.
I hope your optimism proves accurate, but I don't think you understand Hank Leffert. It may well bristle his back to have his
wife taken from him by religion."

"And another thing," hurried on Eleanore, who paid little heed to Will's grim implications, "I must talk to Rachel
Matterson tonight. She's been so downcast. I see her sitting in
the back of the church with circles under her eyes. She won't
sing and she won't talk. I'm worried that she isn't well. Every
time I mean to talk to her, she slips out as if she wants to
avoid me. Tonight, I'm going to sit in the back pew by her and
straighten this out."

"You and Sophie Dean have your hands full of Mattersons,
don't you? I only hope they appreciate your skills as a guardian angel!" said Will. He smiled indulgently and squeezed her
hand.

"Think it funny if you choose, but I aim to make a silk purse out of a sow's ear. Rachel is a remarkable girl, one worth saving from a fate like Sadie's. Sophie thinks she has promise as a singer, and we're doing everything to steer her away from any lesser fate! It's my duty to help her. I don't care if they all think I'm an interfering old hen. Someone must save that girl!"

Once again Will smiled down at Eleanore. His heart was so full of love and longing for the kindly woman that her very presence sometimes filled him with a sorrow. The deepening twilight alone prevented her from seeing the passionate devotion that was clear in his eyes.

Chapter XXIV

THE DEVIL'S NIGHT

LIGHT STREAMED, COMFORTING AND inviting, from the windows of the church. Outside, the usual fanfare and bustle reigned. The churchyard was full of buggies and horses, the porch was cluttered with visitors, and shadows were filled with the shapes of men from the hills who had come to watch the goings-on with amusement and corn liquor fortification. As Will Gray and his troop made for the doorway, distinct hisses and jeers from the outer shadows burned their ears. Some unknown roughneck rudely called, "Hey, did you see what the preacher caught? Wonder if he knows what's under them skirts!" A hoarse round of laughter filled the night. Harvey Littlefield clenched his fists until his knuckles were white. Nelle turned a fiery red.

Every pew was already filled, but a few farm boys in the back gave up their seats to Eleanore and Nelle and the children. Slim Davis and the others who had given up their seats lined up against the wall behind them. Harvey Littlefield walked up the aisle to the pulpit. His entrance was the signal for service to commence. Sophie Dean vigorously attacked the organ and produced the opening bars of the first hymn. The entire crowd joined in unison so boisterous, the tin lamps actually rang with vibration.

Eleanore surveyed the crowd and found Rachel Matterson sitting only a few feet from her. She tried in vain to catch the girl's eyes, but Rachel only stared straight ahead over Sophie's prim shoulders. The only time she saw the girl move was when Rachel turned her head to look at Slim Davis. Rachel instantly flushed and abruptly restored her blind stare ahead. Eleanore was amused. She knew the girl was crazy over the young lad. Although she had never seen him escort her home after services, she was certain that Rachel had a crush on him. That would suffice for the time being as explanation for her peculiar behavior.

Nelle eventually tore her eyes away from Harvey Littlefield in the pulpit. When she did, she saw with horror that grotesque faces were pressed against the windows lining both sides of the room. She shuddered as she pointed them out to Eleanore. "Why are they making those faces? Certainly they mean no harm, but it's most unbecoming. You don't think perhaps they are trying to upset Brother Littlefield, do you? I wonder if Leffert put them up to it?" she asked Eleanore quietly. Eleanore scanned the windows. Each one was filled with pressed faces. The bearded faces were so squashed against the panes that they were as distorted as goblin masks. "I don't know what's going on, Nelle, but it's a sure bet some trouble is brewing. They've done all sorts of uncouth things before, but this is a new line of attack!"

Harvey Littlefield did not sense trouble. He was preoccupied with his duties and filled with fervent desire to bring the Lord to the troubled Hill community. He preached eloquently, gently admonishing the waywardness of the group and encouraging gospel truths with an earnestness that was not light in its impact. His prayer for piety brought tears to many an eye. It was followed by an invitational hymn, "Lord, I'm Coming Home." As the choir drew the song to a close, Littlefield stepped down from his platform and stood at the front of the aisle to wait for confessors to come forward. Children came forth first. They knelt before the man and made confessions of faith in tiny voices. Then there was a stir in a middle pew. From the line of people, there stood a woman, Sadie Leffert. She tenderly laid her sleeping son in old Granny's arms and struggled uneasily through the other occupants of the pew. By the time she reached the center aisle, tears were streaming down her face. She nearly ran up the aisle, dropped on her knees before Littlefield, and lifted her head up to him for guidance.

Littlefield smiled down at her. He raised his hand to halt the renewed singing. "Friends," he said, "My cup overrunneth with joy! The angels in Heaven rejoice with us. Another repentant sinner has joined the fold. For this, we give our thanks to the Lord God." Littlefield looked tenderly down at Sadie. He spoke to her so softly that his words were unclear to the congregation. He said, "Will you confess your faith? Do you believe with all your heart that Jesus Christ is the Son of the Living God?"

In a strangely calm and loud voice, the little woman replied, "Yes, I do believe with all my heart." Her declaration was followed by an angry shout from outside. Glass began splintering. A large stone shot through a window near the pulpit and caught the minister in the temple with force. A look of astonishment on his face, he wavered and then he toppled forward onto Sadie Leffert.

The congregation fell into pandemonium. Women and children screamed, men shouted, and the order turned to bedlam. Suddenly, stones poured through every window. Cries were heard, "Down with the preacher! Down with the possum-faced hypocrites!" Obscenities rang through the hall.

Will Gray, like many a man, rose. He turned to Eleanore and said, "Don't go outside. Stay here. They'll quit throwing sooner or later. Get the children down under the pew." As Will left them, horse hooves could be heard speeding off from the church.

Nelle Adams was horror-stricken. She was not amongst the first to reach Brother Littlefield. It was impossible to pass through the aisle that was congested with men hurrying for the door. She dropped all cares for dignity and heroically jumped from pew to pew like a nimble mountain goat. She knocked off hats, bruised shoulders, and rudely pushed aside the people who had gathered around the fallen preacher to cradle the man's head in her own lap. His forehead was already deeply bruised. Frantically, she pleaded, "Harvey, please wake up. Please! Oh, dear God, don't let my Harvey die!" as she loosened his collar and rubbed his wrists with feverish anxiety.

Sophie Dean pushed her way through. She carried a bucket of water. She calmly began to sprinkle water on the man's face. Nelle soaked her handkerchief in the bucket, wrung it out, and rubbed it over Littlefield's temples. The injured side of his forehead had swollen to the size of a hen's egg. Suddenly, he opened his eyes and muttered weakly, "Nelle, my dear, Nelle..." before he faded back into his faint.

"Oh, Sophie, do you think he'll die?" asked Nelle with terror.

"Lord, no! He fainted again, probably from finding himself in your arms, girl! See, he's coming around again. I advise you to loosen your grip before the rest of his life gets squeezed out of him. It's not proper to act like you've been. You've made quite a spectacle of yourselves already!"

"I don't care a hoot. I don't care who knows that I love him!" said the girl loudly. She turned to the prone man and yelled, "I love you, Harvey Littlefield. Do you hear that?" Her hysterical tears soaked the clergyman's vest. Littlefield opened his eyes and said, "Yes, darling!" The scene between the two lovers was witnessed by a good part of the community. It caused gossip and ridicule for months after, but not a soul would say that it wasn't the sweetest bit of lovemaking ever seen in the hills.

Those who had not witnessed the touching scene had been the ones who went outside to catch the offenders. Most of the crowd soon joined them in the churchyard. Granny Matterson had managed, child in arms, to get a traumatized Sadie settled on a pew. Granny crudely comforted her by saying, "If Hank is the cause of this, he'll pay for it if it's the last thing I get done on Earth!" Rachel murmured, "Sadie, you're not going home to face that devil. You're coming home with us." The two women led Sadie from the church. She covered her face with her worn brown hands and let tears pour through them like water.

When most of the congregation made its way outside, it became apparent that the culprits had escaped with haste. The men who had initially gone out to explore huddled together, trying to piece together the evening's events. Mr. Adams gathered his family together. With the aid of Will and Holderness, Littlefield was lifted into the surrey. Nelle sat by his side.

Will retreated into the church to find Eleanore. She was having difficulty calming her children. Will approached them and said, "I think we should go home now. They can't find out who hit Littlefield, but we're pretty sure Leffert was the instigator. Sam Cooper said he heard Hank swear that he would get the preacher if Sadie joined tonight. We can only guess he did it."

"Is he badly hurt?" asked Eleanore.

"No, I don't think so. He'll certainly have a headache, but from what I've heard, it will be soothed by Nell's loving hands!" he replied with a knowing laugh.

"Well, some good came of it all."

Sophie Dean swooped down on them. "Oh, Eleanore, isn't this just simply awful? There's a terrible fate in store for the man who caused this." Eleanore was quick to agree. Sophie then said, "Will tells me you are all walking tonight. We can make room in our buggy for the children if that would be of any help to you."

"Oh, thank you, Mrs. Dean. I was dreading the walk home with the children. They are still shook up. Janey is so afraid I doubt she would take a step in the dark willingly," accepted Eleanore. Paul suddenly spoke up in grand self defense, "Mama, I wouldn't mind walking. I'm not scared a bit, but if you rather I ride, then I will."

"Paul, you are such a brave boy! It's late, though, so why don't you go along in the buggy and see if you can calm the girls down for Mrs. Dean. Uncle Will will take care of me."

Paul gladly accepted his assignment and took his place in the Deans' buggy. As the final carriages left the churchyard, Will went into the church to put out the lights. He took Eleanore's hand and together they silently walked away from the deserted church. Neither felt comfortable, but they did find reassurance in the presence of the other. The workings of fear and imagination made the night crawl with lurking figures that rustled bushes and made the leaves on the paths crumble with cracking sounds. They paused once or twice to stand shock still and peer in the direction of a snapping twig that broke the regular night noises with clarity.

It was finally at Will's gate that they stopped to rest. Will leaned against the gate and Eleanore stood by his side. They were both breathing hard from taking the path at a fast clip.

They looked skyward and studied the stars. It seemed the easiest way to avoid conversation. Will suddenly spun toward Eleanore, released an audible sigh, and spoke to the woman. "Eleanore, this gate is where you should rest every night. I know I promised not to bother you again about this, but the distance we've created between ourselves is hard to bear. And, if you care for me at all, this must end."

Eleanore refused to tear her eyes away from the stars. She knew that Will would press her again. The time had come. "Will, I do love you. I lay awake at night imagining you by my side. My children adore you. As it goes, they promote you as a husband and a father. The fact remains, however, that I cannot reconcile Bob's death with my life."

"When he first died, I was certain that no man would replace him in my life. Later on, when things got rough, when the crops were threatened, when there wasn't enough money, and when I found myself alone on winter nights, I nearly came to despise him for abandoning me."

"And now? What is Bob to you now? Are you planning to let your life cease with his?" said Will with an unexpected anger.

This time, Eleanore did not shy from his emotions. "Oh, Will, I'm confused. He's not my life anymore. He is a part of a life that I cherished long ago, but he still works in my life. I have only to look at Paul to see Bob. I hear his thinking in Nancy's words. I cannot fairly come to you carrying another man's life like parcels in my children. Any peace we could make would have to be interwoven with Bob."

Will hung his head, but Eleanore pressed on. "I know it is a cruel thing to say or feel, but I would give anything now to free myself of him. I want to pack him away like a childhood memory, a golden thought to tuck away where it would cause no harm. I love you so fiercely that I am nearly tormented and torn to bits."

"I have tried to put this matter aside completely because it always ran into an impasse. It is not right for me. I am unworthy of you, Will, but Lord only knows how I cherish you. I've tried to work it away in the fields, but all the sweat in the world doesn't cleanse this." She waved her hands over the length of her body.

"Eleanore, do you realize that you feel guilty because you have an opportunity for a real life again and Bob does not? Has that ever once occurred to you? Do you know how unfair and unworthy you are being to yourself? Must you persist in wearing your love for me like a horsehair shirt?" asked Will with gentle force.

"Oh, I love you, Will Gray!" cried Eleanore. The two of them suddenly drew together and fully kissed with the passion of the long-denied. There was such yearning that they could not fall apart, but only continue to savor the embrace that spanned from their youth through the past difficult years of desire. A sense of joy filled Eleanore's breast, a feeling that she had never hoped to feel again. But that feeling was cut short. Abruptly, she pulled away and pointed in front of her.

"Look, Will! Something is burning!" No sooner were the words from her mouth when a pistol shot rang out and splintered the air with echoes.

Will turned to face the orange glow that quickly illuminated the sky. He ran down the lane that they had come up and saw flames leaping from treetops in the distance. Eleanore followed him. "It's the church, Ellie!" cried Will with horror. "Those crazy sons-of-bitches burnt the church!"

Will and Eleanore stood side by side, watching flames leap higher. Burning sparks and bits of shingles whipped up into the air and danced, suspended in the force of the fire. "It's too late to do anything. I'm going to take you home." Will grabbed her hand and they ran to her cabin. She trembled with fear and cold. He left her on the doorstep with stern instructions to bolt the door. He kissed her roughly on the mouth before running back toward the church.

The fire had consumed all but a last standing wall. The pews were embers, the handcrafted windows were smashed rubble, and little was left that could even be used to identify the structure as a House of God. Will surveyed the wreckage with a rage in his heart. The heat and smoke was intense. He put a handkerchief over his face and kept a distance from the remaining wall as he trod over the blackened yard. With a huge explosion of noise, the final wall collapsed and fiery bits blew about in the sky.

As Will backed away in the churchyard, he heard a muffled moan. It came from beneath a gnarled old oak that had been spared. A shadow of a figure was lying on the ground beneath the singed boughs. Will gingerly turned the prone figure over. It was Slim Davis. Will tenderly knelt by the young man and cradled his head against his leg. In a very weak voice, a voice that told of the nearness of death, he gasped out, "Hank Leffert…shot me, Mr. Gray." There was a long pause. The moaning ceased. Slim's eyes remained closed, but his mouth moved with extreme laboring. "Please, sir, tell Rachel…I love her. I ain't gonna. . .make it. Bury me in the. . .grave lot. Hank did this. He set the fire." Slim's eyelids fluttered and his mouth moved, but no more words came. Will rubbed the youth's face gently. Slim suddenly opened his eyes and said with a final burst of energy, "Hank done this to me because I saw him set the fire. Please, Mr. Gray, do as I've asked."

The dying young man fell silent again. Will continued to stroke his face as a mother would the soft face of a sick infant. Will, tears in his eyes, spoke to the boy. "Don't worry anymore, Slim. I promise I'll tell Rachel and look after her for you. Don't fret anymore, son. We'll find Hank Leffert. You save your strength now. If anything happens, I'll see to it that you are taken care of as you've asked."

The sound of approaching riders grew louder and louder. They approached the smoldering ruin of the church with excited shouts and cries. One rider bellowed out, "Hey! There's somebody under the tree!" Several men quickly dismounted and ran to gather around Will and the dying boy. Mr. Peterson looked down at Will and asked, "What's going on here? Do you know?"

"Yes, but send one of the men up to Eleanore and tell her to bring her doctor's bag. Tell 'em to be quick. This boy's been shot and he's in bad shape!" ordered Will.

Mr. Peterson knelt down beside Will. "Who shot him, Will?"

"Leffert. He shot him and he burned the church," said Will with anger.

"Why? Has the man gone mad?" asked Peterson.

The rage in his heart grew stronger. "Gone mad? Well, as I see it, Leffert has been allowed to roam like a mad dog for some time now. It's hardly any sudden turn of personality. Like a mad man, he burnt the church because it brought comfort to his wife. Like a mad man, he shot this boy because the boy was a witness. Answer your questions?"

While Will ranted, two of the men left to look for tracks. The churchyard was a rubble of tracks from the meeting. One fellow, however, ventured farther down the lane. He reported that he found a single set of tracks leading up the unused lane that ran to the old Lampit cabin. "Since nobody would have cause to go up there, I think there's a chance it was Leffert looking for a place to hide out. What do you say we go up and catch that mean bastard before he gets away?" The idea was greeted with hearty enthusiasm, but Will quenched it.

Will stopped the eager band and beckoned them to come over to the oak tree. When they had gathered, he said, "I don't think it's a good idea. For one, the man is dangerous. Somebody else will get hurt before the night is out if you manage to corner him. Secondly, Hank Leffert knows every inch of these woods and hills better than we do. Third off, if we wait until day, we can get the deputies rounded up and they'll help. There are some other things, though, that can be done tonight."

Although the postponement of the manhunt was agreed to, it was with some disappointment. Every man in the valley had nurtured a hatred for Leffert that was ready to explode with the slightest provocation. In rural outposts, it was necessary for individual men to assume the duties of civil law enforcement. Abiding citizens felt a keen and burning sense of duty because they—and they alone—maintained the order that protected their families and properties. It was difficult to turn a cheek at the affront, but Will Gray's intelligence was widely respected. Instead of chasing the shadow of Hank Leffert, two men accepted Will's command and they promptly mounted and headed for their own homes and families.

As they were departing, Eleanore and her guide returned with the medical bag. The woman dismounted and ran to Will's side. Will looked up at Eleanore with tears in his eyes. He extended his hand to her and together they dropped beside Slim Davis. Before Eleanore reached for the man's pulse, Will grabbed her arm away. "Ellie, I'm afraid it's too late. Slim is dead."

"Oh, my God! Will, I came as quickly as I could," responded Eleanore, her voice quaking.

"Yes, I'm sure of that, but he was shot at a very close range. He never had a chance, Ellie."

"What an appalling deed! He seemed a decent, hard-working boy. He was always so grateful and polite to me, Will. I think that Rachel was sweet on him. She'll be heartsick. This whole thing makes me so sick, so hateful." She turned fiery eyes to Will. "They said Hank did it."

"Atrocity is more appropriate in describing this, Eleanore. Hank has committed a vile act, an unforgivable deed that shall cause him his own end if any of us have any power in the matter. I think that it is finally clear that this community cannot coexist with him. I'm convinced there's no room for his kind anywhere on this earth," replied Will. The tears that had welled in his eyes gave way to a burning fire, a fire fused by the deepest hatred the gentle man had ever known.

"Will, I want to help. I know there's little a woman can do, but I'll do anything I can to be of help. I'm not inclined to sit at home doing needlework with my doors bolted. Tell me anything there is I can possibly do," declared Eleanore.

"There's something you can do. It would be far less pleasant than chasing down the devil, but it must be done." He touched her arm with great tenderness. "Would you go with me to see Mr. Davis, and then on to see Rachel and Sadie?"

"Certainly, Will."

"Before he died, Slim asked me to take care of a couple matters for him. I'm obliged to honor his requests. He knew he was dying, and he wanted to set things right. He wants to be buried in this churchyard. He also asked that I tell Rachel that he loved her. I'm under promise to him to care for that girl now."

Eleanore felt a great sadness for Slim Davis, but she set her resolve. "Let's get started, Will. The children have been taken over to the Deans for the night, so we needn't worry about them."

Slim's body was wrapped in a gray woolen blanket and loaded with solemn ceremony into the back of Peterson's wagon. Eleanore sat by Mr. Peterson at the reins. Will rode, shotgun in hand, in the rear of the death wagon. They traveled rapidly to the Davis cabin. Peterson set the brake and assisted Eleanore down. As they walked slowly toward the rundown structure, Mr. Davis opened the door. He had a coal lamp in one hand and a gun in the other. "Who comes here?" he bellowed.

Will stepped forward. Davis raised the lamp higher to peer at him. He squinted. "It's me, Mr. Davis. Will Gray." Davis then beckoned them to come closer.

"Mr. Davis, we come with tragic news for you. It's with great grief and sorrow that we must tell you that your son, Slim, has been murdered this night," said Will as he motioned for Eleanore to come forward. "We are awfully sorry for you and your wife, Mr. Davis. Slim was a fine boy."

Davis cleared his throat, but would not make another sound or move. He looked down at his feet. Will and his companions stood equally silent for a long spell. Finally, Will ventured, "Mr. Davis, sir, would it help you if Eleanore here went with you to break the news to your wife? She could stay a bit with her. There are some things we should discuss with you in private. If you like, we will carry Slim's body inside for you."

Davis shook his head in the affirmative and beckoned to Eleanore to follow him inside. Mrs. Davis was up, dressed in a tattered wrapper, sitting at a small table. A tiny stub of candle flickered. Her head was on the table, cradled in her arms. When she heard them enter, she lifted her face. "I thank ye for coming. There's no news to break to me. I heard every word." Rivers of tears streamed down her face. "Put Slim over there on that bed." She rose and turned and went into the lean-to that served as a kitchen. She reached up to a shelf and brought down a bottle of amber liquid, two chipped teacups, and several old jars.

When Peterson and Will carried in the boy's body and placed it on the bed, Mrs. Davis motioned them to go over to the table. Mr. Davis poured each of them some whiskey. His hands shook uncontrollably. The bottle missed its mark over and

over again. Mrs. Davis recovered her son's face and walked over
to the others. "Okay, now you may tell us both what happened."

Will described the night's events. He spared them no details.
He concluded with, "Mr. Davis, we aim to have justice for this."
Before they left the cabin, Will promised that he would build
a casket for Slim and bring it over the next day. Neither Mr.
Davis nor Mrs. Davis seemed to acknowledge his final words.
Mrs. Davis just sat in the plain chair, rocking to and fro, while
Mr. Davis stared at the bottle on the table.

Chapter XXV
NELLE'S NEWS

WILL GRAY, MR. PETERSON, AND ELEANORE went to the Matterson cabin after leaving the Davises to their grief. This visit was equally dreadful, but in a surprising way. The news was taken most peculiarly by Rachel. She seemed to take little comfort in the dying boy's confession of love for her. She shed no tears. She was struck to the quick with fear, with a burning hatred for her brother-in-law, but her composure revealed little to the visitors. In fact, even Granny Matterson found her quiet withdrawal and wordless sobriety disconcerting and odd. Sadie cried out in rage against her husband. She ranted and railed against her master until her father ceased her speech with a curt reminder that Hank Leffert was her chosen husband. Matterson and Sadie entered into a grievous fight. Matterson bid the guests leave the cabin and not return again. As they pulled away in Peterson's rig, Eleanore could hear Matterson thunder at his daughter. "Sadie, ye's a bitch of a gal, not fit fer any man. Leffert is yer husband, better or worse. It is yer duty to abide by him, not show him off to strangers the way ye done. Ye bring shame on this house and on yer husband's name!" It was a manner of thinking that, under the circumstances, struck Eleanore as contemptible.

Will looked down at the moonlit face of the woman he loved. Her distress was plain. "Ellie, you don't understand, do you?"

"What is there to understand? Ignorance? How can Sadie possibly be expected to show loyalty to a brute who has made her life a trial by misery? It is he who has shamed her!" she cried out hoarsely.

Mr. Peterson and Will exchanged knowing looks. Will tried to explain the ways of Hill people, but he feared it would be futile. "Ellie, they think differently than we do. They think it is the duty of a woman to protect her husband, no matter how vile he may appear. They have a sense of loyalty and honor that is never to be broken, but adhered to blindly. It is their strength. They're defensive, embarrassed. Nothing hurts them more than to have their lowness exposed before the Dean's Creek valley people. They will band together now to protect their pride. Don't expect them to welcome our vengeance. A good many of them certainly wish Leffert dead, but they will keep their attitudes shut off from us now. I've seen this happen before over things as simple as missing livestock and raided larders. The magnitude of murder will make them weave together so tightly that they will probably shut themselves off from us for some time."

Eleanore sighed and blew out a puff of air. She pursed her lips and rode in silence to her home. Mr. Peterson went home with Will. They spent the duration of the night making a coffin.

Slim Davis was buried as he wished the next afternoon. The Mattersons did not come to the services. In fact, a good many ridge families were absent. The few that did come stood wordlessly beside the Davises. The valley families and the ridge families kept a distance from each other. Will's words ran through Eleanore's thoughts as she observed the pronounced segregation. It was fortunate, she thought, that the temperate Littlefield presided over the services. Holderness would probably have only riled the uneasy tension that was building. After the burial, the ridge families departed silently and quickly. Eleanore overheard her neighbors talking. Apparently, the plan to capture Leffert had to be abandoned. The authorities in Benchfield declared that it would be an illegal venture because they only had hearsay and no evidence to support the claims that Leffert was guilty. Will himself had talked to both the judge and the sheriff. He broke the news to the eager posse in Dean's Creek with dismay and foreboding. He assured them, as the sheriff had assured him, that Leffert would eventually violate the law again and hopefully it would be a witnessed deed. It was small comfort to anyone.

During the next few weeks, a gloom penetrated the valley. The Indian summer ended. The skies became a continual dreary gray. The leaves that had ornamented the hillside with inspiring jewel colors faded and dropped to the ground, spent and weary from artistic labors. The days shrank. People started rising in the dark. Their days were chopped short by the early sunset. Except to feed chickens and walk to school, the children no longer spent hours playing outside. They spent as much time as possible in the warmth of their homes. Social life came to a standstill with the burning of the church.

Husbands stayed close to their firesides. Extra bolts were added to doors, and squirrel guns were oiled with care. A rumor spread that valley farmers intended to go in and clean out the ridge once and for all, but naught came of it. In fact, it became well known that Hank Leffert, upon hearing the declaration of the law in Benchfield, took up residence again in his cabin with cocky boldness. Sadie and the baby were with him. No one went so far as to even near the cabin.

The wet season began. It rained constantly. Roofs leaked and root cellars turned moldy. Wetness became as familiar as fresh air. Eleanore was grateful for the rain. It flooded the creek and allowed her to keep her children safely home from school without feeling foolish. She fretted constantly. She never allowed them to search for the cow without her. She kept a light burning all night, every night. She had Will make wooden shutters that bolted to cover her windows. She made him add boards to both doors as defense against the cold. Both adults knew that the cold she feared was fear itself. Will made light of her requests. As he finished working on the doors, he laughingly told the children, "I'm building you a fortress against snow-flakes!" Eleanore was far too proud to let Will know her terror, and she was grateful that he pretended that her fortressing was innocent.

All the valley families clung together more tightly that year. The threat of winter was light compared to the threat of Hank Leffert or a feud with the ridge families. Hank, bad as he was, had a loyal following of backwoods hoodlums who mistook his insanity for bravado. Will became a regular member of Eleanore's evening household. She was grateful.

Before the children, Will was his usual gay self. The children accepted his frequent visits as tribute to themselves. Only Nancy had guessed at half his purpose. Once, when her brother said, "Uncle Will is just like a father to us," she had blushed hotly. Will read Brontë and Dickens aloud to them all before the fire. Eleanore usually brought out hot tea, molasses cookies, or gingerbread while they discussed the night's reading or the weather or some neighbor's affairs. Never, even after the children were in bed, did the man or woman discuss themselves or their future. The climate was all against it and they both knew it. It would be too easy to confuse fear with love. They never discussed Hank Leffert, either.

On a typically dreary day, Nelle Adams forded the creek and plodded through the muck up to Eleanore's door. She rode a slightly disgruntled plow horse. With her usual abandon, she burst into Eleanore's parlor. She held her skirts up to her knees. She sat down and pulled off her boots with unladylike hastiness, and she beamed. She kissed Eleanore and each child a dozen or so times and flung herself back into the chair. "I've been dying to see you, Eleanore! You won't believe the news! You'd never guess in a million years! I'm going to be married!"

Eleanore feigned amazement. "Not really!" she cried. "When, my dear, and to whom?"

"At Christmas with Papa's consent and everything, and who else, you silly goose, but Harvey Littlefield!"

"Harvey, eh? Last time we spoke it was Brother Littlefield," teased Eleanore. She congratulated the girl and kissed her on the cheek. She begged for details, which the starry-eyed bride-to-be was only too eager to deliver.

Nelle blushed uncontrollably as she described the aftermath of the minister's injury. He spent several extra days in Dean's Creek recuperating. Nelle's loving care so moved him that he plucked up the courage to propose. "And, Eleanore, you'll never believe what he said! He told me he'd been in love with me since the moment he first laid his eyes on me. The only reason why he never spoke up was because he was afraid of frightening me off! Oh, he's so handsome and so divinely good! I feel as if I've been given a free ticket to Heaven itself. I'm probably not half-good enough for him, but I do love him so!" concluded the girl's description of her courting. Tears shone in her eyes.

"I'm so very happy for you, Nelle. Don't you worry. You will make a fine wife to him. You deserve the best man in the world," soothed Eleanore.

"Do you really think so? We will have to live in Springfield, and I've never even been to a town that big! Brother Holderness says the Littlefields are well-off. Not Harvey's mother and himself, mind you, but the rest of the uncles and cousins, I mean. Harvey's mother is poor as a church mouse, and she'll have to live with us. Aunt Melinda says the rest of the family will probably think I'm some hayseed blown in on a strong wind. Aunt Melinda says I best learn to be more ladylike and a whole lot less flippant. I'm a nervous wreck, Eleanore! If I want to be a preacher's wife, I'll just have to learn not to let go so!" Nelle giggled through her fears and continued, "I mean to be so good. I don't want people to find fault in Harvey on my account. He says he doesn't care how I am so long as I'm myself, but I think he's only seen my better side."

"Really, Nelle, I wouldn't be concerned. After the performance at the church, I think it's safe to say that Harvey has seen every side of you. Apparently it did not damage his love for you, now, did it?" asked Eleanore.

"Well, he did say he hoped I wouldn't change a bit! Aunt Melinda said all men say that before they are married, but that they change their minds right after the ceremony. Of course, I'm not convinced she's much of an authority since she's never been married."

Eleanore studied the excited girl. "Nelle, the less you listen to your Aunt Melinda, the better you'll do."

Eleanore's children, who had shyly been listening to the entire conversation, were wide-eyed. Their mother sent them to the kitchen to wash the dishes left from lunch. They moved as slowly as possible away from the tantalizing conversation between Nelle and their mother. Nancy put a kettle of water on to boil. As she poked listlessly at the damp wood in a faint effort to provoke fire, she murmured dreamily to Paul, "Oh ain't it just too romantic! It's like a fairy tale!"

"Fairy story, nothing! Sounds gosh-awful silly to me. What does she want to go and marry an old preacher for?" replied her brother.

"Oh, but he's charming, Paul. She'll live in a fine place and have servants and everything! I'll miss her, for sure, but I'll never forget her." Nancy, filled with a melodramatic sense of romance, clasped her hands before her and sighed longingly toward the ceiling. Her brother was disgusted—if not a bit jealous.

The two women in the parlor discussed wedding plans with eagerness. Sophie Dean was to create a wedding dress. Aunt Melinda and Mrs. Adams were already sewing trousseau finery. "Mrs. Dean says an afternoon dress or suit would be more appropriate than a white gown for an informal country wedding, so I'm taking her advice since she is a city sort of person. Still, it will be beautiful. The dress, I mean. People around here have seen women married in all sorts of things, even gingham! My outfit is going to be just so because Harvey's family will be coming, and I don't want them to think I'm too rustic!" sighed Nelle.

Nelle could not quit talking. Eleanore enjoyed listening as the girl rambled on. "Brother Holderness will marry us at home since there's no church anymore. I won't be able to have a big party afterwards, not after the incident the night the church burned. I'd be far too afraid someone would slip in and ruin everything or go after Harvey. I just can't get that awful business off my mind. I wish there were a way to clear it up before Christmas!"

"Yes, Nelle, that is a messy situation," agreed Eleanore, who was privy to Will's persistent investigation efforts. "Nelle, there's no living witness and there's no actual evidence as proof that Hank did it. The law has to be careful treading up on the ridge these days. All the ridge people feel as if all the valley people hold them under suspicion. If the law tries to snoop up there to get a witness or evidence, there may be more trouble. Will says our only hope is that Hank will pull something again someday that will get him nailed once and for all. Will's given up hope that any of the Cooney Ridge boys that ran with Leffert will step forward as witnesses."

"Witnesses! It just galls me that Hank Leffert is running free because nobody will say that they saw him do what everyone knows he did. He's a drunken bastard, a cruel lout of a man who has no right to share this earth with the rest of us!" cried Nelle with vehemence.

"Easy there, Nelle! Remember you're trying to make yourself a preacher's wife!" laughed Eleanore. "To tell you the truth, though, I don't rest easy here these days knowing that man is free. Sometimes, I wish I were back in Cedarville where everything was dull and predictable. If anything ever happened to my children over this, I'd never forgive myself."

Chapter XXVI

DOCTORING

COONEY RIDGE FOLK, MOTIVATED by the need for entertainment and the even greater desire to control their lives, spent early fall making the weather predictions that nearly always proved true. Granny Matterson, the most respected forecaster in the region, was the first to declare that the approaching winter was to be the worst in many a year. During the month of October, she studied tree bark, the abundance of walnuts, the thickness of cat's fur, and the antics of wooly worms to draw her conclusions. She supported her theories with additional research that would cast all doubt aside. Granny kept track of the number of fogs they had in August as well as the debut of cicada and katy-did songs. She knew that deer fawns had lost their spots in July that year. She'd encountered brush rabbits gnawing on sassafras. She compiled the evidence and solidly stated that the winter would be cold and the snows would come hard. No one on the ridge doubted her proclamation or her means of discerning. In fact, every person on the ridge and in the valley as well, from the crudest moonshiner to the most pious churchman, accepted the fact that bad times were coming. More than one believer in her skills was quick to note that the burning of the church and the very presence of Hank Leffert were added signs confirming calamity.

November was coming upon the Gray household. Eleanore ticked the days off in the almanac and chewed her lip each time she slashed another date off. She saw to it that plenty of firewood was laid by in neat cord stacks. She and Nancy took pieced quilts out from trunks for repairs and airing. Rows upon rows of canned fruit and vegetables lined her shelf in orderly perfection. None of these preparations, however, dispelled her dread of the cold to come. Even Eleanore placed faith in Granny Matterson's prophesy. The words that had rolled off the old lady's tongue often bewildered Eleanore, but they were always honest, in a Hill-folk way.

On the first night in November, long after the first killing frost of the year, Eleanore sat in a rocker before the fire while her children slumbered in their little room. Neither the warmth of the fire nor the knowledge that she and her children were safe from harm could abate the sense of fear and isolation that mounted daily to circle between her phantoms, the death of Bob, and the eerie sight of the burning church. She had reached a point when labor and fellowship would no longer give relief from plaguing memories.

Eleanore stared into the flames. She imagined the luxury of resting in Will Gray's heavy arms for a moment or two, and then abruptly pulled herself back into the gloom of a cold November night. She pushed aside the longing for Will as one would push aside a pestering child. The woman rose mindful of less dreamlike thinking to put another log on the fire. As she reached for a log, there came a startling pounding on the front door that caused her to drop the wood and stand frozen in her tracks. The pounding persisted, strong and unruly, not the knocking of a polite visitor. For a moment it occurred to her that Hank Leffert himself stood outside her only haven.

Her wits did not fail her. Eleanore got her gun and mechanically stepped forward to open the door. It was not Hank Leffert. Standing before her on the threshold were two women and a small child. Sadie Leffert's face was so badly battered that she was nearly unrecognizable. Both eyes were swollen closed, and blood trickled down her chin. Her features were marred by swelling and discoloration. Standing next to her, half supporting her was Rachel Matterson with a small boy in tow. Rachel looked unnaturally washed out, pale, and small. The tot stared up at Eleanore with blank eyes.

"Oh, dear God in Heaven!" cried out Eleanore. She drew the women and child into the cabin and barred the door. Without hesitation, she laid the thin body of Sadie Leffert on her bed near the fire. She motioned Rachel to take the young boy into Nancy and Paul's room. When Rachel returned, she and Eleanore bathed Sadie's face and undressed her. When Eleanore went to pull a clean gown over the tiny woman's body, she could not avoid examining a multitude of bruises that was already turning a sickly purple hue. She pulled the blanket over Sadie. Sadie never said a word. She lay on the bed like a corpse with widely opened eyes. Rachel's forehead and face were bathed with perspiration.

Eleanore ushered Rachel into the kitchen so they could talk without disturbing Sadie. As Rachel turned toward the door, however, she nearly fainted. She grabbed at the rocker for support and swayed dizzily. Eleanore quickly grabbed her by the waist and guided her to a ladder-back chair. The girl put her head down on the table. When she lifted her face to Eleanore, it became obvious that Rachel Matterson was ill.

"Rachel, what is it? What has happened to you two?"

"Oh, Missus Gray, I've took sick. I…was goin' to have a baby," stammered the girl in a low and broken voice. "I lost it…the baby. Granny fixed me up. I bled so. After I felt better, I went down to stay with Sadie so's my Pa didn't find out about the baby. Hank had got to her. When I got to her cabin it was nearly dark. Her little boy was sitting in the cold, crying. Sadie looked dead. Her eyes were closed, and I couldn't wake her up for ever so long." Rachel had said all she could. Tears poured down her face.

Eleanore felt her head. Rachel had a fever. "Rachel, are you still bleeding?"

"No, not much anymore. Granny knows about these things. She has special medicines. I just don't feel good yet," replied the weary girl.

"Rachel, I'm going to clean you up and put you in bed with Sadie. We have to get you warmed up and calmed down. I don't want you to think about this anymore tonight. Do you hear me? You are both safe here. Sadie's going to be alright."

With the calm efficiency that often follows shock, Eleanore put the girl to bed. She felt Rachel's abdomen. Rachel indicated it was tender, but she did not cry out. "Missus Gray, don't you fret. I know I'm sick, but I'm really better than I was last week. Granny says it takes awhile to work the pizen out. She said all the baby is gone. Wages of sin…" mumbled the girl as she drifted off to sleep.

Eleanore checked on her children. Even Sadie's little one, still fully dressed, slumbered. Eleanore Gray spent the duration of the night huddled under a quilt in the rocker. She slept little and frequently rose to check on the two women in her own bed.

Janey woke shortly after dawn. When Eleanore opened her eyes, she saw her littlest one gently stroking Rachel's hair. She beckoned Janey to her, and the two of them rocked in the chair until the other children came out. Sadie's son, Peter, remained asleep until nearly ten o'clock. Despite the hushed commotion made during the feeding and dressing of the Gray children, neither Sadie nor Rachel woke. Nancy and Paul were anxious for Eleanore to explain the mysterious presence of Sadie and Rachel, but their mother's manner prohibited fussing at her. When the children were finally seated before the fire, Eleanore dropped to the floor to softly explain the previous night to them.

"You don't need to be afraid. Everything is going to be fine. Sadie's husband hurt her, and Rachel is a little sick, but you and I are going to doctor them and make them well. I need for you to be quiet so they can rest. Nancy, when Peter wakes up, I want you to clean him up. Paul, it will be your job to see that the fire stays hot. Sick people need to be kept very warm. Will you help me?"

The Gray children accepted their commissions with seriousness, for the sober concern in their mother's eyes forbade frivolity. While Nancy and Paul silently aided their mother in carrying out morning chores, little Janey crept from room to room on tiptoe. Every time one of their patients murmured or tossed, all eyes would turn to the bed and fingers would crumple against lips to hush any chatter. Whenever Eleanore crossed the parlor floor to feel the foreheads of Sadie and Rachel, the children formed a stiff soldierly line to await their mother's signal that all was well. It had become clear that their home was a hospital, and they were a brigade of nurses and doctors.

When Peter Leffert finally toddled out from the children's room, he instantly ran to his mother's side and reached for her limp hand. Sadie's eyes opened at her son's touch. She extended a weak arm to pat his tousled head. She slowly scanned the room, the unfamiliar whitewash and portraits that swirled before her, and eventually pulled her broke mouth into a smile

when her eyes came to rest on the face of Eleanore Gray. Sadie
Leffert was safe. Her eyes closed peacefully.

Nancy took charge of Peter, a quiet and obedient child. He
was scrubbed, dressed in an odd assortment of clothing contributed by Paul and Janey, and given a hot breakfast. The child
never spoke a word. He ate warm oats and biscuits with jam
as if he had never known such a fine meal. It was Janey who
finally broke the child's stony continence. She plunged a fat finger into the purple jam that drooled from his biscuit and used
it like paint to draw a grand moustache above her own grinning
mouth. The boy smiled, followed her example, and opened his
mouth widely to expose a toothy grin.

When Eleanore left the children at play by the kitchen
stove to check on the patients, she found Rachel wide awake
and sitting up in bed. Eleanore murmured a warm greeting that
received no reply. Rachel's eyes were blank, her face immobile.
Eleanore felt her forehead again, adjusted the pillows behind
her head, and turned to see Sadie's eyes open.

Sadie, quite unlike Rachel, seemed eager to talk about the
night of the beating. It was her small way of repaying her debt
to the woman who gave her shelter. Eleanore learned through
her that Hank had beaten her because he feared she knew of a
witness to his burning of the church. He had left her for dead
without a thought to his son. Sadie claimed no knowledge of a
witness, but it was no defense against the brute. "Even if I did
know somethin', Missus Gray, it wouldn't be of any use. Law
don't take a wife's word agin' her man."

Eleanore did not keep her visitors a secret from neighbors.
In fact, she bundled Paul into warm clothes and sent him to
fetch Will Gray that very afternoon. She had to find out if
Leffert was still in the valley, if there were the possibility of having to face him on her own doorstep. She was determined, once
and for all, to appeal for justice to be done.

When Will returned with Paul, both the boy and the man were winded. Will had obviously come with great haste. He entered the cabin as if he owned it, as if the Devil himself would be inside it. Will glanced at Eleanore, and then ran to the bed where the two women lay. He looked down at them, turned his head to Eleanore, and whispered, "What happened to them?" Anger burned in his eyes, an anger Eleanore had never before seen in the gentle man.

In the warmed kitchen, over hot coffee, Eleanore explained all she knew to Will. Her children and Peter Leffert sat on a bench nearby. The children sat silently listening to every syllable uttered until Eleanore waved her hand at them to go into the other room. They departed obediently, but as slowly as their legs would take them. Although Eleanore carefully guarded Rachel's secret even from Will, she spared him no details of Sadie's beating. "Will, as anyone can plainly see, this is a matter of attempted murder. Leffert meant to kill her. He failed, but that does not alter his intent. The law can surely do something now."

Will pursed his lips and blew out a puff of air in a sigh of obvious futility. "Eleanore, the best we can do is take it to the law, but I'll warn you, beating one's wife is seldom regarded as attempted murder in these parts. A wife is considered a man's property, and he's generally allowed to manage his property however he likes. We've only Sadie's word for it that Hank meant to kill her. A little boy can hardly be called a witness."

"My God! Sadie wouldn't lie about this. Any fool can see that she was very nearly killed!" cried Eleanore.

"Eleanore, I said I'll try my best to convince the authorities of the gravity of this. That's all I can do. I feel as strongly as you, but I'll not be responsible for having men take the law into their own hands. There has been far too much of that around her already. It leads to unruly violence, a violence that may spread far beyond Hank Leffert. Too many are anxious to go up on the ridge to clean out every potential criminal in sight. It gets blind after awhile, beyond control or sense. We don't need that."

"I'll go to Benchfield immediately. In the meantime, if it is suitable with you, I'll have Mr. Adams check on Leffert to find him. The last thing I want is for him to come here. It would put you all in worse danger. Until we get word to you, you are to keep the doors barred. Don't let the children out at all unless you are with them. The gun is to stay loaded. Do you understand?" Will rose, put on his coat, and walked for the door. He stopped to plant a kiss on Eleanore's forehead, and he departed.

Eleanore fumed. She felt like screaming. When Will was gone, she strode around the rooms with her fists balled into her apron pockets. A rage grew inside her, a rage not only against Leffert, but against the attitudes that dwindled law and justice into a mockery. The children watched her pace about.

Finally, she stopped and called the children into the kitchen. She sat them at the table. "Please forgive me. I'm very angry right now. Uncle Will is going to try to help us. Until we hear from him and Mr. Adams, we are going to stay inside the house. If you have to use the outhouse, you aren't to go out. There are chamber pots in the bedroom. Until somebody comes to let us know that everything is okay, we're going to stay right here. If anyone comes, you are to go up the ladder. Paul, you and Nancy are to see to it that everyone gets up there, and you are to pull the ladder up after you. Do you understand?"

Heads nodded in unison. Eleanore took a deep breath to compose her thoughts. "Today we are going to make soup and cookies, so all of you pull out aprons and let's get busy."

Although the children were entertained by the activities in the kitchen, all ears were perked and ready for danger. The hours passed with tenseness. Both Sadie and Rachel woke again and received the affectionate attentions of everyone. Shortly after three o'clock in the afternoon, Toby began barking. The children, without reminder from Eleanore, ran to the ladder. Silently as mice, Nancy and Paul helped the little ones up and followed. They pulled the ladder up. Eleanore pulled the quilt on her bed over Sadie and Rachel in a confused attempt to disguise the bed. As Toby's bark increased, Eleanore frantically piled clothing on the bed to make it appear as if she had been sorting laundry. She got her gun and walked to the door. A soft knock was heard. A second knock followed.

Eleanore trembled so badly that she could barely reach for the latch. "Who's there?" she bellowed.

A reply came. It was a soft voice—a woman's voice. "It's me, Nelle! Nelle Adams, Eleanore!"

There was no denying the voice. It was unmistakably Nelle. Eleanore's heart ceased its thudding. She managed to undo the latch. Her hands shook uncontrollably. Nelle poured into the cabin and the two women embraced. The children were told to come down.

"Where are they, Eleanore? Where are Sadie and Rachel?" asked Nelle.

Eleanore grinned. "In bed, under my laundry!"

When order had been restored, the two patients were propped up against pillows to enjoy Nelle's visit. While the children finished up the dishes in the kitchen, Nelle and Eleanore sat in chairs beside the bed. Nelle hastily explained that Will had gone to Benchfield and that her father had gone with Mr. Peterson and Mr. Dean to find out where Hank was. The authorities in Benchfield had finally agreed to enlist Will as a deputy in charge of organizing a posse to search for Leffert. The other men, in the meantime, had found no sign of Leffert anywhere. They were going to meet at Will's to form a posse that night.

Eleanore beamed. Sadie looked at Nelle and Eleanore and finally said, "They won't ever find him. He has more tricks than a weasel." Rachel nodded in agreement.

"Listen here, you two, something's finally going to be done. It's not going to do either of you any good to take that attitude. Maybe it's just too hard for you to believe that an end is coming to this because you've lived like this all your lives, but I promise you that Will and the others won't let that man do you any more harm. I promise you," said Eleanore with firm sincerity. Sadie responded with a weak smile, but Rachel didn't respond at all.

Nelle sensed the defeat that was taking possession of Rachel. It was clear in the girl's frozen face, in her blank eyes, and her scorning mouth. "Well, ladies, I would like to stay longer, but I promised I'd get home soon. I hope you know that we're doing everything we can to help you." Nelle looked fondly at both patients. "I know that you aren't well now, Rachel, and that you've been ill and under shock, but I have a special favor to ask of you."

Nelle held Rachel's weak hand in her own and looked down at the girl. "Will you do me the honor of singing at my wedding next month?" she asked. Rachel solemnly nodded.

Eleanore walked Nelle outside. Dusk was setting in slowly. It seemed menacing. Eleanore reached behind her to pull the door closed. She turned to Nelle and said, "Thank you, Nelle. Your news has brought me hope. It was good of you to come over alone. If you want to stay the night, please do."

"I'm not afraid, Eleanore. Besides, they'd go crazy if I failed to come home! I'm not sure my visit did much for either one of them. I thought they'd be glad to hear the news. Sadie looks terrible, but Rachel bothers me the most. I thought she'd be happy to sing at my wedding, but maybe it was just a bad time to ask her. I hoped it would cheer her up. How sick is she?"

"Oh, Nelle! That girl is sick inside. She had the grippe and wasn't recovered from that when she had the shock of finding Sadie and bringing her here. It's set her back some. She's turning sour on everything. I think she'll get better, but it may take some time. Asking her to sing was a good idea. It will give her a goal, a reason to get well. We'll see."

Nelle tilted her head and smiled weakly. "I've got to go now. If you need some help or want us to take the children or anything, feel free. You've taken on a big responsibility."

Chapter XXVII

MANHUNT

IN ACCORDANCE WITH THE legal authorities at Benchfield, most men in the valley met at Will Gray's to form a posse to track Leffert. They were authorized to track the man, return him unharmed to the sheriff in Benchfield, and then relinquish any claim upon him. The law, they were assured, would handle extricating a confession of guilt and delivering any punishment declared prudent by the court.

The men filed solemnly into Will's home. Angry murmurings filled the room. Although the men were determined to track Leffert, they feared that the dictates of Benchfield might render the entire search a waste of time. They whispered amongst themselves that they were entitled to the privilege of coercing confession from the man who had ruined the safety of their domain. One bewhiskered farmer spat out his chew and growled, "He's vermin and they'll treat him like the finest gentleman in the land! The kid gloves of the law ain't likely to do to his skin what he's done to Sadie's!"

Mr. Adams, though equally anxious over the issue, looked at the farmer and said, "Calm down, Abner. If we foul up, it may cost us every chance at Leffert. You and I both know that Will here is just as eager as any of us to put an end to this. I say we let him decide our course." Several others nodded in agreement.

Shortly after Will silenced the crowd that had gathered, several men from the ridge shuffled through the door. Every head turned; those with rifles grabbed for them, and every man waited for the ridge men to speak. Slim Davis' father made his way through the chairs toward the front of the room. He put out his hand in a gesture of peace to Will Gray. He cleared his throat and raised his head to speak to the crowd of valley men. "I know we ain't welcome, but we want to help. We've had our losses, too. Ye ain't the only ones who want Hank Leffert finished. Me and these boys come peaceably aiming to help. If ye want us gone, we'll go."

The room again welled with murmurings. Some valley men felt the ridge boys weren't to be trusted. Others were clearly shocked that they had offered help at all. Several commended them loudly. The ridge boys looked down at their boots. Will silently watched and listened to the commotion until he had had enough. He grabbed a log that rested against the fireplace and strongly flung it against the stonework. It made a crashing sound that defied all other noises. Every lip stopped working and all eyes turned to Will at the head of the room.

Glowering, Will slowly scanned the men who had collected to form the legal posse. "Damn it! You clamored for peace here, for an end to the fear and damage that's been done, and now you turn against each other. For once in your lives, you are going to pull together to bring peace to this land."

"Here are the terms. Those of you who fail to see the wisdom of it are asked to leave. Those who are willing to carrying the law out are to stay. This applies equally to those of us from the valley and those of us from the ridge. Mr. Davis comes to us honestly. He's never given any of us trouble before. He's lost a son to Leffert. This is his chance to see to it that another son is not lost to any of us."

Will again scanned the silent audience. He pulled a piece of paper from his pocket and proceeded to deliver the terms of the posse. "First off, our only assignment is to track Leffert and escort him to Benchfield unharmed. There is to be no violence done to the man or the law will find us as guilty as we find Leffert. One wrong move on our part and the entire effort will result in failure. Secondly, we will divide into bands. I will lead one group in the search. Mr. Adams will be responsible for a second band. Mr. Davis will lead a third. You will be randomly assigned to bands and the instructions of the leaders are to be carried out to the letter. Thirdly, any violation of the rules will suspend your right to participate."

Not a man spoke. Will continued. "Now, if any one of you cannot live up to these duties and carry them out with a clear and determined conscience, you will leave this assembly and give us promise that you will not undermine our efforts." Will spoke his piece with the strength and conviction of a Baptist evangelist.

The men whispered to each other, debated the merits and shortcomings of the rules, and glanced around the room to see who would depart. Not a single man rose to leave.

The rest of the evening was spent going over rough maps of the countryside. The search would begin the next day at noon. It was decided that the search would extend as far as Cedarville, Benchfield, and deep into the wooded territories that the ridge people were familiar with. All posse members would return to Dean's Creek on Thanksgiving to regroup if Leffert was not caught before then. The first search, then, was to last six days. After bands were formed and plans were made for setting out the next day, the men organized a small group of older men and young boys to remain as protection in the valley.

At dawn the next day, Will Gray rode to Eleanore's house. He pounded on the door. No one answered. He could hear rustlings in the cabin, but no one came to the door. He again knocked and yelled out, "Ellie, it's Will! Will Gray!" Finally, he heard the latch lift. The door opened a crack. "It's Will, Ellie!" Eleanore, dressed in gown and wrapper, pulled the door open to admit him. Her husband's gun was in her hand.

Will smiled. "I see you took me at my word! Hank's a lucky man not to have come!"

Relief washed over Eleanore's face. "Will, it's not been easy. Come on in the kitchen for coffee and biscuits."

Paul's head peered down from the loft. "Ma, since it's only Will, can we come down?"

"Good Heavens, yes!" replied his mother. The ladder lowered, and down came four children. The pile of clothing on the bed squirmed and heaved until the faces of two frightened women were exposed.

While the children ate their biscuits before the fire and Sadie and Rachel sipped their tea in bed, Will and Eleanore had breakfast in the kitchen. Will quietly filled her in on the plans of the posse and outlined their excursion in great detail.

"Ellie, I'm not in great danger since I'm to head for Cedarville. Pretty unlikely that he's gone for a town of that size—out of his element. We'll be back Thanksgiving day sometime if we don't catch him sooner. Peterson and some of the Smalls will be nearby if you need anything. You're probably handier with a gun than any of them, so you may do well to count on yourself. Hank's far gone from what we can tell, but he may get driven back this way in the chase. You can relax some, but don't go hog wild."

"Will, I hate to think that any of you are in danger, but I know that this must be done. I think you did right to trust Davis. The best we can do is pray for you. Believe me, we'll pray plenty."

"Listen, Ellie, I can't stay any longer. It's been a good farewell breakfast. The Smalls will take care of my place while I'm gone. I'll be back by Thanksgiving at the latest. I assume I'll be invited for a real dinner?"

Eleanore smiled at him. "Of course, Will. You'll be our guest of honor."

Will bid the family and guests farewell and departed quickly. Eleanore ordered the children to dress. She changed into a plain day dress and tackled both the kitchen and the farm chores with only her gun for company.

As Eleanore gathered eggs, she recalled Will at her breakfast table. His skin had been ruddy from the ride in the cold, and it exuded a strong scent that was somehow clean and metallic. His eyes had sparkled with hope, with pride in his strength and belief in his course. Eleanore smiled as she remembered noting that the button on his checked shirt needed to be resewn. It had dangled loosely. She slowly let an egg slip into her basket and her face crumpled. Tears welled in her eyes and spilled down her face. She absentmindedly stroked Toby's head. "Oh, Lord, please keep that man safe. I love him so dearly. I need him." The tears poured unchecked.

As Eleanore threw cobs and hay down for the livestock, she mustered her reserves and coldly lectured herself. "Stop being a fool, woman! He'll be back as sure as snow will fall. You've got a house full of sick people and wild children to think of. Thanksgiving isn't far off. Brandy cakes and pie and mincemeat should knock the selfish pity right out of you." She traded her fear of Leffert for a fear for the safety of a man she loved, and as she stomped back toward her home, her hospital, she once again inventoried the chores that would lift her from gloom. Work had seldom failed her.

During the next five days, there was not a moment's idleness for any hand in her house. Even patients were given tasks, chopping dried fruits and grinding spices. The children fetched and carried, made batters, and sorted potatoes from the root cellar.

On Thanksgiving eve, they attended a community meeting at the Adamses. Rachel and Sadie, with the children, were loaded into the wagon that bumped and wound its way to the neighboring farmhouse. Both patients were sufficiently recovered to make the trek. Nelle Adams urged them all to come. She hinted that something exciting and cheering would be discussed. Eleanore hoped that some word had come back from the posse that would be announced that evening. If not, the trip would be good for Sadie and Rachel anyway. There was no denying that a week together in a cabin had started to dampen spirits.

When they approached the house, they were met by Mr. and Mrs. Peterson, Melinda Britton, and Nelle Adams. Much to Mrs. Peterson's obvious distaste, Joe Peterson assisted the women in helping Sadie and Rachel into the house. Mrs. Peterson coldly examined the two Hill women with uncharitable scrutiny. Eleanore secretly wondered how the woman regarded herself as a Christian.

The house was filled with women and children. Nearly every man in the valley was off on the manhunt. For the first time, it became clear that they were undefended and left completely to their own resources. Eleanore looked around the room, at Sadie reclining on the sofa, at the smiling faces of the Adams women, at the jabbering Mrs. Sloan, and at the children who congregated in every corner. She wondered if they—if any of them—knew how helplessly dependent they truly were upon their men.

Her widowhood had spared her such dependence, but it did not lessen her fears.

The entire house was filled with the aroma of spices, cinnamon, cloves, mince, nutmeg, and ginger. Mrs. Adams entered from the kitchen and proudly held out a large tray of spice cakes and cookies. Nelle smiled at Eleanore and explained, "Mother has been baking for four days getting ready for Thanksgiving! I don't think she could wait another day!"

"Nelle, we've been doing the same ourselves. We've made enough food to feed a city, but it's kept us busy. Working in the kitchen is a healthier past time than brooding over the hunt, don't you think?" replied Eleanore.

"My exact sentiments, but I don't think Mother is even conscious of why she's been so bent on cooking. It worked, though. They'll be home tomorrow, and we'll all rest."

Mr. Peterson, the only gentleman of maturity present, took it upon himself to call the meeting to order. "Ladies and young people, we are gathered together this evening to express our thanks unto the Lord who has blessed our lives this past year. Nelle Adams will play an opening hymn and we will join in a song of praise." Mr. Peterson walked over to the organ and stood next to Nelle. The hymn began. Every person in the room bellowed out the words with heartfelt sincerity.

It had been a long time since the community had gathered for worship. More than one set of eyes filled with tears. The need to worship had not suffered in the absence of a church. Instead, it had mounted to a surprising point that made the desire overwhelming. One hymn was followed by another and another, until all sense of worldly time and place vanished from the hearts and minds of the singers. The rusty and unpracticed voices of the women mingled with the awkward baritone of Mr. Peterson and the wobbly soprano of the children. Notes were punctuated and broken by emotion, but the songs of Thanksgiving flowed from inner wells of faith.

When Nelle finally closed her songbook, Mr. Peterson asked that they all join hands and bow their heads. A prayer poured from the man that spoke for every person in the room. He powerfully prayed that the Lord would guard over the men who had gone on the manhunt, that the Lord would grant strength to those who had remained behind, and that merciful justice would be done to restore peace to the valley and the ridge. It was an unpracticed prayer, but one that moved them all the same.

When they raised their heads, it seemed to them that they had, for a brief time, been removed from the room, removed from the earth altogether. They gazed at each other with tears in their eyes. They ate the refreshments brought out by Mrs. Adams and quietly talked amongst themselves. Eleanore learned that no word at all had been received from the posse. It made her wonder what surprise Nelle had so secretly referred to when she invited them. The children played quietly, grateful for an opportunity to see each other since school had been dismissed for the manhunt.

Mr. Peterson again rose and walked over to the organ. He wiped away a trace of molasses cake that clung to his lips, cleared his throat, and made an announcement that startled and delighted every person present. "As you already know, this assembly was called together for a special reason; I should like to make a proposal. Since the burning of the church, our isolation has grown and our need to worship has likewise increased. The turbulence of this time may be partially responsible, but it is not the sole motivation for our need to worship. I should like to propose that we make plans to build a new church in Dean's Creek. It will take all our efforts and whatever money we may spare, but it needs to be done if we are to survive as a spiritual community. I have talked to Will Gray and other men in the valley during these past weeks and all of us are willing to invest time, money, and labor to see this through. This is our home, the place we have chosen to live, and it is our responsibility to care for our needs."

As Mr. Peterson continued to outline his plans, Eleanore looked at Melinda Britton. Pride shown in her eyes as she watched the man she had once loved speak. Mrs. Peterson, on the other hand, showed no indication of pride. Her husband's plans were obviously a surprise to her. Perhaps, thought Eleanore, his clear commitment to living in Dean's Creek also came as a shock to the wife who hankered for city life. It was pitiful. Nelle's eyes caught Eleanore's. Between them passed the same knowledge and observations.

Mr. Peterson's proposal met with everyone's approval. The room exploded into chatter and enthusiastic planning. Ideas poured from every tongue. Some women dreamed of stained glass windows. Mrs. Dean dreamed of a pipe organ. Nelle, thinking of her intended, amiably described a pulpit that had been described to her. Even the children had contributions. They wanted a room of their own for Sunday school lessons.

After more refreshments and a closing prayer, the gathering faded. Eleanore lingered behind to help tidy up. As she and Nelle took stacks of dishes to the kitchen, they talked of Nelle's wedding and the shock the evening had given to Mrs. Peterson. When Eleanore finally took off her apron and went into the parlor to gather her brood, she found Sadie sleeping. Little Peter and Janey had managed to snuggle beside her. Rachel had fallen asleep in a rocker, her head resting uncomfortably against her chest. Paul and Nancy were fast asleep in a big wing chair. Eleanore smiled at her flock. Mrs. Adams and Melinda came to the doorway and stood behind her. Melinda Britton grabbed Eleanore's hand, put a finger to her mouth to silence her and drew her back into the kitchen.

"Eleanore, let them stay the night here. The best Thanksgiving gift I could have would be a swarm of children. They'd be no bother. Nelle here is anxious to talk to Rachel about the wedding music, and Sadie is a joy to have around. All of you should stay and have Thanksgiving here with us tomorrow."

Mrs. Adams beamed in agreement. "Eleanore, as you have seen, there's more than enough food here. There's no way on Earth we can eat this all alone, and I hate to see my work go to waste!"

Eleanore swept a lock of hair off her forehead. The prospect of hauling the band home in the rickety wagon was not pleasing. It would be difficult to get the women into the house alone. Sadie and Rachel still needed their rest, and it seemed unfair to wake the children. Finally, she looked up and said, "They can stay, but I have to go home. I'll be back tomorrow with more food. They're all yours! I must say, I could do with a night's sleep in my own bed again!"

Nelle grinned, but suddenly looked very serious. "Eleanore, why do you have to go back? Won't you be afraid?"

"First of all, Will expects us to be home. He's to be our guest of honor at dinner tomorrow. With your permission, I have to leave a note to invite him here. And, I also want to fix up two of my old dresses for Sadie and Rachel tomorrow. They don't have any decent clothes and I thought it would cheer them up."

"My dear, Will Gray is very welcome to come here, and we understand quite well how dresses can improve spirits!" said Mrs. Adams. "We will plan then to see you by noon. We will hold dinner until the men come in. Have a safe trip home."

The women saw Eleanore off. They assured her that they would put everyone to bed properly and that she needn't worry. Eleanore took the reins in her hands and headed off into the dark for her own cabin.

*****

While those who remained in Dean's Creek gathered at the Adamses on the eve of Thanksgiving Day, Will Gray rode his horse recklessly across the roads that went between Cedarville and Dean's Creek. The cold night air whipped his face raw. His eyes teared in the wind. He had not changed his clothes or bathed for days. The stench of stale perspiration rose to fill his nostrils. He rode alone. Two men from his band of the posse had been sent back earlier. They would not have reached Dean's Creek yet. Their horses were not as capable as his. The remaining members of the posse band had opted to camp at nightfall and complete the journey in the light of day.

His mind turned with the events of the manhunt. The band of the posse that had been least likely to find Leffert, his own that went for Cedarville, had come the closest to the man's trail. While Will and his men meandered through the small dots of communities and bare open spaces that spread between Cedarville and Dean's Creek, Hank Leffert had been in Cedarville. In Leffert's wake, a man died in the tavern in Cedarville. There were twelve witnesses to Leffert's latest deed. While Will stopped to see Emmy Gray, Leffert departed. By the time Will learned of the tavern murder, a posse had formed in Cedarville to chase the murderer. The Dean's Creek posse joined with the Cedarville posse to scour the countryside. Not a solitary trace of Leffert was found, and all efforts were temporarily disbanded. Facing failure when one had been so close to success was not easy, and Will Gray brooded. With every rise and fall of his horse's hooves, there chanted through his skull the nightmarish reminder that Hank Leffert could be back in Dean's Creek.

He did not get back to Dean's Creek until nearly ten o'clock in the morning Thanksgiving Day. He stopped to wash his face and exchange the stale shirt for a fresh one beside the freezing waters of the creek before going on to Eleanore's. Although he was exhausted, fear shot an energy through him that drove him on.

It was a clear and cold morning. The sun actually filtered down for one rare day. The sight of Eleanore's cabin brought relief to him. From a distance, he could spy the roof. Suddenly, he pulled his horse to a halt. He could see no smoke from the chimney. He drove the weary beast on as quickly as he could. Horror flooded his heart. The door of the cabin stood wide open. The horse-hitched wagon stood before the open door. The hens cackled. Toby ran out towards him, tongue wagging and tail thumping. As he dismounted, the dog rubbed against his legs and whimpered.

"Ellie! It's me, Will!" he shouted as he neared the doorway. He turned and went for his gun when no reply came. Slowly, he went through the open door. The sight that appeared before him was the materialization of his worst fears, his most tormented imaginings. The curtains were torn from the windows. The pillows and feather ticks were slashed. Down covered every inch of the room. A smoldering log had burned and scorched the cherished blue rug. Chairs were broken and piled about like limbs in a flooded river. The portraits that had lined the walls were smashed. Jar after jar of preserves and canned vegetables lay broken and strewn everywhere. Will's eyes worked quickly. In a second's time, he had scanned the room and his eyes came to rest on two bodies that lay lifelessly twisted together below the loft.

Hank Leffert laid face up, arms and legs flung wide. His eyes were open, staring in horror. The front of his chest was a gelatinous mound of purple-red blood. Caught beneath his body, entangled in the broken loft ladder, was Eleanore Gray. Her face was turned away from Will. He moved toward her, slowly at first, then as rapidly as he could. His heart pounded. His entire body trembled. He roughly pulled the massive corpse off from her and slowly turned the body of his beloved over. Her eyes were closed. The side of her head was bruised nearly black. He put his head to her chest, but he could not hear her heartbeat above his own pounding heart. He forced himself to be still as he fearfully watched her chest. It subtly heaved up and down, almost imperceptibly. He watched again. It repeated. His eyes filled with tears and he cried out, "Oh, God, she's alive! She's alive!"

Chapter XXVIII
THE WEDDING

Eleanore could not open her right eye. She moved her left eye around slowly. Massive pink hydrangeas, blurred and blocked by the swelling of her eyelid, seemed to envelop her. The world, it seemed, had filled with hydrangeas of extraordinary size during her leave of absence.

"Well, I do declare! 'Bout time ye woke yeself up! Been a sleepin' off and on fer two days, Miz Gray!" cackled an ugly but familiar voice. "Lawd o' mercy! Done yerself up fine. They sent for that city doctor with the driving machine, but he took so long gettin' here he ain't here yet. Good thing fer ye my Rachel had sense enough to come fetch me. Yessir, damn good thing," continued the dried-up voice.

Eleanore pried open her one good eye and tried to wrench her head in the direction of the sound. Her eye passed over nothing but more hydrangeas. She smelled pipe smoke. "Granny Matterson, is that you?"

Quite suddenly, there appeared before Eleanore's eye the wizened features of the toothless old woman. The face loomed closer and closer until it was less than six inches from the eye. "It's me. Who else around here would know about doctoring! Only you and me, Miz Gray, and ye's sure not the doctor woman this time! Ha, ha!"

"Flowers. Hydrangeas. There were hydrangeas at my grandmother's house," murmured Eleanore.

"If ye be meaning these pink flowers on the wallpaper, ye best git it clear that they's just paper. Ain't no hand...han... whatevers ye said around here. It's snowing outside."

Eleanore could hear the old woman rise and close the door. She heard voices whispering and moments later the door opened. Heavy footsteps crossed the floor. She could hear fabric rustling.

A strong hand—a hand so warm that it seemed to be fiery hot—engulfed her own. "Ellie, are you awake?" asked Will Gray.

Eleanore struggled to focus. Her eye kept rolling. It hurt to turn her head. Pain tore up her arm. "Will!" she cried out.

"Stay still, Ellie. Don't move or excite yourself. You've got a concussion, we think. Your face is pretty injured on the right side, but it's just bruised and swollen. Your arm's hurt, but Granny tended it. You are going to recover just fine. You need to sleep," he soothed in a soft and serious voice.

"Hank Leffert, Will. Is he dead?" she asked, choking on her terror.

"Yes, thank God. Now, don't you talk anymore. Nelle is bringing in a cup of herb tea that Granny brewed. It should make you sleepy. Just rest. We'll talk later." Will released his grip and rose.

During the next few days, Eleanore slowly began to recover. The bruises changed color, the swelling that blocked her vision eased, and she grew restless, eager to move about. As she rested in the bed in Melinda Britton's room, her children came to visit her. They were never allowed to stay long. Nelle Adams read to her. Granny sat by her side for hours, smoking her pipe and talking endlessly about her medical experiences. Will Gray appeared at odd hours of the day and night. He forbade her to talk much. He simply held her hand. Outside her room, she could hear Rachel Matterson's perfect voice repeating the same songs over and over again. Once she heard Janey crying, but she was too weak to rise to go to her child. Finally, after a torturous week of confinement, Will came into the room and said, "Today, Eleanore Gray, you are invited to the front parlor."

She was led out on his arm. It was difficult to balance on wobbly legs, and the trip from the downstairs bedroom into the front parlor lasted an eternity. The parlor was filled with her family, the Adamses, Rachel, and Sophie. The children clapped and clamored at her appearance. The afternoon produced celebration. Her children eagerly showered her with trinkets and pencil sketches they had made during her confinement. Nelle played the organ, while Nancy and Rachel sang a duet. Mr. Adams spoke of the plans for rebuilding the church. There was cake, cider, and wedges of custard pie. Eleanore basked in the long-awaited afternoon until it became clear to all but herself that she was exhausted. Will Gray escorted her back to her room.

She wished the pink hydrangeas were real. He guided her into the bed and drew a flounced coverlet, a blanket peppered with delicate pink rosebuds, up to her neck. He stirred the fire and sat by her side. Eleanore reached her hand out to grab his.

"Ellie, are you ready to talk about what happened? Do you remember anything at all?" he asked.

"I remember far more than I'd like to," she replied. "We came here to the Adamses on Thanksgiving eve for a church meeting. It was grand. Everyone was too tired to go home afterwards, so I left them here and went home alone to finish up some things I needed to do and to leave you a note to meet us here for Thanksgiving dinner. When I got home, I knew something was wrong. I shouldn't have gone inside. The door was ajar, but no lights were burning. When I stepped inside, I lit the lamp and the whole room seemed nothing but a mass of debris. Everything was hacked up. There were feathers and broken things everywhere, but I didn't think anyone was there with me until I bent down to pick up a piece of a cup that had belonged to my mother. It was smashed."

She had to clear her throat before she could continue. "I heard him breathing behind me, behind the door. I knew it was him. Somehow I think I put the light out. It was dark, very dark. His hands brushed my skirt. He laughed. I got the gun, though. It was on the hook by the bed. I hid it in my cloak so he wouldn't know I'd gotten it. After a bit, I realized that the fire was still going, just enough to let me see. That meant he could see, too. Oh, God, I was so terrified!

"Hank grabbed me and he laughed again. It was the evilest laugh in the world. He pressed against me. He smelled dirty. His breath had liquor on it. I couldn't get him away from me. He kept saying, 'Come on, now, ye must need some lovin', little widow lady. Ye owes me that much. I knows ye been keepin' my Sadie here, widow lady. She's told ye plenty. Ye jes' pay me off, now.' I got away. I kicked him hard and I got away. I ran to get up to the loft. I was going to take the ladder up with me so he couldn't get to me, but before I got all the way up, he pulled the ladder and I fell to the floor. My arm wouldn't work. I laid there, watching him come down to the floor near me. Somehow, I think I shot him. I heard a noise and I felt him fall on me and then I can't remember anything."

Eleanore's face was covered with tears. She looked longingly at Will, hoping that he could somehow abolish her remembrance, tell her it was a dream.

"You shot him, Ellie. You saved your own life. I'm sure he would have killed you. He's killed over far less. He shot a man in Cedarville, and we couldn't catch him," said Will. "Killing a man is not easy, Ellie, but you did what had to be done."

"I know you're right, but it was so horrible. It was like being seized by Satan and having to ask the Lord if there wasn't an easier way out. There wasn't anything else I could do."

Will rose and looked down at her. He tenderly brushed the hair back from her forehead. "It's over. I love you. Rest, now."

Eleanore rested and rested until she could rest no more. She itched to be busy, to have work to relieve her from reliving her nightmare. Will urged the Adams women to draw her out, to plunge her into the thick of wedding and Christmas preparations that busied the entire household.

Sadie and Rachel, with little Peter, left the Adams household to return to the Leffert cabin. With Eleanore and Nelle's help, and with a bit of volunteered labor from Mr. Dean, they repaired the cabin, whitewashed the walls, sewed curtains from a piece of fabric that Melinda Britton donated, and quickly transformed the dingy cabin into a home that would be the center of a new life for them.

Sadie never mourned the death of her husband. Once, in fact, she drew near to even thanking Eleanore for saving her life by killing the man, but Rachel silenced her before she spoke the awful truth aloud. Sadie was, for the first time in her adult life, at peace. She radiated cheer.

Rachel, though busy with Nelle's wedding, did not recover the easy gaiety that had once been the beacon of her presence. She took to wearing a bitter expression, a stony face that told the world that she had endured and survived more trouble in her young life than anyone would imagine possible. She never sang during her work anymore. She rose early every day, donned her sour outlook, and busied her hands as if they would give her salvation. Eleanore noticed it all, saw fragments of herself in the girl, but was unable to minimize the hurt and torment that plagued Rachel.

Days passed before Eleanore entered her own cabin again. She lacked the strength to face it. One afternoon, after work at Sadie's had ended, she walked over to her home. At first she hesitated to open the door. Then she whipped out an arm, pushed the door wide, and strode inside. Someone had removed the debris. The floors had been swept clean. The burn in the blue rug was covered by a small hooked rug. There were unfamiliar pillows and a quilt on the bed. Jars of fruit and vegetables, jars that had never been touched by her own hands, stood neatly on the pantry shelves. Curtains of light blue and cream-printed calico were at every window. It was as if the cabin had never been the site for the killing, or if she had walked into someone else's cabin. She never learned who had restored her home.

Eleanore and her children continued to stay with the Adamses for another week. When Eleanore asked Nelle if she knew who had fixed up her home, Nelle only replied, "Friends, Ellie. You don't need to go back until you want to. Having you and the children here has been a joy and we shall hate to see you leave."

During the week, the Grays helped with wedding and Christmas preparations. The work seemed endless. During the days, the children made ornaments and little gifts under Nelle's guidance, while Eleanore assisted Mrs. Adams in the kitchen. In the evenings, long after the children were fast asleep, Melinda and Eleanore stayed up by the fire in the parlor, putting the finishing touches of embroidery on Nelle's trousseau. Eleanore's capable fingers had not lost their skill during the years of farm-

ing. She held up a lace-edged pillowslip that had been decorated with primroses and French knots of baby's breath. It was
as fine a piece of work as even Melinda might produce. Melinda
gave the work a side glance. "Eleanore, if you stay here any longer, you will be the finest artist in the valley!"

"Melinda, thank you. I had almost forgotten that I once did
this all winter long. I'm afraid farm life doesn't give a woman
much time for such idleness," replied Eleanore. Eleanore looked
down at her pillowslip and smiled. She knew that Nelle Adams
would have a perfect life with Harvey Littlefield. That very pillowslip would rest under their heads some night. She hoped
that every ounce of care she had worked into it would seep out
and bless them. She sighed. "Melinda, it's nearly Christmas. I
want the children to spend Christmas at home. We've stayed far
too long. I am so very grateful for all the care and kindness you
have given us, but we must go home on Monday."

Eleanore and her children boarded the rickety wagon after
breakfast on Monday morning. They were all quiet during the
ride home, but the sight of the cabin at the end of the lane was
a welcome one that prompted the children to scramble down
and run the last length of the hill to the door. Smoke rolled
lazily up from the chimney, and Eleanore knew that her homecoming had been anticipated. When she went through the door,
the first thing that greeted her was a huge tree that Will Gray
had brought for their Christmas. Sitting before a roaring fire in
a new rocking chair was the tall, lean frame of Will Gray. He
rose and swept his arms in a low formal bow. "Welcome home,
Ellie."

While the children inspected every inch of the house and
marveled at new furnishings, Will and Eleanore sat by the fire.
Will told Eleanore that he was making a final trip to Benchfield
to get some shopping done before the wedding. "I think, Ellie,
that I'm going to break down and buy myself a new suit of

clothes. I wouldn't want to spoil Nelle's big day by showing up like the country bumpkin! There isn't perchance anything you'd like me to pick up while I'm in town, is there? You know, like peppermint sticks or rag dolls?"

"Well, actually, I'm afraid I haven't got much for the children this year. I've got ten dollars saved up, but no place to spend it. You wouldn't be able to play Santa for me, would you?" said Eleanore as she rose and went into the kitchen. She lifted a brick from the back wall behind the stove and withdrew her precious cache. When she returned to the front room, she found her children dragging the box of Christmas ornaments out from under the bed. She smiled. "Children, would you be so kind as to run out to the henhouse to get the eggs before we trim the tree? Heaven only knows how many eggs have been sitting out there!"

Once the children had rushed to their chore, Eleanore turned to Will. "Here's my money. What we need will be candy for certain, a new dolly for Janey, a pair of good boots for Paul, and some picture books for Nancy. Use whatever is left over to get anything else you think the children might like. Paul wears a size five boot, and Nancy likes romantic books. Oh! And we'll be needing some lengths of pink satin ribbon for the wedding for the girls. Too much to handle?"

Will shot her a pretend hurt look. "Not on your life. It will be a pleasure. I'm heading out today. I should be back by nightfall. If you need anything, Sadie and Rachel are just down the lane. By the way, before I forget again, I've had a letter to you from Emmy Gray in my pocket ever since I was in Cedarville. I thought you might just like to have it."

Will left. The children returned and were permitted to start trimming the tree. Although Eleanore usually reserved that pleasure for Christmas Eve, she wanted to make the homecoming a special event. While Paul unwound lengths of silver paper, Janey played with the tiny angels that would be hung from every bough, and Nancy polished the glass baubles that would make the tree shimmer in the firelight. Eleanore gave them free reign. She nestled into the new chair and carefully opened the letter from Emmy. She read the letter twice, folded it as if it were a hundred dollar bill, and put it up on the mantle. The news it contained would be kept a secret present to her family that would be guarded until Christmas.

Nelle and Harvey Littlefield were to marry on Christmas Eve at the Adams home. They were going to be married in the early evening by the light of candles that would line the entire front parlor. As early as ten o'clock that morning, preparations began in the Gray house. Sadie and Rachel arrived at Eleanore's by noon. Eleanore had promised to help them with their dresses and take them over to the Adams farm by three o'clock. A contagious fever of excitement spread through the house during preparations. It struck everyone except Rachel.

Rachel practiced her song for them, but it lacked the swell of emotion that usually made her singing such a joy. Although every note was perfected, they all rang flat, deadened by the girl's gloom. Everyone knew it, but no one dared speak of it. Eleanore hoped it would not be so noticeable that evening.

Sophie Dean, Melinda Britton, and Eleanore had spent weeks working on a dress for Rachel. It was her first formal dress gown, of a light blue fabric. It gathered below her bosom empire-style, and fell into a narrow train that was accented by layers of horizontal tucks. From under the blue, high-collared yoke poured layers of a filmy white-laced fabric that formed the sleeves. They were full, but transparent and graceful. The same lace fabric fell behind her down the back of the gown. A pale blue satin sash was bound around the high empire waist. She had white kid slippers, white gloves, and a wide-brimmed hat to complete the ensemble. It took two women to get her into the gown. When she finally emerged from the bedroom and stood in Eleanore's parlor, every mouth gaped in wonder. The girl looked as if she were lifted from one of Nancy's picture books. Her beauty, though marred by a stern face, was undeniable.

The wedding, the most anticipated event in the valley, brought friends and neighbors together from every part of the valley and beyond. Before the ceremony, the valley people in all their finery mingled with the city Littlefields. Whatever social graces the country people may have lacked went unnoticed in the warmth and hospitality that they exuded.

With some amusement, Eleanore and Will watched Granny Matterson, by far the most peculiar thing city eyes had ever fallen on, flirt with an elderly Littlefield uncle. He had a childishly pink complexion that turned crimson every time Granny reached over to swat him on the sleeve during one of her jokes. Eleanore suspected his snowy moustache covered a mouth that was either grimacing or grinning at each onslaught. Granny's cackle disconcerted him, and he frequently turned to gaze around the room in embarrassment. When Granny's pipe fell from a side pocket in her dress, he gallantly stooped to retrieve it, returned it to the baffling old woman with dignified ceremony, and drifted off into the crowd in hopes of escaping.

The most surprising and pleasing thing to occur before the ceremony took place when Henry Adams introduced a young gentleman to Rachel Matterson. Eldon Littlefield, younger cousin to Harvey Littlefield, was the handsomest youth Eleanore had ever encountered. In him, each of Harvey's fine features was magnified. His brown eyes had more depth, his smile a broader sweep, his auburn hair a higher luster. Beaming, he bowed to Rachel and whispered some polite expression that Eleanore could not hear. It was Rachel's response that brought sudden joy to Eleanore. For the first time in many weeks, the girl smiled with genuine pleasure. Eleanore watched Rachel's gaze follow the man as he drifted off into the crowd.

When Rachel sang that evening, it was with her heart. Eleanore could not avoid noticing that the girl seemed to see only Eldon Littlefield when she let the notes pour into the room. Her eyes were fastened on the young man who stood at the back of the room. Sadie, who stood next to Eleanore, nudged Eleanore in the side with her finger and cocked an eyebrow. Sadie had also noticed the effect of Eldon Littlefield.

Melinda Britton cried uncontrollably during the exchange of vows. She hid her eyes in a gauzy handkerchief and did not raise her head until it was certain that her niece and Harvey were pronounced man and wife. Mr. and Mrs. Adams held hands throughout the ceremony and beamed. It was clear that Harvey Littlefield was the ideal husband in their minds for the precious Nelle.

The ceremony was concluded and followed by refreshments. Although the crowd was small, gifts were heaped upon the side tables. Mrs. Adams had made a three-tier vanilla cake that could have been envied by the most capable pastry chef in the country. It was adorned with crystallized violets and sugared mint leaves. As the guests sat eating the delicacy and sipping sherry, they spoke of the wedding and of their wishes for the bride and groom. Granny Matterson, undone by spirits, waved a crumb-covered fork about as she loudly proclaimed, "Purtiest wedding I ever been to, and I been to many a wedding in my day. City folk know how to do it up! Lord o' mercy, that Nelle and her beau, why they looks as if they's enchanted and stabbed by the pixies!" Her pronouncement was loud enough to still everyone in the room for a moment. It was followed by hearty laughter from every corner.

Eleanore could not keep her eyes off Rachel. The girl stood in a corner, talking to another young woman and Eldon Littlefield. Her cheeks were pink and her talk was animated.

When Will escorted Eleanore and her passengers out to the buggy after the celebration, he wished her a safe journey home and whispered that Santa Claus could be expected in their household early the next morning. The ride home was pleasant. Rachel, though silent, smiled as they bumped down the lane. The children, full of cake, drowsed.

Long after the children were tucked into bed, Eleanore sat before the fire. The wedding she had helped prepare for so many weeks had ended in a matter of hours. She smiled as she thought of Harvey and Nelle. They would wake in the bedroom of pink hydrangeas the next morning to face a new life together. The girl who had stood before the crowd that evening, who had seemed so terribly beautiful and serene in the cream-colored dress, was launched into a life that she had only before dreamed of and longed for.

As Eleanore removed her heavy wrapper and pulled back the unfamiliar star pattern quilt on her bed, she was struck by the image of Will Gray. In the finery of the new Norfolk suit that he had purchased for the wedding, he had seemed taller, prouder, and far more handsome than she could ever remember him being before. She wondered if, like Nelle and Harvey, there was even a slight chance that they, too, would embark on a new life, a life for which she was starting to hanker. Before she blew out the lamp, her eye turned to meet the picture of Bob Gray, now cracked by Hank Leffert's fist, which rested on the side table. With a heaviness of heart, she slept.

Chapter XXIX

HOLY NIGHT

ELEANORE GRAY ROSE IN the dark on Christmas morning. She dressed and went into the kitchen. By the light of a kerosene lamp, she handled tin pans with silent gentleness. For Christmas breakfast, there would be the traditional stollen that her own mother had prepared each holiday. It was a sweet yeasty bread that was fused with spices, raisins, and a delectable hodge-podge of dried fruits. When Eleanore was a girl, she had regarded this creation as a special gift in itself. As she folded the dough, she could taste, from memory, the special mingling of fruit and spice that had earmarked her own childhood Christmases.

Toby, who had patiently snored near the warm stove throughout her work, uttered a low growl. Eleanore placed her cup of coffee on the worn tabletop, brushed floury hands against her apron, and ran as silently as possible to the front door. Will Gray had arrived as promised, early. She admitted the frosty man with only a warm smile and a cautionary finger to her lips as a greeting. He stamped his feet with exaggerated quietness and entered the dark and silent cabin. Together, like conspirators, Eleanore and Will untied the bundle that was flung over his shoulder. Beneath the tree they arranged a mound of gaily ribboned and wrapped gifts. Eleanore lit candles and lined them around the parlor. The effect was pleasing, almost magical enough to make this Christmas rise above the turmoil that had warped the preceding weeks.

As Will sat in the kitchen sipping the steaming cup of black brew, Eleanore again worked the dough that had risen into a white mountain in an earthenware bowl. She kneaded it, flattened it, filled it, and wound it up. She decorated the top and placed it in the dark, hot oven.

Her children rose as the sun began to peek through the darkness. They rose to the scent of baking, the sight of a room aglow with wax candles, and the precious piles of parcels wrapped in bright papers and printed flour sacking. Their still sleepy eyes widened. "Oh, Mama, it is so beautiful!" screamed Nancy. Janey ran to touch every treasure beneath the tree. Paul shook a box that bore his name.

"Enough of that! You'll get dressed and eat breakfast before you open a single gift!" forbade Eleanore with mock curtness.

Will smiled as he and Eleanore watched bare feet and flannel retreat. "I think we are a success, Eleanore!" he whispered. "I've never seen them look so excited. The train in Benchfield didn't even warrant that much enthusiasm. And that smell coming from the stove is something from another world."

Will teased the children unmercifully during breakfast. Between large mouthfuls of the rich stollen, he managed to stir their curiosity to an unprecedented pitch. "Janey," he said, "I met the most peculiar man on my way up your lane this morning. He drove a red wagon with the queerest team of horses I've ever laid eyes on. Every one of the creatures had antlers like old tree branches sprouting from their heads. The man himself was mighty odd, too. He wore a red suit and had full whiskers that were as white as snow itself. When I tipped my hat at him and said good morning, all he said was, 'Ho-ho-ho!' and then he went on down your lane."

Janey's eyes widened. "Mama, who was it? Did he come here?" Eleanore studied her tiny daughter's face, and then seriously replied, "Well, somebody sure did! I was terribly busy in the kitchen and didn't hear a thing, but when I went into the parlor to light the candles, there were packages everywhere that seemed to have come from out of the blue! It gave me quite a turn!"

Nancy, the older and wiser, nearly rolled her eyes in disbelief. She caught herself and decided to aid the fabrication. "Mama, do you think it was St. Nick?"

Eleanore threw her hands wide in a gesture of uncertainty. "You know, nobody else fits that description, and Will himself saw it!"

Paul, who was skeptical but not unwilling, searched Will's face for some sign that a joke was at work. Will's features gave him no clues. The man sipped his coffee and tackled a third slice of stollen.

When breakfast was over, the dishes were left undone. Eleanore rose and ordered, "Everyone stay put a little longer." As she had done for years, she fetched a battered black leather Bible and seated herself. As she read the Nativity story from the book of St. Matthew, her children listened with quiet reverence. As soon as the final words were uttered, however, the youngsters erupted and scrambled madly for the parlor. Their excitement could be contained no longer.

Nancy, the eldest, was allowed to open her gifts first. The books that Will selected were immediately cherished. The girl could barely be coerced to set them aside long enough to open her other gifts. She unwrapped her share of penny candy, the light blue woolen stockings that the Benchfield clerk had selected for Will, a beaded brooch from the Adamses, various colored lengths of hair ribbon and a delicate music box from Will himself. She murmured her thanks and distributed kisses of gratitude, then retreated to the rocker to suck a stick of peppermint and pour over the books that had caught her heart.

Paul was next. While Janey was pacified with a piece of candy and the honor of sitting in Will's broad lap, Paul pranced about in his new boots. Will beckoned to the boy and pointed a sturdy finger at a long parcel wrapped in a plain brown paper. "Better open that one, Paul. Sometimes our best treasures come to us in plain coverings."

The boy's fingers shredded the paper until they came to rest on the smooth, polished wood of a rifle stock. The boy stroked his first gun with wonder and pride. He held it up and practiced aiming at the mantle. "We're going squirrel hunting, ain't we, Uncle Will?"

"You bet, Paul. I'm going to make you the best shot in the hills," replied Will with pleasure. Will winked at Eleanore. The woman's eyes filled with tears.

"Oh, Will, I can't thank you enough for making my son so happy!" she cried out and hurried over to the man and wrapped her arms around both Will and Janey. "Thank you."

Janey was slow to open her packages. Her fingers, though small, were not nimble enough to undo the ribbons that bound the papers. With her mother's help, they eventually laid bare a doll with blonde curls and rolling blue glass eyes. "Mama, it's Nelle!" squealed the tot. The little girl rode the Nelle doll around the room on a new stick horse that Will had made, and crooned an off-key song that was hopelessly unrecognizable.

Under the fat boughs of the tree rested only two very small packages that were bedecked with glittered paper and fancy bows. One bore Eleanore's name in fine script, the other bore Will's name in identical script. "You first, Ellie. It looked like

Santa shopped at the same store for both of us!" announced Will. Paul and Janey ceased their play and Nancy even tore her eyes away from her romance long enough to watch the two adults open their own gifts.

All eyes were upon Eleanore as she undid the fashionable bow that ran around her box. Inside was a pendant, a brilliant garnet set in a simple gold frame. Eleanore looked up from the jeweler's box to meet Will's gaze. "This is magnificent! Truly magnificent!" Much to the children's surprise and delight, their mother scooped up the remaining gift that lay beneath the tree, crossed the room, laid a kiss upon the gentleman's forehead, and handed him her gift to him.

Will opened the little jeweler's box. Nestled against the velvet that lined the box was a gold watch. The cover piece was etched with an ornate hunting scene. Will whistled and held the fine object up for the children to admire. When he pushed the catch to open the watch face, his eyes fastened on an inscription on the inside of the cover piece. It read, "To Will to keep our time by." The man turned to face his beloved. "Ellie, this is the most precious gift I have ever received, and I'll keep it with me always." He pulled Eleanore to him in a modest embrace and murmured into her hair, "I love you, dear one. Merry Christmas." The children applauded the embrace. Eleanore, grateful that Will's words were for her ears only, pushed back a strand of hair and blushed.

The children retreated into their room and reentered the parlor with a show of ceremony as they presented Will and Eleanore with the gifts that they had secreted away for this special day. Eleanore admired a tatted hankie, a crocheted doily, a crude clay pot, and a pastel picture that her children had produced for her. Will praised and thanked the youngsters for a cheap pocket knife that they had somehow managed to acquire from the Benchfield general store. Paul proudly offered explanation. "We saved back some of our birthday money from Aunt Emmy and Mr. Adams got this in Benchfield for us!"

The rest of Christmas day was filled with more merriment and cheer than any of them had imagined possible. Rachel, Sadie, and little Peter came for hot wild turkey, carols, and mulled cider. Will and Eleanore waltzed to the tune of Nancy's music box. The children played dominoes and marbles. In the early evening, while the guests were finishing their wedges of mincemeat pie with top cream, Will took Eleanore outside.

They opened the door of the cabin to face a whirl of heavy snow that had silently covered the trees and slopes with dazzling beauty during the afternoon's celebrations. "Right on cue, Mrs. Gray!" said Will as they stepped off the porch. "There's a little something else for you in my wagon."

When Will pulled back a tarp that covered the wagon bed, he exposed a pine chest that gleamed golden. Fat snowflakes flocked it as they fell. As Eleanore's eyes swept the length and breadth of the perfectly worked wood, Will's fingers made a heart in the snow that had fallen on it. He worked their initials in the snow until he produced the crude emblem of love that many a Hill youth had left etched into the bark of a tree. Eleanore leaned against him, took in the warmth and scent of her gentle giant, and held onto him as if she never wished to separate from his side. Will stroked her hair. He finally hooked a finger under her chin and raised her head to meet his, and they kissed with all the passion that had been postponed.

The evening closed in on a day that had equaled only their greatest hopes. Rachel sang "Silent Night" in the glow of the parlor, and everyone raised the final refrains in unison. Before the guests took their leave, Will asked that they all join him in the barn. It was a mysterious request that caused eyebrows to raise, but it was heeded.

Wrapped in scarves and covered with coats and snow, the entire group made its way through the snow that piled up. "Now, ladies, I'm going to take you home in the wagon and in a moment you will see why," offered Will with an air of mystery. Inside the barn, near Jersey and her offspring, stood a black and white cow.

Will patted the beast on the head. "This critter isn't likely to talk, but she will give milk. This is my present to you, Rachel and Sadie. It's something long overdue down at your place, from what I hear!"

"Lawd o' mercy!" cried Sadie. "Oh, Mister Gray, I can't begin to thank you!" The woman shyly patted the cow's head, then abruptly stood on tiptoe and laid an embarrassed kiss on Will's cheek. "Lawd o' mercy!" she cried again.

As the guests piled into the wagon and as Will tied the cow to the back, Paul and Nancy fetched feed to tide them over. Eleanore helped Will. When the job was completed, Will Gray took Eleanore's hand in his. "I want to thank you for giving me the finest Christmas I have ever known. I have to go away for a few days, Ellie. Matter in Cedarville over Leffert. Authorities want me to help tie up some loose ends in their paperwork. Trip may take a little longer than usual because of the weather, but I promise to be back by the New Year. You stay well and don't worry about me." He placed a kiss on the top of her snowy head and mounted the wagon.

As the wagon departed, they all shouted "Merry Christmas" and waved to each other. Only when the wagon was out of sight did Eleanore finally follow her children inside to the warmth of the parlor. The wreckage of a day's festivities awaited their hands, but Eleanore urged no one to sort through the debris or to wash the plates and pans that lay heaped on the kitchen table. She bade her youngsters to wash and dress for bed.

By the light of the fire, they again read the Christmas story. Her children's faces, aglow in the heat that leaped and spat, studied her as her mouth moved over the familiar phrases of St. Matthew. As Eleanore closed the book and rose to place it on the mantle, her eyes caught sight of the letter from Emmy Gray. She whirled around to face her flock. "I nearly forgot the biggest surprise of all!" she cried. "Your Aunt Emmy is coming to visit this spring!"

Chapter XXX

PEACE ON EARTH

OF ALL THE MONUMENTAL days that clutter a calendar year, New Year's Day—the entry date—is the most important in Hill folklore. Generation after generation of Hill people have believed, beyond any rational evidence to the contrary, that New Year's Day holds the key to the entire passage of the duration of the year. It is believed that to hang a new calendar on the wall before sun up on New Year's Day will lead one to disaster. Almanacs, the most respected sources of information about planting for the coming year, remain unopened until the year is truly begun lest curiosity drive one to pursue bad luck. Unexpected visitors on New Year's Day mean that the year will be filled with unexpected surprises, both good and bad. Even the most driven housewife refrains from doing laundry on the first day of the year; to do so would insure that the rest of the year would contain nothing but drudgery.

On the other hand, Hill folk believe that to remain too idle on the advent of the year will lead one to spend the rest of the year in wasteful laziness. No matter how cold or wet it may be outside, the windows of homes are thrown wide just before midnight of New Year's Day to let out the spirits of ill luck and to admit the spirits of good luck. It is not uncommon to see families hauling wood and water for New Year's Day on New Year's Eve. To carry things in and out of the house on New Year's Day is considered by most to lead one to certain poverty. For good luck, many a family eats black-eyed peas on New Year's Day. Some place dimes under the dinner plates for added fortune. If one drinks liquor on New Year's Day, it will bring drunkenness for the rest of the year. In sum, it is believed that how the first day of the year is passed will be indicative of how the remainder of the year will pass. It is not a matter that Hill folk regard lightly.

"Needs more black pepper, Missus Gray!" shouted Sadie as she stirred a blackened kettle of black-eyed peas and hog jowl over Eleanore's fire. "Black pepper and maybe some salt, too," she added as she wiped her hands across her skirt and started rummaging through the pantry shelves.

"They're down there on the bottom shelf, Sadie. You ever going to call me by my first name?" replied Eleanore with a smile.

"Never have before, but I reckon since it's New Year's and I'm a standin' in yer house cooking hoppin' john that it's time. Eleanore is a purty name. Rolls off the tongue, don't it?" replied Sadie. As a matter of habit, she raised her hand to conceal the toothless gaps in her smile.

The children played in the parlor. Rachel sat in the rocker reading a romance borrowed from Nancy. Eleanore, anxious for Will Gray's promised arrival, lifted her skirts to trespass through the glass and clay marbles that littered the blue carpet to go to the window to see if there was any sign of his wagon or horse yet. It was nearly noon and the white carpet of snow that had fallen since the arrival of Sadie and Rachel remained unmarked. With some disappointment, Eleanore lifted the latch and let Toby out. She wondered if, in accordance with the superstitions of the hills, she would spend the remainder of the New Year waiting for the man.

Like a child who had no concept of time or patience, she kept glancing up at the clock. Twenty minutes passed as slowly as twenty days. Toby barked to be let in. Again she went to the door, lifted the latch and opened it. At the bottom of the lane was a wagon loaded with furniture that seemed to dangle and escape the strappings of a flimsy tarp that covered the entire wagon bed. Eleanore stepped out for a better look.

The cold nearly struck her down. It went for her bones. Wet winds of snow and drizzle whipped her hair over her eyes. The wagon seemed to be coming up the lane, but at a snail's pace. She looked down at Toby and said, "If that's Will, it looks as if he brought me more furniture or something. That man is full of surprises!"

As the wagon progressed, it became clear that two people were in the front seat. Eleanore squinted. It was impossible to recognize their faces. Both were covered with scarves and broad-rimmed hats. She could, however, recognize Will's horses. She waved and one of the figures waved back. Toby leapt off the porch steps and galloped toward the heavily laden wagon that rocked ever so slowly up the lane. Eleanore, nearly frozen in her dress and shawl, ran into the house. "Sadie, put hot coffee on! We've got company! Nancy, set another place at the table!" she commanded.

After Will drove the team and wagon into the barn, he and the other passenger scurried to the cabin door. Will rapped hard on the door and stood back. Ellie opened the door and let out a delighted scream. Before her, wrapped in thick layers of men's clothing, stood Emmy Gray. The two women threw their arms around each other before Eleanore ushered her welcome guests to the fire.

That New Year's Day proved to be the most eventful in Eleanore's entire life. When the nine people crowded into the kitchen and seated themselves to heaping plates of black-eyed peas, each of them knew that the coming year would be unlike all others. Eleanore could scarcely eat. She alternately beamed at Will Gray and Emmy Gray with more pleasure and more lightness of heart than she could contain.

"Oh, Will, I simply can't take this in!" she cried aloud later as they sat about the parlor.

Emmy Gray, the only person in Cedarville who had ever mattered to her after the death of her husband, had come, not to visit, but to live in Dean's Creek. Will, under the pretext of a legal visit to Cedarville, had loaded the woman, lock, stock and barrel, into his wagon and delivered her to Eleanore. Will and Emmy had had a rough journey across the snowy roads and paths that led to Dean's Creek. They were both, finally and at last, home.

Emmy, unbecomingly dressed in man's clothing, pushed back the thick hair that was turning gray and sighed. "Eleanore," she said, "I know this is quite a shock and probably quite an inconvenience right now, but I'm so terribly glad that I decided to leave Cedarville to the mercy of the hounds!"

She nervously looked around the room, at the unfamiliar furnishings and faces, and continued. "This past year was more than I could bear. My business went from bad to worse. It was a good thing you never decided to go into the shop with me. You'd have to love hats an awful lot to put up with what I have. First of all, business was slower than ever. People took to ordering ready-mades from the catalogs. It's not like it used to be. You don't have to wait six months for your parcel to come!

And I couldn't compete with the prices those catalogs charged. It was impossible."

"To add insult to injury, the bank came after me when I fell behind in payments on a loan that I had to take out. I had to sell the shop. It was the hardest thing I ever did in my life. And you talk about gossip! Even the people I had regarded as close friends took to sneering at me when I fell on hard times. I had to leave. I simply had to pack up and go."

"I was planning to come in the spring to see this place and to see if I could find a little house out here, but I couldn't hold on any longer. I got word to Will and, God bless him, he came and got me!" concluded the woman weakly. Tears brimmed in her eyes.

Eleanore smiled warmly. "Emmy, I don't care what brought you here. I want to keep you here. My house is yours."

"Well, I'm not coming empty handed. Every piece of equipment I own is out in that wagon. I've got plans, big plans. Starting this spring, I'll be shipping out hats to all parts of the country. I've got orders from catalogs and from some fancy shops in Chicago and St. Louis and Kansas City! All I need is a place to work and some women to put to work. Will said I'd find both here. He said that there's a town not far from here where a train comes through. With all that, and a bit of your hospitality, I'll be set up mighty well."

Will Gray stretched his long frame and leaned against the back of a battered stick-and-ball corner chair. His eyes met Eleanore's then flickered toward Sadie Leffert. Sadie, silent as a mouse, was clearly afire with hopes. Her eyes studied Emmy Gray. Will cleared his throat and said, "If you're needing a hard worker, Emmy, Sadie over here is just your woman!"

"I ain't much of a bargain. I can't read or write, and I don't know a darned thing about hat making. I never even owned a hat 'cept fer a split bonnet to work outside in! I work hard, though, and I ain't never sick, and I sure do like money!" announced Sadie in confusion.

"You'll do just fine, then!" smiled Emmy.

Will, obviously pleased with the match of employer and employee, rose and excused himself. "Ellie, I've got to be going. There's a meeting tonight at Frank's and I planned on going no matter how tired I was. I'll leave the wagon here and ride one of my horses. I'll be back by tomorrow." The tall man turned to face Emmy and said, "Pleasure to have my kin here. You won't regret coming here. No one else has."

Eleanore saw him to the door. She stood on the porch by his side, linked her arm through his and murmured, "It's a pleasure to have you here, too. I missed you." She rose on tiptoe and planted a kiss on his wind-reddened cheek. "By the way, what's this meeting about?"

Will smiled down at her, brushed his large palm across her dark head, and announced, "We're going to build a church."

Everyone went to bed early that night. The day's excitement had drained even the most energetic child. Emmy, Nancy, and Janey slept in the children's room. Paul slept on a pallet before the fire. Toby snored on the blue rug. Eleanore, who had fallen asleep as soon as she pulled the quilt up to her chin, woke shortly after three o'clock in the morning. The sound of the night, the routine snores and tossings of sleepers, was broken by a rustling outside the cabin. Eleanore listened; the unfamiliar rustle persisted. Toby stirred, uttered a low growl and padded his way over to the door. Eleanore rose, pulled on her boots and wrapper, and grabbed the gun. She and Toby stood on the porch listening. Both of them knew that something was going on in the barn. Finally, Eleanore whispered, "Well, Toby, you feel like going out with me to defend the chickens?"

Eleanore took a lantern down from its hook on the porch, lit it, and crept across the yard behind Toby. She held the light high to survey the barn. One of Will Gray's horses stood in a · stall. Her own beasts seemed undisturbed. The chickens were silent but clearly unharmed. "Oh, Toby! We've got the spooks!"

As she whirled around to depart, she faced Will Gray. For an instant, her mouth opened in a silent scream before she recovered. She chuckled at herself and walked toward him. "What on earth are you doing here at this hour?" she asked.

Will neither smiled nor spoke. He crossed his arms and leaned against the door frame. He reeked of liquor. One foot gave way under his weight, but he caught his balance in a weak effort to conceal the state of his intoxication. "Eleanore, I've come here tonight to take one last try. It's a new year, as you and I well know. Are you going to marry me or aren't you?" he slurred.

"Will Gray, you are drunk as a skunk. If your racket hadn't got me out of bed, would you have spent the night out here waiting to ask me that?" she replied.

"Maybe," he said with a playful pout.

"You were supposed to be at a church meeting. Where have you been?"

"At a church meeting."

"I find it hard to believe that you got in this state at a church meeting."

"We had a meeting and we're going to have a church this year. We start working on it in the spring when the grown... er...ground taws...I mean, thaws. After midnight, to celebrate, we had refreshments."

Eleanore smiled with amusement and shook her head from side to side as she announced, "I'll marry you when the church gets built, and only if I never have to see you in this condition again."

The events of that New Year's Day were indeed indicative of the events that filled their lives during the rest of the year.

During the winter months, huddled in the parlor over worktables and shaping molds, Sadie Leffert and Emmy Gray made hats. Rachel processed orders, filled labels, and kept accounts for the blooming enterprise. They produced hats of every conceivable shape, size, and color, and they stored carton after carton of tagged creations in Sadie's cabin until spring. By the end of May, the business proved so profitable that the women were able to afford a stained glass window for the new Dean's Creek Church. In July, Emmy purchased Eleanore's farmhouse and a portion of the eroded land to expand her new millinery establishment.

The church planning meetings persisted throughout that winter. People trudged through the worst snows and coldest winds on record to plot and plan and dream in the warmth of the Adams house. They raised money and hopes, broke ground in the spring, and erected by that summer the sort of structure that they had only dared dream of. It was a real church, a white gabled building, complete with a bell tower, stained glass windows, and a pipe organ. The pipe organ had been donated by some unknown individual. Although no card was attached to the huge crate that arrived via Benchfield, the station master did know that it had arrived from Chicago. The mystery persisted for some time.

Rachel Matterson, who had spent New Year's Day reading romances, had one of her own. In April, Nelle Littlefield invited the Hill girl to stay in Springfield for a spell. Rachel went and never returned. Several years after her departure, a man came to fix the Dean's Creek pipe organ. He knew quite well the tale of its mysterious appearance in Dean's Creek. Quite by accident, he discovered the unknown donor. On the underside of the organ proper was a brass placard no bigger than a dollar bill. The inscription on it read, "A gift from Mr. and Mrs. Eldon Littlefield of Chicago, Illinois." Rachel Matterson had become, only a few months after leaving the hills, the wife of Chicago's most prominent attorney. Nelle Littlefield knew, of course, but she had kept her mouth sealed in girlish conspiracy.

Will and Eleanore were to be married on a sweltering summer day shortly after the completion of the new church. Some days before the ceremony, the Gray children met down by the spring, their voices lowered in conspiratorial whispers.

"What are we gonna call Uncle Will?" Paul was the first to speak. "After he marries Mama?"

Nancy trailed her toes in the water. "Do you think he'll mind if we call him Daddy?"

Paul leapt into the water, splashing Janey, much to the young girl's delight. When he surfaced, he asked, "Who? Uncle Will?"

"No," Nancy replied curtly. "Our father. Do you think he'll mind? In heaven?"

This question brought an uncomfortable silence over the three children. Finally, Janey, in her childlike wisdom, said, "Unca Will is a good daddy. He makes Mama smile. That's good." And she plunged her little body into the water, splashing the thoughtful older children with glee.

That settled it for the children.

Although sweltering on the day Will and Eleanore Gray exchanged vows, every seat in the new church was filled. Valley people sat next to ridge people, all silently dabbing their eyes as the vows were exchanged. Nancy sang; Janey stood next to her mother with a small bouquet of hydrangeas, smiling widely the entire time. Paul walked his mother down the aisle, and stayed to stand with Will.

When the vows were pronounced and the union sealed with a kiss, Will wrapped his family in his arms. "I'm so lucky to have you all."

"We're lucky, too, Daddy," Nancy said, her voice catching.

Tears filled Will's eyes. "Come on, my children," he said, kissing them all on the forehead. "Let's go home."

While the wedding preparations had kept her plenty busy, Eleanore hadn't let herself get lost in them. Instead, she kept a happy eye on the future—a future with Will as her husband. The work would be hard, she knew. Farming the rocky hills and depleted valleys would wear on her as the years passed. Her children would grow up and move on with their own lives. But with Will by her side, Eleanore knew she wouldn't have to face that future alone. And that was more than enough to make her happy.

This I Remember:

A COLLECTIVE BIOGRAPHY OF GOLDIE LUCAS

BY HER CHILDREN AND GRANDCHILDREN

"The facts are the best I can do, and if they are slanted in any way,
it is because that's how I remember them."
Elroy Lucas, February 2006

Goldie M. Lucas
1908–1960

Goldie M. Lucas was born October 9, 1908, at home in Dean's Creek in Camden County, Missouri. Goldie was the eighth child of Lillian and John Wright. John worked as a traveling home and barn painter, leaving Lillian to raise the children mostly alone.

Goldie attended a one-room schoolhouse named George School, where she completed the eighth grade. Around this time, Lillian died and Goldie moved to Tuscumbia, Missouri, where she attended ninth grade. It was her final year of formal schooling.

Once Goldie left school, she moved to Crescent, Missouri, and worked at a boarding house. It was there she met a young man named Walter Lucas. They met on July 7, 1924 and married two weeks later in Hillsboro, Missouri.

Goldie and Walter had a lot of close relatives in Crescent. Later, they moved to Manchester, Missouri, and had their first child, Elroy (1927–2006). They then moved to Des Peres, and had four additional children: Don (1929–present), Naomi (1930–2005), Mary (1932–present), and James (1934–present).

Walter lost his job because the three oldest children angered their father's boss.

Walter got a new job in Kirkwood, and the Lucas family moved into a two-room house with five kids. This house would remain in the Lucas family for several decades. Walter added an additional four rooms, and Goldie added another four children: David (1936 to 2006), Joyce (1941–present), John (1943–present), and Jeannie (1946–present).

Goldie died on February 22, 1960, after a long battle with rheumatoid arthritis. Walter died almost seventeen years later, on February 1, 1977. Goldie and Walter are buried at Glover's Chapel Church of Christ, where Goldie had attended services as a child.

Elroy "Luke" F. Lucas
October 16, 1927–March 27, 2006

In the days of the Great Depression, there were many out of work and 'on the bum.' The hobos would come to the backyard and knock on the door for a handout. Mom always had a loaf of homemade bread, homemade butter, and usually cold meat. She made a couple of sandwiches, gave them a jar of water, and off they went. We were poor, but between the garden and a hog or two, we always had food.

We owned a Jersey cow named Jersey—although we shortened that to Jery. In the spring, there was a hill above our lot that was covered with wild pansies and little wild violets. One day, a group of ladies came to the house for cookies, gossip, and a little social time. Mom mentioned the hillside of pansies, and the ladies decided to go see the flowers. Mom held the top wire of the barbed wire fence up and held her foot on the middle wire so the ladies could pass through the fence. Just like the Hill folk in *Eleanore Gray*, the ladies didn't believe in gates. They had all passed through the fence without a problem, and then Mom passed through. They had all gone about five yards and here came old Jery at a full gallop.

Cows run with their feet flying every which way, and Jery's approach was eyed by the ladies with real misgivings. Collectively, they decided to flee back to the fence. Mom stood her ground and, sure enough, with a sound like "Baugh," old Jery slid to a stop and put her head down for Mom to scratch.

Mom turned her head to see that all the ladies were on the other side of that barbed wire fence. Mom never knew how they made it so fast, when they had been so slow and careful going the other way. The ladies did cross the fence again and saw the wild flowers. The retelling of this story always brought a smile to Mom's face, thinking of those ladies leaping over the fence and diving between the wires.

The Great Drought was in full swing back in those days. The sun was often red from the Kansas topsoil blowing over. Dad had a poor potato crop one year, so in the fall, he planted turnips. There must have been the right amount of moisture at the right time, because he was rewarded with a wagon box heaping full of turnips. Dad piled them in the back yard, covered them first with straw and then with dirt, and then he made a trench around the mound for water to get away from the mound. Mom, Dad, or I would burrow into the mound and get a pan of turnips, as needed. It seemed to me that there was always a pan of turnips on the stove.

Looking back, I expect those turnips were overcooked, but nothing Mom did could cover the taste of turnips. We ate them raw, boiled, in a casserole, baked, and every other way Mom could think of to cook them. Sixty-five years later, I still pass when the turnip bowl is passed to me, but those turnips got us through that winter.

We kids got to work in the garden picking dew berries and other things we grew. Mom always canned 800 to 1,000 jars of fruit and vegetables every year, so even when sugar was rationed during World War II, we had enough coupons that we could trade some to a neighbor for pork. We still had cows, so we had lots of milk, butter, and cottage cheese. While I might have been a little thin growing up, Mom made sure we always had enough to eat.

Walter "Don" Lucas
January 9, 1929— 8-17-2011

I was nine or ten years old late in the summer. I was a young kid with nothing to do but look for trouble. I decided to make myself a corncob pipe. So I got a corncob and dried it out and cut about two and a half inches. I hollowed it out with my pocketknife, and cut a hole in the side at the bottom. My dad had brought home some green hollow sticks from the greenhouse where he worked. The green sticks were used to support the plants. I took one and used it for my stem.

The next day or two I decided to put my corncob pipe to use, so I went about 300 feet south of my house where there were several vacant lots filled with just weeds. I went in the field, laid on my belly facing the road, got my matches out, and stuffed the pipe with grass. I went to light it and, in lighting it and puffing away, I must have dropped the match in the grass. I tried to put the fire out, but it got away from me.

I ran back to the house and told my mom. She came out with a wash tub as full as she could carry it and walked the 300 feet down the road and threw the tub of water on the fire. By that time, the neighbor, Mr. Doerr, got his hose out and stretched it across the rode and put out the fire. By the time my mother got back to the house with the empty tub, she was so wore out that she didn't even spank me. I think she made me sit in the corner for a while.

While Mom kept us kids in line, she also defended us. Once, my brother Elroy and I were catching trouble from a bully. I was in first grade and Elroy was in second. The bully was beating on us something awful, so we made a plan. Elroy got an early start and hid behind a shed built next to the sidewalk. I was to run and lead the bully to where Elroy was waiting. Our plan worked beyond our wildest expectations.

I ran by and Elroy tripped the bully. Down he went, hard on the sidewalk! Elroy and I jumped on him, banging away with our fists and feet. We ran for home, leaving the bully with a bloody face and broken glasses.

The bully's mother came to our house and talked really rude to Mom. Mom just smiled and told her that if she didn't get off the place, Mom would slap her face off her head. Mom told her that her son had bullied us for several months, and he would get the same treatment if he tried it again. I always remembered my mother sticking up for me.

Naomi Lucas Davis
May 27, 1930–2005

On Naomi's wedding day, she was so excited she was giddy. Mom and Pop went outside with Naomi and cut flowers, including Lily of the Valley. Then the flowers were arranged for wedding flowers. Mom and Charlie had gotten the black Cadillac from Pfitzsinger Funeral Home, and Naomi arrived in that at the Church. Some of the family wanted Mom to be wheeled down the aisle, but she told them no, and walked all the way down the aisle, as she wanted to do so for Naomi. It was the last time the kids saw her walk. Her love for her kids was boundless.

Mary Lucas Hofstetter
May 21, 1932—

Goldie Marie Wright Lucas was a large woman with a large heart of gold. When she was named Goldie, no one could imagine how perfect the name would be.

As I was growing up in the family that would in time include eight brothers and sisters and me, the overriding memory I have of Mom is her tremendous generosity and thoughtfulness.

During the Great Depression of the 1930s, Mom and Dad had lots of relatives who had even less than we did. Mom always helped the others with food or any other thing she could spare or share. I remember hobos would come to our door, begging for some food, and even though food was scarce for us, she would always give them a sandwich before sending them on their way.

Before and during World War II, many of the "country" relatives would come into the "Big City" where we lived to be able to go to school. Mom had not been able to finish high school before the babies had started coming along, so whenever anyone in the entire family graduated, Mom always made sure they had a graduation party. On Sunday, they could be found at Aunt Goldie's. Many nephews and cousins were taken in by Mom and Dad during this time, too. Some stayed at our house for as much as four to six months to get jobs and earn money. During the War, several relatives who came into St. Louis before being transported into the services would spend a night or two at our house.

Mom seemed to know just the right things to offer to folks. In 1945 and 1946, one of our nephews met a girl from New York, and Mom helped them by taking care of the wedding plans so they could have a nice wedding.

One of the fondest memories of Mom that shaped our family so much was her love of books and writing. Dad and Mom would walk all the way to Kirkwood Library each week and bring home a load of books for all of us to read. Mom was very talented artistically and wrote poetry, some of which was published. She also wrote letters to the editor and the book *Eleanore Gray*. I am so lucky that she was my Mom.

James N. Lucas
January 22, 1934—

My mom was a supermom. In addition to caring for a large family with very limited money, she was good at making the best of it. She sewed for all of us, however at the age of ten, I refused to wear the homemade sun suits anymore.

I recall my mom playing the piano. She only could play by ear using chords. Her favorite music was old ballads, such as "Old Nellie Gray," "Put My Little Shoes Away," and "On a Cold Winter Night," along with countless others.

Mom was always working on a very secret project—the book that no one was supposed to peek at lest all hell break out.

When the older kids were driving Mom crazy, she told us to get out of the house and do something—so we did. That's when we went to work on the basement. We dug out the basement and put up concrete blocks. Be careful of what you ask for!

My mom was a very good cook. While baking pies, she would make ten or more at one time. All in all, she was indeed a great person to have as a mother and friend.

David A. Lucas
June 11, 1936–June 9, 2006
As told by his wife Marie Lucas (April 1, 1933—),
married on October 15, 1960

I can still look out in my back yard and see a massive bush of Goldie's thornless roses. David took cuttings from them, and, as hard as it is to grow roses, these thrived. Several other family members had also taken cuttings off of them, and the rose lives on. Pop and Goldie's kitchen table was always the scene of pinochle games. Goldie always kept up with Pop's competitiveness. Amazingly, her gnarled hands held those cards.

David and I were always amazed at what she could do with those hands. We were most amazed at her making salad—lots of salad. Her hands cut those vegetables into small pieces with no apparent effort. Her hands never stopped her from doing things, but in time, she asked David to make the pies when she could not. She would always tell him how many to make. It became standard that David would always make more for her. He loved making the pies to help out and feed the large family. It became their own private little tradition.

Joyce Lucas Preiss
April 13, 1941—

The family always had to heat water on the stove back when. When I was two and a half, a tub of boiling water just off the stove was on the floor and I stuck both feet in it. I got severe burns on both feet. A neighbor took me to the doctor, where my feet were covered with sulfa. When Mom got home, she calmly sprung into action, and made a solution of incredibly dark strong tea. When it cooled, she tore strips of sheets and soaked them in the tea. She had learned this as a child, and it worked. Mom tended to me and kept my feet in the soaked bandages, and I began to heal. It was so bad that I had to re-learn to walk, but Mom and her healing touch got me through it. She always knew home remedies, and nursed us back to health with such love and care.

John C. Lucas
December 16, 1943—

Goldie Wright Lucas had nine children—four girls and five boys. I was the eighth child and the fifth boy. Mother always told me I was the eighth child of the eighth child of the eighth child, and so on. She never said if that was a blessing or a curse.

Mom brought me home on Christmas Day, 1943. Since she had not been able to buy a present for my brother David, I was his present. Boy, was he disappointed; David never let me forget that.

I never remember Mother walking, although there are pictures of her taking me by the hand. When rheumatoid arthritis confined her to bed, she actually slowed down only a little. Around the house, her name was "Sarge." She could give orders on how to peel the apples, sweep the floor, and fry the eggs. Her motto was "let your head save your feet."

Mom could not sit very long. Dad had cut the arms off her wheelchair so we could slide her in and out of the bed and car. The car seat was her most comfortable seating. She went everywhere. When we went to the Tuscumbia picnic or the State Fair in Sedalia, she slept in the front seat and the kids slept on the ground with the critters. We even pushed and carried her wheelchair into a riffle on the Glaize Creek so she could cool off like she did in the old days.

The worst punishment Mom ever meted out to me was a spanking with her crippled hands. I don't remember what I did, but it must have been a corker. The spanking did not hurt—but her pain was unbearable to me.

Mom would spend hours telling Joyce, Jeanne, and me—her youngest kids—stories about her childhood, her family, and life in the Ozarks. We would snuggle in bed with her and she would sing the old-time hymns she learned at the Glover Chapel near Dean's Creek. She talked about working as a cook for Pevely

Dairy in Crescent, Missouri, (where she met Dad). One story she told was about a lady who kept coming in to sample "a little of this and a little of that." Mom said she would rather feed "five hungry men than one woman with a comin' appetite."

When I was growing up, Mom's hands were so gnarled and swollen she could barely write, but write she did. Every event, big or small, seemed to inspire another poem. I especially remember the Hungarian revolt of 1956 that inspired "The Tiger in the Streets." The death of a St. Louis Zoo favorite brought forth the whimsical "Phil the Gorilla."

Mom was always supportive of me and all her kids in school. When the school resisted allowing me to take Geometry or Trigonometry, Mom insisted they admit me and they did. When my guidance counselor suggested I was not college material, she called him and told him I was going and he couldn't stop me. He didn't. I always thought my teaching degree was hers; I only wish she could have been there to see it.

Carol Jeanne Lucas Toothman
November 4, 1946—

My thoughts of Mom are not so much memories as flashes of events. What I remember about Mom was not ever seeing her walk. She was always either in the wheelchair or in her bed. She didn't attend events because "Handicapped Access" was a thing of the future that she would not live to see. I remember climbing into her bed to play "phone calls" to Elroy, who was off in the Army.

I remember when my folks purchased the farm and how we spent forever cleaning it up. I stepped on a nail and punctured an artery. Mom saw me pull the nail from my shoe and knew I was hurt, even though I didn't feel it. I remember sweeping the walking stones in the back. I looked down to discover one of the stones was a headstone that said, "Here lies John Estes/He is not dead/He only sleepth." That scared the hell out of me.

I remember always having company staying at the house, folks from the country who were visiting for a week or more. I remember Walter Tabor would bring students to St. Louis to see the big city "lights," and of course they stayed at the house. One little girl was my age, and I thought she was beautiful. Sadly she was accidentally killed with a rifle a few weeks later, and that event sealed my fear of guns.

I remember the time Cousin Ronald was visiting Uncle Paul. Mom sent a pan of her special cinnamon rolls over to Uncle Paul's but Ronnie baked them and ate them all before Uncle Paul got home from work and hid the evidence. When Mom asked about them, Uncle Paul knew nothing.

Of course, I remember when Mom died. We had been home from school for Washington's birthday, and it was wet and cold. Mom was sick, but that didn't stop Joyce, John, and me from fighting. Mom told us to go to bed and to "Pray for the long-horn cows." Now I realize she was burning up with fever and delirious. That is the last I ever heard her say. It is such a silly thing to remember.

Sarah M. Lucas Anderson
(Goldie's granddaughter)
May 19, 1976—

I never knew Goldie; for a long time, I wasn't even sure who she was. She was the mother to my father, John. She had died a long time ago, while my dad was still a kid. Pop—that's what we called Dad's father—had remarried long before I came to be. Mema Maggie was my grandmother; I have a vague, surprised memory of one day learning Mema wasn't Dad's real mom.

As I got older, however, Goldie became more a part of my life. I remember going on a fishing trip with Dad and taking a few unplanned turns. Suddenly we were back at the old family farm in the Ozarks, where Goldie had grown up. Dad remembered coming back to that farm a few times when he was growing up.

When I was in my early teens, my Uncle Luke got all of the old family photos reproduced—this was before computer scanners were $100 at Walmart. We had a family reunion at our house every summer (because we had a swimming pool) and I remember my cousin Raymond (Mary's youngest son) setting up a complicated tripod so he could take new photos of all the old ones that had been scattered around with the aunts and uncles. I think that was the first time Goldie became a real part of my life, because it was the first time I saw her picture. One of my favorites is of her standing with the help of a cane, holding my father's hand. I think Dad was about four in the picture.

Goldie was always smiling in the pictures, no matter how sick she was. She was a joyful, giving woman, a trait she passed on to all of her children. When I graduated from college, my aunt Naomi gave me a small china cup. It's a chocolate cup, a delicate pink rose painted on a cream and teal surface. It had belonged to Goldie. Naomi was keeping Goldie's tradition of marking educational milestones alive. I still have the cup, along with several of Goldie's pictures on my walls. She is never far from me now.

She was also a creative woman. She published poetry; her whole family was gifted with words. Now that my own novels are being published, my aunts and uncles tell me how much it means to see Goldie's literary spark show up in the family.

When Uncle Jim asked me to take *Eleanore Gray* and see if I could edit it for publication, I was honored. He had a typed draft, but he also sent me the original draft that Goldie had written longhand. He'd kept it in a closet for several decades.

Time was not kind to the manuscript. The pages are crumbling, and, clearly, at some point a mouse made off with some action verbs. Each page is in a protective case in a binder now, no longer in a closet, but on a shelf.

I've found a way to connect with a woman I never knew. Many of the things that happen in *Eleanore Gray* were things from her childhood growing up in Hill country. While the events are fiction, the settings, the people are all representative of things she knew and remembered.

For another example, she only wrote on one side of each sheet of paper, saving the other side for edits or doodles. I don't know if the women she drew are supposed to be Eleanore or if they were just flights of fancy. Looking at them is like watching my grandmother think on paper. My grandparents were not rich. Despite having nine kids to feed, Pop made sure Goldie had enough paper to write on. To me, it says if it was important to Goldie, it was important to Pop.

This book was important to Goldie, and it is important to me. After all, she was my grandmother.

3-3-13

This book. "Eleanore Gray", was written by my dearly-beloved, Aunt Goldie M. Lucas nee Wright. She was a sister to my mother, Annie Elizabeth Willoughby nee Wright. Although Aunt Goldie was bed written - in later life - one never really remembered her in that manner. She was always so cheerful and full of plans. Not only for herself and family but for her numerous nieces, nephews, friends and neighbors. She helped me cut out and sew baby clothes for my first-born, Martin Lee. I always loved her and her family so much!

Fond memories, - 5 Children
11 Grandchildren
4 Great ",
Billie Poloski

10055154R0017

Made in the USA
Charleston, SC
03 November 2011